The Masterpieces of

GEORGE SAND

AMANDINE LUCILLE AURORE DUPIN,
BARONESS DUDEVANT

VOLUME I

Edition de Nohant

LIMITED TO ONE THOUSAND NUMBERED COPIES

WITH THE

PHOTOGRAVURES ON JAPAN PAPER

INDIANA

MADAME DELMARE DRESSES DE RAMIÈRE'S WOUNDS

A mattress was placed on several chairs, and Indiana, assisted by her women, busied herself in dressing the wounded hand, while Sir Ralph, who had some surgical knowledge, drew a large quantity of blood from him.

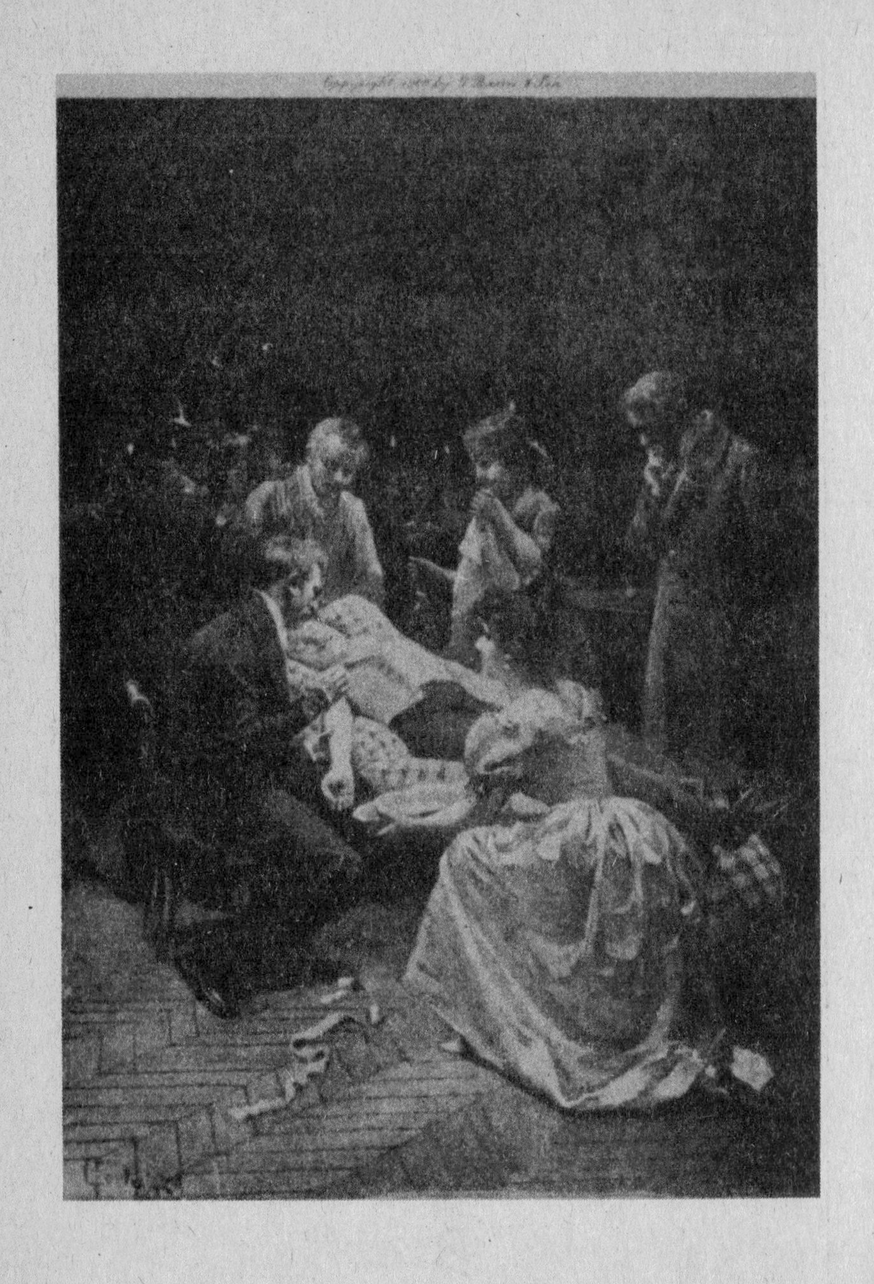

GEORGE SAND
INDIANA

TRANSLATED BY
GEORGE BURNHAM IVES

WITH A CHRONOLOGY OF HER LIFE AND WORK

Published by
Academy Chicago Publishers
213 West Institute Place
Chicago, Illinois 60610

First Printing: 1978
Second Printing: 1984
Third Printing: 1992

Cover illustration: Constantin Guys, "Lady and
Gentleman Riding in the Bois de Boulogne" c. 1860.

Library of Congress Cataloging-in-Publication Data

Sand, George, pseud. of Mme. Dudevant, 1804-1876.
Indiana.

Reprint of 1900 ed. published by G. Barrie,
Philadelphia, which was issued as v.1 of The
Masterpieces of George Sand.
Bibliography: p.
I. Ives, George Burnham, 1856-1930. II Title
[PZ3.S21In 1978] [PQ2404] 843'.8 77-27987
ISBN: 0-915864-58-4 lib.bdg.
ISBN: 0-915864-57-6 pbk.

GEORGE SAND: CHRONOLOGY

1804
July 1 Birth at 15 Rue de la Meslay, Paris. Daughter of Maurice Dupin and Sophie Delaborde. Christened Amandine Aurore Lucie Dupin.
Family moves to Rue de la Grange-Batelière, Paris.

1808
Aurore travels to Spain with her mother. They join her father at Palace de Goday in Madrid, where he is serving in Napoleon's army under General Murat.

1809
The family goes to Nohant in France, the home of Maurice Dupin's mother, born Marie-Aurore de Saxe, Comtesse de Horn, the daughter of the illegitimate son of King Frederic-Augustus II of Poland. Death of Maurice Dupin in a fall from a horse.

1810
Sophie Dupin gives custody of Aurore to Madame Dupin in return for a pension.

1810-1814
Winters in Paris at Rue Neuve-des-Mathurins with her grandmother and visits from Sophie. Summers at Nohant.

1817-1820
Educated at the English Convent des Augustines in Paris.

1820
Returns to Nohant. Studies with her father's tutor Deschartres.

1821
Death of Madame Dupin. Aurore inherits some money, a house in Paris and the house at Nohant.
Moves in with her mother at 80 Rue St.-Lazare, Paris.

1822
Meets Casimir Dudevant on a visit to the Duplessis family.
September 10 Marries Dudevant, son of Baron Dudevant. They move to Nohant.

1823
June 30 Maurice is born at Hotel de Florence, 56 Rue Neuve-des-Mathurins, Paris.

1824
Spring and summer at the Duplessis' at Plessis-Picard near Melun; autumn at a Parisian suburb, Ormesson; winter in an apartment at Rue du Faubourg-Saint-Honoré.

1825
Spring at Nohant. Aurore is ill in the summer. Dudevants travel to his family home in Gascony. She meets Aurélian de Sèze, and recovers her health.
November 5 Writes long confession to Casimir about de Sèze. She gives him up.
Winter in Gascony.

1826
Moves to Nohant. Casimir travels, Aurore manages the estate and writes to de Sèze.

1827
Illness again. The water cure at Clermont-Ferraud, where she writes *Voyage En Auvergne,* autobiographical sketch.

1827-1829
Winter at Le Châtre. Summer at Nohant.

1828
September 13 Birth of Solange.

1830
Visit to Bordeaux to Aurélian de Sèze. Their correspondence ceases. She writes a novel *Aimée*.
December Discovery of Casimir's will, filled with antipathy to her.

1831
January 4 Moves to Paris to 31 Rue de Seine.
Joins staff of *Le Figaro*. Writes three short stories: *La Molinara* (in *Figaro*); *La Prima Donna* (in *Revue de Paris)* and *La Fille d'Albano* (in *La Mode*).
April Returns to Nohant for three months. Writes *Indiana*.
July Moves to 25 Quai Saint-Michel, Paris.
December Publishes *Rose Et Blanche* in collaboration with Jules Sandeau. Book is signed Jules Sand.

1832
Travel between Paris and Nohant.
April Solange is brought to Paris.
November Move to 19 Quai Malaquais with Solange.
Indiana and *Valentine* published. Maurice sent by Casimir to Henry IV Military Academy in Paris.

1833
January Break with Sandeau.
June Meets Alfred de Musset.
Publishes *Lelia*.
September Fontainebleau with de Musset.
December 12 To Italy with de Musset.

1834
January 19 The Hotel Danieli in Venice. Musset attempts a break with Aurore, becomes ill. His physician is Pietro Pagello.
March 29 de Musset returns to Paris. Aurore remains with Pagello.
Writes *André, Mattéa, Jacques, Léone Léoni* and the first *Lettres d'Un Voyageur.*
August 15 Return to Paris with Pagello.
August 24 de Musset goes to Baden.
August 29 Aurore to Nohant.
October Return to Paris. Musset return from Baden. Pagello returns to Venice.
November 25 Begins journal to de Musset.
December Return to Nohant.

1835
January Return to Paris.
March 6 Final break with Musset.
Meets Michel of Bourges, her lawyer and political mentor. Writes *Simon.*
Autumn Return to Nohant for Maurice's holiday.
October 19 Casimir threatens her physically. Begins suit for legal separation.
December 1 Judgment in her favor won by default.

1836
February 16 She wins second judgment. Casimir bring suit.
May 10, 11 Another verdict in her favor from civil court of La Châtre. Casimir appeals to a higher court.
July 25, 26 Trial in royal court of Bourges. Jury divided. Out of court settlement. Her fortune is divided with Casimir.
August To Switzerland with Maurice and Solange and Liszt and d'Agoult.
Autumn Hotel de la France, 15 Rue Lafitte, Paris with Liszt and d'Agoult. Meets Chopin.

1837

January Return to Nohant. Publishes *Mauprat* in spring. Writes *Les Maîtres Mosaïstes*. Liszt and d'Agoult visit Nohant. Fatal illness of Sophie in Paris. Visit to Fontainebleau, writes *La Dernière Aldini*. Trip to Gascony to recover Solange, who has been kidnapped by Casimir.

1838

Writes *L'Orco* and *L'Uscoque,* two Venetian novels.
May To Paris. Romance with Chopin.
November Trip to Majorca with children and Chopin. Writes *Spiridion*.

1839

February Leaves Majorca for three months in Marseilles. Then to Nohant. Publishes *Un Hiver À Majorque, Pauline* and *Gabriel-Gabrielle*.
October Occupies adjoining apartments with Chopin until spring of 1841 at 16 Rue Pigalle, Paris, in winter. Summer is spent at Nohant with Chopin as guest.

1840

Writes *Compagnon Du Tour De France* and *Horace*. Influenced by Pierre Leroux.

1841

Moves from Rue Pigalle to 5 and 9 Rue St.-Lazare, Square d'Orléans, with Chopin.

1842

Consuelo published.

1843

La Comtesse De Rudolstadt published, a sequel to *Consuelo*.

1844

Jeanne published, a foreshadowing of pastoral novels.

1845
Têvêrino, Pêché de M. Antoine and *Le Meunier D'Angibault,* the latter two socialist novels.

1846
La Mare Au Diable published and *Lucrezia Floriani.* Solange married to Auguste-Jean Clésinger. Estrangement from Chopin.

1847
Francois Le Champi published.

1848
Writes government circulars, contributes to *Bulletins de la Republique* and publishes her own newspaper *La Cause du Peuple,* all for the Second Republic. Death of Solange's son. *La Petite Fadette* published.

1849
Her play based on *François Le Champi* performed at the Odéon. First of a series of successful plays.

1850
Chateau des Désertes published in the *Revue Des Deux Mondes.*

1851
Republic falls. She uses her influence to save her friends from political reprisals. Plays *Claudie* and *Le Mariage De Victorine* presented.

1852
Return to Nohant.

1853
Published *Les Maitres Sonneurs.* Play *Le Pressoir* presented.

1855
Four volume autobiography *Histoire De Ma Vie* published, carries her life to Revolution of 1848.
January 13 Death of Solange's daughter Jeanne.
Visit to Italy with Maurice and Alexandre Manceau.

1856
Does French adaptation of *As You Like It*.

1858
Holidays at Gargilesse on River Creuse at cottage given her by Alexander Manceau.

1859
Writes *Elle Et Lui*. Publishes *Jean De La Roche* and *L'Homme De Neige*.

1860
Writes *La Ville Noire* and *Marquis De Villemer*.
November Contracts typhoid fever.

1862
May 16 Marriage of Maurice Sand and Caroline Calametta.

1863
July 14 Marc-Antoine Sand born, son of Maurice and Caroline.
Mademoiselle La Quintinie published, anti-clerical novel. Begins friendship with Flaubert.

1864
Play *Le Marquis De Villemer* presented. Death of Marc-Antoine Sand. Moves from 3 Rue Racine near the Odéon to 97 Rue des Feuillantines. Exchanges Gargilesse for a house at Palaiseau with Manceau.

1865
Death of Manceau.

1866
Visits Flaubert at Croisset, dedicates *Le Dernier Amour* to him. Birth of Aurore Sand.

1867
Return to Nohant to live with Maurice and Caroline. Writes two novels a year.

1868
Birth of Gabrielle Sand.

1870
The play *L'Autre* with Sarah Bernhardt, presented at the Theatre Francais.

1870-1871
Franco-German War. Removal to Boussac because of a small-pox epidemic at Nohant.

1876
June 8 Dies.

INTRODUCTION

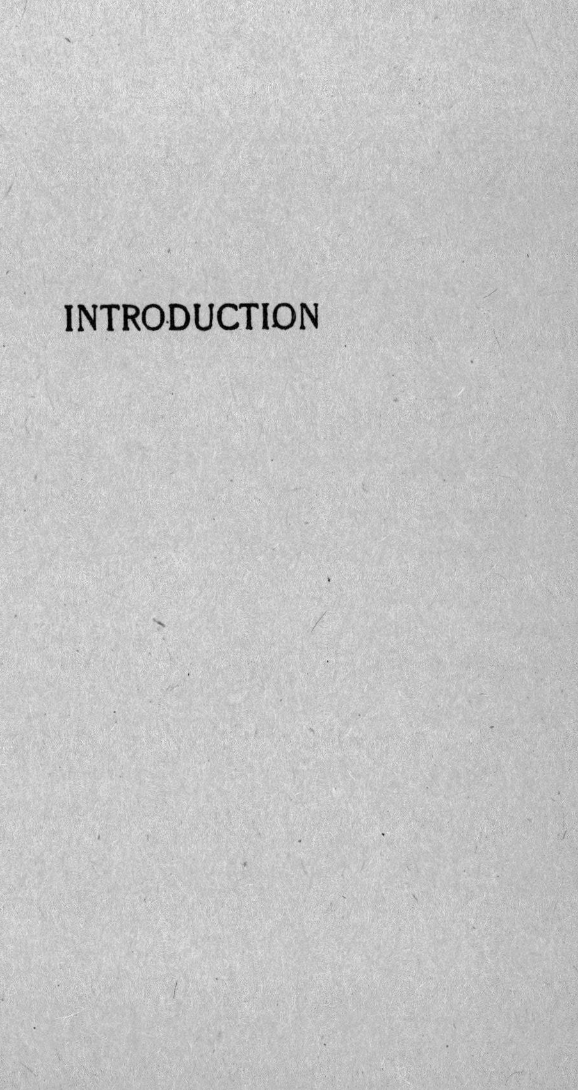

INTRODUCTION

I wrote *Indiana* during the autumn of 1831. It was my first novel; I wrote it without any fixed plan, having no theory of art or philosophy in my mind. I was at the age when one writes with one's instincts, and when reflection serves only to confirm our natural tendencies. Some people chose to see in the book a deliberate argument against marriage. I was not so ambitious, and I was surprised to the last degree at all the fine things that the critics found to say concerning my subversive purposes. Criticism is far too acute; that is what will cause its death. It never passes judgment ingenuously on what has been done ingenuously. It looks for noon at four o'clock, as the old women say, and must cause much suffering to artists who care more for its decrees than they ought to do.

Under all régimes and in all times there has been a race of critics, who, in contempt of their own talent, have fancied that it was their duty to ply the trade of denouncers, of purveyors to the prosecuting attorney's office; extraordinary functions for men of letters to assume with regard to their confrères! The rigorous measures of government against the press never satisfy these savage critics. They would have them directed not only against works but against persons as well, and, if their advice were followed, some of us would be forbidden to write anything whatsoever.

INTRODUCTION

At the time that I wrote *Indiana,* the cry of Saint Simonism was raised on every pretext. Later they shouted all sorts of other things. Even now certain writers are forbidden to open their mouths, under pain of seeing the police agents of certain newspapers pounce upon their work and hale them before the police of the constituted powers. If a writer puts noble sentiments in the mouth of a mechanic, it is an attack on the bourgeoisie; if a girl who has gone astray is rehabilitated after expiating her sin, it is an attack on virtuous women; if an impostor assumes titles of nobility, it is an attack on the patrician caste; if a bully plays the swashbuckling soldier, it is an insult to the army; if a woman is maltreated by her husband, it is an argument in favor of promiscuous love. And so with everything. Kindly brethren, devout and generous critics! What a pity that no one thinks of creating a petty court of literary inquisition in which you should be the torturers! Would you be satisfied to tear the books to pieces and burn them at a slow fire, and could you not, by your urgent representations, obtain permission to give a little taste of the rack to those writers who presume to have other gods than yours?

Thank God, I have forgotten the names of those who tried to discourage me at my first appearance, and who, being unable to say that my first attempt had fallen completely flat, tried to distort it into an incendiary proclamation against the repose of society. I did not expect so much honor, and I consider that I owe to those critics the thanks which the hare proffered the frogs, imagining from their alarm that he was entitled to deem himself a very thunderbolt of war.

GEORGE SAND.

Nohant, May, 1852.

PREFACE TO THE EDITION OF 1832

If certain pages of this book should incur the serious reproach of tending toward novel beliefs, if unbending judges shall consider their tone imprudent and perilous, I should be obliged to reply to the criticism that it does too much honor to a work of no importance; that, in order to attack the great questions of social order, one must either be conscious of great strength of purpose or pride one's self upon great talent, and that such presumption is altogether foreign to a very simple tale, in which the author has invented almost nothing. If, in the course of his task, he has happened to set forth the lamentations extorted from his characters by the social malady with which they were assailed; if he has not shrunk from recording their aspirations after a happier existence, let the blame be laid upon society for its inequalities, upon destiny for its caprices! The author is merely a mirror which reflects them, a machine which reverses their tracing, and he has no reason for self-reproach if the impression is exact, if the reflection is true.

Consider further that the narrator has not taken for text or devise a few shrieks of suffering and wrath scattered through the drama of human life. He does not claim to conceal serious instruction beneath the exterior form of a tale; it is not his aim to lend a hand in constructing the edifice which a doubtful future is preparing for us and to give a sly kick at that of the past which is crumbling away. He knows too well that we live in an epoch of moral deterioration, wherein the reason of mankind has need of curtains to soften the too bright glare which dazzles it. If he had felt sufficiently learned to write a genuinely useful book, he would have toned down the truth, instead of presenting it in its crude tints and with its startling effects. That book would have performed the functions of blue spectacles for weak eyes.

He does not abandon the idea of performing that honorable and laudable task some day; but, being still a young man, he simply tells you to-day what he has seen, not presuming to draw his conclusions concerning the great controversy between the future and the past, which perhaps no man of the present generation is especially competent to do. Too conscientious to conceal his doubts from you, but too timid to transform them into certainties, he relies upon your reflections and abstains from weaving into the woof of his narrative preconceived opinions, judgments all formed. He plies with exactitude his trade of narrator. He will tell you everything, even painful truths; but, if you should wrap him in the philosopher's robe, you would find that he was exceedingly confused, simple story-teller that he is, whose mission is to amuse and not to instruct.

Even were he more mature and more skilful, he would not dare to lay his hand upon the great sores of dying civilization. One must be so sure of being able to cure them when one ventures to probe them! He would much prefer to arouse your interest in old discarded beliefs, in old-fashioned, vanished forms of devotion, to employing his talent, if he had any, in blasting overturned altars. He knows, however, that, in these charitable times, a timorous conscience is despised by public opinion as hypocritical reserve, just as, in the arts, a timid bearing is sneered at as an absurd mannerism; but he knows also that there is honor, if not profit, in defending lost causes.

To him who should misunderstand the spirit of this book, such a profession of faith would sound like an anachronism. The narrator hopes that few auditors, after listening to his tale to the end, will deny the *moral* to be derived from the facts, a moral which triumphs there as in all human affairs; it seemed to him, when he wrote the last line, that his conscience was clear. He flattered himself, in a word, that he had described social miseries without too much bitterness, human passions without too much passion. He placed the mute under his strings when they echoed too loudly; he tried to stifle certain notes of the soul which should remain mute, certain voices of the heart which cannot be awakened without danger.

Perhaps you will do him justice if you agree that the being who tries to free himself from his lawful curb is represented as very wretched indeed, and the heart that rebels against the decrees of its destiny as in sore distress. If he has not given the best imaginable rôle to that one of his characters who represents *the law,* if that one who represents *opinion* is even less cheerful, you will see a third representing *illusion,* who cruelly thwarts the vain hopes and enterprises of passion. Lastly, you will see that, although he has not strewn rose-leaves on the ground where the law pens up our desires like a sheep's appetite, he has scattered thistles along the roads which lead us away from it.

These facts, it seems to me, are sufficient to protect this book from the reproach of immorality; but, if you absolutely insist that a novel should end like one of Marmontel's tales, you will perhaps chide me on account of the last pages; you will think that I have done wrong in not casting into misery and destitution the character who has transgressed the laws of mankind through two volumes. In this regard, the author will reply that before being moral he chose to be true; he will say again, that, feeling that he was too new to the trade to compose a philosophical treatise on the manner of enduring life, he has restricted himself to telling you the story of *Indiana,* a story of the human heart, with its weaknesses, its passions, its rights and its wrongs, its good qualities and its evil qualities.

Indiana, if you insist upon an explanation of every thing in the book, is a type; she is woman, the feeble being whose mission it is to represent *passions* repressed, or, if you prefer, suppressed by *the law;* she is desire at odds with necessity; she is love dashing her head blindly against all the obstacles of civilization. But the serpent wears out his teeth and breaks them in trying to gnaw a file; the powers of the soul become exhausted in trying to struggle against the positive facts of life. That is the conclusion you may draw from this tale, and it was in that light that it was told to him who transmits it to you.

But despite these protestations the narrator anticipates reproaches. Some upright souls, some honest men's consciences will be alarmed perhaps to see virtue so harsh, reason so downcast, opinion so unjust. He is dismayed at the prospect; for the thing that an author should fear more than anything in the world is the alienating from his works the confidence of good men, the awakening of an ominous sympathy in embittered souls, the inflaming of the sores, already too painful, which are made by the social yoke upon impatient and rebellious necks.

PREFACE

The success which is based upon an unworthy appeal to the passions of the age is the easiest to win, the least honorable to strive for. The historian of *Indiana* denies that he has ever dreamed of it; if he thought that he had reached that result, he would destroy his book, even though he felt for it the artless fatherly affection which swaddles the rickety offspring of these days of literary abortions.

But he hopes to justify himself by stating that he thought it better to enforce his principles by real examples than by poetic fancies. He believes that his tale, with the depressing atmosphere of frankness that envelopes it, may make an impression upon young and ardent brains. They will find it difficult to distrust a historian who forces his way brutally through the midst of facts, elbowing right and left, with no more regard for one camp than for the other. To make a cause odious or absurd is to persecute it, not to combat it. It may be that the whole art of the novelist consists in interesting the culprits whom he wishes to redeem, the wretched whom he wishes to cure, in their own story.

It would be giving overmuch importance to a work that is destined doubtless to attract very little notice, to seek to protect it against every sort of accusation. Therefore the author surrenders unconditionally to the critics; a single charge seems to him too serious to accept, and that is the charge that he has written a dangerous book. He would prefer to remain in a humble position forever to building his reputation upon a ruined conscience. He will add a word therefore to repel the blame which he most dreads.

Raymon, you will say, is society; egoism is substituted for morality and reason. Raymon, the author will reply, is the false reason, the false morality by which society is governed; he is the man of honor as the world understands the phrase, because the world does not examine closely enough to see everything. The good man you have beside Raymon; and you will not say that he is the enemy of order; for he sacrifices his happiness, he loses all thought of self before all questions of social order.

Then you will say that virtue is not rewarded with sufficient blowing of trumpets. Alas! the answer is that we no longer witness the triumph of virtue elsewhere than at the boulevard theatres. The author will tell you that he has undertaken to exhibit society to you, not as virtuous, but as necessary, and that honor has become as difficult as heroism in these days of moral degeneration. Do you think that this truth will cause great souls to loathe honor? I think just the opposite.

PREFACE TO THE EDITION OF 1842

In allowing the foregoing pages to be reprinted, I do not mean to imply that they form a clear and complete summary of the beliefs which I hold to-day concerning the rights of society over individuals. I do it simply because I regard opinions freely put forth in the past as something sacred, which we should neither retract nor cry down nor attempt to interpret as our fancy directs. But to-day, having advanced on life's highway and watched the horizon broaden around me, I deem it my duty to tell the reader what I think of my book.

When I wrote *Indiana*, I was young; I acted in obedience to feelings of great strength and sincerity which overflowed thereafter in a series of novels, almost all of which were based on the same idea: the ill-defined relations between the sexes, attributable to the constitution of our society. These novels were all more or less inveighed against by the critics, as making unwise assaults upon the institution of marriage. *Indiana*, notwithstanding the narrowness of its scope and the ingenuous uncertainty of its grasp, did not escape the indignation of several self-styled serious minds, whom I was strongly disposed at that time to believe upon their simple statement and to listen to with docility. But, although my reasoning powers were developed hardly enough to write upon so grave a subject, I was not so much of a child that I could not pass judgment in my turn on the thoughts of those persons who passed judgment on mine. However simple-minded a man accused of crime may be and however shrewd the magistrate, the accused has enough common-sense to know whether the magistrate's sentence is equitable or inequitable, wise or absurd.

Certain journalists of our day who set themselves up as representatives and guardians of public morals—I know not by virtue of what mission they act, since I know not by what faith they are commissioned—pronounced judgment pitilessly against my poor tale, and, by representing it as an argument against social order, gave it an importance and a sort of echo which it would not otherwise have obtained. They thereby imposed a very serious and weighty rôle upon a young author hardly initiated in the most elementary social ideas, whose whole literary and philosophical baggage consisted of a little imagination, courage and love of the truth. Sensitive to the reproofs and almost grateful for the lessons which they were pleased to administer, he examined the arguments which arraigned the moral character of his thoughts before the bar of public opinion, and, by virtue of that examination, which he conducted entirely without pride, he gradually acquired convictions which were mere feelings at the outset of his career and which to-day are fundamental principles.

During ten years of investigations, of scruples, and of irresolution, often painful but always sincere, shunning the rôle of pedagogue which some attributed to me to make me ridiculous, abhorring the imputation of pride and spleen with which others pursued me to make me odious, proceeding according to the measure of my artistic faculties, to seek the synthesis of life by analyzing it, I related facts which have sometimes been acknowledged to be plausible, and drew characters which have often been described as having been studied with care. I restricted myself to that, striving to establish my own conviction rather than to shake other people's, and saying to myself that, if I were mistaken, society would find no lack of loud voices to overturn my arguments and to repair by judicious answers the evil that my imprudent questions might have done. Numerous voices did, in fact, arise to put the public on its guard against the dangerous writer, but, as for the judicious answers, the public and the author are still awaiting them.

A long while after I wrote the preface to *Indiana* under the influence of a remnant of respect for constituted society, I was still seeking to solve this insoluble problem : *the method of reconciling the welfare and the dignity of individuals oppressed by that same society without modifying society itself.* Leaning over the victims and mingling his tears with theirs, making himself their interpreter with his readers, but, like a prudent advocate, not striving overmuch to palliate the wrong-doing of his clients, and addressing himself to the clemency of the judges rather than to their austerity, the novelist is really the advocate of the abstract beings who represent our passions and our sufferings before the tribunal of superior force and the jury of public opinion. It is a task which has a gravity of its own beneath its trivial exterior, and a task which it is exceedingly difficult to confine to its true path, pestered as you are at every step by those who accuse you of being too serious in respect to form and by those who accuse you of being too frivolous in respect to substance.

I do not flatter myself that I performed this task skilfully; but I am sure that I attempted it in all seriousness, amid inward hesitations wherein my conscience, sometimes dismayed by its ignorance of its rights, sometimes inspired by a heart enamored of justice and truth, marched forward to its goal, without swerving too far from the straight road and without too many backward steps.

To enlighten the public as to this inward struggle by a series of prefaces and discussions would have been a puerile method, wherein the vanity of talking about one's self would have taken too much space to suit me. I could but abstain from it as well as from touching too hastily upon the points which were still obscure in my mind. Conservators called me too bold, innovators too timid. I confess that I had respect and sympathy for the past and the future alike, and in the battle I found no peace of mind until the day when I fully realized that the one should not be the violation and the annihilation of the other, but its continuation and development.

After this novitiate of ten years, being initiated at last in broader ideas which I derived not from myself but from the philosophical progress which had taken place around me—and particularly from a few vast intellects which I religiously questioned, and, generally speaking, from the spectacle of the sufferings of my fellowmen,—I realized at last that, although I may have done well to distrust myself and to hesitate to put forth my views at the epoch of ignorance and inexperience when I wrote *Indiana*, my present duty is to congratulate myself on the bold utterances to which I allowed myself to be impelled then and afterwards; bold utterances for which I have been reproached so bitterly, and which would have been bolder still had I known how legitimate and honest and sacred they were.

To-day therefore, having re-read the first novel of my youth with as much severity and impartiality as if it were the work of another person, on the eve of giving it a publicity which it has not yet derived from the popular edition, having resolved beforehand not to retract—one should never retract what was said or done in good faith—but to condemn myself if I should discover that my former tendencies were mistaken or dangerous, I find myself so entirely in accord with myself with respect to the sentiment which dictated *Indiana* and which would dictate it now if I had that story to tell to-day for the first time, that I have not chosen to change anything in it save a few ungrammatical sentences and some inappropriate words. Doubtless many more of the same sort remain, and the literary merits of my writings I submit without reserve to the animadversions of the critics; I gladly accord to them all the competence in that regard which I myself lack. That there is an incontestable mass of talent in the daily press of the present day, I do not deny and I delight to acknowledge it. But that there are many philosophers and moralists in this array of polished writers, I do positively deny, with due respect to those who have condemned me, and who will condemn me again on the first opportunity, from their lofty plane of morality and philosophy.

I repeat then, I wrote *Indiana*, and I was justified in writing it; I yielded to an overpowering instinct of outcry and rebellion which God had implanted in me, God who makes nothing that is not of some use, even the most insignificant creatures, and who interposes in the most trivial as well as in great causes. But what am I saying? is this cause that I am defending so very trivial, pray? It is the cause of half of the human race, nay, of the whole human race; for the unhappiness of woman involves that of man, as that of the slave involves that of the master, and I strove to demonstrate it in *Indiana*.

Some persons said that I was pleading the cause of an individual; as if, even assuming that I was inspired by personal feeling, I was the only unhappy mortal in this peaceful and radiant human race! So many cries of pain and sympathy answered mine that I know now what to think concerning the supreme felicity of my fellowman.

I do not think that I have ever written anything under the influence of a selfish passion; I have never even thought of avoiding it. They who have read me without prejudice understand that I wrote *Indiana* with a feeling, not deliberately reasoned out, to be sure, but a deep and genuine feeling that the laws which still govern woman's existence in wedlock, in the family and in society are unjust and barbarous. I had not to write a treatise on jurisprudence but to fight against public opinion; for it is that which postpones or advances social reforms. The war will be long and bitter; but I am neither the first nor the last nor the only champion of so noble a cause, and I will defend it so long as the breath of life remains in my body.

This feeling which inspired me at the beginning I reasoned out and developed as it was combated and reproved. Unjust and malevolent critics taught me much more than I should have discovered in the calm of impunity. For this reason therefore I offer thanks to the bungling judges who enlightened me. The motives that inspired their judgments cast a bright light upon my mind and enveloped my conscience in a sense of profound security. A sincere mind turns everything to advantage, and facts that would discourage vanity redouble the ardor of genuine devotion.

Let no one look upon the reproof which, from the depths of a heart that is to-day serious and tranquil, I have just addressed to the majority of journalists of my time, as implying even a suggestion of protest against the right of censorship with which public morality invests the French press. That criticism often ill performs and ill comprehends its mission in the society of the present day, is evident to all; but that the mission is in itself providential and sacred, no one can deny unless he be an atheist in the matter of progress, unless he be an enemy of the truth, a blasphemer of the future and an unworthy child of France! Liberty of thought, liberty to write and to speak, blessed conquest of the human mind! what are the petty sufferings and the fleeting cares engendered by thy errors or abuses compared to the infinite blessings which thou hast in store for the world!

INDIANA

PART FIRST

I

On a certain cool, rainy evening in autumn, in a small château in Brie, three pensive individuals were gravely occupied in watching the wood burn on the hearth and the hands of the clock move slowly around the dial. Two of these silent guests seemed to give way unreservedly to the vague ennui that weighed upon them; but the third gave signs of open rebellion: he fidgeted about on his seat, stifled half audibly divers melancholy yawns, and tapped the snapping sticks with the tongs, with a manifest intention of resisting the common enemy.

This person, who was much older than the other two, was the master of the house, Colonel Delmare, an old warrior on half-pay, once a very handsome man, now over-corpulent, with a bald head, gray moustache and awe-inspiring eye; an excellent master before whom everybody trembled, wife, servants, horses and dogs.

At last he left his chair, evidently vexed because he did not know how to break the silence, and began to walk heavily up and down the whole length of the salon, without laying aside for an instant the rigidity which characterizes all the movements of an ex-soldier, resting his weight on his loins and turning the whole body at once, with the unfailing self-satisfaction peculiar to the man of show and the model officer.

But the glorious days had passed, when Lieutenant

Delmare inhaled triumph with the air of the camps; the retired officer, forgotten now by an ungrateful country, was condemned to undergo all the consequences of marriage. He was the husband of a young and pretty wife, the proprietor of a commodious manor with its appurtenances, and, furthermore, a manufacturer who had been fortunate in his undertakings; in consequence whereof the colonel was ill-humored, especially on the evening in question; for it was very damp, and the colonel had rheumatism.

He paced gravely up and down his old salon, furnished in the style of Louis XV., halting sometimes before a door surmounted by nude Cupids in fresco, who led in chains of flowers well-bred fawns and good-natured wild boars; sometimes before a panel overladen with paltry, over-elaborated sculpture, whose tortuous vagaries and endless intertwining the eye would have wearied itself to no purpose in attempting to follow. But these vague and fleeting distractions did not prevent the colonel, whenever he turned about, from casting a keen and searching glance at the two companions of his silent vigil, resting upon them alternately that watchful eye which for three years past had been standing guard over a fragile and priceless treasure, his wife.

For his wife was nineteen years of age; and if you had seen her buried under the mantel of that huge fire-place of white marble inlaid with burnished copper; if you had seen her, slender, pale, depressed, with her elbow resting on her knee, a mere child in that ancient household, beside that old husband, like a flower of yesterday that had bloomed in a gothic vase, you would have pitied Colonel Delmare's wife, and the colonel even more perhaps than his wife.

The third occupant of this lonely house was also sitting

under the same mantel, at the other end of the burning log. He was a man in all the strength and all the bloom of youth, whose glowing cheeks, abundant golden hair and full whiskers presented a striking contrast to the grizzly hair, weather-beaten complexion and harsh countenance of the master of the house; but the least *artistic* of men would none the less have preferred Monsieur Delmare's harsh and stern expression to the younger man's regular but insipid features. The bloated face carved in relief on the sheet of iron that formed the back of the fire-place, with its eye fixed constantly on the burning logs, was less monotonous perhaps than the pink and white fair-haired character in this narrative, absorbed in like contemplation. However, his strong and supple figure, the clean-cut outline of his brown eyebrows, the polished whiteness of his forehead, the tranquil expression of his limpid eyes, the beauty of his hands, and even the rigorously correct elegance of his hunting costume, would have caused him to be considered a very comely *cavalier* in the eyes of any woman who had conceived a passion for the so-called *philosophic* tastes of another century. But perhaps Monsieur Delmare's young and timid wife had never as yet examined a man with her eyes; perhaps there was an entire absence of sympathy between that pale and unhappy woman and that sound sleeper and hearty eater. Certain it is that the conjugal Argus wearied his hawklike eye without detecting a glance, a breath, a palpitation, between these two very dissimilar beings. Thereupon, being assured that he had not the slightest pretext for jealousy to occupy his mind, he relapsed into a state of depression more profound than before, and abruptly plunged his hands into his pockets.

The only cheerful and attractive face in the group was

that of a beautiful hunting dog, of the large breed of pointers, whose head was resting on the knees of the younger man. She was remarkable by reason of her long body, her powerful hairy legs, her muzzle, slender as a fox's, and her intelligent face, covered with disheveled hair, through which two great tawny eyes shone like topazes. Those dog's eyes, so fierce and threatening during the chase, had at that moment an indefinable expression of affectionate melancholy; and when her master, the object of that instinctive love, sometimes so superior to the deliberate affection of man, ran his fingers through the beautiful creature's silky silver locks, her eyes sparkled with pleasure, while her long tail swept the hearth in regular cadence, and scattered the ashes over the inlaid floor.

It was a fitting subject for Rembrandt's brush, that interior, dimly lighted by the fire on the hearth. At intervals fugitive white gleams lighted up the room and the faces, then, changing to the red tint of the embers, gradually died away; the gloom of the salon varying as the fitful gleams grew more or less dull. Each time that Monsieur Delmare passed in front of the fire, he suddenly appeared, like a ghost, then vanished in the mysterious depths of the salon. Strips of gilding stood forth in the light now and then on the oval frames, adorned with wreaths and medallions and fillets of wood, on furniture, inlaid with ebony and copper, and even on the jagged cornices of the wainscoting. But when a brand went out, resigning its brilliancy to some other blazing point, the objects which had been in the light a moment before withdrew into the shadow, and other projections stood forth from the obscurity. Thus one could have grasped in due time all the details of the picture, from the console supported by three huge gilded tritons, to the frescoed ceiling, representing a sky studded with stars and clouds, and to the heavy hangings of crimson damask, with long tassels, which shimmered like satin, their ample folds seeming to sway back and forth as they reflected the flickering light.

One would have said, from the immobility of the two figures in bold relief before the fire, that they feared to disturb the immobility of the scene; that they had been turned to stone where they sat, like the heroes of a fairy tale, and that the slightest word or movement would bring the walls of an imaginary city crumbling about their ears. And the dark-browed master, who alone broke the silence and the shadow with his regular tread, seemed a magician who held them under a spell.

At last the dog, having obtained a smile from her master, yielded to the magnetic power which the eye of man exerts over that of the lower animals. She uttered a low whine of timid affection and placed her fore paws on her beloved's shoulders with inimitable ease and grace of movement.

"Down, Ophelia, down!"

And the young man reproved the docile creature sternly in English, whereupon she crawled toward Madame Delmare, shamefaced and repentant, as if to implore her protection. But Madame Delmare did not emerge from her reverie, and allowed Ophelia's head to rest on her two white hands, as they lay clasped on her knee, without bestowing a caress upon her.

"Has that dog taken up her quarters in the salon for good?" said the colonel, secretly well-pleased to find a pretext for an outburst of ill-humor, to pass the time. "Be off to your kennel, Ophelia! Come, out with you, you stupid beast!"

If anyone had been watching Madame Delmare closely

he could have divined, in that trivial and commonplace incident of her private life, the painful secret of her whole existence. An imperceptible shudder ran over her body, and her hands, in which she unconsciously held the favorite animal's head, closed nervously around her rough, hairy neck, as if to detain her and protect her. Whereupon Monsieur Delmare, drawing his hunting-crop from the pocket of his jacket, walked with a threatening air toward poor Ophelia, who crouched at his feet, closing her eyes, and whining with grief and fear in anticipation. Madame Delmare became even paler than usual; her bosom heaved convulsively, and, turning her great blue eyes upon her husband with an indescribable expression of terror, she said:

"In pity's name, monsieur, do not kill her!"

These few words gave the colonel a shock. A feeling of chagrin took the place of his angry impulse.

"That, madame, is a reproof which I understand very well," he said, "and which you have never spared me since the day that I killed your spaniel in a moment of passion while hunting. He was a great loss, was he not? A dog that was forever forcing the hunting and rushing after the game! Whose patience would he not have exhausted? Indeed, you were not nearly so fond of him until he was dead; before that you paid little attention to him; but now that he gives you a pretext for blaming me—"

"Have I ever reproached you?" said Madame Delmare in the gentle tone which we adopt from a generous impulse with those we love, and from self-esteem with those whom we do not love.

"I did not say that you had," rejoined the colonel in a half-paternal, half-conjugal tone; "but the tears of some women contain bitterer reproaches than the fiercest imprecations of others. *Morbleu!* madame, you know perfectly well that I hate to see people weeping about me."

"I do not think that you ever see me weep."

"Even so! don't I constantly see you with red eyes? On my word, that's even worse!"

During this conjugal colloquy the young man had risen and put Ophelia out of the room with the greatest tranquillity; then he returned to his seat opposite Madame Delmare after lighting a candle and placing it on the chimney-piece.

This act, dictated purely by chance, exerted a sudden influence upon Monsieur Delmare's frame of mind. As soon as the light of the candle, which was more uniform and steadier than that of the fire, fell upon his wife, he observed the symptoms of suffering and general prostration which were manifest that evening in her whole person: in her weary attitude, in the long brown hair falling over her emaciated cheeks and in the purple rings beneath her dull, inflamed eyes. He took several turns up and down the room, then returned to his wife and, suddenly changing his tone:

"How do you feel to-day, Indiana?" he said, with the stupidity of a man whose heart and temperament are rarely in accord.

"About as usual, thank you," she replied, with no sign of surprise or displeasure.

"'As usual' is no answer at all, or rather it's a woman's answer; a Norman answer, that means neither yes nor no, neither well nor ill."

"Very good; I am neither well nor ill."

"I say that you lie," he retorted with renewed roughness; "I know that you are not well; you have told Sir Ralph here that you are not. Tell me, isn't that the truth? Did she not tell you so, Monsieur Ralph?"

"She did," replied the phlegmatic individual addressed, paying no heed to the reproachful glance which Indiana bestowed upon him.

At that moment a fourth person entered the room: it was the factotum of the household, formerly a sergeant in Monsieur Delmare's regiment.

He explained briefly to Monsieur Delmare that he had his reasons for believing that charcoal thieves had been in the park the last few nights at the same hour, and that he had come to ask for a gun to take with him in making his nightly round before locking the gates. Monsieur Delmare, scenting powder in the adventure, at once took down his fowling-piece, gave Lelièvre another, and started to leave the room.

"What!" said Madame Delmare in dismay, "you would kill a poor peasant on account of a few bags of charcoal?"

"I will shoot down like a dog," retorted Delmare, irritated by this remonstrance, "any man whom I find prowling around my premises at night. If you knew the law, madame, you would know that it authorizes me to do it."

"It is a horrible law," said Indiana, warmly. But she quickly repressed this impulse and added in a lower tone: "But your rheumatism? You forget that it rains, and that you will suffer for it to-morrow if you go out to-night."

"You are terribly afraid that you will have to nurse your old husband," replied Delmare, impatiently opening the door.

And he left the room, still muttering about his age and his wife.

II

The two personages whom we have mentioned, Indiana Delmare and Sir Ralph, or, if you prefer, Monsieur Rodolphe Brown, continued to face each other, as calm and cold as if the husband were standing between them. The Englishman had no idea of justifying himself, and Madame Delmare realized that she had no serious grounds for reproaching him, for he had spoken with no evil intention. At last, making an effort, she broke the silence and upbraided him mildly.

"That was not well done of you, my dear Ralph," she said. "I had forbidden you to repeat the words that I let slip in a moment of pain, and Monsieur Delmare is the last person in the world whom I should want told of my trouble."

"I can't understand you, my dear," Sir Ralph replied; "you are ill and you refuse to take care of yourself. I had to choose between the chance of losing you and the necessity of letting your husband know."

"Yes," said Madame Delmare, with a sad smile, "and you decided to *notify the authorities.*"

"You are wrong, you are wrong, on my word, to allow yourself to inveigh so against the colonel; he is a man of honor, a worthy man."

"And who says that he's not, Sir Ralph?"

"Why, you do, without meaning to. Your depression, your ailing condition, and, as he himself observes, your red eyes, tell everybody every hour in the day that you are not happy."

"Hush, Sir Ralph, you go too far. I have never given you permission to find out so much."

"I anger you, I see; but what would you have! I am not clever; I am not acquainted with the subtle distinctions of your language, and then, too, I resemble your husband in many ways. Like him I am utterly in the dark as to what a man must say to a woman, either in English or in French, to console her. Another man would have conveyed to your mind, without putting it in words, the idea that I have just expressed so awkwardly; he would have had the art to insinuate himself into your confidence without allowing you to detect his progress, and perhaps he would have succeeded in affording some relief to your heart, which puts fetters on itself and locks itself up before me. This is not the first time that I have noticed how much more influence words have upon women than ideas, especially in France. Women more than——"

"Oh! you have a profound contempt for women, my dear Ralph. I am alone here against two of you, so I must make up my mind never to be right."

"Put us in the wrong, my dear cousin, by recovering your health, your good spirits, your bloom, your animation of the old days; remember Ile Bourbon and that delightful retreat of ours, Bernica, and our happy childhood, and our friendship, which is as old as you are yourself."

"I remember my father, too," said Indiana, dwelling sadly upon the words and placing her hand in Sir Ralph's.

They relapsed into profound silence.

"Indiana," said Ralph, after a pause, "happiness is always within our reach. Often one has only to put out his hand to grasp it. What do you lack? You have modest competence, which is preferable to great wealth, an excellent husband, who loves you with all his heart, and, I dare to assert, a sincere and devoted friend."

Madame Delmare pressed Sir Ralph's hand faintly, but she did not change her attitude; her head still hung forward on her breast and her tear-dimmed eyes were fixed on the magic effects produced by the embers.

"Your depression, my dear friend," continued Sir Ralph, "is due purely to physical causes; which one of us can escape disappointment, vexation? Look below you and you will see people who envy you, and with good reason. Man is so constituted that he always aspires to what he has not."

I spare you a multitude of other commonplaces which the excellent Sir Ralph put forth in a tone as monotonous and sluggish as his thoughts. It was not that Sir Ralph was a fool, but he was altogether out of his element. He lacked neither common sense nor shrewdness; but the rôle of consoler of women was, as he himself acknowledged, beyond his capacity. And this man had so little comprehension of another's grief, that with the best possible disposition to furnish a remedy, he could not touch it without inflaming it. He was so conscious of his awkwardness that he rarely ventured to take notice of his friend's sorrows; and on this occasion he made superhuman efforts to perform what he considered the most painful duty of friendship.

When he saw that Madame Delmare was obliged to make an effort to listen to him, he held his peace, and naught could be heard save the innumerable little voices whispering in the burning wood, the plaintive song of the log as it becomes heated and swells, the crackling of the bark as it curls before breaking, and the faint phosphorescent explosions of the alburnum, which emits a bluish flame. From time to time the baying of a dog mingled with the whistling of the wind through the cracks of the door and the beating of the rain against the window-panes. That evening was one of the saddest that Madame Delmare had yet passed in her little manor-house in Brie.

Moreover, an indefinable vague feeling of suspense weighed upon that impressionable soul and its delicate fibres. Weak creatures live on alarms and presentiments. Madame Delmare had all the superstitions of a nervous, sickly Creole; certain nocturnal sounds, certain phases of the moon were to her unfailing presages of specific events, of impending misfortunes, and the night spoke to that dreamy, melancholy creature a language full of mysteries and phantoms which she alone could understand and translate according to her fears and her sufferings.

"You will say again that I am mad," she said, withdrawing her hand, which Sir Ralph still held, "but some disaster, I don't know what, is preparing to fall upon us. Some danger is impending over someone—myself, no doubt—but, look you, Ralph, I feel intensely agitated, as at the approach of a great crisis in my destiny. I am afraid," she added, with a shudder, "I feel faint."

And her lips became as white as her cheeks. Sir Ralph, terrified, not by Madame Delmare's presentiments, which he looked upon as symptoms of extreme mental exhaustion, but by her deathly pallor, pulled the bell-rope violently to summon assistance. No one came, and as Indiana grew weaker and weaker, Sir Ralph, more alarmed in proportion, moved her away from the fire, deposited her in a reclining chair, and ran through the house at random, calling the servants, looking for water or salts, finding nothing, breaking all the bell-ropes, losing his way in the labyrinth of dark rooms, and wringing his hands with impatience and anger against himself.

At last it occurred to him to open the glass door that led into the park, and to call alternately Lelièvre and Noun, Madame Delmare's Creole maid.

A few moments later Noun appeared from one of the dark paths in the park, and hastily inquired if Madame Delmare were worse than usual.

"She is really ill," replied Sir Ralph.

They returned to the salon and devoted themselves to the task of restoring the unconscious Madame Delmare, one with all the ardor of useless and awkward zeal, the other with the skill and efficacy of womanly affection.

Noun was Madame Delmare's foster-sister; the two young women had been brought up together and loved each other dearly. Noun was tall and strong, glowing with health, active, alert, overflowing with ardent, passionate creole blood; and she far outshone with her resplendent beauty the frail and pallid charms of Madame Delmare; but the tenderness of their hearts and the strength of their attachment killed every feeling of feminine rivalry.

When Madame Delmare recovered consciousness, the first thing that she observed was the unusual expression of her maid's features, the damp and disordered condition of her hair and the excitement which was manifest in her every movement.

"Courage, my poor child," she said kindly; "my illness is more disastrous to you than to myself. Why, Noun, you are the one to take care of yourself; you are growing thin and weeping as if it were not your destiny to live; dear Noun, life is so bright and fair before you!"

Noun pressed Madame Delmare's hand to her lips effusively, and said, in a sort of frenzy, glancing wildly about the room:

"*Mon Dieu!* madame, do you know why Monsieur Delmare is in the park?"

"Why?" echoed Indiana, losing instantly the faint flush that had reappeared on her cheeks. "Wait a moment—I don't know—You frighten me! What is the matter, pray?"

"Monsieur Delmare declares that there are thieves in the park," replied Noun in a broken voice. "He is making the rounds with Lelièvre, both armed with guns."

"Well?" said Indiana, apparently expecting some shocking news.

"Why, madame," rejoined Noun, clasping her hands frantically, "isn't it horrible to think that they are going to kill a man?"

"Kill a man!" cried Madame Delmare, springing to her feet with the terrified credulity of a child frightened by it's nurse's tales.

"Ah! yes, they will kill him," said Noun, stifling her sobs.

"These two women are mad," thought Sir Ralph, who was watching this strange scene with a bewildered air. "Indeed," he added mentally, "all women are."

"But why do you say that, Noun," continued Madame Delmare; "do you believe that there are any thieves there?"

"Oh! if they were really thieves! but some poor peasant perhaps, who has come to pick up a handful of wood for his family!"

"Yes, that would be ghastly, as you say! But it is not probable; right at the entrance to Fontainebleau forest, when it is so easy to steal wood there, nobody would take the risk of a park enclosed by walls. Bah! Monsieur Delmare won't find anybody in the park, so don't you be afraid."

But Noun was not listening; she walked from the window to her mistress's chair, her ears strained to catch the slightest sound; she seemed torn between the longing to run after Monsieur Delmare and the desire to remain with the invalid.

Her anxiety seemed so strange, so uncalled-for to Monsieur Brown, that he laid aside his customary mildness of manner, and said, grasping her arm roughly:

"Have you lost your wits altogether? don't you see that you frighten your mistress and that your absurd alarms have a disastrous effect upon her?"

Noun did not hear him; she had turned her eyes upon her mistress, who had just started on her chair as if the concussion of the air had imparted an electric shock to her senses. Almost at the same instant the report of a gun shook the windows of the salon, and Noun fell upon her knees.

"What miserable woman's terrors!" cried Sir Ralph, worn out by their emotion; "in a moment a dead rabbit will be brought to you in triumph, and you will laugh at yourselves."

"No, Ralph," said Madame Delmare, walking with a firm step toward the door, "I tell you that human blood has been shed."

Noun uttered a piercing shriek and fell upon her face.

The next moment they heard Lelièvre's voice in the park:

"He's there! he's there! Well aimed, my colonel! the brigand is down!"

Sir Ralph began to be excited. He followed Madame Delmare. A few moments later a man covered with blood and giving no sign of life was brought under the peristyle.

"Not so much noise! less shrieking!" said the colonel

with rough gayety to the terrified servants who crowded around the wounded man; "this is only a joke; my gun was loaded with nothing but salt. Indeed I don't think I touched him; he fell from fright."

"But what about this blood, monsieur?" said Madame Delmare in a profoundly reproachful tone, "was it fear that caused it to flow?"

"Why are you here, madame?" cried Monsieur Delmare, "what are you doing here?"

"I have come to repair the harm that you have done, as it is my duty to do," replied Madame Delmare coldly.

She walked up to the wounded man with a courage of which no one of the persons present had as yet felt capable, and held a light to his face. Thereupon, instead of the plebeian features and garments which they expected to see, they discovered a young man with noble features and fashionably dressed, albeit in hunting costume. He had a trifling wound on one hand, but his torn clothes and his swoon indicated a serious fall.

"I should say as much!" said Lelièvre; "he fell from a height of twenty feet. He was just putting his leg over the wall when the colonel fired, and a few grains of small shot or salt in the right hand prevented his getting a hold. The fact is, I saw him fall, and when he got to the bottom he wasn't thinking much about running away, poor devil!"

"Would any one believe," said one of the female servants, "that a man so nicely dressed would amuse himself by stealing?"

"And his pockets are full of money!" said another, who had unbuttoned the supposed thief's waistcoat.

"It is very strange," said the colonel, gazing, not without emotion, at the man stretched out before him.

"If the man is dead it's not my fault; examine his hand, madame, and see if you can find a particle of lead in it."

"I prefer to believe you, monsieur," replied Madame Delmare, who, with a self-possession and moral courage of which no one would have deemed her capable, was closely scrutinizing his pulse and the arteries of his neck. "Certainly," she added, "he is not dead, and he requires speedy attention. The man hasn't the appearance of a thief and perhaps he deserves our care; even if he does not deserve it, our duty calls upon us women to care for him none the less."

Thereupon Madame Delmare ordered the wounded man to be carried to the billiard room, which was nearest. A mattress was placed on several chairs, and Indiana, assisted by her women, busied herself in dressing the wounded hand, while Sir Ralph, who had some surgical knowledge, drew a large quantity of blood from him.

Meanwhile, the colonel, much embarrassed, found himself in the position of a man who has shown more ill-temper than he intended to show. He felt the necessity of justifying himself in the eyes of the others, or rather of making them justify him in his own eyes. So he had remained under the peristyle, surrounded by his servants, and indulging with them in the excited, prolix and perfectly useless disquisitions which are always forthcoming after the event. Lelièvre had already explained twenty times, with the most minute details, the shot, the fall and its results, while the colonel, who had recovered his good-nature among his own people, according to his custom after giving way to his anger, impeached the purposes of a man who entered private property in the night-time over the wall. Every one agreed with the master, when the gardener, quietly leading him aside, assured him that the thief was the living image of a young land-owner who had recently settled in the neighborhood, and whom he had seen talking with Mademoiselle Noun three days before at the rustic fête at Rubelles.

This information gave a different turn to Monsieur Delmare's ideas; on his ample forehead, bald and glistening, appeared a huge swollen vein, which was always the precursor of a tempest.

"Morbleu!" he said, clenching his fists, "Madame Delmare takes a deal of interest in this puppy, who sneaks into my park over the wall!"

And he entered the billiard room, pale and trembling with wrath.

III

"You may be reassured, monsieur," said Indiana; "the man you killed will be quite well in a few days; at least we hope so, although he is not yet able to talk."

"That's not the question, madame," said the colonel, in a voice that trembled with suppressed passion; "I insist upon knowing the name of this interesting patient of yours, and how it came about that he mistook the wall of my park for the avenue to my house."

"I have absolutely no idea," replied Madame Delmare with such a cold and haughty air that her redoubtable spouse was bewildered for an instant.

But his jealous suspicions soon regained the upper hand.

"I shall find out, madame," he said in an undertone; "you may be sure that I shall find out."

Thereupon, as Madame Delmare pretended not to notice his rage and continued her attentions to the wounded man, he left the room, in order not to explode before the women, and recalled the gardener.

"What is the name of the man who, you say, resembles our prowler?"

"Monsieur de Ramière. It is he who has just bought Monsieur de Cercy's little English house."

"What sort of man is he? a nobleman, a fop, a fine gentleman?"

"A fine gentleman, monsieur; noble, I think."

"Undoubtedly," rejoined the colonel with emphasis. "Monsieur de Ramière! Tell me, Louis," he added, lowering his voice, "have you ever seen this fop prowling about here?"

"Last night, monsieur," Louis replied, with an embarrassed air, "I certainly saw—as to its being a fop, I can't say, but it was a man, sure enough."

"And you saw him?"

"As plainly as I see you, under the windows of the orangery."

"And you didn't fall upon him with the handle of your shovel?"

"I was just going to do it, monsieur; but I saw a woman in white come out of the orangery and go to meet him. At that I said to myself: 'Perhaps it's monsieur and madame, who have taken a fancy to walk a bit before daybreak;' and I went back to bed. But this morning I heard Lelièvre talking about a thief whose tracks he had seen in the park, and I said to myself: 'There's something under this.'"

"And why didn't you tell me immediately, stupid?"

"*Dame!* monsieur, there are some things in life that are *so delicate!*"

"I understand—you presume to have doubts. You are a fool; if you ever have another insolent idea of this sort I'll cut off your ears. I know very well who the thief is and why he came into the garden. I have put all these questions to you simply to find out what care you take of your orangery. Remember that I have some rare plants there that madame sets great store by, and that there are collectors who are insane enough to rob their neighbors' hothouses; it was I whom you saw last night with Madame Delmare."

And the poor colonel walked away, more tormented, more exasperated than before, leaving his gardener far from convinced that there are horticulturists fanatical enough to risk a bullet in order to purloin a shoot or a cutting.

Monsieur Delmare returned to the billiard-room and, paying no heed to the symptoms of returning consciousness which the wounded man displayed at last, he was preparing to search the pockets of his jacket which lay on a chair, when he put out his hand and said in a faint voice:

"You wish to know who I am, monsieur, but it is useless. I will tell you when we are alone. Until then spare me the embarrassment of making myself known in my present disagreeable and absurd position."

"It is a great pity in truth!" retorted the colonel sourly; "but I confess that I hardly appreciate it. However, as I trust that we shall meet again, and alone, I consent to defer an acquaintance until then. Meanwhile will you kindly tell me where I shall have you taken."

"To the public house in the nearest village, if you please."

"But monsieur is no condition to be moved, is he, Ralph?" said Madame Delmare hastily.

"Monsieur's condition affects you far too much, madame," said the colonel. "Leave the room, all of you," he said to the women in attendance. "Monsieur feels better, and he will find strength now to explain his presence on my premises."

"Yes, monsieur," rejoined the wounded man, "and I beg all those who have been kind enough to bestow any care upon me to listen to my acknowledgment of my misconduct. I feel that is of much importance that there should be no misunderstanding here of my motives, and it is of importance to myself that I should not be deemed what I am not. Let me tell you then what rascally scheme brought me to your park. You have installed, monsieur, by methods of extreme simplicity, known to you alone, a factory which is immeasurably superior to all similar factories in the province, both in respect to its processes and its product. My brother owns a very similar establishment in the south of France, but the cost of running it is enormous. His business was approaching shipwreck when I learned of the success of your venture; whereupon I determined to come and ask you to give me advice on certain points,—a generous service which could not possibly injure your own interests, as my brother's output is of an entirely different nature from yours. But the gate of your English garden was rigorously closed to me; and when I asked for an interview with you, I was told that you would not even allow me to look over your establishment. Repelled by these discourteous refusals, I determined to save my brother's life and honor even at the peril of my own; I entered your premises at night by scaling the wall, and tried to obtain entrance to the factory in order to examine the machinery. I had determined to hide in a corner; to bribe your workmen, to steal your secret,—in a word, to enable an honest man to profit by it without injuring you. Such was my crime. Now, monsieur, if you demand any other reparation than that which you have just taken, I am ready to offer it to you as soon as I am strong enough; indeed, I may perhaps demand it."

"I think that we should cry quits, monsieur," replied the colonel, half relieved from a great anxiety. "Take notice, all of you, of the explanation monsieur has given me. I am over-avenged, assuming that I require any revenge. Go now and leave us to discuss my profitable business operations."

The servants left the room; but they alone were deceived by this reconciliation. The wounded man, weakened by his long speech, was not capable of appreciating the tone of the colonel's last words. He fell back into Madame Delmare's arms and lost consciousness a second time. She leaned over him, not deigning to raise her eyes to her angry husband, and the two strikingly contrasted faces of Monsieur Delmare and Monsieur Brown, the one pale and distorted by anger, the other calm and expressionless as usual, questioned each other in silence.

Monsieur Delmare did not need to say a word to make himself understood; however he drew Sir Ralph aside and said, crushing his fingers in his grasp:

"This is an admirably woven intrigue, my friend. I am delighted, perfectly delighted with this young fellow's quick wit, which enabled him to save my honor in the eyes of my servants. But, *mordieu!* he shall pay dear for the insult, which I feel in the depths of my heart. And that woman nursing him, who pretends not to know him! Ah! how true it is that cunning is inborn in those creatures!"

Sir Ralph, utterly nonplussed, walked methodically up and down the room three times. At his first turn he drew the conclusion: *improbable;* at the second: *impossible;* at the third: *proven.* Then, returning with his impassive face to the colonel, he pointed to Noun, who was standing behind the wounded man, wringing her hands, with haggard eyes and livid cheeks, in the immobility of despair, terror and misery.

A real discovery carries with it such a power of swift and overwhelming conviction, that the colonel was more impressed by Sir Ralph's emphatic gesture than he would have been by the most persuasive eloquence. Doubtless Sir Ralph had more than one means of striking the right scent; he recalled the fact that Noun was in the park when he called her, her wet hair, her damp, muddy shoes, which testified to a strange fancy for walking abroad in the rain—trivial details which had made but slight impression on him at the time that Madame Delmare fainted, but which recurred to his memory now. Then, too, the extraordinary terror she had manifested, her convulsive agitation, and the cry she had uttered when she heard the shot.

Monsieur Delmare did not require all this evidence; being more penetrating because he had more interest in the matter, he had only to look at the girl's face to see that she alone was guilty. But his wife's assiduity in ministering to the hero of this amorous adventure became more and more distasteful to him.

"Leave us, Indiana," he said. "It is late and you are not well. Noun will remain with monsieur to take care of him during the night, and to-morrow, if he is better, we will see about having him taken home."

There was nothing to say in reply to this unexpected complaisance. Madame Delmare, who was so determined in her resistance to her husband's violence, always yielded to his milder moods. She requested Sir Ralph to remain a little longer with the patient, and withdrew to her bedroom.

Not without ulterior motives had the colonel arranged things thus. An hour later, when everybody had gone to bed and the house was still, he stole softly into the room where Monsieur de Ramière lay, and, hiding behind a curtain, was speedily convinced, by the young man's conversation with the lady's-maid, that an amorous intrigue between the two was in progress. The young creole's unusual beauty had created a sensation at the rustic balls in the neighborhood. She had not lacked offers of homage, even from members of some of the first families of the province. More than one handsome officer of lancers, in garrison at Melun, had put himself out to please her; but Noun was still to have her first love affair, and only one of her suitors had succeeded in pleasing her: Monsieur de Ramière.

Colonel Delmare was by no means desirous of following the development of their liaison; so he retired as soon as he had made sure that his wife had not for an instant occupied the thoughts of the Almaviva of this adventure. He heard enough of it, however, to realize the difference between the love of poor Noun, who threw herself into the affair with all the vehemence of her passionate nature, and that of the well-born youth, who yielded to the impulse of a day without abjuring the right to resume his reason on the morrow.

When Madame Delmare awoke she found Noun beside her bed, embarrassed and downcast. But she had ingenuously given credence to Monsieur de Ramière's explanation, the more readily as persons interested in Monsieur Delmare's line of trade had previously tried to surprise the secrets of the Delmare factory, by stratagem or by fraud. She attributed her companion's embarrassment therefore to the excitement and fatigue of the night, and Noun took courage when she saw the colonel calmly enter his wife's room and discuss the affair of the previous evening with her as a perfectly natural occurrence.

In the morning Sir Ralph had satisfied himself as to the patient's condition. The fall, although a severe one, had had no serious result; the wound in the hand had already closed; Monsieur de Ramière had expressed a desire to be taken to Melun, and he had distributed the contents of his purse among the servants to induce them to keep quiet concerning his adventure, in order, he said, that his mother, who lived within a few leagues, might not be alarmed. Thus the story became known very slowly, and in several different versions. Certain information concerning the English factory of Monsieur de Ramière, the brother, added weight to the fiction the intruder had happily improvised. The colonel and Sir Ralph had the delicacy to keep Noun's secret, without even letting her know that they knew it; and the Delmare family soon ceased to give any thought to the incident.

IV

You will find it difficult to believe perhaps that Monsieur de Ramière, a young man of brilliant intellect, considerable talents and many estimable qualities, accustomed to salon triumphs and to adventures in perfumed boudoirs, had conceived a very durable passion for the housekeeper in the household of a small manufacturer in Brie. And yet Monsieur de Ramière was neither fop nor libertine. We have said that he was intelligent—that is to say, he appreciated the advantages of birth at their real value. He was a man of high principle when he argued with himself; but vehement passions often carried him beyond the bounds of his theories. At such times he was incapable of reflection, or he avoided appearing before the tribunal of his conscience: he went astray, as if without his own knowledge, and the man of yesterday strove to deceive him of to-morrow. Unfortunately the most salient feature in his character was not his principles, which he possessed in common with many other white-gloved philosophers and which no more preserved him from inconsistency than they preserve them; but his passions, which no principles could stifle, and which made of him a man apart in that degenerate society where it is so difficult to depart from the beaten path without appearing ridiculous. Raymon had the art of being often culpable without arousing hatred, often eccentric without being offensive; indeed he sometimes succeeded in arousing the pity of people who had the most reason to complain of him. There are men who are humored thus by every one who approaches them. Sometimes an attractive face and animated speech make up the sum total of their sensibility. We do not presume to judge Monsieur Raymon de Ramière so harshly, nor to draw his portrait before exhibiting him in action. We are examining him now at a distance, like the multitude who pass him in the street.

Monsieur de Ramière was in love with the young creole with the great black eyes, who had aroused the admiration of the whole province at the fête of Rubelles; but he was in love and nothing more. He had made her acquaintance because he had nothing else to do, perhaps, and success had kindled his desires; he had obtained more than he asked, and on the day that he triumphed over that easily vanquished heart he returned home dismayed by his victory, and said to himself, striking his forehead:

"God grant that she doesn't love me!"

Thus it was not until after he had accepted all the proofs of her love that he began to suspect the existence of that love. Then he repented, but it was too late; he must either resign himself to what the future might have in store, or retreat like a coward toward the past. Raymon did not hesitate; he allowed himself to be loved, he loved in return for gratitude; he scaled the walls of the Delmare estate from love of danger; he had a terrible fall from awkwardness; and he was so touched by his lovely young mistress's grief that he deemed himself justified thenceforth in his own eyes in continuing to dig the pit into which she was destined to fall.

When he had recovered, winter had no storms, darkness no perils, remorse no stings which could deter him from passing through the corner of the forest to meet the young creole and swear to her that he had never loved any other woman; that he preferred her to the queens of society, and a thousand other exaggerations which will always be fashionable with poor and credulous maidens. In January Madame Delmare went to Paris with her husband; Sir Ralph Brown, their excellent neighbor, betook himself to his own estate, and Noun, being left in charge of her master's country house, was able to absent herself on various pretexts. It was unfortunate for her, and this facility of intercourse with her lover greatly abridged the ephemeral happiness which she was destined to enjoy. The forest with its poetic shadows, its arabesques of hoar-frost, its moonlight effects, the mysterious going and coming by the little gate, the furtive departure in the morning when Noun's little feet, as she accompanied him to the gate, left their prints on the snow in the park—all these accessories of an amorous intrigue served to prolong Monsieur de Ramière's intoxication. Noun, in white *déshablilé*, with her long black hair for ornament, was a lady, a queen, a fairy; when he saw her come forth from that red brick castle, a heavy, square structure of the time of the Regency, with a semi-feudal aspect, he could easily fancy her a châtelaine of the Middle Ages, and in the summer-house filled with rare flowers, where she made him drunk with the seductions of youth and passion, he readily forgot all that he was destined to remember later.

But when Noun, disdaining precautions and defying danger in her turn, came to him at his home, with her white apron and neckerchief coquettishly arranged according to the fashion of her country, she was nothing more than a maid and a maid in the service of a pretty woman —a circumstance that always makes a soubrette seem like a makeshift. And yet Noun was very lovely, it was in that dress that he had first seen her at that village fête where he had forced his way through the crowd of curious bystanders, and had enjoyed the petty triumph of carrying her off from a score of rivals. Noun would lovingly remind him of that day; she did not know, poor child, that Raymon's love did not date back so far, and that her day of pride had been only a day of vanity to him. And then the courage with which she sacrificed her reputation to him—that courage which should have made him love her all the more—displeased Monsieur de Ramière. The wife of a peer of France who should sacrifice herself so recklessly would be a priceless conquest; but a lady's maid! That which is heroism in the one becomes brazen-faced effrontery in the other.

With the one a world of jealous rivals envies you; with the other a rabble of scandalized flunkeys condemns you. The lady of quality sacrifices twenty previous lovers to you; the lady's maid sacrifices only a husband that she might have had.

What can you expect? Raymon was a man of fashionable morals, of elegant manners, of poetic passion. In his eyes a grisette was not a woman, and Noun, by virtue of a beauty of the first order, had taken him by surprise on a day of popular merrymaking. All this was not Raymon's fault; he had been reared to shine in society, all his thoughts had been directed toward an exalted goal, all his faculties had been moulded to enjoy princely good fortune, and the ardor of his blood had led him into bourgeois amours against his will. He had done all that he possibly could do to prolong his enjoyment, but he had failed; what was he to do now? Ideas extravagant in generosity had passed through his brain; on the days when he was most in love with his mistress he had thought seriously of raising her to his level, of legitimizing their union. Yes, upon my honor, he had thought of it; but love, which legitimizes everything, was growing weaker now; it was passing away with the perils of the intrigue and the piquant charm of mystery. Marriage was no longer possible; and note this: Raymon reasoned very cogently and altogether in his mistress's favor.

If he had really loved her, he could, by sacrificing to her his future, his family and his reputation, still have found happiness, and, consequently, have made her happy; for love is a contract no less than marriage. But, his ardor having cooled as he felt that it had, what future could he create for her? Should he marry her and display day after day a gloomy face, a cold heart, a comfortless home? Should he marry her and make her odious to her family, contemptible in the eyes of her equals, and a laughing-stock to her servants; take the risk of introducing her in a social circle where she would feel that she was out of place; where humiliation would kill her; and, lastly, overwhelm her with remorse by forcing her to realize all the trials she had brought upon her lover?

No, you will agree with him that it was impossible, that it would not have been generous, that a man cannot contend thus with society, and that such heroic virtue resembles Don Quixote breaking his lance against a windmill; an iron courage which a breath of wind scatters; the chivalry of another age which arouses the pitying contempt of this age.

Having thus weighed all the arguments, Monsieur de Ramière concluded that it would be better to break that unfortunate bond. Noun's visits were beginning to be painful to him. His mother, who had gone to Paris for the winter, would not fail to hear of the little scandal before long. Even now she was surprised at his frequent visits to Cercy, their country estate, and at his passing whole weeks there. He had, to be sure, alleged as a pretext, an important piece of work which he was finishing away from the noise of the city; but that pretext was beginning to be worn out. It grieved Raymon to deceive so kind a mother, to deprive her for so long a time of his filial attentions; and—how shall I tell you?—he left Cercy and did not return.

Noun wept and waited, and as the days and weeks passed, unhappy creature that she was, she ventured so far as to write. Poor girl! that was the last stroke. A letter from a lady's maid! Yet she had taken satin-finished paper and perfumed wax from Madame Delmare's desk, and her style from her heart. But the spelling! Do you know how much energy a syllable more or less adds to or detracts from the sentiments? Alas! the poor half-civilized girl from Ile Bourbon did not know even that there were rules for the use of language. She believed that she wrote and spoke as correctly as her mistress, and when she found that Raymon did not return she said to herself:

"And yet my letter was well adapted to bring him."

That letter Raymon lacked courage to read to the end. It was a masterpiece of ingenuous and graceful passion; it is doubtful if Virginia wrote Paul a more charming one after she left her native land. But Monsieur de Ramière made haste to throw it in the fire, fearful lest he should blush for himself. Once more, what do you expect? This is a prejudice of education, and self-love is a part of love just as self-interest is a part of friendship.

Monsieur de Ramière's absence had been noticed in society; that is much to say of a man, in respect to this society of ours where all men resemble one another. One may be a man of intelligence and still care for society, just as one may be a fool and despise it. Raymon liked it, and he was justified in his liking, for he was a favorite and was much sought after; and that multitude of indifferent or sneering masks assumed for him attentive and interested smiles. Unfortunate men may be misanthropes, but those persons of whom one is fond are rarely ungrateful; at least so Raymon thought. He was grateful for the slightest manifestations of attachment, desirous of universal esteem, proud of having a large number of friends.

In this society, whose prejudices are absolute, everything had succeeded in his case, even his faults; and when he sought the cause of this universal affection which had always encompassed him, he found it in himself, in his longing to obtain it, in the joy it caused him, in the hearty kindliness which he dealt out lavishly without exhausting it.

He owed it in some measure to his mother too, whose superior intelligence, sparkling conversation and private virtues made her an exceptional woman. It was from her that he inherited those excellent principles which always led him back to the right path and prevented him, despite the impetuosity of his twenty-five years, from ever forfeiting his claim to public esteem. Moreover, people were more indulgent to him than to others because his mother had the knack of apologizing for him while blaming him, of commanding indulgence when she seemed to implore it. She was one of those women who had lived through different epochs so utterly dissimilar that their minds become as flexible as their destinies; who have grown rich on experience of misfortune; who have escaped the scaffolds of '93, the vices of the Directory, the vanities of the Empire and the enmities of the Restoration; rare women, whose kind is dying out.

It was at a ball at the Spanish ambassador's that Raymon reappeared in society.

"Monsieur de Ramière, if I am not mistaken," said a pretty woman to her neighbor.

"He is a comet who appears at irregular intervals," was the reply. "It is centuries since any one heard of the pretty fellow."

The lady who spoke thus was a middle-aged foreigner. Her companion blushed slightly.

"He's very good-looking, is he not, madame?" she said.

"Charming, on my word," replied the old Sicilian.

"You are talking about the hero of the eclectic salons,

the dark-eyed Raymon, I'll be bound," said a dashing colonel of the guard.

"He has a fine head to study," rejoined the younger woman.

"And what pleases you even more, I dare say," said the colonel, "a wicked head."

The young woman was his wife.

"Why a wicked head?" queried the Sicilian.

"Full of genuine Southern passions, madame, worthy of the bright sunlight of Palermo."

Two or three young women put forward their flower-laden heads to hear what the colonel was saying.

"He made ravages in the garrison last year, I promise you," he continued. "We fellows shall be obliged to pick a quarrel with him, in order to get rid of him."

"If he's a Lovelace, so much the worse for him," said a young lady with a satirical cast of countenance; "I can't endure men whom everybody loves."

The ultramontane countess waited until the colonel had walked away, when she tapped Mademoiselle de Nangy's fingers lightly with her fan and said:

"Don't speak so; you don't know here what to think of a man who wants to be liked."

"Do you think, pray, that all they have to do is to want it?" said the damsel with the long sardonic eyes.

"Mademoiselle," said the colonel, coming up again to invite her to dance; "take care that the charming Raymon does not overhear you."

Mademoiselle de Nangy laughed; but during the rest of the evening the pretty group of which she was one dared not mention Monsieur de Ramière's name again.

V

Monsieur de Ramière wandered amid the undulating waves of that gayly-dressed crowd without distaste and without ennui.

Nevertheless, he was fighting against a feeling of chagrin. On returning to his own sphere he had a species of remorse, of shame for all the wild ideas which a misplaced attachment had suggested to him. He looked at the women so brilliantly beautiful in the bright light; he listened to their refined and clever conversation; he heard their talents highly praised; and in those marvellous specimens of their sex, those almost royal costumes, those exquisitely appropriate remarks, he found on all sides an implied reproach for having been untrue to his destiny. But, despite this species of mental bewilderment, Raymon suffered from more genuine remorse; for his intentions were always kind and considerate to the last degree, and a woman's tears broke his heart, hardened as it was.

The honors of the evening were universally accorded to a young woman whose name no one knew, and who enjoyed the privilege of monopolizing attention because her appearance in society was a novelty. The simplicity of her costume alone would have sufficed to make her a distinguished figure amid the diamonds, feathers and flowers in which the other women were arrayed. Strings of pearls woven into her black hair were her only jewels. The lustreless white of her necklace, her crêpe dress and her bare shoulders blended at a little distance, and the heated atmosphere of the apartments had barely succeeded in bringing to her cheeks a faint flush of as delicate a shade as that of a Bengal rose blooming on the snow. She was a tiny, dainty, slender creature; a salon type of beauty to which the bright light of the candles gave a fairylike touch, and which a sunbeam would have dimmed. When she danced she was so light that a breath would have whisked her away; but in her lightness there was no animation, no pleasure. When she was seated she bent forward as if her too flexible body lacked strength to support itself, and when she spoke she smiled sadly. Fantastic tales were at the very height of their vogue at this period. Accordingly, those who were learned in that line compared this young woman to a fascinating apparition evoked by sorcery, which would fade away and vanish like a dream when the first flush of dawn appeared on the horizon.

Meanwhile they crowded about her to invite her to dance.

"Make haste," said a dandy of a romantic turn to one of his friends; "the cock will crow soon, and even now your partner's feet have ceased to touch the floor. I'll wager that you can't feel her hand in yours."

"Pray look at Monsieur de Ramière's dark, strongly-marked face," said an *artistic* lady to her neighbor. "Contrast him with that pale, slender young woman, and see if the *solid* tone of the one doesn't make an admirable foil for the *delicate* tone of the other."

"That young woman," said a woman who knew everybody and who played the part of an almanac at social functions, "is the daughter of that old fool, De Carvajal, who tried to play Joséphin, and who died ruined at Ile Bourbon. This lovely exotic flower has made a foolish marriage, I believe; but her aunt stands well at court."

Raymon had drawn near the fair Indian. A peculiar emotion seized him every time that he looked at her; he had seen that pale, sad face; perhaps in some dream, but at all events he had seen it, and his eyes rested upon it with the delight we all feel on seeing once more a charming vision which we thought that we had lost forever.

Raymon's gaze disturbed her who was the object of it; she was awkward and shy, like a person unaccustomed to society, and the sensation that she caused seemed to embarrass rather than to please her. Raymon made the circuit of the salon, succeeded finally in learning that her name was Madame Delmare, and went and asked her to dance.

"You do not remember me," he said, when they were alone in the midst of the crowd; "but I have not been able to forget you, madame. And yet I saw you for an instant only, through a cloud; but in that instant you seemed so kind, so compassionate."

Madame Delmare started.

"Oh! yes, monsieur," she said quickly, "it is you! I recognized you, too."

Then she blushed and seemed to fear that she had offended the proprieties. She looked around as if to see whether anyone had heard her. Her timidity enhanced her natural charm, and Raymon was touched to the heart by the tone of that creole voice, slightly husky, but so sweet that it seemed made to pray or to bless.

"I was afraid," he said, "that I should never have an opportunity to thank you. I could not call upon you and I knew that you went but little into society. I feared, also, that if I made your acquaintance I should come in contact with Monsieur Delmare, and our previous relations could not fail to make that contact disagreeable.

How glad I am for this moment, which enables me to pay the debt of my heart!"

"It would be much pleasanter for me," said she, "if Monsieur Delmare also could enjoy it; and if you knew him better you would know that he is as kind as he is brusque. You would forgive him for having been your involuntary assailant, for his heart certainly bled more freely than your wound."

"Let us not talk of Monsieur Delmare, madame; I forgive him with all my heart. I injured him and he took the law into his own hands. I have nothing more to do but to forget; but as to you, madame, who lavished such delicate and generous attentions upon me, I choose to remember all my life your treatment of me, your pure features, your angelic gentleness, and these hands which poured balm upon my wounds and which I dared not kiss."

While he spoke Raymon held Madame Delmare's hand, to be prepared to walk through their figure in the contra-dance. He pressed that hand gently in his, and all the young woman's blood rushed to her heart.

When he led Madame Delmare back to her seat, her aunt, Madame de Carvajal, had gone; the crowd was thinning. Raymon sat down beside her. He had that ease of manner which a wide experience in affairs of the heart imparts; it is the violence of our desires, the precipitate haste of our love, that makes us stupid when we are with women. The man who has rubbed the edge off his emotions a little is more anxious to please than to love. Nevertheless Monsieur de Ramière felt more deeply moved in the presence of that simple, unspoiled woman than he had ever been. Perhaps this swift impression was due to his memory of the night he had passed at her house; but it is certain that, while he talked to her with animation, his heart did not lead his mouth astray. However, the habit he had acquired with other women gave to his words a power of persuasion to which the untutored Indiana yielded, not understanding that it had not all been invented expressly for her.

In general—and women are well aware of it—a man who talks wittily of love is only moderately in love. Raymon was an exception; he expressed passion artistically and felt it ardently. But it was not passion that rendered him eloquent, it was eloquence that made him passionate. He knew that he had a weakness for women, and he would become eloquent in order to seduce a woman and fall in love with her while seducing her. It was sentiment of the sort dealt in by advocates and preachers, who weep hot tears when they perspire freely. He sometimes fell in with women who were shrewd enough to distrust these heated improvisations; but he had committed what are called follies for love's sake: he had run away with a girl of noble birth; he had compromised women of very high station; he had had three sensational duels; he had displayed to a crowded evening party, to a whole theatre full of spectators, the bewilderment of his heart and the disarray of his thoughts. A man who does all this without fear of ridicule or of curses, and who succeeds in avoiding both, is safe from all assault; he can take any risk and hope for anything. Thus the most skilfully constructed defences yielded to the consideration that Raymon was madly in love when he meddled with love at all. A man capable of making a fool of himself for love is a rare prodigy in society, and one that women do not disdain.

I do not know how it happened, but when he escorted Madame de Carvajal and Madame Delmare to their carriage he succeeded in putting Indiana's little hand to his lips. Never before had a man's furtive, burning kiss breathed upon that woman's fingers, although she was born in a fiery climate and was nineteen years old; nineteen years of Ile Bourbon, which are equivalent to twenty-five in our country.

Ill and nervous as she was, that kiss almost extorted a shriek from her, and she had to be assisted into the carriage. Raymon had never come in contact with such a delicate organization. Noun, the creole, was in robust health, and Parisian women do not faint when their hands are kissed.

"If I should see her twice," he said to himself as he walked away, "I should lose my head over her."

The next morning he had completely forgotten Noun.

All that he knew about her was that she belonged to Madame Delmare. The pale-faced Indiana engrossed all his thoughts, filled all his dreams. When Raymon began to feel the shafts of love he was in the habit of seeking to distract his thoughts, not in order to stifle the budding passion, but, on the contrary, to drive away the reasoning power that urged him to weigh its consequences. Of an ardent temperament, he pursued his object hotly. He had not the power to quell the tempests which arose in his bosom, nor to rekindle them when he felt that they were dying away and vanishing.

He succeeded the next day in learning that Monsieur Delmare had gone to Brussels on a business trip, and had left his wife in charge of Madame de Carvajal, of whom he was not at all fond, but who was Madame Delmare's only relative. He, an upstart soldier, belonged to a poor and obscure family, of which he seemed to be ashamed, simply because he repeated so often that he was not ashamed of it. But, although he passed his life reproaching his wife for alleged scorn of him which she did not entertain, he was conscious that he ought not to compel her to live on terms of intimacy with his uneducated kindred. Moreover, despite his dislike for Madame de Carvajal, he could not refuse to treat her with great deference for these reasons.

Madame de Carvajal, who was descended from a noble Spanish family, was one of those women who cannot make up their minds to be of no account in the world. In the days when Napoleon ruled Europe she had burned incense to the glory of Napoleon, and with her husband and brother-in-law had joined the party of the Joséphinos; but her husband had lost his life at the fall of the conqueror's short-lived dynasty, and Indiana's father had taken refuge in the French colonies. Thereupon Madame de Carvajal, being a clever and active person, had repaired to Paris, and there, by some fortunate speculations on the Bourse, had built up for herself a new competence on the ruins of her past splendors. By dint of shrewd wit, intrigues and piety she had also obtained some favor at Court, and her establishment, while it was by no means brilliant, was one of the most respectable of all those presided over by protégés of the Civil List.

When Indiana arrived in France after her father's death, as the bride of Colonel Delmare, Madame de Carvajal was but moderately pleased by so paltry an alliance. Nevertheless she saw that Monsieur Delmare, whose good sense and activity in business were worth a dowry, prospered with his slender capital; and she purchased for Indiana the little château of Lagny and the factory connected with it. In two years, thanks to Monsieur Delmare's technical knowledge and certain funds advanced by Sir Rodolphe Brown, his wife's cousin by marriage, the colonel's affairs took a fortunate turn; he began to pay off his debts, and Madame de Carvajal, in whose eyes fortune was the first recommendation, manifested much affection for her niece and promised her the remnant of her wealth. Indiana, who was devoid of ambition, was devotedly kind and attentive to her aunt from gratitude, not from self-interest; but there was at least as much of one as of the other in the colonel's manœuvres. He was a man of iron in the matter of his political opinions; he would listen to no argument concerning the unassailable glory of his great emperor, and he upheld that glory with the blind obstinacy of a child of sixty years. He was obliged therefore to put forth all his patience to refrain from breaking out again and again in Madame de Carjaval's salon, where the Restoration was lauded to the skies. What Delmare suffered at the hands of five or six pious old women is beyond description. His vexation on this account was in part the cause of his frequent ill-humor against his wife.

So much for Madame de Carvajal; we return now to Monsieur de Ramière. At the end of three days he had learned all these domestic details, so actively had he followed up everything likely to put him in the way of an intimate acquaintance with the Delmare family. He learned that by acquiring Madame de Carvajal's favor he could obtain opportunities of meeting Indiana. On the evening of the third day he procured an introduction to the aunt.

In her salon there were four or five barbarians solemnly playing *reversi,* and two or three young men of family, as utterly vapid as it is allowable for a man to be who has sixteen quarterings of nobility. Indiana was at work patiently filling in the background of a piece of embroidery on her aunt's frame. She was leaning over her work, apparently absorbed by that mechanical operation, and, it may be, well pleased to escape in this way the dull chatter of her neighbors. For aught I know, behind the long black hair that fell over the flowers of her embroidery, she was reviewing in her mind the emotions of that fleeting instant which had opened the door of a new life to her, when the servant's voice, announcing several new arrivals, made it necessary for her to rise. She did so mechanically, for she had paid no heed to the names, and barely lifted her eyes from her embroidery; but a voice at her side made her start as if she had received an electric shock, and she was obliged to lean on her work-table to avoid falling.

VI

Raymon was not prepared for that silent salon, peopled only by a few taciturn guests. It was impossible to utter a word which was not heard in every corner of the room. The dowagers who were playing cards seemed to be there for the sole purpose of embarrassing the conversation of the younger guests, and Raymon fancied that he could read on their stern features the secret satisfaction which old age takes in avenging itself by blocking other people's pleasure. He had counted upon a less constrained, tenderer interview than that of the ball, and it was just the opposite. This unexpected difficulty gave greater intensity to his desires, more fire to his glances, more animation and vivacity to the roundabout remarks he addressed to Madame Delmare. The poor child was altogether unused to this style of attack. She could not possibly defend herself, because nothing was asked of her; but she was forced to listen to the proffer of an ardent heart, to learn how dearly she was loved, and to allow herself to be encompassed by all the perils of seduction without making any resistance. Her embarrassment increased with Raymon's boldness. Madame de Carvajal, who made some reasonably well-founded claims to wit, and to whom Monsieur de Ramière's wit had been highly praised, left the card-table to challenge him to a refined discussion concerning love, into which she introduced much Spanish heat and German metaphysics. Raymon eagerly accepted the challenge, and, on the pretext of answering the aunt, said to the niece all that she would have refused to hear. The poor young wife, without a protector and exposed to so lively and skilful an assault on all sides, could not muster strength to take part in that thorny discussion. In vain did her aunt, who was anxious to exhibit her to advantage, call upon her to testify to the truth of certain subtle theories of sentiment; she confessed blushingly that she knew nothing about such things, and Raymon, intoxicated with joy to see her cheeks flush and her bosom heave, swore inwardly that he would teach her.

Indiana slept less that night than she had done for the last two or three nights; as we have said, she had never been in love, and her heart had long been ripe for a sentiment which none of the men she had met hitherto had succeeded in arousing. She had been brought up by a father of an eccentric and violent character, and had never known the happiness which is derived from the affection of another person. Monsieur de Carvajal, drunk with political passions, consumed by ambitious regrets, had become the most cruel planter and the most disagreeable neighbor in the colonies; his daughter had suffered keenly from his detestable humor. But, by dint of watching the constant tableau of the evils of slavery, of enduring the weariness of solitude and dependence, she had acquired a superficial patience, proof against every trial, an adorable kindliness toward her inferiors, but also an iron will and an incalculable power of resistance to everything that tended to oppress her. By marrying Delmare she simply changed masters; by coming to live at Lagny, she changed her prison and the locus of her solitude. She did not love her husband, perhaps for the very reason that she was told that it was her duty to love him, and that it had become with her a sort of second nature, a principle of conduct, a law of conscience, to resist mentally every sort of moral constraint. No one had attempted to point out to her any other law than that of blind obedience.

Brought up in the desert, neglected by her father, surrounded by slaves, to whom she could offer no other assistance or encouragement than her compassion and her tears, she had accustomed herself to say: "A day will come when everything in my life will be changed, when I shall do good to others, when some one will love me, when I shall give my whole heart to the man who gives me his; meanwhile, I will suffer in silence and keep my love as a reward for him who shall set me free." This liberator, this Messiah had not come; Indiana was still awaiting him. She no longer dared, it is true, to confess to herself her whole thought. She had realized under the clipped hedge-rows of Lagny that thought itself was more fettered there than under the wild palms of Ile Bourbon; and when she caught herself saying, as she used to say: "A day will come—a man will come"—she forced that rash longing back to the depths of her heart, and said to herself: "Death alone will bring that day!"

And so she was dying. A strange malady was consuming her youth. She was without strength and unable to sleep. The doctors looked in vain for any discoverable disorder, for none existed; all her faculties were failing away in equal degree, all her organs were gradually degenerating; her heart was burning at a slow fire, her eyes were losing their lustre, the circulation of her blood was governed entirely by excitement and fever; a few months more and the poor captive bird would surely die. But, whatever the extent of her resignation and her discouragement, the need remained the same. That silent, broken heart was still calling involuntarily to some generous youthful heart to revivify it. The being whom she had loved most dearly hitherto was Noun, the cheery and brave companion of her tedious solitude; and the man who had manifested the greatest liking for her was her phlegmatic cousin Sir Ralph. What food for the all-consuming activity of her thoughts—a poor girl, ignorant and neglected like herself, and an Englishman whose only passion was fox-hunting!

Madame Delmare was genuinely unhappy, and the first time that she felt the burning breath of a young and passionate man enter her frigid atmosphere, the first time that a tender and caressing word delighted her ear, and quivering lips left a mark as of a red-hot iron on her hand, she thought neither of the duties that had been laid upon her, nor of the prudence that had been enjoined upon her, nor of the future that had been predicted for her; she remembered only the hateful past, her long suffering, her despotic masters. Nor did it occur to her that the man before her might be false or fickle. She saw him as she wished him to be, as she had dreamed of him, and Raymon could easily have deceived her if he had not been sincere.

But how could he fail to be sincere with so lovely and loving a woman? What other had ever laid bare her heart to him with such candor and ingenuousness? With what other had he been able to look forward to a future so captivating and so secure? Was she not born to love him, this slave who simply awaited a sign to break her chains, a word to follow him? Evidently heaven had made for Raymon this melancholy child of Ile Bourbon, whom no one had ever loved, and who but for him must have died.

Nevertheless a feeling of terror succeeded this all-pervading, feverish joy in Madame Delmare's heart. She thought of her quick-tempered, keen-eyed, vindictive husband, and she was afraid,—not for herself, for she was inured to threats, but for the man who was about to undertake a battle to the death with her tyrant. She knew so little of society that she transformed her life into a tragic romance; a timid creature, who dared not love for fear of endangering her lover's life, she gave no thought to the danger of destroying herself.

This then was the secret of her resistance, the motive of her virtue. She made up her mind on the following day to avoid Monsieur de Ramière. That very evening there was a ball at the house of one of the leading bankers of Paris. Madame de Carvajal, who, being an old woman with no ties of affection, was very fond of society, proposed to attend with Indiana; but Raymon was to be there and Indiana determined not to go. To avoid her aunt's persecution, Madame Delmare, who was never able to resist except in action, pretended to assent to the plan; she allowed herself to be dressed and waited until Madame de Carvajal was ready; then she changed her ball dress for a robe de chambre, seated herself in front of the fire and resolutely awaited the conflict. When the old

Spaniard, as rigid and gorgeous as a portrait by Van Dyck, came to call her, Indiana declared that she was not well and did not feel that she could go out. In vain did her aunt urge her to make an effort.

"I would be only too glad to go," she said, "but you see that I can hardly stand. I should be only a trouble to you to-night. Go to the ball without me, dear aunt; I shall enjoy the thought of your pleasure."

"Go without you!" said Madame de Carvajal, who was sorely distressed at the idea of having made an elaborate toilet to no purpose, and who shrank from the horrors of a solitary evening. "Why, what business have I in society, an old woman whom no one speaks to except to be near you? What will become of me without my niece's lovely eyes to give me value?"

"Your wit will fill the gap, my dear aunt," said Indiana.

The Marquise de Carvajal, who only wanted to be urged, set off at last. Whereupon, Indiana hid her face in her hands and began to weep; for she had made a great sacrifice and believed that she had already blasted the attractive prospect of the day before.

But Raymon would not have it so. The first thing that he saw at the ball was the old marchioness's haughty aigrette. In vain did he look for Indiana's white dress and black hair in her vicinity. He drew near and heard her say in an undertone to another lady:

"My niece is ill; or rather," she added, to justify her own presence at the ball, "it's a mere girlish whim. She wanted to be left alone in the salon with a book in her hand, like a sentimental beauty."

"Can it be that she is avoiding me?" thought Raymon.

He left the ball at once. He hurried to the marchioness's house, entered without speaking to the concierge, and asked the first servant that he saw, who was half asleep in the antechamber, for Madame Delmare.

"Madame Delmare is ill."

"I know it. I have come at Madame de Carvajal's request to see how she is."

"I will tell madame."

"It is not necessary. Madame Delmare will receive me."

And Raymon entered the salon unannounced. All the other servants had retired. A melancholy silence reigned in the deserted apartments. A single lamp, covered with its green silk shade, lighted the main salon dimly. Indiana's back was turned to the door; she was completely hidden in the depths of a huge easy-chair, sadly watching the burning logs, as on the evening when Raymon entered the park of Lagny over the wall; sadder now, for her former undefined sufferings, aimless desires had given place to a fleeting joy, a gleam of happiness that was not for her.

Raymon, his feet encased in dancing shoes, approached noiselessly over the soft, heavy carpet. He saw that she was weeping, and, when she turned her head, she found him at her feet, taking forcible possession of her hands, which she struggled in vain to withdraw from his clasp. Then, I agree, she was overjoyed beyond words to find that her scheme of resistance had failed. She felt that she passionately loved this man who paid no heed to obstacles and who had brought happiness to her in spite of her efforts. She blessed heaven for rejecting her sacrifice, and, instead of scolding Raymon, she was very near thanking him.

As for him, he knew already that she loved him. He needed not to see the joy that shone through her tears to realize that he was master, and that he could venture.

He gave her no time to question him, but, changing rôles with her, vouchsafing no explanation of his unlooked-for presence, and no apology intended to make him seem less guilty than he was, he said:

"You are weeping, Indiana. Why do you weep? I insist upon knowing."

She started when he called her by her name; but there was additional joy in the surprise which that audacity caused her.

"Why do you ask?" she said. "I must not tell you."

"Well, I know, Indiana. I know your whole history, your whole life. Nothing that concerns you is unknown to me, because nothing that concerns you is indifferent to me. I resolved to know everything about you, and I have learned nothing that was not revealed to me during the brief moment that I passed under your roof, when I was brought, all crushed and bleeding, to your feet, and your husband was angry to see you, so lovely and so kind, support me with your soft arms and pour balm upon my wounds with your sweet breath. He was jealous? oh! I can readily understand it; I should have been, in his place, Indiana; or rather, in his place, I would kill myself; for to be your husband, madame, to possess you, to hold you in his arms, and not to deserve you, not to win your heart, is to be the most miserable or the most dastardly of men!"

"O heaven! hush," she cried, putting her hand over his mouth; "hush! for you make me guilty. Why do you speak to me of him? why seek to teach me to curse him? If he should hear you! But I have said no evil of him; I have not authorized you to commit this crime! I do not hate him; I esteem him, I love him!"

"Say rather that you are horribly afraid of him; for

the despot has broken your spirit, and fear has sat at your bedside ever since you became that man's prey. You, Indiana, profaned by the touch of that boor, whose iron hand has bowed your head and ruined your life! Poor child! so young and so lovely, to have suffered so horribly! for you cannot deceive me, Indiana, who look at you with other eyes than those of the common herd; I know all the secrets of your destiny, and you cannot hope to hide the truth from me. Let those who look at you because you are lovely say, when they notice your pallor and your melancholy: 'She is ill;'—well and good; but I, who follow you with my heart, whose whole soul encompasses you with solicitude and love, I am well aware what your disease is. I know that, if God had willed it so, if he had given you to me, unlucky wretch that I am, who deserve to have my head broken for having come so late, you would not be ill. On my life I swear, Indiana, I would have loved you so that you would have loved me the same and that you would have blessed the chain that bound us. I would have carried you in my arms to prevent your feet from being wounded; I would have warmed them with my breath. I would have held you against my breast to save you from suffering. I would have given all my blood to make up your lack of it, and if you had lost sleep with me, I would have passed the night saying soft words to you, smiling on you to restore your courage, weeping the while to see you suffer. When sleep had breathed upon your silken eyelids, I would have brushed them with my lips to close them more softly, and I would have watched over you, kneeling by your bed. I would have forced the air to caress you gently, golden dreams to throw flowers to you. I would have kissed noiselessly your lovely tresses, I would have counted with ecstatic joy the palpitations of your breast, and, at your awakening, Indiana, you would have found me at your feet, guarding you like a jealous master, waiting upon you as a slave, watching for your first smile, seizing upon your first thought, your first glance, your first kiss."

"Enough! enough!" said Indiana, agitated and quivering with emotion, "you make me faint."

And yet, if people died of happiness, Indiana would have died at that moment.

"Do not speak so to me," she said—"to me who am destined never to be happy; do not depict heaven upon earth to me who am doomed to die."

"To die!" cried Raymon vehemently, seizing her in his arms; "you, die! Indiana! die before you have lived—before you have loved! No, you shall not die; I will not let you die, for my life is bound to yours henceforth. You are the woman of whom I dreamed, the purity that I adored, the chimera that always fled from me, the bright star that shone before me and said to me: 'Go forward in this life of wretchedness and heaven will send one of its angels to bear you company.' You were always destined for me; your soul was always betrothed to mine, Indiana! Men and their iron laws have disposed of you; they have snatched from me the mate God would have chosen for me, if God did not sometimes forget his promises. But what do we care for men and laws if I love you still in another's arms, if you can still love me, accursed and unhappy as I am in having lost you! I tell you, Indiana, you belong to me; you are the half of my heart, which has long been struggling to join the other half. When you dreamed of a friend on Ile Bourbon, you dreamed of me; when, at the word husband, a sweet thrill of fear and hope passed through your heart, it was because I was destined to be your husband. Do you not recognize me? Does not it seem to you that we must have met twenty years ago? Did I not recognize you, my angel, when you stanched my blood with your veil, when you placed your hand on my dying heart to bring back its heat and its life? Ah! I remember distinctly enough. When I opened my eyes I said to myself: 'There she is! she has been like that in all my dreams—pale, melancholy and kind-hearted. She is my own; it is she who is destined to fill my cup with unknown joys.' And the physical life which returned to me then was your work. For we were brought together by no commonplace circumstances, you see; it was neither chance nor caprice, but fatality, death, which opened the gates of this new life to me. It was your husband—your master—who, guided by his destiny, brought me all bleeding in his arms and threw me at your feet, saying: 'Here is something for you!' And now nothing can part us."

"Yes, he can part us!" hastily interposed Madame Delmare, who, carried away by her lover's transports, had listened to him in ecstasy. "Alas! alas! you do not know him; he is a man who knows nothing of pardon—a man who cannot be deceived; He will kill you, Raymon!"

She hid her face in his bosom, sobbing. Raymon embraced her passionately.

"Let him come!" he cried; "let him come and snatch this moment of happiness from me! I defy him! Stay here, Indiana—here against my heart; let it be your refuge and your protection. Love me and I shall be invulnerable. You know that it is not in that man's power to kill me; I have already been exposed defenceless to his blows. But you, my good angel, were hovering over me, and your wings protected me. Have no fear, I say, we shall find a way to turn aside his wrath;

and now I am not even afraid for you, for I shall be at hand. And when this master of yours attempts to oppress you, I will protect you against him. I will rescue you, if necessary, from his cruel laws. Would you like me to kill him? Tell me that you love me, and I will be his executioner if you sentence him to death."

"Hush! hush! you make me shudder! If you wish to kill some one, kill me; for I have lived one whole day and I ask nothing more."

"Die, then, but let it be of happiness!" cried Raymon, pressing his lips to Indiana's.

But the storm was too severe for so fragile a plant; she turned pale, put her hand to her heart and swooned.

At first Raymon thought that his caresses would call her blood back into her icy veins; but in vain did he cover her hand with kisses; in vain did he call her by the sweetest names. It was not a premeditated swoon of the sort we so often see. Madame Delmare had been seriously ill for a long time, and was subject to nervous paroxysms which sometimes lasted whole hours. Raymon, in desperation, was reduced to the necessity of calling for help. He rang; a maid appeared; but the phial that she held escaped from her hands, and a cry from her throat, when she recognized Raymon. He, recovering instantly all his self-possession, put his mouth to her ear.

"Hush, Noun! I knew that you were here and I came to see you. I did not expect to see your mistress, who was, as I supposed, at the ball. When I came in I frightened her and she fainted. Be prudent; I am going away."

Raymon fled, leaving each of the two women in possession of a secret which was destined to carry despair to the heart of the other.

VII

The next morning Raymon, on waking, received a second letter from Noun. He did not toss this one disdainfully aside; on the contrary, he opened it eagerly: it might have something to say of Madame Delmare. So, in fact, it did; but in what an embarrassing position this complication of intrigues placed Raymon! It had become impossible to conceal the girl's secret. Already suffering and terror had thinned her cheeks. Madame Delmare observed her ailing condition, but was unable to discover its cause. Noun dreaded the colonel's severity, but she dreaded her mistress's gentleness even more. She was very sure that she would obtain forgiveness, but she would die of shame and grief in being forced to make the confession. What would become of her if Raymon were not careful to protect her from the humiliations that were certain to overwhelm her! He must give some thought to her, or she would throw herself at Madame Delmare's feet and tell her the whole story.

The fear of this result had a powerful effect upon Monsieur de Ramière. His first thought was to separate Noun from her mistress.

"Be very careful not to speak without my consent," he wrote in reply. "Try and be in Lagny this evening. I will be there."

On his way thither he reflected as to the course he had better pursue. Noun had common sense enough not to expect a reparation—that was out of the question. She had never dared to utter the word marriage, and because she was discreet and generous, Raymon deemed himself less guilty. He said to himself that he had not deceived her, and that Noun must have foreseen what her fate must be. The cause of Raymon's embarrassment was not any hesitation about offering the poor girl half of his fortune; he was ready to enrich her, to take all the care of her that the most sensitive delicacy could suggest. What made his position so painful was the necessity of telling her that he no longer loved her; for he did not know how to dissemble. Although his conduct at this crisis seems two-faced and treacherous, his heart was sincere, and had always been. He had loved Noun with his senses; he loved Madame Delmare with all his heart. Thus far he had lied to neither. His aim now was to avoid beginning to lie, and Raymon felt equally incapable of deceiving Noun and of dealing her the fatal blow. He must make a choice between a cowardly and a barbarous act. Raymon was very unhappy. He had come to no decision when he reached the gate of Lagny park.

Noun, for her part, had not expected so prompt a reply, and had recovered a little hope.

"He still loves me," she said to herself, "he doesn't mean to abandon me. He had forgotten me a little, that's not to be wondered at; in Paris, in the midst of merry-making, with all the women in love with him, as they are sure to be, he has allowed himself to be led away from the poor creole for a few moments. Alas! who am I that he should sacrifice to me all those great ladies who are much lovelier and richer than I am? Who knows," she said to herself artlessly, "perhaps the Queen of France is in love with him!"

By dint of meditating upon the seductions which luxurious surroundings probably exerted on her lover, Noun thought of a scheme for making herself more agreeable to him. She arrayed herself in her mistress's clothes, lighted a great fire in the room that Madame Delmare occupied at Lagny, decorated the mantel with the loveliest flowers she could find in the greenhouse, prepared a collation of fruit and choice wines, in a word resorted to all the dainty devices of the boudoir, of which she had never thought before; and when she looked at herself in a great mirror, she did herself no more than justice in deciding that she was fairer than the flowers with which she had sought to embellish her charms.

"He has often told me," she said to herself, "that I needed no ornaments to make me lovely, and that no woman at court, in all the splendor of her diamonds, was worth one of my smiles. And yet those same women that he used to despise fill his thoughts now. Come, I must be cheerful, I must seem lively and happy; perhaps I shall reconquer to-night all the love I once aroused in him."

Raymon, having left his horse at a charcoal-burner's cabin in the forest, entered the park, to which he had a key. This time he did not run the risk of being taken for a thief; for almost all the servants had gone with their masters, he had taken the gardener into his confidence, and he knew all the approaches to Lagny as well as those to his own estate.

It was a cold night; the trees in the park were enveloped in a dense mist, and Raymon could hardly distinguish their black trunks through the white mist which swathed them in diaphanous robes. He wandered some time through the winding paths before he found the door of the summer-house where Noun awaited him. She was wrapped in a pelisse with the hood thrown over her head.

"We cannot stay here," she said, "it is too cold. Follow me and do not speak."

Raymon felt an extreme reluctance to enter Madame Delmare's house as the lover of her maid. However, he could not but comply; Noun was walking lightly away in front of him, and this interview was to be the last.

She led him across the courtyard, quieted the dogs, opened the doors noiselessly, and, taking his hand, guided him in silence through the dark corridors; at last she ushered him into a circular room, furnished simply but with refinement, where flowering orange-bushes exhaled their sweet perfume; transparent wax candles were burning in the candelabra.

Noun had strewn the floor with the petals of Bengal roses, the divan was covered with violets, a subtle warmth entered at every pore, and the glasses gleamed on the table amid the fruit, whose ruddy cheeks were daintily blended with green moss.

Dazzled by the sudden transition from darkness to brilliant light, Raymon stood for a moment bewildered; but it was not long ere he realized where he was. The exquisite taste and chaste simplicity which characterized the furniture; the love stories and books of travel scattered over the mahogany shelves; the embroidery frame covered with a bright, pretty piece of work, the diversion of hours of patient melancholy; the harp whose strings seemed still to quiver with strains of love and longing; the engravings representing the pastoral attachment of Paul and Virginie, the peaks of Ile Bourbon and the blue shores of Saint-Paul; and, above all, the little bed half-hidden behind its muslin curtains, as white and modest as a maiden's bed, and over the headboard, by way of consecrated boxwood, a bit of palm, taken perhaps from some tree in her native island, on the day of her departure;—all these revealed the presence of Madame Delmare, and Raymon was seized with a strange thrill as he thought that that cloak-enveloped woman who had led him thither might be Indiana herself. This extravagant supposition seemed to be confirmed when he saw, in the mirror opposite, a white figure, the phantom of a woman entering a ball-room and laying aside her cloak, to appear, radiant and half-nude, in the dazzling light. But it was only a momentary error—Indiana would have concealed her charms more carefully; her modest bosom would have been visible only through the triple gauze veil of her corsage; she would perhaps have dressed her hair with natural camellias, but they would not have frisked about on her head in such seductive disorder; she might have encased her feet in satin shoes, but her chaste gown would not have betrayed thus shamelessly the mysteries of her shapely legs.

Taller and more powerfully built than her mistress, Noun was dressed, not clothed in her finery. She was graceful but lacked nobility of bearing; she was lovely with the loveliness of women, not of fairies; she invited pleasure and gave no promise of sublime bliss.

Raymon, after scrutinizing her in the mirror without turning his head, turned his eyes upon everything that was calculated to give forth a purer reflection of Indiana—the musical instruments, the paintings, the narrow, maidenly bed. He was intoxicated by the vague perfume her presence had left behind in that sanctuary; he shuddered with desire as he thought of the day when Indiana herself should throw open its delights to him; and Noun, standing behind him with her arms folded, gazed ecstatically at him, fancying that he was overwhelmed with delight at the sight of all the pains she had taken to please him.

But he broke the silence at last.

"I thank you," he said, "for all the preparations you have made for me; I thank you especially for bringing me here, but I have enjoyed this pleasant surprise long enough. Let us leave this room; we are not in our proper place here, and I must have some respect for Madame Delmare, even in her absence."

"That is very cruel," said Noun, who did not understand him, but remarked his cold and displeased manner; "it is very hard to have had such hopes of pleasing you and to see that you spurn me."

"No, dear Noun, I shall never spurn you; I came here to have a serious talk with you and to show you the deep affection that I owe you. I am grateful for your desire to please me; but I loved you better adorned by your youth and your natural charms than in this borrowed finery."

Noun half understood and wept.

"I am a miserable creature," she said; "I hate myself, for I no longer please you. I should have foreseen that you would not love me long, being, as I am, a poor, uneducated girl. I do not reproach you for anything. I knew well enough that you would not marry me; but if you would have kept on loving me, I would have sacrificed everything without a regret, endured everything without complaining. Alas! I am ruined! I am dishonored! perhaps I shall be turned out-of-doors. I am going to give life to a creature who will be even more unfortunate than I am, and no one will pity me. Everyone will feel that he has a right to trample on me. But I would joyfully submit to all that, if you still loved me."

Noun talked thus a long while. Perhaps she did not repeat the same words, but she said the same things, and said them a hundred times more eloquently than I can say them. Where are we to look for the secret of the eloquence which suddenly reveals itself to an ignorant, inexperienced mind in the crisis of a genuine passion and a profound sorrow ? At such times words have a greater value than in all the other scenes of life ; at such times trivial words become sublime by reason of the sentiment that dictates them and the accent with which they are spoken. At such times the woman of the lowest rank, abandoning herself to the frenzy of her emotions, becomes more pathetic and more convincing than her to whom education has taught moderation and reserve.

Raymon was flattered to find that he had inspired so generous an attachment, and gratitude, compassion, perhaps a little vanity, rekindled love for a moment.

Noun was suffocated by her tears ; she had torn the flowers from her hair which fell in disorder over her broad and dazzling shoulders. If Madame Delmare had not had her slavery and her sufferings to heighten her charms, Noun would have surpassed her immeasurably in beauty at that moment ; she was resplendent with grief and love. Raymon was vanquished ; he drew her into his arms, made her sit beside him on the sofa, moved the little decanter-laden table nearer to them, and poured a few drops of orange-flower water in a silver cup for her. Comforted by this mark of interest far more than by the calming potion, Noun wiped away her tears and threw herself at Raymon's feet.

"Do love me," she said, passionately embracing his knees ; "tell me that you still love me and I shall be cured, I shall be saved. Kiss me as you used to, and I will not regret having ruined myself to give you a few days of pleasure."

She threw her cool, brown arms about him, she covered him with her long hair; her great black eyes emitted a burning languor and betrayed that ardor of the blood, that purely oriental lust which is capable of triumphing over all the efforts of the will, all the chaste delicacy of the thought. Raymon forgot everything—his resolutions, his new love and his surroundings. He returned Noun's delirious caresses. He moistened his lips at the same cup, and the heady wines which were close at hand completed the dethronement of their reason.

Little by little a vague and shadowy memory of Indiana was blended with Raymon's drunkenness. The two glass panels which repeated Noun's image *ad infinitum* seemed to be peopled by a thousand phantoms. He gazed into the depths of that multiple reflection, looking for a slenderer figure there, and it seemed to him that he could distinguish, in the last hazy and confused shadow of Noun's image the graceful and willowy form of Madame Delmare.

Noun, herself bewildered by the strong liquors which she knew not how to use, no longer noticed her lover's strange remarks. If she had not been as drunk as he, she would have understood that in his wildest flights Raymon was thinking of another woman. She would have seen him kiss the scarf and the ribbons Indiana had worn, inhale the perfume which reminded him of her, crumple in his burning hands the tissue that had covered her breast; but Noun appropriated all these transports to herself, when Raymon saw naught of her but Indiana's dress. If he kissed her black hair, he fancied that he was kissing Indiana's black hair. It was Indiana whom he saw in the fumes of the punch which Noun's hand had lighted; it was she who smiled upon him and beckoned him from behind those white muslin curtains; and it was she of whom he dreamed upon that chaste and spotless bed, when, yielding to the influence of love and wine, he led thither his dishevelled creole.

When Raymon woke, a sort of half light was shining through the cracks of the shutters, and he lay a long while without moving, absorbed by a vague feeling of surprise and gazing at the room in which he was and the bed in which he had slept, as if they were a vision of his slumber. Everything in Madame Delmare's chamber had been put in order. Noun, who had fallen asleep the sovereign mistress of that place, had waked in the morning a lady's-maid once more. She had taken away the flowers and put the remains of the collation out of sight; the furniture was all in place, nothing suggested the amorous debauch of the night, and Indiana's chamber had resumed its innocent and virtuous aspect.

Overwhelmed with shame, he rose and attempted to leave the room, but he was locked in; the window was thirty feet from the ground, and he must needs remain in that remorse-laden atmosphere, like Ixion on his wheel. Thereupon he fell on his knees with his face toward that disarranged, tumbled bed which made him blush.

"O Indiana!" he cried, wringing his hands, "how I have outraged you! Can you ever forgive me for such infamous conduct? Even if you should forgive me, I can never forgive myself. Resist me now, my gentle, trustful Indiana; for you do not know the baseness and brutality of the man to whom you would surrender the treasures of your innocence! Repulse me, trample on me, for I have not respected the sanctuary of your sacred modesty; I have befuddled myself with your wine like a footman, sitting beside your maid; I have sullied your spotless robe with my accursed breath, and your chaste girdle with my infamous kisses on another's breast; I have not shrunk from poisoning the repose of your lonely nights, and from shedding, even upon this bed, which your husband himself respected, the influences of seduction and adultery! What safety will you find henceforth behind these curtains whose mysteries I have not shrunk from profaning? What impure dreams, what bitter and consuming thoughts will cling fast to your brain and wither it! What phantoms of vice and shamelessness will crawl upon the virginal linen of your couch! And your sleep, pure as a child's—what chaste divinity will care to protect it now? Have I not put to flight the angel who guarded your pillow? Have I not thrown your alcove open to the demon of lust? Have I not sold him your soul? And will not the insane passion which consumes the vitals of this lascivious creole cling to yours, like Dejanira's robe and gnaw at them! Oh! miserable wretch! miserable, guilty wretch that I am! if only I could wash away with my blood the stain I have left on this couch!"

And Raymon sprinkled it with his tears.

At that moment Noun returned, in her neckerchief and apron; she fancied, when she saw Raymon kneeling, that he was praying. She did not know that society people do not pray. She stood waiting in silence, until he should deign to notice her presence.

Raymon, when he saw her, had a feeling of embarrassment and irritation, but without the courage to scold her, without the strength to say a friendly word to her.

"Why did you lock me in this room?" he said at last. "Do you forget that it is broad daylight and that I cannot go out without compromising you openly?"

"So you're not to go out," said Noun caressingly. "The house is deserted and no one can see you; the gardener never comes to this part of the building to which I alone have the keys. You must stay with me all day; you are my prisoner."

This arrangement drove Raymon to despair; he had no other feeling for his mistress than a sort of aversion. However, he could do nothing but submit, and it may be that, notwithstanding what he suffered in that room, an invincible attraction detained him there.

When Noun left him to go and find something for breakfast, he set about examining by daylight all those dumb witnesses of Indiana's solitude. He opened her books, turned the leaves of her albums, then closed them precipitately; for he still shrank from committing a profanation and violating some feminine mystery. At last he began to pace the room and noticed, on the wooden panel opposite Madame Delmare's bed, a large picture, richly framed and covered with a double thickness of gauze.

Perhaps it was Indiana's portrait. Raymon, in his eagerness to see it, forgot his scruples, stepped on a chair, removed the pins, and was amazed to see a full-length portrait of a handsome young man.

VIII

"It seems to me that I know that face," he said to Noun, struggling to assume an indifferent attitude.

"Fi! monsieur," said the girl, as she placed on a table the tray that she brought containing the breakfast; "it is not right to try and find out my mistress's secrets."

This remark made Raymon turn pale.

"Secrets!" he said. "If this is a secret, it has been confided to you, Noun, and you were doubly guilty in bringing me to this room."

"Oh! no, it's not a secret," said Noun with a smile; "for Monsieur Delmare himself assisted in hanging Sir Ralph's portrait on that panel. As if madame could have any secrets with a husband so jealous!"

"Sir Ralph, you say? Who is Sir Ralph?"

"Sir Rodolphe Brown, madame's cousin, her playmate in childhood, and my own, too, I might say; he is such a good man!"

Raymon scrutinized the picture with surprise and some uneasiness.

We have said that Sir Ralph was an extremely comely person, physically; with a red and white complexion and abundant hair, a tall figure, always perfectly dressed, and capable, if not of turning a romantic brain, of satisfying the vanity of an unromantic one. The peaceable baronet was represented in hunting costume, about as we saw him in the first chapter of this narrative, and surrounded by his dogs, the beautiful pointer Ophelia in the foreground, because of the fine silver-gray tone of her silky coat and the purity of her Scotch blood. Sir Ralph had a hunting-horn in one hand and in the other the rein of a superb, dapple-gray English hunter, who filled almost the whole background of the picture. It was an admirably executed portrait, a genuine family picture with all its perfection of detail, all its puerile niceties of resemblance, all its bourgeois minutiæ; a picture to make a nurse weep, dogs bark and a tailor faint with joy. There was but one thing on earth more insignificant than the portrait, and that was the original.

Nevertheless it kindled a violent flame of wrath in Raymon.

"Upon my word!" he said to himself, "this dapper young Englishman enjoys the privilege of being admitted to Madame Delmare's most secret apartment! His vapid face is always here, looking coldly on at the most private acts of her life! He watches her, guards her, follows her every movement, possesses her every hour in the day! At night he watches her asleep and surprises the secret of her dreams; in the morning, when she comes forth, all white and quivering, from her bed, he sees the dainty bare foot that steps lightly on the carpet; and when she dresses with all precaution—when she draws the curtains at her window and forbids even the daylight from entering her presence too boldly—when she believes that she is quite alone, hidden from every eye—that insolent face is there, feasting on her charms! That man, all booted and spurred, presides over her toilet. Is this gauze usually spread over the picture?" he asked the maid.

"Always," she replied, "when madame is absent. But don't take the trouble to replace it, for madame is coming in a few days."

"In that case, Noun, you would do well to tell her that the expression of the face is very impertinent. If I had been in Monsieur Delmare's place I wouldn't have consented to leave it here unless I had cut out the eyes. But that's just like the stupid jealousy of the ordinary husband! They imagine everything and understand nothing."

"For heaven's sake, what have you against good Monsieur Brown's face?" said Noun, as she made her mistress's bed; "he is such an excellent master! I used not to care much for him, because I always heard madame say that he was selfish; but ever since the day that he took care of you——"

"True," Raymon interrupted her, "it was he who helped me that day; I remember him perfectly now. But I owe his interest only to Madame Delmare's prayers."

"Because she is so kind-hearted," said poor Noun. "Who could help being kind-hearted after living with her?"

When Noun spoke of Madame Delmare, Raymon listened with an interest of which she had no suspicion.

The day passed quietly enough, but Noun dared not lead the conversation to her real object. At last, toward evening, she made an effort and compelled him to declare his intentions.

Raymon had no other intention than to rid himself of a dangerous witness and of a woman whom he no longer loved. But he proposed to assure her future, and in fear and trembling he made her the most liberal offers.

It was a bitter affront to the poor girl; she tore her hair, and would have beaten her head against the wall if Raymon had not put forth all his strength to hold her. Thereupon, employing all the resources of language and intellect with which nature had endowed him, he made her understand that it was not for her, but for the child she was to bring into the world, that he desired to make provision.

"It is my duty," he said; "I hand the funds over to you as the child's heritage, and you would fail in your duty to him if a false sense of delicacy should lead you to reject them."

Noun became calmer and wiped her eyes.

"Very well," she said, "I will accept the money if you will promise to keep on loving me; for, just by doing your duty to the child, you will not do it to the mother. Your gift will keep him alive, but your indifference will kill me. Can't you take me into your service? I am not exacting; I don't aspire to all that another woman in my place might have had the skill to obtain. But let me be your servant. Obtain a place for me in your mother's family. She will be satisfied with me, I give you my word; and, even if you don't love me, I shall at least see you."

"What you ask is impossible, my dear Noun. In your present condition you cannot think of entering anyone's service; and to deceive my mother—to play upon her confidence in me—would be a base act to which I shall never consent. Go to Lyon or Bordeaux; I will undertake to see to it that you want nothing until such time as you can show yourself again. Then I will obtain a place for you with some one of my acquaintances—at Paris, if you wish, if you insist upon being near me—but as to living under the same roof, that is impossible."

"Impossible!" echoed Noun, wringing her hands in a passion of grief. "I see that you despise me—that you blush for me. But no, I will not go away, alone and degraded, to die abandoned in some distant city where you will forget me. What do I care for my reputation? Your love is what I wanted to retain."

"Noun, if you fear that I am deceiving you, come with me. The same carriage shall take us to whatever place you choose. I will go with you anywhere, except to Paris or to my mother's, and I will bestow upon you all the care and attention that I owe you."

"Yes, to abandon me on the day after you have put me down, a useless burden, in some foreign land!" she rejoined, smiling bitterly. "No, monsieur, no, I will stay here; I do not choose to lose everything at once. I should sacrifice, by following you, the person whom I loved best in the world before I knew you; but I am not anxious enough to conceal my dishonor to sacrifice both my love and my friendship. I will go and throw myself at Madame Delmare's feet; I will tell her all, and she will forgive me, I know, for she is kind and she loves me. We were born on almost the same day, and she is my foster-sister. We have never been separated, and she will not want me to leave her. She will weep with me; she will take care of me, and she will love my child —my poor child! Who knows! she has not the good fortune to be a mother; perhaps she will bring it up as her own! Ah! I was mad to think of leaving her, for she is the only person on earth who will take pity on me!"

This determination plunged Raymon in horrible perplexity; but suddenly the rumbling of a carriage was heard in the courtyard. Noun, in dismay, ran to the window.

"It's Madame Delmare!" she cried; "go instantly!"

In that moment of excitement the key to the secret staircase could not be found. Noun took Raymon's arm and hurriedly pulled him into the hall; but they were not half way to the stairs when they heard footsteps in the same passage; they heard Madame Delmare's voice ten steps in front of them, and a candle carried by a servant who attended her cast its flickering light almost on their terrified faces. Noun had barely time to retrace her steps, still pulling Raymon after her, and to return with him to the bedroom.

A dressing room, with a glass door, might afford a place of refuge for a few moments; but there was no way of locking the door, and it was possible that Madame Delmare might go to the dressing-room at once. To avoid being detected instantly, Raymon was obliged to rush into the alcove and hide behind the curtains. It was not probable that Madame Delmare would retire at once, and meanwhile Noun might find an opportunity to help him to escape.

Indiana bustled into the room, tossed her hat on the bed and kissed Noun with the familiarity of a sister. There was so little light in the room that she did not notice her companion's emotion.

"You expected me, did you?" she said, going to the fire; "how did you know I was coming?—Monsieur Delmare," she added, not waiting for a reply, "will be here to-morrow. I started at once on receiving his letter. I have certain reasons for receiving him here and not in Paris. I will tell you what they are. But, in heaven's name, why don't you speak to me? you don't seem so glad to see me as usual."

"I am low-spirited," said Noun, kneeling by her mistress to remove her shoes. "I have something to tell you, too, but later; come to the salon now."

"God forbid! what an idea! it's deathly cold there!"

"No, there's a good fire."

"You are dreaming! I just came through it."

"But your supper is waiting for you."

"I don't want any supper; besides, there is nothing ready. Go and get my boa, I left it in the carriage."

"In a moment."

"Why not now? Go, I say, go!"

As she spoke, she pushed Noun toward the door with a playful air; and the maid, seeing that she must be bold and self-possessed, went out for a few moments. But she had no sooner left the room than Madame Delmare threw the bolt and removed her cloak, placing it on the bed beside her hat. As she did it, she went so near to Raymon, that he instinctively stepped back, and the bed, which apparently rested on well-oiled castors, moved with a slight noise. Madame Delmare was surprised but not frightened, for it was quite possible that she had herself moved the bed; she stretched forth her neck, drew the curtain aside and revealed a man's head outlined against the wall in the half-light cast by the fire on the hearth.

In her terror she uttered a shriek and rushed to the mantel to seize the bell-cord and summon help. Raymon would have preferred to be taken for a thief again than to be recognized in that situation. But if he did not make himself known, Madame Delmare would call her servants and compromise her own reputation. He placed his trust in the love he had inspired in her, and, rushing to her, tried to stop her shrieks and to keep her away from the bell-cord, saying to her in an undertone, for fear of being heard by Noun, who was probably not far away:

"It is I, Indiana; look at me and forgive me! Indiana! forgive an unhappy wretch whose reason you have led astray, and who could not make up his mind to give you back to your husband until he had seen you once more."

And while he held Indiana in his arms, no less in the hope of moving her than to keep her from ringing, Noun was knocking at the door in an agony of apprehension. Madame Delmare, extricating herself from Raymon's arms, ran and opened the door, then sank into a chair.

Pale as death and almost fainting, Noun threw herself against the door to prevent the servants, who were running hither and thither, from interrupting this strange scene; paler than her mistress, with trembling knees and her back glued to the door, she awaited her fate.

Raymon felt that with due address he might still deceive both women at once.

"Madame," he said, falling on his knees before Indiana, "my presence here must seem to you an outrageous insult; here at your feet I implore your forgiveness. Grant me an interview of a few moments and I will explain——"

"Hush, monsieur, and leave this house," cried Madame Delmare, recovering all the dignity befitting her situation; "leave this house openly. Open the door, Noun, and allow monsieur to go, so that all my servants may see him and that the disgrace of such a proceeding may fall upon him."

Noun, believing that she was detected, threw herself on her knees by Raymon's side. Madame Delmare looked at her in amazement, but said nothing.

Raymon tried to take her hand; but she indignantly withdrew it. Flushed with anger, she rose and pointed to the door.

"Go, I tell you!" she said; "go, for your conduct is despicable. So these are the means you chose to employ! you, monsieur, hiding in my bedroom, like a thief! It seems that it is a habit of yours to introduce yourself into families in this way! and this is the pure attachment that you offered me the night before last! This is the way you were to protect me, respect me and defend me! This is the way you worship me! You see a woman who has nursed you with her hands, who, to restore you to life, defied her husband's anger; you deceive her by a pretence of gratitude, you promise her a love worthy of her, and as a reward for her attentions, as the price of her credulity, you seek to surprise her in her sleep and to hasten your triumph by indescribable infamy! You bribe her maid, you almost creep into her bed, like a lover already favored; you do not shrink from admitting her servants to the secret of an intimacy that does not exist.

Go, monsieur; you have taken pains to undeceive me very quickly! Go, I say! do not remain another moment under my roof! And you, wretched girl, who have so little regard for your mistress's honor—you deserve to be dismissed. Stand away from that door, I tell you!"

Noun, half dead with surprise and despair, gazed fixedly at Raymon as if to ask him for an explanation of this incredible mystery. Then, with a wild gleam in her eyes, hardly able to stand, she dragged herself to Indiana and seized her arm fiercely.

"What was that you said?" she cried, her teeth clenched with rage; "this man loved you?"

"Eh! you must have known that he did!" said Madame Delmare, pushing her away contemptuously and with all her strength; "you must have known what reasons a man has for hiding behind a woman's curtains. Ah! Noun," she added, noticing the girl's evident despair, "it was a dastardly thing, and one of which I would never have believed you to be capable; you consented to sell her honor who had such perfect faith in yours!"

Madame Delmare was shedding tears, tears of indignation as well as of grief. Raymon had never seen her so lovely; but he hardly dared look at her, for her haughty air, the air of an insulted woman, forced him to lower his eyes. He was terror-stricken, too, petrified by Noun's presence. If he had been alone with Madame Delmare, he might perhaps have been able to soften her. But Noun's expression was terrifying; her features were distorted by rage and hatred.

A knock at the door startled them all three. Noun rushed forward once more to keep out intruders; but Madame Delmare, pushing her aside imperatively, motioned to Raymon to withdraw to the corner of the room. Then, with the self-possession which made her so remarkable at critical moments, she wrapped herself in a shawl, partly opened the door herself, and asked the servant who had knocked what he had to say to her.

"Monsieur Rodolphe Brown is here," was the reply; "he wishes to know if madame will receive him."

"Say to Monsieur Rodolphe Brown that I am delighted that he has come and that I will join him at once. Make a fire in the salon and bid them prepare some supper. One moment! Go and get the key to the small park."

The servant retired. Madame Delmare remained at the door, holding it open, not deigning to listen to Noun and imperiously enjoining silence on Raymon.

The servant returned in a few moments. Madame Delmare, still holding the door open between him and Monsieur de Ramière, took the key from him, bade him hurry up the supper, and, as soon as he had gone, turned to Raymon.

"The arrival of my cousin, Sir Rodolphe Brown," she said, "saves you from the public scandal which I intended to inflict on you; he is a man of honor, who would eagerly assume the duty of defending me; but as I should be very sorry to expose a man like him to danger at the hands of such a man as you, I will allow you to go without scandal. Noun, who admitted you, will find a way to let you out. Go!"

"We shall meet again, madame," replied Raymon with an attempt at self-assurance; "and although I am culpable, you will perhaps regret the harshness with which you treat me now."

"I trust, monsieur, that we shall never meet again," she rejoined.

And still standing at the door, not deigning to bow, she watched him depart with his miserable and trembling accomplice.

When he was alone with Noun in the obscurity of the park, Raymon expected reproaches from her; but she did not speak to him. She led him to the gate of the small park, and, when he tried to take her hand, she had already vanished. He called her in a low voice, for he was anxious to learn his fate; but she did not reply, and the gardener, suddenly appearing, said to him:

"Come, monsieur, you must be off; madame is here and you may be discovered."

Raymon took his departure with death in his heart; but in his despair at having offended Madame Delmare he almost forgot Noun and thought of nothing but possible methods of appeasing her mistress; for it was a part of his nature to be irritated by obstacles and never to cling passionately except to things that were well-nigh desperate.

At night, when Madame Delmare, after supping silently with Sir Ralph, withdrew to her own apartments, Noun did not come, as usual, to undress her; she rang for her to no purpose, and when she had concluded that the girl was resolved not to obey, she locked her door and went to bed. But she passed a horrible night, and, as soon as the day broke, went down into the park. She was feverish and agitated; she longed to feel the cold enter her body and allay the fire that consumed her breast. The day before, at that hour, she was happy, abandoning herself to the novel sensations of that intoxicating love. What a ghastly disillusionment in twenty-four hours! First of all, the news of her husband's return several days earlier than she expected; those four or five days which she had hoped to pass in Paris were to her a whole lifetime of never-ending bliss, a dream of love never to be interrupted by an awakening; but in the morning she had had to abandon the hope, to resume the yoke, and to go to meet her master in order that he might not meet Raymon at Madame de Carvajal's; for Indiana thought that it would be impossible for her to deceive her husband if he should see her in Raymon's presence. And then this Raymon, whom she loved as a god—it was by him of all men that she was thus basely insulted! And lastly, her life-long companion, the young creole whom she loved so dearly, suddenly proved to be unworthy of her confidence and her esteem!

Madame Delmare had wept all night long. She sank upon the turf, still whitened by the morning rime, on the bank of the little stream that flowed through the park. It was late in March and nature was beginning to awake; the morning, although cold, was not devoid of beauty; patches of mist still rested on the water like a floating scarf, and the birds were trying their first songs of love and springtime.

Indiana felt as if relieved of a heavy weight, and a wave of religious feeling overflowed her soul.

"God willed it so," she said to herself; "in His providence he has given me a harsh lesson, but it is fortunate for me. That man would perhaps have led me into vice, he would have ruined me; whereas now the vileness of his sentiments is revealed to me, and I shall be on my guard against the tempestuous and detestable passion that fermented in his breast. I will love my husband! I will try to love him! At all events I will be submissive to him, I will make him happy by never annoying him, I will avoid whatever can possibly arouse his jealousy; for now I know what to think of the false eloquence that men know how to lavish on us. I shall be fortunate, perhaps, if God will take pity on my sorrows and send death to me soon."

The clatter of the mill-wheel that started the machinery

in Monsieur Delmare's factory made itself heard behind the willows on the other bank. The river, rushing through the newly opened gates, began to boil and bubble on the surface; and, as Madame Delmare followed with a melancholy eye the swift rush of the stream, she saw floating among the reeds something like a bundle of cloth which the current strove to hurry along in its train. She rose, leaned over the bank and distinctly saw a woman's clothes,—clothes that she knew too well. Terror nailed her to the spot; but the stream flowed on, slowly drawing a body from the reeds among which it had caught, and bringing it toward Madame Delmare.

A piercing shriek attracted the workmen from the factory to the spot; Madame Delmare had fainted on the bank, and Noun's body was floating in the water at her feet.

PART SECOND

IX

Two months have passed. Nothing is changed at Lagny, in that house to which I introduced you one winter evening, except that all about its red brick walls with their frame of gray stone and its slated roofs yellowed by venerable moss, the springtime is in its bloom. The family is scattered here and there, enjoying the mild and fragrant evening air; the setting sun gilds the window-panes and the roar of the factory mingles with the various noises of the farm. Monsieur Delmare is seated on the steps, gun in hand, practising at shooting swallows on the wing. Indiana, at her embroidery frame near the window of the salon, leans forward now and then to watch with a sad face the colonel's cruel amusement in the courtyard. Ophelia leaps about and barks, indignant at a style of hunting so contrary to her habits; and Sir Ralph, astride the stone railing, is smoking a cigar and, as usual, looking on impassively at other people's pleasure or vexation.

"Indiana," cried the colonel, laying aside his gun, "do for heaven's sake put your work away; you tire yourself out as if you were paid so much an hour."

"It is still broad daylight," Madame Delmare replied.

"No matter; come to the window, I have something to tell you."

Indiana obeyed, and the colonel, drawing near the

window, which was almost on a level with the ground, said to her with as near an approach to playfulness of manner as an old and jealous husband can manage:

"As you have worked hard to-day and as you are very good, I am going to tell you something that will please you."

Madame Delmare struggled hard to smile; her smile would have driven a more sensitive man than the colonel to despair.

"You will be pleased to know," he continued, "that I have invited one of your humble adorers to breakfast with you to-morrow, to divert you. You will ask me which one; for you have a very pretty collection of them, you flirt!"

"Perhaps it's our dear old curé?" said Madame Delmare, whose melancholy was enhanced by her husband's gayety.

"Oh! no, indeed!"

"Then it must be the mayor of Chailly or the old notary from Fontainebleau."

"Oh! the craft of women! You know very well that it would be none of those people. Come, Ralph, tell madame the name she has on the tip of her tongue but doesn't choose to pronounce herself."

"You need not go through so much preparation to announce a visit from Monsieur de Ramière," said Sir Ralph, tranquilly, as he threw away his cigar; "I suppose that it's a matter of perfect indifference to her."

Madame Delmare felt the blood rush to her cheeks; she made a pretence of looking for something in the salon, then returned to the window with as calm a manner as she could command.

"I fancy that this is a jest," she said, trembling in every limb.

"On the contrary I am perfectly serious; you will see him here at eleven o'clock to-morrow."

"What! the man who stole into your premises to obtain unfair possession of your invention, and whom you almost killed as a criminal! You must both be very pacific to forget such grievances!"

"You set me the example, dearest, by receiving him very graciously at your aunt's, where he called on you."

Indiana turned pale.

"I do not by any means appropriate that call," she said earnestly, "and I am so little flattered by it that, if I were in your place, I would not receive him."

"You women are all false and cunning just for the pleasure of being so. You danced with him during one whole ball, I was told."

"You were misinformed."

"Why, it was your aunt herself who told me! However, you need not defend yourself so warmly; I have no fault to find, as your aunt desired and assisted to bring about this reconciliation between us. Monsieur de Ramière has been seeking it for a long while. He has rendered me some very valuable services with respect to my business, and he has done it without ostentation and almost without my knowledge; so, as I am not so savage as you say, and also as I do not choose to be under obligations to a stranger, I determined to make myself square with him."

"How so?"

"By making a friend of him; by going to Cercy this morning with Sir Ralph. We found his mother there, who seems a delightful woman; and the house is furnished with refinement and comfort, but without ostentation and without a trace of the pride that attaches to venerable names. After all, this Ramière's a good fellow, and I have invited him to come and breakfast with us and inspect the factory. I hear favorable accounts of his brother, and I have made sure that he cannot injure me by adopting the same methods that I use; so I prefer that that family should profit by them rather than any other. You see no secrets are kept very long, and mine will soon be like a stage secret if progress in manufacturing continues at the present rate."

"For my part," said Sir Ralph, "I have always disapproved of this secrecy, as you know; a good citizen's discovery belongs to his country as much as to himself, and if I——"

"*Parbleu!* that is just like you, Sir Ralph, with your practical philanthropy! You will make me think that your fortune doesn't belong to you, and that, if the nation takes a fancy to it to-morrow, you are ready to exchange your fifty thousand francs a year for a wallet and staff! It looks well for a *buck* like you, who are as fond of the comforts of life as a sultan, to preach contempt of wealth!"

"What I say," rejoined Sir Ralph, "is not meant to be philanthropic at all; my point is that selfishness properly understood leads us to do good to others to prevent them injuring us. I am selfish myself, as everybody knows. I have accustomed myself not to blush for it, and, after analyzing all the virtues, I find personal interest at the foundation of them all. Love and devotion, which are two apparently generous passions, are perhaps the most selfish passions that exist; nor is patriotism less so, my word for it. I care little for men; but not for anything in the world would I undertake to prove it to them, my fear of them is inversely proportional to my esteem for them. We are both selfish therefore but I admit it, whereas you deny it."

A discussion arose between them wherein each sought by all the arguments of selfishness to demonstrate the selfishness of the others. Madame Delmare took advantage of it to retire to her room and to abandon herself to all the reflections to which news so entirely unexpected naturally gave birth.

It will be well not only to admit you to the secret of her thoughts, but also to enlighten you as to the situation of the various persons whom Noun's death had affected in greater or less degree.

It is almost proven, so far as the reader and I myself are concerned, that that unfortunate creature threw herself into the stream through despair, in one of those moments of frenzy when extreme resolutions are most easily formed. But, as she evidently did not return to the house after leaving Raymon—as no one had met her and had an opportunity to divine her purpose—there was no indication of suicide to throw light upon the mystery of her death.

Two persons were in a position to attribute it with moral certainty to her own act—Monsieur de Ramière and the gardener of Lagny. The grief of the former was concealed beneath a pretence of illness; the terror and remorse of the other enjoined silence upon him. This man who, from cupidity, had connived at the intercourse of the lovers throughout the winter, was the only person who had been in a position to remark the young creole's secret misery. Justly fearing the reproaches of his employers and the criticisms of his equals, he held his peace in his own interest; and when Monsieur Delmare, who had some suspicions after the discovery of this intrigue, questioned him as to the lengths to which it had been carried during his absence, he boldly denied that it had continued at all. Some people in the neighborhood—a very lonely neighborhood, by the way—had noticed Noun walking toward Crecy at unreasonable hours; but apparently there had been no relations between her and Monsieur de Ramière since the end of January, and her death occurred on the 28th of March. So far as appeared, her death was attributable to chance; as she was walking through the park at nightfall, she might have been deceived by the dense fog that had prevailed for several days, have lost her way and missed the English bridge over the stream, which was quite narrow but had very steep banks and was swollen by recent rains.

Although Sir Ralph, who was more observant than his reflections indicated, had found in his private thoughts grounds for strong suspicion of Monsieur de Ramière, he communicated them to no one, regarding as useless and cruel any reproachful words addressed to a man who was so unfortunate as to have such a source of remorse in his life. He even succeeded in convincing the colonel, who expressed in his presence some suspicions in that regard, that it was most urgent, in Madame Delmare's delicate condition, to continue to conceal from her the possible causes of her old playmate's suicide. So it was with the poor girl's death as with her love affair. There was a tacit agreement never to mention it before Indiana, and ere long it ceased to be talked about at all.

But these precautions were of no avail, for Madame Delmare had her own reasons for suspecting a part of the truth; the bitter reproaches she had heaped on the unhappy girl on that fatal evening seemed to her a sufficient explanation of her sudden resolution. So it was that, at the ghastly moment when she discovered the dead body floating in the water, Indiana's repose, already so disturbed, and her heart, already so sad, had received the final blow; her lingering disease was progressing actively;

and this woman, young and perhaps strong, refusing to be cured, concealing her sufferings from her husband's undiscerning and far from delicate affection, sank voluntarily beneath the burden of sorrow and discouragement.

"Woe is me!" she cried as she entered her room, after learning of Raymon's impending visit. "A curse on that man, who has entered this house only to bring despair and death! O God! why dost Thou permit him to come between Thee and me, to take command of my destiny at his pleasure, so that he has only to put out his hand and say: 'She is mine! I will derange her reason, I will bring desolation into her life; and if she resists me I will spread mourning around her, I will encompass her with remorse, regrets and alarms!' O God! it is not fair that a poor woman should be so persecuted!"

She wept bitterly; for the thought of Raymon revived the memory of Noun, more vivid and heartrending than ever.

"Poor Noun! my poor playmate! my countrywoman, my only friend!" she exclaimed sorrowfully; "that man is your murderer. Unhappy child! his influence was fatal to you as to me! You loved me so dearly, you were the only one who could divine my sorrows and mitigate them by your artless gayety! Woe to me who have lost you! Was it for this that I brought you from so far away! By what wiles did that man surprise your good faith and induce you to do such a despicable thing? Ah! he must have deceived you shamefully, and you did not realize your error until you saw my indignation! I was too harsh, Noun; I was so harsh that I was downright cruel; I drove you to despair, I killed you! Poor girl! why did you not wait a few hours until the wind had blown away my resentment like a wisp of straw! Why did you not come and weep on my bosom and say:

'I was deceived; I acted without knowing what I was doing, but you know well enough that I respect you and love you!'—I would have taken you in my arms, we would have wept together, and you would not be dead. Dead! dead so young and so lovely and so full of life! Dead at nineteen and such a ghastly death!"

While thus weeping for her companion, Indiana, unknown to herself, wept also for her three days of illusion, the loveliest days of her life, the only days when she had really lived; for during those three days she had loved with a passion which Raymon, had he been the most presumptuous of men, could never have imagined. But the blinder and more violent that love had been, the more keenly had she felt the insult she had received; the first love of a heart like hers contains so much modesty and sensitive delicacy!

And yet Indiana had yielded to a burst of shame and anger rather than to a well-matured determination. I have no doubt that Raymon would have obtained his pardon had he been allowed a few more minutes in which to plead for it. But fate had defeated his love and his address, and Madame Delmare honestly believed now that she hated him.

X

For his part, it was neither in a spirit of bravado nor because of the injury to his self-esteem that he aspired more ardently than ever to Madame Delmare's love and forgiveness. He believed that they were unattainable, and no other woman's love, no other earthly joy seemed to him their equivalent. Such was his nature. An insatiable craving for action and excitement consumed his life. He loved society with its laws and its fetters, because it offered him material for combat and resistance; and if he had a horror of license and debauchery, it was because they promised insipid and easily obtained pleasure.

Do not believe, however, that he was insensible to Noun's ruin. In the first impulse, he conceived a horror of himself and loaded his pistols with a very real purpose of blowing out his brains; but a praiseworthy feeling stayed his hand. What would become of his mother, his aged, feeble mother, the poor woman whose life had been so agitated and so sorrowful, who lived only for him, her only treasure, her only hope? Must he break her heart, shorten the few years that still remained to her? No, surely not. The best way to redeem his wrongdoing was to devote himself thenceforth solely to his mother, and it was with that purpose in mind that he returned to her at Paris, and put forth all his energies to make her forget his desertion of her during a large part of the winter.

Raymon exerted an incredible influence over everybody about him; for, take him for all in all, with his faults and his youthful escapades, he was above the average of society men. We have not as yet told you upon what his reputation for wit and talent was based, because it was aside from the events we had to describe; but it is time to inform you that this Raymon, whose weaknesses you have followed and whose frivolity you have censured, is one of the men who have had the most control and influence over your thoughts, whatever your opinions to-day may be. You have devoured his political pamphlets, and, while reading the newspapers of the period, you have often been captivated by the irresistible charm of his style and the grace of his courteous and worldly logic.

I am speaking of a time already far away, in these days when time is no longer reckoned by centuries, nor even by reigns, but by ministries. I am speaking of the Martignac year, of that epoch of repose and doubt, interjected in the middle of a political era, not like a treaty of peace, but like an armistice; of those fifteen months of the reign of doctrines, which had such a strange influence on principles and on morals, and which may perhaps have paved the way for the extraordinary result of our latest revolution.

It was in those days that men saw the blooming of certain youthful talents, unfortunate in that they were born in a period of transition and of compromise; for they paid their tribute to the conciliatory and wavering tendencies of the time. Never, so far as I know, was knowledge of mere words and ignorance, or pretended ignorance, of things carried so far. It was the reign of restrictions, and it is beyond my power to say who made the fullest use of them, short-gowned Jesuits or long-gowned lawyers. Political moderation had become a part of the national character, like courteous manners, and it was the same with the first variety of courtesy as with the second: it served as a mask for secret antipathies, and taught them how to fight without scandal and publicity. We must say, however, in defence of the young men of that period, that they were often towed like light skiffs in the wake of great ships, with no very clear idea of where they were being taken, proud and happy to be cleaving the waves and swelling out their new sails.

Placed by his birth and his wealth among the partisans of absolute royalty, Raymon made a sacrifice to the *youthful* ideas of his time by clinging religiously to the Charter; at all events that was what he thought that he was doing and what he exerted himself to prove. But conventions that have fallen into desuetude are subject to interpretation, and the Charter of Louis XVIII was already in the same plight as the Gospel of Jesus Christ; it was simply a text upon which everybody practised his powers of eloquence, and a speech thereon created a precedent no more than a sermon. A period of luxurious living and indolence, when civilization lay sleeping on the brink of a bottomless abyss, eager to enjoy its last pleasures.

Raymon had taken his stand upon the line between abuse of power and abuse of licence, a shifting ground upon which good men still sought, but in vain, a shelter from the tempest that was brewing. To him, as to many other experienced minds, the rôle of conscientious statesman still seemed possible. A manifest error at a time when people pretended to defer to the voice of reason only to stifle it the more surely on every side. Being without political passions, Raymon fancied that he was without interests to promote; but he was mistaken, for society, constituted as it then was, was agreeable and advantageous to him; it could not be disturbed without a diminution in the sum total of his well-being, and that perfect contentment with one's social position, which communicates itself to the thought, is a wonderful promoter of moderation. Who is so ungrateful to Providence as to reproach it for the misfortunes of other people, if it has only smiles and benefactions for him? How was it possible to persuade those young supporters of the constitutional monarchy that the constitution was already antiquated, that it weighed heavily on the social body and fatigued it, while they found its burdens light and reaped only its advantages?

Nothing is so easy and so common as to deceive one's self when one does not lack wit and is familiar with all the niceties of the language. Language is a prostitute queen who descends and rises to all rôles, disguises herself, arrays herself in fine apparel, hides her head and effaces herself; an advocate who has an answer for everything, who has always foreseen everything, and who assumes a thousand forms in order to be right. The most honorable of men is he who thinks best and acts best, but the most powerful is he who is best able to talk and write.

As his wealth relieved him from the necessity of writing for money, Raymon wrote from a liking for it, and—he said it with perfect good faith—from a sense of duty. The rare faculty that he possessed, of refuting positive truth by sheer talent, had made him an invaluable man to the ministry, whom he served much better by his impartial criticism than did its creatures by their blind devotion; and even more invaluable to that fashionable young society which was quite willing to abjure the absurdities of its former privileges, but wished at the same time to retain the benefit of its present advantageous position.

They were in very truth men of great talent who still supported society, tottering on the brink of the precipice, and who, being themselves suspended between two reefs, struggled calmly and with perfect self-possession against the harsh reality that was on the point of engulfing them. To succeed in such wise as to create a conviction against every sort of probability and to keep that conviction alive for some time among men of no convictions, is the art which most impresses and surpasses the understanding of an uncultivated, vulgar mind which has studied none but commonplace truths.

Thus Raymon had no sooner returned to that society, which was his element and his home, than he felt its vital and exciting influences. The petty love affairs that had engrossed him vanished for a moment in the face of broader and more brilliant interests. He carried into these the same boldness of attack, the same ardor; and when he saw that he was more eagerly sought than ever by all the most distinguished people in Paris, he felt that he loved life more than ever. Was he to be blamed for forgetting a secret remorse while reaping the reward he had merited for services rendered his country? He felt life overflowing through every pore of his young heart, his active brain, his whole vigorous and buoyant being, he felt that destiny was making him happy in spite of himself; and he would crave forgiveness of an indignant ghost that came sometimes and bewailed her fate in his dreams, for having sought in the affection of the living a protection against the terrors of the grave.

But he had no sooner returned to life, as it were, than he felt, as in the past, the need of mingling thoughts of love and plans of intrigue with his political meditations, his dreams of ambition and philosophy. I say ambition, not meaning ambition for honor and wealth, for which he had no use, but for reputation and aristocratic popularity.

He had at first despaired of ever seeing Madame Delmare again after the tragic ending of his double intrigue. But, as he measured the extent of his loss, as he brooded over the thought of the treasure that had escaped him, he conceived the hope of grasping it once more, and, at the same time he regained determination and confidence.

He calculated the obstacles he should encounter, and realized that the most difficult to overcome at the outset would come from Indiana herself; therefore he must use the husband to protect him from the attack. This was not a new idea, but it was sure; jealous husbands are particularly well adapted to this service.

A fortnight after he had conceived this idea, Raymon was on the way to Lagny, where he was expected to breakfast. You will not require me to describe to you in detail the shrewdly proffered services by which he had succeeded in making himself agreeable to Monsieur Delmare; I prefer, as I am describing the features of the characters in this tale, to draw a hasty sketch of the colonel for you.

Do you know what they call an *honest man* in the provinces? He is a man who does not encroach on his neighbor's field; who does not demand from his debtors a sou more than they owe him; who raises his hat to every person who bows to him; who does not ravish maidens in the public roads; who sets fire to no other man's barn; who does not rob wayfarers at the corner of his park. Provided that he religiously respects the lives and purses of his fellow-citizens, nothing more is demanded of him. He may beat his wife, maltreat his servants, ruin his children, and it is nobody's business. Society punishes only those acts which are injurious to it; private life is beyond its jurisdiction.

Such was Monsieur Delmare's theory of morals. He had never studied any other social contract than this: *Every man is master in his own house.* He treated all affairs of the heart as feminine puerilities, sentimental subtleties. Being a man devoid of wit, of tact and of education, he enjoyed greater consideration than a man obtains by dint of talent and amiability. He had broad shoulders and a strong wrist; he handled the sword and the sabre perfectly, and was exceedingly quick to take offence. As he did not always understand a joke, he was constantly haunted by the idea that people were making fun of him. Being incapable of suitable repartee, he had but one way of defending himself: to enforce silence by threats. His favorite epigrams always turned upon cowhidings to be administered and affairs of honor to be settled; wherefore the province always prefixed to his name the epithet *brave*, because military valor apparently consists in having broad shoulders and long moustaches, in swearing fiercely, and in putting one's hand to the sword on the slightest pretext.

God forbid that I should believe that camp life makes all men brutes! but I may be permitted to believe that one must have a large stock of tact and discretion to resist the habit of passive and brutal domination. If you have served in the army, you are familiar with what the troops call *skin-breeches*, and will agree that there are large numbers of them among the remains of the old imperial cohorts. Those men who, when brought together and urged forward by a powerful hand, performed such magnificent exploits, towered like giants amid the smoke of the battle-field; but, having returned to civil life, the heroes became mere soldiers once more, bold, vulgar fellows who reasoned like machines; and it was fortunate if they did not behave in society as in conquered territory. It was the fault of the age rather than theirs. Ingenuous minds, they had faith in the adulation of victory, and allowed themselves to be persuaded that they were great patriots because they defended their country —some against their will, others for money and honors. But how did they defend it, those tens of thousands of men who blindly embraced the error of a single man, and who, after saving their country, basely destroyed it? And again, if a soldier's devotion to his captain seems to you a great and noble thing, well and good, so it does to me; but I call that fidelity, not patriotism. I congratulate the conquerors of Spain, I do not thank them. As for the honor of the French name, I by no means understand that method of safeguarding it among neighbors, and I find it difficult to believe that the Emperor's generals were very deeply engrossed by it at that deplorable stage of our glory; but I know that we are forbidden to discuss these matters impartially; I hold my peace, posterity will pass judgment on them.

Monsieur Delmare had all the good qualities and all the failings of these men. He was innocent to childishness concerning certain refinements of the point of honor, yet he was very well able to conduct his affairs to the best possible end without disturbing himself as to the good or evil which might result therefrom to others. His whole conscience was the law; his whole moral code was his rights under the law. His was one of those rigid, unbending probities which never borrow for fear of not returning, and never lend for fear of not recovering. He was the honest man who neither takes nor gives aught; who would rather die than steal a bundle of sticks in the king's forest, but would kill you without ceremony for picking up a twig in his. He was useful to himself alone, harmful to nobody. He took part in nothing that was going on about him, lest he might be compelled to do somebody a favor. But, when he deemed himself in honor bound to do it, no one could go about it with more energy and zeal and a more chivalrous spirit. At once trustful as a child and suspicious as a despot, he would believe a false oath and distrust a sincere promise. As in the military profession, form was everything with him.

Public opinion governed him so exclusively that common sense and argument counted for nothing in his decisions, and when he said: "Such things are done," he thought that he had stated an irrefutable argument.

Thus it will be seen that his nature was most antipathetic to his wife's, his heart entirely unfitted to understand her, his mind entirely incapable of appreciating her. And yet it is certain that slavery had engendered in her woman's heart a sort of virtuous and unspoken aversion which was not always just. Madame Delmare doubted her husband's heart overmuch; he was only harsh and she deemed him cruel. There was more roughness than anger in his outbreaks, more vulgarity than impertinence in his manners. Nature had not made him evil-minded: he had moments of compassion which led him to repentance, and in his repentance he was almost sensitive. It was camp life that had raised brutality to a principle in him. With a less refined, less gentle wife he would have been as gentle as a tame wolf; but this woman was disheartened with her fate; she did not take the trouble to try to make it happier.

XI

As he alighted from his tilbury in the courtyard at Lagny, Raymon's heart failed him. So he was once more to enter that house which recalled such awful memories! His arguments, being in accord with his passions, might enable him to overcome the impulses of his heart, but not to stifle them, and at that moment the sensation of remorse was as keen as that of desire.

The first person who came forward to meet him was Sir Ralph Brown, and when he spied him in his everlasting hunting costume, flanked by his hounds and sober as a Scotch laird, he fancied that the portrait he had seen in Madame Delmare's chamber was walking before his eyes. A few moments later the colonel appeared, and the breakfast was served without Indiana. As he passed through the vestibule, by the door of the billiard room, and recognized the places he had previously seen under such different circumstances, Raymon was so distressed that he could hardly remember why he had come there now.

"Is Madame Delmare really not coming down?" the colonel asked his factotum Lelièvre, with some asperity.

"Madame slept badly," replied Lelièvre, "and Mademoiselle Noun—that devil of a name keeps coming to my tongue!—Mademoiselle Fanny, I mean, just told me that madame is lying down now."

"How does it happen then that I just saw her at her window? Fanny is mistaken. Go and tell madame that breakfast is served; or stay—Sir Ralph, my dear kinsman, be pleased to go up and see for yourself if your cousin is really ill."

While the unfortunate name that the servant had mentioned from habit caused Raymon's nerves a painful thrill, the colonel's expedient caused him a strange sensation of jealous anger.

"In her bedroom!" he thought. "He doesn't confine himself to hanging the man's portrait there, but sends him there in person. This Englishman has privileges here which the husband himself seems to be afraid to claim."

"Don't let that surprise you," said Monsieur Delmare, as if he had divined Raymon's reflections; "Monsieur Brown is the family physician; and then he's our cousin too, a fine fellow whom we love with all our hearts."

Ralph remained absent ten minutes. Raymon was distraught, ill at ease. He did not eat and kept looking at the door. At last the Englishman reappeared.

"Indiana is really ill," he said; "I told her to go back to bed."

He took his seat tranquilly and ate with a robust appetite. The colonel did likewise.

"This is evidently a pretext to avoid seeing me," thought Raymon. "These two men don't suspect it, and the husband is more displeased than worried about his wife's condition. Good! my affairs are progressing more favorably than I hoped."

This resistance rearoused his determination and Noun's image vanished from the dismal hangings, which, at the beginning, had congealed his blood with terror. Soon he saw nothing but Madame Delmare's slender form. In the salon he sat at her embroidery frame, examined the flowers she was making—talking all the while and feigning deep interest—handled all the silks, inhaled the perfume her tiny fingers had left upon them. He had seen the same piece of work before, in Indiana's bedroom; then it was hardly begun, now it was covered with flowers that had bloomed beneath the breath of fever, watered by her daily tears. Raymon felt the tears coming to his own eyes, and, by virtue of some unexplained sympathy, sadly raising his eyes to the horizon, at which Indiana was in the habit of gazing in melancholy mood, he saw in the distance the white walls of Cercy standing out against a background of dark hills.

The colonel's voice roused him with a start.

"Well, my excellent neighbor," he said, "it is time for me to pay my debt to you and keep my promises. The factory is in full swing and the hands are all at work. Here are paper and pencils, so that you can take notes."

Raymon followed the colonel, inspected the factory with an eager, interested air, made comments which proved that chemistry and mechanics were equally familiar to him, listened with incredible patience to Monsieur Delmare's endless dissertations, coincided with some of his ideas, combated some others, and in every respect so conducted himself as to persuade his guide that he took an absorbing interest in these things, whereas he was hardly thinking of them and all his thoughts were directed toward Madame Delmare.

It was a fact that he was familiar with every branch of knowledge, that no invention was without interest for him; moreover he was forwarding the interests of his brother, who had really embarked his whole fortune in a similar enterprise, although of much greater extent. Monsieur Delmare's technical knowledge, his only claim to superiority, pointed out to him at that moment the best method of taking advantage of this interview.

Sir Ralph, who was a poor business man but a very shrewd politician, suggested during the inspection of the factory some economical considerations of considerable importance. The workmen, being anxious to display their skill to an expert, surpassed themselves in deftness and activity. Raymon looked at everything, heard everything, answered everything, and thought of nothing but the love affair that brought him to that place.

When they had exhausted the subject of machinery the discussion fell upon the volume and force of the stream. They went out and climbed upon the dam, bidding the overseer raise the gates and mark the different depths.

"Monsieur," said the man, addressing Monsieur Delmare, who fixed the maximum at fifteen feet, "I beg pardon, but we had it seventeen once this year."

"When was that? You are mistaken," said the colonel.

"Excuse me, monsieur, it was on the eve of your return from Belgium, the very night Mademoiselle Noun was found drowned; what I say is proved by the fact that the body passed over that dike yonder and did not stop until it got here, just where monsieur is standing."

Speaking thus, with much animation, the man pointed to where Raymon stood. The unhappy young man turned pale as death; he cast a horrified glance at the water flowing at his feet; it seemed to him that the livid face was reflected in it, that the body was still floating there; he had an attack of vertigo and would have fallen into the river had not Monsieur Brown caught his arm and pulled him away.

"Very good," said the colonel, who noticed nothing, and who gave so little thought to Noun that he did not suspect Raymon's emotion; "but that was an extraordinary instance, and the average depth of the water is— But what the devil's the matter with you two?" he inquired, suddenly interrupting himself.

"Nothing," replied Sir Ralph; "as I turned I trod on monsieur's foot; I am distressed, for I must have hurt him terribly."

Sir Ralph made this reply in so calm and natural a tone that Raymon was convinced that he thought he was telling the truth. A few courteous words were exchanged and the conversation resumed its course.

Raymon left Lagny a few hours later without seeing

Madame Delmare. It was better than he hoped; he had feared that he should find her calm and indifferent.

However he repeated his visit with no better success. That time the colonel was alone; Raymon put forth all the resources of his wit to captivate him, and shrewdly descended to innumerable little acts of condescension—praised Napoléon, whom he did not like, deplored the indifference of the government, which left the illustrious remnant of the Grande Armée in oblivion and something like contempt, carried opposition tenets as far as his opinions would permit him to go, and selected from his various beliefs those which were likely to flatter Monsieur Delmare's. He even provided himself with a character different from his real one, in order to attract his confidence. He transformed himself into a *bon vivant*, a "hail fellow well met," a careless good-for-naught.

"What if that fellow should ever make a conquest of my wife!" said the colonel to himself as he watched him drive away.

Then he began to chuckle inwardly and to think that Raymon was a *charming fellow*.

Madame de Ramière was at Cercy at this time: Raymon extolled Madame Delmare's charms and wit to her, and without urging her to call upon her, had the art to suggest the thought.

"I believe she is the only one of my neighbors whom I do not know," she said; "and as I am a new arrival in the neighborhood it is my place to begin. We will go to Lagny together next week."

The appointed day arrived.

"She cannot avoid me now," thought Raymon.

In truth Madame Delmare could not escape the necessity of receiving him, for when she saw an elderly woman she did not know step from the carriage, she went out on the stoop herself to meet her. At the same moment she recognized Raymon in the man who accompanied her; but she realized that he must have deceived his mother to induce her to take that step, and her displeasure on that account gave her strength to be dignified and calm. She received Madame de Ramière with a mixture of respect and affability; but her coldness to Raymon was so absolutely glacial that he felt that he could not long endure it. He was not accustomed to disdain and his pride took fire at being unable to conquer with a glance those who were prepossessed against him. Thereupon, deciding upon his course like a man who cared nothing for a woman's whim, he asked permission to join Monsieur Delmare in the park and left the two women together.

Little by little, vanquished by the charm which a superior intellect, combined with a noble and generous heart, is capable of exerting even in its least intimate relations, Indiana became affable, affectionate and almost playful with Madame de Ramière. She had never known her mother, and Madame de Carvajal, despite her presents and her words of praise, was far from being a mother to her; so she felt a sort of fascination of the heart with Raymon's mother.

When he joined her as she was stepping into her carriage he saw Indiana put to her lips the hand that Madame de Ramière offered her. Poor Indiana felt the need of having some one to cling to. Everything that offered a prospect of interest and of companionship in her lonely and unhappy life was welcomed by her with the keenest delight; and then she said to herself that Madame de Ramière would preserve her from the snare into which Raymon sought to lure her.

"I will throw myself into this good woman's arms,"

she was thinking already, "and, if necessary, I will tell her everything. I will implore her to save me from her son, and her prudence will stand guard over him and over me."

Such was not Raymon's reasoning.

"Dear mother!" he said to himself, as he drove back with her to Cercy, "her charm and her goodness of heart perform miracles. What do I not owe to them already! my education, my success in life, my standing in society. I lacked nothing but the happiness of owing to her the heart of such a woman as Indiana."

Raymon, as we see, loved his mother because of his need of her and of the well-being he owed to her; so do all children love their mothers.

A few days later Raymon received an invitation to pass three days at Bellerive, a beautiful country seat owned by Sir Ralph Brown, between Cercy and Lagny, where it was proposed, in concert with the best hunters of the neighborhood, to destroy a part of the game that was devouring the owner's woods and gardens. Raymon liked neither Sir Ralph nor hunting, but Madame Delmare did the honors of her cousin's house on great occasions, and the hope of meeting her soon decided Raymon to accept the invitation.

The fact was that Sir Ralph did not expect Madame Delmare on this occasion; she had excused herself on the ground of her wretched health. But the colonel, who took umbrage when his wife sought diversion on her own account, took still greater umbrage when she declined such diversions as he chose to allow her.

"Do you want to make the whole province think that I keep you under lock and key?" he said to her. "You make me appear like a jealous husband; it's an absurd rôle and one that I do not propose to play any longer.

Besides, what does this lack of courtesy to your cousin mean? Does it become you, when we owe to his friendship the establishment and prosperity of our business, to refuse him such a service? You are necessary to him and you hesitate! I cannot understand your whims. All the people whom I don't like are sure of a hearty welcome from you; but those whom I esteem are unfortunate enough not to please you."

"That reproach has very little application to the present case, I should say," replied Madame Delmare. "I love my cousin like a brother, and my affection for him was of long standing when yours began."

"Oh! yes, yes, more of your fine words; but I know that you don't find him sentimental enough, the poor devil! you call him selfish because he doesn't like novels and doesn't cry over the death of a dog. However, he's not the only one. How did you receive Monsieur de Ramière? a charming young fellow, on my word! Madame de Carvajal introduces him to you and you receive him with the greatest affability; but I have the ill-luck to think well of him and you pronounce him unendurable, and when he calls upon you, you go to bed! Are you trying to make me appear a perfect boor? It is time for this to come to an end and for you to begin to live like other people."

Raymon deemed it inadvisable, in view of his plans, to show too much eagerness; threats of indifference are successful with almost all women who think that they are loved. But the hunting had been in progress since morning when he reached Sir Ralph's, and Madame Delmare was not expected until dinner time. He employed the interval in preparing a plan of action.

It occurred to him that he must find some method of justifying his conduct, for the critical moment was at hand. He had two days before him and he determined to apportion the time thus: the rest of the day that was nearly ended to make an impression, the next day to persuade and the following day to be happy. He even consulted his watch and calculated almost to an hour the time when his enterprise would succeed or fail.

XII

He had been two hours in the salon when he heard Madame Delmare's sweet and slightly husky voice in the adjoining room. By dint of reflecting on his scheme of seduction he had become as passionately interested as an author in his subject or a lawyer in his cause, and the emotion that he felt at the sight of Indiana may be compared to that of an actor thoroughly imbued with the spirit of his rôle who finds himself in the presence of the principal character of the drama and can no longer distinguish artificial stage effects from reality.

She was so changed that a feeling of sincere compassion found its way into Raymon's being, amid the nervous tremors of his brain. Unhappiness and illness had left such deep traces on her face that she was hardly pretty, and that he felt that there was more glory than pleasure to be gained by the conquest. But he owed it to himself to restore this woman to life and happiness.

Seeing how pale and sad she was, he judged that he had no very strong will to contend against. Was it possible that such a frail envelope could conceal great power of moral resistance?

He reflected that it was necessary first of all to interest her in herself, to frighten her concerning her depression and her failing health, in order the more easily to open her mind to the desire and the hope of a better destiny.

"Indiana!" he began, with secret assurance perfectly concealed beneath an air of profound melancholy, "to think that I should find you in such a condition as this! I did not dream that this moment to which I have looked forward so long, which I have sought so eagerly, would cause me such horrible pain!"

Madame Delmare hardly anticipated this language; she expected to surprise Raymon in the attitude of a confused and shrinking culprit; and lo! instead of accusing himself—of telling her of his grief and repentance—his sorrow and pity were all for her! She must be sorely cast down and broken in spirit to inspire compassion in a man who should have implored hers!

A French woman—a woman of the world—would not have lost her head at such a delicate juncture; but Indiana had no tact; possessed neither the skill nor the power of dissimulation necessary to preserve the advantage of her position. His words brought before her eyes the whole picture of her sufferings and tears glistened on the edge of her eyelids.

"I am ill, in truth," she said, as she seated herself, feebly and wearily, in the chair Raymon offered her; "I feel that I am very ill, and, in your presence, monsieur, I have the right to complain."

Raymon had not hoped to progress so fast. He seized the opportunity by the hair, as the saying is, and, taking possession of a hand which felt cold and dry in his, he replied:

"Indiana! do not say that; do not say that I am the

cause of your illness, for you make me mad with grief and joy."

"And joy!" she repeated, fixing upon him her great blue eyes overflowing with melancholy and amazement.

"I should have said hope; for, if I have caused you unhappiness, madame, I can perhaps bring it to an end. Say a word," he added, kneeling beside her on a cushion that had fallen from the divan, "ask me for my blood, my life!"

"Oh! hush!" said Indiana bitterly, withdrawing her hand; "you made a shameful misuse of promises before; try to repair the evil you have done!"

"I intend to do it; I will do it!" he cried, trying to take her hand again.

"It is too late," she said. "Give me back my companion, my sister; give me back Noun, my only friend!"

A cold shiver ran through Raymon's veins. This time he had no need to encourage her emotion; there are emotions which awake unbidden, mighty and terrible, without the aid of art.

"She knows all," he thought, "and she has judged me."

Nothing could be more humiliating to him than to be reproached for his crime by the woman who had been his innocent accomplice; nothing more bitter than to see Noun's rival lamenting her death.

"Yes, monsieur," said Indiana, raising her face, down which the tears were streaming, "you were the cause—"

But she paused when she observed Raymon's pallor. It must have been most alarming, for he had never suffered so keenly.

Thereupon all the kindness of her heart and all the involuntary emotion which he aroused in her resumed their sway over Madame Delmare.

"Forgive me!" she said in dismay; "I hurt you terribly; I have suffered so myself! Sit down and let us talk of something else."

This sudden manifestation of her sweet and generous nature rendered Raymon's emotion deeper than ever. He sobbed aloud; he put Indiana's hand to his lips and covered it with tears and kisses. It was the first time that he had been able to weep since Noun's death, and it was Indiana who relieved his breast of that terrible weight.

"Oh! since you, who never knew her, weep for her so freely," she said; "since you regret so bitterly the injury you have done me, I dare not reproach you any more. Let us weep for her together, monsieur, so that, from her place in heaven, she may see us and forgive us."

Raymon's forehead was wet with cold perspiration. If the words *you who never knew her* had delivered him from painful anxiety, this appeal to his victim's memory, in Indiana's innocent mouth, terrified him with a superstitious terror. Sorely distressed, he rose and walked feverishly to a window and leaned on the sill to breathe the fresh air. Indiana remained in her chair, silent and deeply moved. She felt a sort of secret joy on seeing Raymon weep like a child and display the weakness of a woman.

"He is naturally kind," she murmured to herself; "he is fond of me; his heart is warm and generous. He did wrong, but his repentance expiates his fault, and I ought to have forgiven him sooner."

She gazed at him with a softened expression; her confidence in him had returned. She mistook the remorse of the guilty man for the repentance of love.

"Do not weep any more," she said, rising and walking up to him; "it was I who killed her; I alone am guilty. This remorse will sadden my whole life. I gave way to an impulse of suspicion and anger; I humiliated her, wounded her to the heart. I vented upon her all my spleen against you; it was you alone who had offended me, and I punished my poor friend for it. I was very hard to her!"

"And to me," said Raymon, suddenly forgetting the past to think only of the present.

Madame Delmare blushed.

"I should not perhaps have reproached you for the cruel loss I sustained on that awful night," she said; "but I cannot forget the imprudence of your conduct toward me. The lack of delicacy in your romantic and culpable project wounded me very deeply. I believed then that you loved me!—and you did not even respect me!"

Raymon recovered his strength, his determination, his love, his hopes; the sinister presentiment, which had made his blood run cold, vanished like a nightmare. He awoke once more, young, ardent, overflowing with desire, with passion, and with hopes for the future.

"I am guilty if you hate me," he said, vehemently, throwing himself at her feet; "but, if you love me, I am not guilty—I never have been. Tell me, Indiana, do you love me?"

"Do you deserve it?" she asked.

"If, in order to deserve it," said Raymon, "I must love you to adoration—"

"Listen to me," she said, abandoning her hands to him and fastening upon him her great eyes, swimming in tears, wherein a sombre flame gleamed at intervals. "Do you know what it is to love a woman like me? No, you do not know. You thought that it was merely a matter of gratifying the caprice of a day. You judged my heart by all the surfeited hearts over which you have hitherto exerted your ephemeral domination. You do not know that I have never loved as yet and that I will not give my untouched virgin heart in exchange for a ruined, withered heart, my enthusiastic love for a lukewarm love, my whole life for one brief day!"

"Madame, I love you passionately; my heart too is young and ardent, and, if it is not worthy of yours, no man's heart will ever be. I know how you must be loved; I have not waited until this day to find out. Do I not know your life? did I not describe it to you at the ball, the first time that I ever had the privilege of speaking to you? Did I not read the whole history of your heart in the first one of your glances that ever fell upon me? And with what did I fall in love, think you? with your beauty alone? Ah! that is surely enough to drive an older and less passionate man to frenzy; but for my part, if I adore that gracious and charming envelope, it is because it encloses a pure and divine soul, it is because a celestial fire quickens it, and because I see in you not a woman simply, but an angel."

"I know that you possess the art of praising; but do not hope to move my vanity. I have no need of homage, but of affection. I must be loved without a rival, without reserve and forever; you must be ready to sacrifice everything to me, fortune, reputation, duty, business, principles, family—everything, monsieur, because I shall place the same absolute devotion in my scale, and I wish them to balance. You see that you cannot love me like that!"

It was not the first time that Raymon had seen a woman take love seriously, although such cases are rare, luckily for society; but he knew that promises of love do not bind the honor, again luckily for society. Sometimes too the women who had demanded from him these solemn pledges had been the first to break them. He did not take fright therefore at Madame Delmare's demands, or rather he gave no thought either to the past or the future. He was borne along by the irresistible fascination of that frail, passionate woman, so weak in body, so resolute in heart and mind. She was so beautiful, so animated, so imposing as she dictated her laws to him, that he remained as if fascinated at her knees.

"I swear," he said, "that I will be yours body and soul; I devote my life, I consecrate my blood to you, I place my will at your service; take everything, do as you will with my fortune, my honor, my conscience, my thoughts, my whole being."

"Hush!" said Indiana hastily, "here is my cousin."

As she spoke the phlegmatic Sir Ralph Brown entered the room with his usual tranquil air, expressing great surprise and pleasure to see his cousin, whom he had not hoped to see. Then he asked permission to kiss her by way of manifesting his gratitude, and, leaning over her with methodical moderation, he kissed her on the lips, according to the custom among children in his country.

Raymon turned pale with anger and Ralph had no sooner left the room to give some order, than he went to Indiana and tried to remove all trace of that impertinent kiss. But Madame Delmare calmly pushed him away.

"Remember," she said, "that you owe much reparation if you wish me to believe in you."

Raymon did not understand the delicacy of this rebuff; he saw in it nothing but a rebuff and he was angry with Sir Ralph. Shortly after he noticed that, when Sir Ralph spoke to Indiana in an undertone, he used the more familiar form of address, and he was on the verge of mistaking the reserve which custom imposed upon Sir Ralph at other times, for the precaution of a favored lover. But he blushed for his insulting suspicions as soon as he met the young woman's pure glance.

That evening Raymon displayed his intellectual powers. There was a large company and people listened to him; he could not escape the prominence which his talents gave him. He talked, and if Indiana had been vain she would have had her first taste of happiness in listening to him. But on the contrary her simple, straightforward mind took fright at Raymon's superiority; she struggled against the magic power which he exerted over all about him, a sort of magnetic influence which heaven, or hell, accords to certain men—a partial and ephemeral royalty, so real that no mediocre mind can escape its ascendancy, so fleeting that no trace of it remains after them, and that when they die we are amazed at the sensation they made during their lives.

There were many times when Indiana was fascinated by such a brilliant display; but she at once said to herself sadly that she was eager for happiness, not for glory. She asked herself in dismay if this man, for whom life had so many different aspects, so many absorbing interests, could devote his whole mind to her, sacrifice all his ambitions to her. And while he defended step by step, with such courage and skill, such ardor and self-possession, doctrines purely speculative and interests entirely foreign to their love, she was terrified to see that she was of so little account in his life while he was everything in hers. She said to herself in terror that she was to him a three days' fancy and that he had been to her the dream of a whole life.

When he offered her his arm as they were leaving the

salon, he whispered a few words of love in her ear; but she answered sadly:

"You have a great mind!"

Raymon understood the reproof and passed the whole of the following day at Madame Delmare's feet. The other guests, being engrossed by their hunting, left them entirely to themselves.

Raymon was eloquent; Indiana had such a craving to believe, that half of his eloquence was wasted. Women of France, you do not know what a creole is; you would undoubtedly have yielded less readily to conviction, for you are not the ones to be deceived or betrayed!

XIII

When Sir Ralph returned from hunting and as usual felt Madame Delmare's pulse, Raymon, who was watching him closely, detected an almost imperceptible expression of surprise and pleasure on his placid features. And then, in obedience to some mysterious secret impulse, the two men looked at each other, and Sir Ralph's light eyes, fastened like an owl's upon Raymon's black ones, forced them to look down. During the rest of the day the baronet's manner toward Madame Delmare, beneath his apparent imperturbability, was keenly observant, indicative of something which might be called interest or solicitude if his face had been capable of reflecting a decided sentiment. But Raymon exerted himself in vain to discover if fear or hope were uppermost in his thoughts; Ralph was impenetrable.

Suddenly, as he stood a few steps behind Madame Delmare's chair, he heard her cousin say to her in an undertone:

"You would do well, cousin, to go out in the saddle to-morrow."

"Why, I have no horse just now, as you know," she said.

"We will find one for you. Will you hunt with us?"

Madame Delmare resorted to various pretexts to escape. Raymon understood that she preferred to remain with him, but he thought at the same time that her cousin seemed to display extraordinary persistence in preventing her from doing so. So he left the persons with whom he was talking, walked up to her and joined Sir Ralph in urging her to go. He had a feeling of bitter resentment against this importunate chaperon, and determined to tire out his watchfulness.

"If you will agree to follow the hunt," he said to Indiana, "you will embolden me to follow your example, madame. I care little for hunting; but to have the privilege of being your esquire——"

"In that case I will go," replied Indiana, heedlessly.

She exchanged a meaning glance with Raymon; but, swift as it was, Sir Ralph caught it on the wing, and Raymon was unable, during the rest of the evening, to glance at her or address her without encountering Monsieur Brown's eyes or ears. A feeling of aversion, almost of jealousy, arose in his heart. By what right did this cousin, this friend of the family, assume to act as a school-master with the woman whom *he* loved! He swore that Sir Ralph should repent, and he sought an opportunity to insult him without compromising Madame Delmare; but that was impossible. Sir Ralph did the honors of his establishment with a cold and dignified courtesy which offered no handle for an epigram or a contradiction.

The next morning, before the rising-bell had rung, Raymon was surprised to see his host's solemn face enter his room. There was something even stiffer than usual in his manner, and Raymon felt his heart beat fast with longing and impatience at the prospect of a challenge. But he came simply to talk about a horse which Raymon had brought to Bellerive and had expressed a desire to sell. The bargain was concluded in five minutes; Sir Ralph made no objection to the price but produced a *rouleau* of gold from his pocket and counted down the amount on the mantel with a coolness of manner that was altogether extraordinary, not deigning to pay any heed to Raymon's remonstrances concerning such scrupulous promptness. As he was leaving the room, he turned back to say:

"Monsieur, the horse belongs to me from this morning!"

At that Raymon fancied that he could detect a purpose to prevent him from hunting, and he observed dryly that he did not propose to follow the hunt on foot.

"Monsieur," replied Sir Ralph, with a slight trace of affectation, "I am too well versed in the laws of hospitality."

And he withdrew.

On going down into the courtyard Raymon saw Madame Delmare in her riding-habit, playing merrily with Ophelia, who was tearing her handkerchief. Her cheeks had taken on a faint rosy tinge, her eyes shone with a brilliancy that had long been absent from them. She had already recovered her beauty; her curly black hair escaped from beneath her little hat, in which she was charming; and the cloth habit buttoned to the chin outlined her slender, graceful figure. The principal charm of the creoles, to my mind, consists in the fact that the excessive delicacy of their features and their proportions enables them to retain for a long while the daintiness of childhood. Indiana, in her gay and laughing mood, seemed to be no more than fourteen.

Raymon, impressed by her charms, felt a thrill of triumph and paid her the least insipid compliment he could invent upon her beauty.

"You were anxious about my health," she said to him in an undertone; "do you not see that I long to live?"

He could not reply otherwise than by a happy, grateful glance. Sir Ralph himself brought his cousin her horse; Raymon recognized the one he had just sold.

"What!" said Madame Delmare in amazement, for she had seen him trying the animal the day before in the courtyard, "is Monsieur de Ramière so polite as to lend me his horse?"

"Did you not admire the creature's beauty and docility yesterday?" said Sir Ralph; "he is yours from this moment. I am sorry, my dear, that I couldn't have given him to you sooner."

"You are growing facetious, cousin," said Madame Delmare; "I do not understand this joke at all. Whom am I to thank—Monsieur de Ramière, who consents to lend me his horse, or you, who perhaps asked him for it?"

"You must thank your cousin," said Monsieur Delmare, "who bought this horse for you and makes you a present of him."

"Is it really true, my dear Ralph?" said Madame Delmare, patting the pretty creature with the delight of a girl at receiving her first jewels.

"Didn't we agree that I should give you a horse in

exchange for the piece of embroidery you are doing for me? Come, mount him, have no fear. I have studied his disposition, and I tried him only this morning."

Indiana threw her arms around Sir Ralph's neck, then leaped upon Raymon's horse and fearlessly made him prance.

This whole domestic scene took place in a corner of the courtyard before Raymon's eyes. He was conscious of a paroxysm of violent anger when the simple and trustful affection of those two displayed itself before him; passionately in love as he was and with less than a whole day in which to have Indiana to himself.

"How happy I am!" she said, calling him to her side on the avenue. "It seems my dear Ralph divined what gift would be most precious to me. And aren't you happy too, Raymon, to see the horse you have ridden pass into my hands? Oh! how I will love him and care for him! What do you call him? Tell me; for I prefer not to take away the name you gave him."

"If there is a happy man here," rejoined Raymon, "it should be your cousin, who gives you presents and whom you kiss so heartily."

"Are you really jealous of our friendship and of those loud smacks?" she said with a laugh.

"Jealous? perhaps so, Indiana; I am not sure. But when that red-cheeked young cousin puts his lips to yours, when he takes you in his arms to seat you on the horse that he *gives* you and I *sell* you, I confess that I suffer. No, madame, I am not happy to see you the mistress of the horse I loved. I can understand that one might be happy in giving him to you; but to play the tradesman in order to provide another with the means of making himself agreeable to you, is a very cleverly managed humiliation on Sir Ralph's part. If I did not believe that all this cunning was quite involuntary, I would like to be revenged on him."

"Oh! fie! this jealousy is not becoming to you! How can our commonplace intimacy arouse any feeling in you, in you who should be, so far as I am concerned, outside of the common life of mankind and should create for me a world of enchantment—in you of all men! I am displeased with you already, Raymon; I perceive that there is something like wounded self-esteem in this angry feeling displayed toward this poor cousin. It seems to me that you are more jealous of the lukewarm preference which I display for him in public than of the exclusive affection which I might secretly entertain for another."

"Forgive me, forgive me, Indiana, I am wrong! I am not worthy of you, angel of goodness and gentleness! but I confess that I have suffered cruelly because of the right that man has seemed to assume."

"He assume rights, Raymon! Do you not know what sacred gratitude binds us to him? do you not know that his mother was my mother's sister? that we were born in the same valley; that in our early years he was my protector; that he was my mainstay, my only teacher, my only companion at Ile Bourbon; that he has followed me everywhere; that he left the country which I left, to come and live where I lived; in a word, that he is the only being who loves me and who takes any interest in my life?"

"Curse him! all that you tell me, Indiana, inflames the wound. So he loves you very dearly, does this Englishman, eh? Do you know how I love you?"

"Oh! let us not compare the two. If an attachment of the same nature made you rivals, I should owe the preference to the one of longer standing. But have no fear, Raymon, that I shall ever ask you to love me as Ralph loves me."

"Tell me about the man, I beg you; for who can penetrate his stone mask?"

"Must I do the honors for my cousin?" she said with a smile. "I confess that I do not altogether like the idea of describing him; I love him so dearly that I would like to flatter him; as he is, I am afraid that you will not find him a very noble figure. Do try to help me; come, how does he seem to you?"

"His face—forgive me if I wound you—indicates absolute nonentity; but there are signs of good sense and education in his conversation when he deigns to speak; but he speaks so hesitatingly, so coldly, that no one profits by his knowledge, his delivery is so depressing and tiresome. And then there is something commonplace and dull in his thoughts which is not redeemed by measured purity of expression. I think that his is a mind imbued with all the ideas that have been suggested to him, but too apathetic and too mediocre to have any of his own. He is just the sort of man that one must be to be looked upon in society as a serious-minded person. His gravity forms three-fourths of his merit, his indifference the rest."

"There is some truth in your portrait," said Indiana, "but there is prejudice too. You boldly solve doubts which I should not dare to solve, although I have known Ralph ever since I was born. It is true that his great defect consists in looking frequently through the eyes of others; but that is not the fault of his mind but of his education. You think that, without education, he would have been an absolute nonentity; I think that he would have been less so than he is. I must tell you one fact in his life which will help to explain his character. He was unfortunate to have a brother whom his parents openly preferred to him; this brother had all the brilliant qualities that he lacks. He learned easily, he had a taste for all the arts, he fairly sparkled with wit; his face, while less regular than Ralph's, was more expressive. He was affectionate, zealous, active, in a word, he was lovable. Ralph, on the contrary, was awkward, melancholy, undemonstrative; he loved solitude, learned slowly and did not make a display of what little knowledge he possessed. When his parents saw how different he was from his older brother, they maltreated him; they did worse than that: they humiliated him. Thereupon, child as he was, his character became gloomy and pensive and an unconquerable timidity paralyzed all his faculties. They had succeeded in inspiring in him self-aversion and self-contempt; he became discouraged with life, and, at the age of fifteen, he was attacked by the spleen, a malady that is wholly physical under the foggy sky of England, wholly mental under the revivifying sky of Ile Bourbon. He has often told me that one day he left the house with a determination to throw himself into the sea; but as he sat on the shore collecting his thoughts, as he was on the point of carrying out his plan, he saw me coming toward him in the arms of the negress who had been my nurse. I was then five years old. I was pretty, they say, and I manifested a predilection for my taciturn cousin which nobody shared. To be sure, he was attentive and kind to me in a way I was not accustomed to in my father's house. As we were both unhappy, we understood each other even then. He taught me his father's language, and I lisped mine to him. This blending of Spanish and English may be said to express Ralph's character. When I threw my arms around his neck, I saw that he was weeping, and, without knowing why, I began to weep too. Thereupon he pressed me to his heart and, so he told me afterward, made a vow to live for me, a neglected if not hated child, to whom his friendship would at all events be a kindness and his life of some benefit. Thus I was the first and only tie in his sad life. After that day we were hardly ever apart; we passed our days leading a free and healthy life in the solitude of the mountains. But perhaps these tales of our childhood bore you, and you would prefer to join the hunt and have a gallop."

"Foolish girl," said Raymon, seizing the bridle of Madame Delmare's horse.

"Very well, I will go on," said she. "Edmond Brown, Ralph's older brother, died at the age of twenty; his mother also died of grief, and his father was inconsolable. Ralph would have been glad to mitigate his sorrow, but the coldness with which Monsieur Brown greeted his first attempts increased his natural timidity. He passed whole hours in melancholy silence beside that heart-broken old man, not daring to proffer a word or a caress, he was so afraid that his consolation would seem misplaced or trivial. His father accused him of lack of feeling, and Edmond's death left Ralph more wretched and more misunderstood than ever. I was his only consolation."

"I cannot pity him, whatever you may do," Raymon interrupted; "but there is one thing in his life and yours that I cannot understand: it is that you never married."

"I can give you a very good reason for that," she replied. "When I reached a marriageable age, Ralph, who was ten years older than I—an enormous difference in our climate, where the childhood of girls is so brief—Ralph, I say, was already married."

"Is Sir Ralph a widower? I never heard anyone mention his wife."

"Never mention her to him. She was young and rich and lovely, but she had been in love with Edmond—she had been betrothed to him; and when, in order to serve family interests and family sentiment, she was made to marry Ralph, she did not so much as try to conceal her aversion for him. He was obliged to go to England with her, and when he returned to Ile Bourbon after his wife's death, I was married to Monsieur Delmare and just about to start for Europe. Ralph tried to live alone, but solitude aggravated his misery. Although he has never mentioned Mistress Ralph Brown to me, I have every reason to believe that he was even more unhappy in his married life than he had been in his father's house, and that his natural melancholy was increased by recent and painful memories. He was attacked with the spleen again; whereupon he sold his coffee plantation and came to France to settle down. His manner of introducing himself to my husband was original, and would have made me laugh if my good Ralph's attachment had not touched me deeply. 'Monsieur,' he said, 'I love your wife; it was I who brought her up; I look upon her as my sister and even more as my daughter. She is my only remaining relative and the only person to whom I am attached. Allow me to establish myself near you and let us three pass our lives together. They say that you are a little jealous of your wife, but they say also that you are a man of honor and uprightness. When I tell you that I have never had any other than brotherly love for her, and that I shall never have, you can regard me with as little anxiety as if I were really your brother-in-law. Isn't it so, monsieur?' Monsieur Delmare, who is very proud of his reputation for soldierly frankness, greeted this outspoken declaration with a sort of ostentatious confidence. But several months of careful watching were necessary before that confidence became as genuine as he boasted that it was. Now it is as impregnable as Ralph's steadfast and pacific heart."

"Are you perfectly sure, Indiana," said Raymon, "that Sir Ralph is not deceiving himself the least bit in the world when he swears that he never loved you?"

"I was twelve years old when he left Ile Bourbon to go with his wife to England; I was sixteen when he returned to find me married, and he manifested more joy than sorrow. Now, Ralph is really an old man."

"At twenty-nine?"

"Don't laugh at what I say. His face is young, but his heart is worn out by suffering, and he no longer loves anybody, in order to avoid suffering."

"Not even you?"

"Not even me. His friendship is simply a matter of habit; it was generous in the old days when he took upon himself to protect and educate my childhood, and then I loved him as he loves me to-day because of the need I had of him. To-day my whole heart is bent upon paying my debt to him, and my life is passed in trying to beautify and enliven his. But, when I was a child, I loved him with the instinct rather than with the heart, and he, now that he is a man, loves me less with the heart than with the instinct. I am necessary to him because I am almost alone in loving him; and to-day, as Monsieur Delmare manifests some attachment to him, he is almost as fond of him as of me. His protection, formerly so fearless in face of my father's despotism, has become lukewarm and cautious in face of my husband's. He never reproaches himself because I suffer, provided that I am near him. He does not ask himself if I am unhappy; it is enough for him to see that I am alive. He does not choose to lend me a support, which, while it would make my lot less cruel, would disturb his serenity by making trouble between him and Monsieur Delmare. By dint of hearing himself say again and again that his heart is dry, he has persuaded himself that it is true, and his heart has withered in the inaction in which he has allowed it to fall asleep from distrust. He is a man whom the affection of another person might have developed; but it was withdrawn from him and he shrivelled up. Now he asserts that happiness consists in repose, pleasure, in the comforts of life. He asks no questions about cares that he has not. I must say the word: Ralph is selfish."

"Very good, so much the better," said Raymon; "I am no longer afraid of him; indeed I will love him if you wish."

"Yes, love him, Raymon," she replied; "he will appreciate it; and, so far as we are concerned, let us never trouble ourselves to explain why people love us, but how they love us. Happy the man who can be loved, no matter for what reason!"

"What you say, Indiana," replied Raymon, grasping her slender, willowy form, "is the lament of a sad and solitary heart; but, in my case, I want you to know both why and how, especially why."

"To give me happiness, is it not?" she said, with a sad but passionate glance.

"To give you my life," said Raymon, brushing Indiana's floating hair with his lips.

A blast upon the horn near by warned them to be on their guard; it was Sir Ralph, who saw them or did not see them.

XIV

Raymon was amazed at what seemed to take place in Indiana's being as soon as the hounds were away. Her eyes gleamed, her cheeks flushed, the dilation of her nostrils betrayed an indefinable thrill of fear or pleasure, and suddenly, driving her spurs into her horse's side, she left him and galloped after Ralph. Raymon did not know that hunting was the only passion that Ralph and Indiana had in common. Nor did he suspect that in that frail and apparently timid woman there abode a more than masculine courage, that sort of delirious intrepidity which sometimes manifests itself like a nervous paroxysm in the feeblest creatures. Women rarely have the physical courage which consists in offering the resistance of inertia to pain or danger; but they often have the moral courage which attains its climax in peril or suffering. Indiana's delicate fibres delighted above all things in the tumult, the rapid movement and the excitement of the chase, that miniature image of war with its fatigues, its stratagems, its calculations, its hazards and its battles. Her dull, ennui-laden life needed this excitement; at such times she seemed to wake from a lethargy and to expend in one day all the energy that she had left to ferment uselessly in her blood for a whole year.

Raymon was terrified to see her ride away so fast, abandoning herself fearlessly to the impetuous spirit of a horse that she hardly knew, rushing him through the thickets, avoiding with amazing skill the branches that lashed at her face as they sprang back, leaping ditches

THE BOAR HUNT

Raymond was terrified to see her ride away so fast, abandoning herself fearlessly to the impetuous spirit of a horse that she hardly knew, rushing him through the thickets, avoiding with amazing skill the branches that lashed at her face as they sprang back, leaping ditches without hesitation, venturing confidently on clayey, slippery ground, heedless of the risk of breaking her slender limbs, but eager to be first on the smoking scent of the boar.

without hesitation, venturing confidently on clayey, slippery ground, heedless of the risk of breaking her slender limbs, but eager to be first on the smoking scent of the boar. So much determination alarmed him and nearly disgusted him with Madame Delmare. Men, especially lovers, are addicted to the innocent fatuity of preferring to protect weakness rather than to admire courage in womankind. Shall I confess it? Raymon was terrified at the promise of high spirit and tenacity in love which such intrepidity seemed to afford. It was not like the resignation of poor Noun, who preferred to drown herself rather than to contend against her misfortunes.

"If there's as much vigor and excitement in her tenderness as there is in her diversions," he thought; "if her will clings to me, fierce and palpitating, as her caprice clings to that boar's quarters, why society will impose no fetters on her, the law will have no force; my destiny will have to succumb and I shall have to sacrifice my future to her present."

Cries of terror and distress, among which he could distinguish Madame Delmare's voice, roused Raymon from these reflections. He anxiously urged his horse forward and was soon overtaken by Ralph, who asked him if he had heard the outcries.

At that moment several terrified whippers-in rode up to them, crying out confusedly that the boar had charged and overthrown Madame Delmare. Other huntsmen, in still greater dismay, appeared, calling for Sir Ralph, whose surgical skill was required by the injured person.

"It's of no use," said a late arrival. "There is no hope, your help will be too late."

In that moment of horror, Raymon's eyes fell upon the pale, gloomy features of Monsieur Brown. He did not cry out, he did not foam at the mouth, he did not wring his hands ; he simply took out his hunting-knife and with a *sang-froid* truly English was preparing to cut his own throat, when Raymon snatched the weapon from him and hurried him in the direction from which the cries came.

Ralph felt as if he were waking from a dream when he saw Madame Delmare rush to meet him and urge him forward to the assistance of her husband, who lay on the ground, apparently lifeless. Sir Ralph made haste to bleed him ; for he had speedily satisfied himself that he was not dead ; but his leg was broken and he was taken to the château.

As for Madame Delmare, in the confusion her name had been substituted by accident for that of her husband, or perhaps Ralph and Raymon had erroneously thought that they heard the name in which they were most interested.

Indiana was uninjured, but her fright and consternation had almost taken away her power of locomotion. Raymon supported her in his arms and was reconciled to her womanly heart when he saw how deeply affected she was by the misfortune of a husband whom she had much to forgive before pitying him.

Sir Ralph had already recovered his accustomed tranquillity ; but an extraordinary pallor revealed the violent shock he had experienced ; he had nearly lost one of the two human beings whom he loved.

Raymon, who alone, in that moment of confusion and excitement, had retained sufficient presence of mind to understand what he saw, had been able to judge of Ralph's affection for his cousin, and how little it was balanced by his feeling for the colonel. This observation, which positively contradicted Indiana's opinion, did not depart from Raymon's memory as it did from that of the other witnesses of the scene.

However Raymon never mentioned to Madame Delmare the attempted suicide of which he had been a witness. In this ungenerous reserve there was a suggestion of selfishness and bad temper which you will forgive perhaps in view of the amorous jealousy which was responsible for it.

After six weeks the colonel was with much difficulty removed to Lagny; but it was more than six months thereafter before he could walk; for before the fractured femur was fairly reduced he had an acute attack of rheumatism in the injured leg, which condemned him to excruciating pain and absolute immobility. His wife lavished the most loving attentions upon him; she never left his bedside and endured without a complaint his bitter fault-finding humor, his soldier-like testiness and his invalid's injustice.

Despite the ennui of such a depressing life, her health became robust and flourishing once more and happiness took up its abode in her heart. Raymon loved her, he really loved her. He came every day; he was discouraged by no difficulty in the way of seeing her, he bore with the infirmities of her husband, her cousin's coldness, the constraint of their interviews. A glance from him filled Indiana's heart with joy for a whole day. She no longer thought of complaining of life; her heart was full, her youthful nature had ample employment, her moral force had something to feed upon.

The colonel gradually came to feel very friendly to Raymon. He was simple enough to believe that his neighbor's assiduity in calling upon him was a proof of the interest he took in his health. Madame de Ramière also came occasionally, to sanction the liaison by her presence, and Indiana became warmly and passionately attached to Raymon's mother. At last the wife's lover became the husband's friend.

As a result of being thus constantly thrown together, Raymon and Ralph perforce became intimate in a certain sense; they called each other "my dear fellow," they shook hands morning and night. If either of them desired to ask a slight favor of the other, the regular form was this: "I count upon your friendship," etc. And when they spoke of each other they said: "He is a friend of mine."

But, although they were both as frank and outspoken as a man can be in the world, they were not at all fond of each other. They differed essentially in their opinions on every subject; they had no likes or dislikes in common; and, although they both loved Madame Delmare, they loved her in such a different way that that sentiment divided them instead of bringing them together. They found a singular pleasure in contradicting each other and in disturbing each other's equanimity as much as possible by reproaches which were none the less sharp and bitter because they took the form of generalities.

Their principal and most frequent controversies began with politics and ended with morals. It was in the evening, when they were all assembled around Monsieur Delmare's easy-chair, that discussions arose on the most trivial pretexts. They always maintained the external courtesy which philosophy imposed on the one and social custom on the other: but they sometimes said to each other, under the thin veil of allusions, some very harsh things, which amused the colonel; for he was naturally bellicose and quarrelsome and loved disputes in default of battles.

For my part, I believe that a man's political opinion is the whole man. Tell me what your heart and your head are and I will tell you your political opinions. In whatever rank or political party chance may have placed us at our birth, our character prevails sooner or later over the prejudice or artificial beliefs of education. You will call that a very sweeping statement perhaps; but how could I persuade myself to augur well of a mind that clings to certain theories which a generous spirit rejects? Show me a man who maintains the usefulness of capital punishment, and, however conscientious and enlightened he may be, I defy you ever to establish any sympathetic connection between him and me. If such a man attempts to instruct me as to facts which I do not know, he will never succeed; for it will not be in my power to give him my confidence.

Ralph and Raymon differed on all points, and, yet, before they knew each other, they had no clearly defined opinions. But, as soon as they were at odds, each of them maintained the contrary of what the other advanced, and in that way they would form for themselves an absolute, unassailable conviction. Raymon was on all occasions the champion of existing society, Ralph attacked its structure at every point.

The explanation was simple: Raymon was happy and treated with the utmost consideration, Ralph had known nothing of life but its evils and its bitterness; one found everything very satisfactory, the other was dissatisfied with everything. Men and things had maltreated Ralph and heaped benefits upon Raymon; and, like two children, they referred everything to themselves, setting themselves up as a court of last resort in regard to the great questions of social order, although they were equally incompetent.

Thus Ralph always upheld his visionary scheme of a republic from which he proposed to exclude all abuses, all prejudices, all injustice; a scheme founded entirely upon the hope of a new race of men. Raymon upheld his doctrine of an hereditary monarchy, preferring, he said, to endure abuses, prejudice and injustice, to seeing scaffolds erected and innocent blood shed.

The colonel was almost always on Ralph's side at the beginning of the discussion. He hated the Bourbons and imparted to all his opinions all the animosity of his sentiments. But soon Raymon would adroitly bring him over to his side by proving to him that the monarchy was in principle much nearer the Empire than the Republic. Ralph was so lacking in the power of persuasion, he was so sincere, so bungling, the poor baronet! his frankness was so unpolished, his logic so dull, his principles so rigid! He spared no one, he softened no harsh truth.

"*Parbleu!*" he would say to the colonel, when that worthy cursed England's intervention, "what in heaven's name have you, a man of some common sense and reasoning power, I suppose, to complain of because a whole nation fought fairly against you?"

"Fairly?" Delmare would repeat the word, grinding his teeth together and brandishing his crutch.

"Let us leave political questions to be decided by the powers concerned," Sir Ralph would say, "as we have adopted a form of government which forbids us to discuss our interests ourselves. If a nation is responsible for the faults of its legislature, what one can you find that is guiltier than yours?"

"And so I say, monsieur, shame upon France, which abandoned Napoléon and submitted to a king proclaimed by the bayonets of foreigners!" the colonel would exclaim.

"For my part, I do not say shame upon France," Sir Ralph would rejoin, "but woe to her! I pity her because she was so weak and so diseased, on the day she was purged of her tyrant, that she was compelled to accept your rag of a constitutional Charter, a mere shred of liberty which you are beginning to respect now that you must throw it aside and conquer your liberty over again."

Thereupon Raymon would pick up the gauntlet that Sir Ralph threw down. A knight of the Charter, he chose to be a knight of liberty as well, and he proved to Ralph with marvelous skill that one was the expression of the other; that, if he shattered the Charter he overturned his own idol. In vain would the baronet struggle in the unsound arguments in which Monsieur de Ramière entangled him; with admirable force he would argue that a greater extension of the suffrage would infallibly lead to the excesses of '93, and that the nation was not yet ripe for liberty, which is not the same as license. And when Sir Ralph declared that it was absurd to attempt to confine a constitution within a certain number of articles, that what was sufficient at first would eventually become insufficient, supporting his argument by the example of the convalescent, whose needs increased every day, Raymon would reply to all these commonplaces expressed with difficulty by Monsieur Brown that the Charter was not an immovable circle, that it would stretch with the necessities of France, attributing to it an elasticity which, he said, would afford later a means of satisfying the demands of the nation, but which in fact satisfied only those of the crown.

As to Delmare, he had not advanced a step since 1815. He was a stationary mortal, as full of prejudices and as obstinate as the émigrés at Coblentz, the never-failing subjects of his implacable irony. He was like an old child and had failed utterly to comprehend the great drama of the downfall of Napoléon. He had seen naught but the fortune of war in that crisis when the power of public opinion triumphed. He was forever talking of treason and of selling the country, as if a whole nation could betray a single man, as if France would have allowed herself to be sold by a few generals! He accused the Bourbons of tyranny and sighed for the glorious days of the Empire, when arms were lacking to till the soil and families were without bread. He declaimed against Franchet's police and extolled Fouché's. He was still at the day after Waterloo.

It was really a curious thing to listen to the sentimental idiocies of Delmare and Monsieur de Ramière, philanthropic dreamers both, one under the sword of Napoléon, the other under the sceptre of Saint-Louis; Monsieur Delmare planted at the foot of the Pyramids, Raymon seated under the monarchic shadow of the oak of Vincennes. Their Utopias, which clashed at first, became reconciled in due time: Raymon limed the colonel with his chivalrous sentiments; for one concession he exacted ten, and he accustomed him little by little to the spectacle of twenty-five years of victory ascending in a spiral column under the folds of the white flag. If Ralph had not constantly cast his abrupt, rough observations into the centre of Monsieur de Ramière's flowery rhetoric, he would infallibly have won Delmare over to the throne of 1815; but Ralph irritated his self-esteem, and the bungling outspokenness with which the Englishman strove to shake his convictions served only to anchor him more firmly in his imperialism. Thus all Monsieur de Ramière's efforts were wasted; Ralph trod heavily upon the flowers of his eloquence and the colonel returned with renewed enthusiasm to his tri-color. He swore that he would shake off the dust from it some fine day, that he would spit on the lilies and restore the Duc de Reichstadt to the throne of *his fathers;* he would begin anew the conquest of the world ; and he always concluded by lamenting the disgrace that rested upon France, the rheumatism that glued him to his chair and the ingratitude of the Bourbons to the old moustaches whom the sun of the desert had burned and who had swarmed over the ice-floes of the Moskowa.

"My poor fellow!" Ralph would say, "for heaven's sake be fair; you complain because the Restoration did not pay for services rendered the Empire and because it did reimburse its *émigrés.* Tell me, if Napoléon could come to life again to-morrow in all his power, would you like it if he should withdraw his favor from you and bestow it on the partisans of legitimacy? Every one for himself and his own; these are business discussions, disputes concerning private interests, which have little interest for France, now that you are almost all as incapacitated as the *voltigeurs* of the emigration, and that, whether gouty, married or sulking, you are all equally useless to her. However, she must support you all, and you see who can complain the loudest of her. When the day of the Republic dawns, she will clear her skirts of all your demands, and it will be no more than justice."

These trivial but self-evident observations offended the colonel like so many personal affronts; and Ralph who, with all his good sense, did not realize that the pettiness of spirit of a man whom he esteemed could go so far, fell into the habit of irritating him without mercy.

Before Raymon's arrival there had been a tacit agreement between the two to avoid every subject of controversy in which there might be some clashing and wounding of delicate sensibilities. But Raymon brought into their conversation all the subtleties of the language, all the petty artifices of civilization. He taught them that people can say anything to one another, indulge in all sorts of reproaches and shield themselves behind the pretext of legitimate discussion. He introduced among them the habit of disputation, then tolerated in the salons, because the vindictive passions of the Hundred Days had finally become appeased, had assumed divers milder shades. But the colonel had retained all the vehemence of his passions, and Ralph made a sad mistake in thinking that it was possible for him to listen to reason. Monsieur Delmare became daily more sour toward him and drew nearer to Raymon, who, without making too extensive concessions, knew how to assume an appearance of graciousness in order to spare the other's self-esteem.

It is a great imprudence to introduce politics as a pastime in the domestic circle. If there exist to-day any peaceful and happy families, I advise them to subscribe to no newspaper; not to read a single line of the budget, to bury themselves in the depth of their country estates as in an oasis, and to draw between themselves and the rest of society a line that none may pass; for, if they allow the echoes of our disputes to meet their ears, it is all over with their union and their repose. It is hard to imagine how much gall and bitterness political differences cause between near kindred. Most of the time they simply afford them an opportunity for reproaching one another for defects of character, mental obliquities and vices of the heart.

They would not dare to call one another knave, imbecile, ambitious villain or poltroon. They express the same idea by such names as *jesuit, royalist, revolutionist* and *trimmer*. These are different words, but the insult is the same, and all the more stinging because they may pursue and attack one another in this fashion without restraint, without mercy. There is an end to all mutual toleration of failings, all charitable spirit, all generous and delicate reserve; nothing is overlooked, everything is attributed to political feeling, and beneath that mask hatred and vengeance are freely exhaled. O ye blessed dwellers in the country, if there still be any country in France, shun, shun politics, and read the *Peau d'Ane* by your firesides! But the contagion is so great that there is no retreat obscure enough, no solitude profound enough to hide and shelter the man who would find a refuge for his amiable heart from the tempests of our civil dissensions.

In vain had the little château in Brie defended itself for years against this ill-omened invasion; it lost in time its heedlessness, its active domestic life, its long evenings of silence and meditation. Noisy disputes awoke its slumbering echoes; bitter and threatening words terrified the faded cherubs who had smiled amid the dust of the hangings for a hundred years past. The excitements of present-day life found their way into that ancient dwelling, and all those old-fashioned splendors, all those relics of a period of pleasure and frivolity saw with dismay the advent of an epoch of doubt and declamation, represented by three men who shut themselves up together every day to quarrel from morning till night.

XV

Despite these never-ending dissensions, Madame Delmare clung with the confidence of her years to the hope of a happy future. It was her first happiness; and her ardent imagination, her rich young heart, were able to supply it with all that it lacked. She was ingenious in creating keen and pure joys for herself—in bestowing upon herself the complement of the precarious favors of her destiny. Raymon loved her. In truth he did not lie when he told her that she was the only love of his life; he had never loved so innocently nor so long. With her he forgot everything but her. The world and politics were blotted out by the thought of her; he enjoyed the domestic life, the being treated like one of the family, as she treated him. He admired her patience and her strength of will; he wondered at the contrast between her mind and her character; he wondered especially that, after importing so much solemnity into their first compact, she was so unexacting, satisfied with such furtive and infrequent joys, and that she trusted him so blindly and so absolutely. But love was a novel and generous passion in her heart, and a thousand noble and delicate sentiments were included in it and gave it a force which Raymon could not understand.

For his own part, he was annoyed at first by the constant presence of the husband or the cousin. He had intended that this love should be like all his previous loves, but Indiana soon compelled him to rise to her level. The resignation with which she endured the constant surveillance, the happy air with which she glanced at him by stealth, her eyes which spoke to him in eloquent though silent language, her sublime smile when a sudden allusion in conversation brought their hearts nearer together—these soon became keen pleasures which Raymon craved and appreciated, thanks to the refinement of his mind and the culture of education.

What a difference between that chaste creature who seemed not to contemplate the possibility of a *dénoûment* to her love and all those other women who were intent only upon hastening it while pretending to shun it! When Raymon happened to be alone with her, Indiana's cheeks did not turn a deeper red, nor did she avert her eyes in confusion. No, her tranquil, limpid eyes were always fixed upon him in ecstasy; an angelic smile played always about her lips, as ruddy as a little girl's who has known no kisses but her mother's. When he saw her so trustful, so passionate, so pure, living solely with the heart and not realizing that her lover's heart was in torment when he was at her feet, Raymon dared not be a man, lest he should seem to her inferior to her dreams of him, and, through self-love, he became as virtuous as she.

Madame Delmare, ignorant as a genuine creole, had never dreamed hitherto of considering the momentous questions that were now discussed before her every day. She had been brought up by Sir Ralph, who had a poor opinion of the intelligence and reasoning power of womankind, and who had confined himself to imparting some positive information likely to be of immediate use. Thus she had a very shadowy idea of the world's history, and any serious discussion bored her to death. But when she heard Raymon apply to those dry subjects all the charm of his wit, all the poesy of his language, she listened and tried to understand; then she ventured timidly to ask ingenuous questions which a girl of ten brought up according to worldly ideas would readily have answered. Raymon took pleasure in enlightening that virgin mind which seemed destined to open to receive his principles; but, despite the power he exerted over her untrained, artless mind, his sophisms sometimes encountered resistance from her.

Indiana opposed to the interests of civilization, when raised to the dignity of principles of action, the straightforward ideas and simple laws of good sense and humanity; her arguments were characterized by an unpolished freedom which sometimes embarrassed Raymon and always charmed him by its childlike originality. He applied himself as to a task of serious importance to the attempt to bring her around gradually to his principles, to his beliefs. He would have been proud to dominate her conscientious and naturally enlightened convictions; but he had some difficulty in attaining his end. Ralph's generous theories, his unbending hatred of the vices of society, his keen impatience for the reign of other laws and other morals were sentiments to which Indiana's unhappy memories responded. But Raymon suddenly unhorsed his adversary by demonstrating that this aversion for the present was the work of selfishness; he described with much warmth his own attachments, his devotion to the royal family, which he had the art to clothe with all the heroism of a perilous loyalty, his respect for the persecuted faith of his fathers, his religious sentiments, which were not the fruit of reasoning, he said, but to which he clung by instinct and from necessity. And the joy of loving one's fellow-creatures, of being bound to the present generation by all the ties of honor and philanthropy; the pleasure of serving one's country by repelling dangerous innovations, by maintaining domestic peace, by giving, if need be, all one's blood to save the shedding of one drop of that of the lowest of one's countrymen! he depicted all these attractive Utopian visions with so much art and charm that Indiana submitted to be led on to the feeling that she must love and respect all that Raymon loved and respected. It was fairly proved that Ralph was an egotist; when he maintained a generous idea, they smiled; it was clear that at such times his heart and his mind were in contradiction. Was it not better to believe Raymon, who had such a big, warm, expansive heart?

There were moments, however, when Raymon almost forgot his love to think only of his antipathy. When he was with Madame Delmare, he could see nobody but Sir Ralph, who presumed, with his rough, cool common sense, to attack him, a man of superior talents, who had overthrown such doughty adversaries! He was humiliated to find himself engaged with so paltry an adversary, and thereupon would overwhelm him with the weight of his eloquence; he would bring into play all the resources of his talent, and Ralph, bewildered, slow in collecting his ideas, slower still in expressing them, would be made painfully conscious of his weakness.

At such moments it seemed to Indiana that Raymon's thoughts were altogether diverted from her; she had spasms of anxiety and terror as she reflected that perhaps all those noble and high-sounding sentiments so eloquently declaimed were simply the pompous scaffolding of words, the ironical harangue of the lawyer, listening to himself and practising the comedy which is to take by surprise the good-nature of the tribunal. She was especially fearful when, as her eyes met his, she fancied that she saw gleaming in them, not the pleasure of having been understood by her, but the triumphant self-satisfaction of having made a fine argument. She was afraid at such times, and her thoughts turned to Ralph, the egotist, to whom they had perhaps been unjust; but Ralph was not tactful enough to say anything to prolong this uncertainty, and Raymon was very skilful in removing it.

Thus there was but one really perturbed existence, but one really ruined happiness in that domestic circle: the existence and happiness of Sir Ralph Brown, a man born to misfortune, for whom life had displayed no brilliant aspects, no intense, heart-filling joys; a victim of great but secret unhappiness, who complained to no one and whom no one pitied; a truly accursed destiny, in the poetic sense without thrilling adventures; a commonplace, bourgeois, melancholy destiny, which no friendship had sweetened, no love charmed, which was endured in silence, with the heroism which the love of life and the need of hoping give; a lonely mortal who had had a father and mother like everybody else, a brother, a wife, a son, a friend, and who had reaped no benefit, retained nothing of all those ties; a stranger in life who went his way melancholy and indifferent, having not even that exalted consciousness of his misfortune which enables one to find some fascination in sorrow.

Despite his strength of character, he sometimes felt discouraged with virtue. He hated Raymon, and it was in his power to drive him from Lagny with a word; but he did not say it, because he had one belief, a single one, which was stronger than Raymon's countless beliefs. It was neither the church, nor the monarchy, nor society, nor reputation, nor the law, which dictated his sacrifices and his courage—it was his conscience.

He had lived so alone that he had not accustomed himself to rely upon others; but he had learned, in his isolation, to know himself. He had made a friend of his own heart; by dint of self-communion, of asking himself the cause of the unjust acts of others, he had assured himself that he had not earned them by any vice; he had ceased to be irritated by them, because he set little store by his own personality, which he knew to be insipid and commonplace. He understood the indifference of which he was the object, and he had chosen his course with regard to it; but his heart told him that he was capable of feeling all that he did not inspire, and, while he was disposed to forgive everything in others, he had decided to tolerate nothing in himself. This wholly inward life, these wholly private sensations gave him all the outward appearance of a selfish man; indeed nothing resembles selfishness more closely than self-respect.

However, as it often happens that, because we attempt to do too much good, we do much less than enough, it happened that Sir Ralph made a great mistake from over-scrupulousness and caused Madame Delmare an irreparable injury from dread of burdening his own conscience with a cause of reproach. That mistake was his failure to enlighten her as to the real reasons of Noun's death. Had he done so she would doubtless have reflected on the perils of her love for Raymon; but we shall see later why Monsieur Brown dared not inform his cousin and what painful scruples led him to keep silence on so momentous a question. When he decided to break his silence it was too late; Raymon had had time to establish his empire.

An unforeseen event occurred to cloud the future prospects of the colonel and his wife; a business house in Belgium, upon which all the prosperity of the Delmare establishment depended, had suddenly failed, and the colonel, who had hardly recovered his health, started in hot haste for Antwerp.

He was still so weak and ill that his wife wished to accompany him; but Monsieur Delmare, being threatened with complete ruin and resolved to honor all his obligations, feared that his journey would then seem too much like a flight; so he determined to leave his wife at Lagny as a pledge of his return. He even declined the company of Sir Ralph and begged him to remain and stand by Madame Delmare in case of any trouble on the part of anxious or over-eager creditors.

At this painful crisis Indiana was alarmed at nothing save the possibility of having to leave Lagny and be separated from Raymon; but he comforted her by convincing her that the colonel would surely go to Paris. Moreover he gave her his word that he would follow her, on some pretext or other, wherever she might go, and the credulous creature deemed herself almost happy in a misfortune which enabled her to put Raymon's love to the test. As for him, a vague hope, a persistent, importunate thought had absorbed his mind ever since he had heard of this event: he was to be alone with Indiana at last, the first time for six months. She had never seemed to attempt to avoid a tête-à-tête, and although he was in no haste to triumph over a love whose ingenuous chastity had for him the attraction of novelty, he was beginning to feel that his honor was involved in bringing it to some conclusion. He honorably repelled any malicious insinuation concerning his relations with Madame Delmare; he declared very modestly that there was nothing more than a placid and pleasant friendship between them; but not for anything in the world would he have admitted, even to his best friend, that he had been passionately in love for six months and had as yet obtained no fruit of that love.

He was somewhat disappointed in his anticipations when he saw that Sir Ralph seemed determined to replace Monsieur Delmare so far as surveillance was concerned, that he appeared at Lagny in the morning and did not return to Bellerive until night; indeed, as their road was the same for some distance, Ralph, with an intolerable affectation of courtesy, insisted upon timing his departure by Raymon's. This constraint soon became intensely disagreeable to Monsieur de Ramière, and Madame Delmare fancied that she could detect in it not only a suspicion insulting to herself, but a purpose to assume despotic control over her conduct.

Raymon dared not request a secret interview; whenever he had made the attempt, Madame Delmare had reminded him of certain conditions agreed upon between them. Meanwhile a week had passed since the colonel's departure; he might return very soon; the present opportunity must be turned to advantage. To allow Sir Ralph the victory would be a disgrace to Raymon. One morning he slipped this letter into Madame Delmare's hand:

"Indiana! do you not love me as I love you? My angel! I am unhappy and you do not see it. I am sad, anxious concerning your future, not my own; for, wherever you may be, there I shall live and die. But the thought of poverty alarms me on your account; ill and frail as you are, my poor child, how will you endure privation? You have a rich and generous cousin: your husband will perhaps accept at his hands what he will refuse at mine. Ralph will ameliorate your lot, and I shall be able to do nothing for you!

"Be sure, be sure, my dear love, that I have reason to

be depressed and disappointed. You are heroic, you laugh at everything, you insist that I must not grieve. Ah! how I crave your gentle words, your sweet glances, to sustain my courage! But, by a monstrous fatality, these days that I hoped to pass freely at your feet, have brought me nothing but a constraint that grows ever more galling.

"Say a word, Indiana, so that we may be alone at least an hour, that I may weep upon your white hands and tell you all that I suffer, and that a word from you may console and comfort me.

"And then, Indiana, I have a childish caprice, a genuine lover's caprice. I would like to enter your room. Oh! don't be frightened, my gentle creole! It is my bounden duty not only to respect you, but to fear you; that is the very reason why I would like to enter your room, to kneel in that place where you were so angry with me, and where, bold as I am, I dared not look at you. I would like to prostrate myself there, to pass a meditative, happy hour there; I would crave no other favor, Indiana, than that you should place your hand on my heart and cleanse it of its crime, pacify it if it beats too rapidly, and give it your confidence once more if you find me worthy of you at last. Yes! I would like to prove to you that now I am worthy, that I know you through and through, that I worship you with an adoration as pure and holy as ever maiden conceived for her Madonna! I would like to be sure that you no longer fear me, that you esteem me as much as I revere you; I would like to live an hour as angels live, with my head upon your heart. Tell me, Indiana, may I? One hour—the first, perhaps the last!

"It is time to forgive me, Indiana, to give me back your confidence, so cruelly snatched from me, so dearly redeemed. Are you not satisfied with me? Have I not passed six months behind your chair, confining my desires to a glance at your snow-white neck through the curls of your black hair, as you leaned over your work, to a breath of the perfume which emanates from you and which the air from the window at which you sit brings faintly to my nostrils? Does not such submission deserve the reward of a kiss? a sister's kiss, if you will, a kiss on the forehead? I will remain true to our agreements, I swear it. I will ask for nothing. But, cruel one, will you grant me nothing? Are you afraid of yourself?"

Madame Delmare went to her room to read this letter; she replied to it instantly, and handed him the reply with a key to the park-gate, which he knew too well.

"I afraid of you, Raymon? Oh! no, not now. I know too well that you love me, I am too blissfully happy in the belief that you love me. Come then, for I am not afraid of myself either; if I loved you less, perhaps I should be less calm; but I love you with a love of which you yourself have no idea. Go away early, so that Ralph may suspect nothing. Return at midnight; you are familiar with the park and the house; here is the key of the small gate; lock it after you."

This ingenuous, generous confidence made Raymon blush. He had tried to inspire it, with the purpose of abusing it; he had counted on the darkness, the opportunity, the danger. If Indiana had shown any fear, she was lost; but she was perfectly calm; she placed her trust in his good faith; he swore that he would give her no cause to repent. But the important point was to pass a night in her bedroom, in order not to be a fool in his own eyes, in order to defeat Ralph's prudence, and to be able to laugh at him in his sleeve. That was a personal gratification which he craved.

XVI

But Ralph was really intolerable on this particular evening; he had never been more stupid and dull and tiresome. He could say nothing apropos, and, to cap the climax of his loutishness, he gave no sign of taking his leave even when the evening was far advanced. Madame Delmare began to be ill at ease; she glanced alternately at the clock, which had struck eleven—at the door, which had creaked in the wind—and at the expressionless face of her cousin, who sat opposite her in front of the fire, placidly watching the blaze without seeming to suspect that his presence was distasteful.

But Sir Ralph's tranquil mask, his petrified features, concealed at that moment a profound and painful mental agitation. He was a man whom nothing escaped because he observed everything with perfect self-possession. He had not been deceived by Raymon's pretended departure; he perceived very plainly Madame Delmare's anxiety at that moment. He suffered more than she did herself, and he moved irresolutely between the impulse to give her a salutary warning and the fear of giving way to feelings which he disavowed; at last his cousin's interest carried the day, and he summoned all his moral courage in order to break the silence.

"That reminds me," he said abruptly, following out the line of thought with which his mind was busy, "that it was just a year ago to-day that you and I sat in this chimney-corner as we are sitting now. The clock marked almost the same hour; the weather was cold and threatening as it is to-night. You were ill, and were disturbed by melancholy ideas; a fact that almost makes me believe in the truth of presentiments."

"What can he be coming to?" thought Madame Delmare, gazing at her cousin with mingled surprise and uneasiness.

"Do you remember, Indiana," he continued, "that you felt even less well than usual that night? Why, I can remember your words as if I had just heard them. 'You will call me insane,' you said, 'but some danger is hovering about us and threatening some one of us—threatening me, I have no doubt,' you added; 'I feel intensely agitated, as if some great crisis in my destiny were at hand—I am afraid!' Those are your very words."

"I am no longer ill," said Indiana, who had suddenly turned as pale as at the time of which Sir Ralph spoke; "I no longer believe in such foolish terrors."

"But I believe in them," he rejoined, "for you were a true prophet that night, Indiana; a great danger did threaten us—a disastrous influence surrounded this peaceful abode."

"*Mon Dieu!* I do not understand you!"

"You soon will understand me, my poor girl. That was the evening that Raymon de Ramière was brought here. Do you remember in what condition?"

Ralph paused a few seconds, but dared not look at his cousin. As she made no reply, he continued:

"I was told to bring him back to life and I did so, as much to satisfy you as to obey the instincts of humanity; but, in truth, Indiana, it was a great misfortune that I saved that man's life! It was I who did all the harm."

"I don't know what you mean by harm!" rejoined Indiana, dryly.

She was deeply moved in advance by the explanation which she foresaw.

"I mean that unfortunate creature's death," said Ralph. "But for him she would still be alive; but for his fatal love the lovely, honest girl who loved you so dearly would still be at your side."

Thus far Madame Delmare did not understand. She was exasperated beyond measure by the strange and cruel method which her cousin adopted to reproach her for her attachment to Monsieur de Ramière.

"Enough of this," she said, rising.

But Ralph apparently took no notice of her remark.

"What always astonished me," he continued, "was that you never guessed the real motive that led Monsieur de Ramière to scale the walls."

A suspicion darted through Indiana's mind; her legs trembled under her, and she resumed her seat.

Ralph had buried the knife in her breast and made a ghastly wound. He no sooner saw the effect of his work than he hated himself for it; he thought only of the injury he had inflicted on the person whom he loved best in all the world; he felt that his heart was breaking. He would have wept bitterly if he could have wept; but the poor fellow had not the gift of tears; he had naught of that which eloquently translates the language of the heart. The external coolness with which he performed the cruel operation gave him the air of an executioner in Indiana's eyes.

"This is the first time," she said bitterly, "that I have known your antipathy for Monsieur de Ramière to lead you to employ weapons that are unworthy of you; but I do not see how it assists your vengeance to stain the memory of a person who was dear to me, and whom her melancholy end should have made sacred to us. I have asked you no questions, Sir Ralph; I do not know what you refer to. With your permission I will listen to no more."

She rose and left Monsieur Brown bewildered and crushed.

He had foreseen that he could not enlighten Madame Delmare except at his own expense. His conscience had told him that he must speak, whatever the result might be, and he had done it with all the abruptness of method, all the awkwardness of execution of which he was capable. What he had not fully appreciated was the violence of a remedy so long delayed.

He left Lagny in despair and wandered through the forest in a sort of frenzy.

It was midnight; Raymon was at the park gate. He opened it, but as he opened it he felt his brow grow chill. For what purpose had he come to this rendezvous? He had made divers virtuous resolutions, but would he be amply rewarded by a chaste interview, by a sisterly kiss, for the torture he was undergoing at that moment? For, if you remember under what circumstances he had previously passed through those garden paths, stealthily, at night, you will understand that it required a certain degree of moral courage to go in search of pleasure along such a road and amid such memories.

Late in October the climate of the suburbs of Paris becomes damp and foggy, especially at night and in the neighborhood of streams. Chance decreed that the fog should be as dense on this night as on certain other nights in the preceding spring. Raymon felt his way along the mist-enveloped trees. He passed a summer-house which contained a fine collection of geraniums in winter. He glanced at the door, and his heart beat fast at the extravagant idea that it might open and give egress to a woman wrapped in a pelisse. Raymon smiled at this superstitious weakness and went his way. Nevertheless the cold seized him, and he felt an unpleasant tightness at his throat as he approached the stream.

He had to cross it to reach the flower-garden, and the only means of crossing in that vicinity was a narrow wooden bridge. The fog became more dismal than ever over the river-bed, and Raymon clung to the railing of the bridge in order not to go astray among the reeds that grew along the banks. The moon was just rising, and, as it strove to pierce the vapors, cast an uncertain light on the plants which the wind and the current moved to and fro. In the breeze which rustled the leaves and ruffled the surface of the water there was a sort of wailing sound like human words half-spoken. There was a faint sob close beside Raymon and a sudden movement among the reeds; it was a curlew flying away at his approach. The cry of that shore-bird closely resembles the moaning of an abandoned child; and when it comes up from among the reeds you would say that it was the last effort of a drowning man. Perhaps you will consider that Raymon was very weak and cowardly; his teeth chattered and he nearly fell; but he soon realized the absurdity of his terror and crossed the bridge.

He was half-way across when a human figure appeared in front of him, at the end of the rail, as if waiting for him to approach. Raymon's ideas became confused; his bewildered brain had not the strength to reason. He retraced his steps and hid among the trees, gazing with a fixed, terrified stare at that ill-defined apparition which remained in the same place, as vague and uncertain as the river mist and the trembling rays of the moon. He was beginning to believe that in his mental preoccupation he had been deceived, and that what he took for a human form was only a tree-trunk or the stalk of a shrub, when he distinctly saw it move and walk toward him.

At that moment, had not his legs absolutely refused to act, he would have fled in as great a panic as the child who passes a cemetery at night and fancies that he hears mysterious steps running after him on the tips of the blades of grass. But he felt as if he were paralyzed, and, to support himself, threw his arms around the trunk of the willow behind which he was hidden. The next moment Sir Ralph, wrapped in a light cloak which gave him the aspect of a phantom at three yards, passed very close to him and took the path by which he had just come.

"Bungling spy!" thought Raymon, as he saw him looking for his footprints. "I will escape your cowardly surveillance, and while you are mounting guard here I will be enjoying myself yonder."

He crossed the bridge as lightly as a bird, and with the confidence of a lover. His terrors were at an end; Noun had never existed; real life was awakening all about him; Indiana awaited him yonder; and Ralph was on sentry-go to keep him from entering.

"Watch closely," said Raymon, gayly, as he saw him in the distance going in the opposite direction. "Watch for me, dear Sir Rodolphe Brown; protect my good fortune, O my officious friend; and, if the dogs are restless, if the servants wake, pacify them, keep them quiet by saying: 'It is I who am watching, sleep in peace.'"

Scruples, remorse, virtue were at an end for Raymon; he had paid dearly enough for the hour that was striking. His blood that had frozen in his veins flowed now toward his brain with maddening violence. A moment ago the pallid terrors of death, dismal visions of the tomb; now the impetuous realities of love, the keen joys of life. Raymon felt as bold and full of animation as in the morning, when an ugly dream has enveloped us in its shroud and suddenly a merry sunbeam awakens and revivifies us.

"Poor Ralph!" he thought as he ascended the secret staircase with a bold, light step, "you would have it so!"

PART THIRD

XVII

On leaving Sir Ralph, Madame Delmare had locked herself into her room, and a thousand tempestuous thoughts had invaded her mind. It was not the first time that a vague suspicion had cast its ominous light upon the fragile edifice of her happiness. Monsieur Delmare had previously let slip in conversation some of those indelicate jests which pass for compliments. He had complimented Raymon on his knightly triumphs in a way to give the cue to ears that knew naught of the incident. Every time that Madame Delmare had spoken to the gardener, Noun's name had been injected, as if by an unavoidable necessity, into the most trivial details, and then Monsieur de Ramière's had always glided in by virtue of some mysterious junction of ideas which seemed to have taken possession of the man's brain and to beset him in spite of himself. Madame Delmare had been struck by his strange and bungling questions. He became confused in his speech on the slightest pretext; he seemed to be oppressed by a burden of remorse which he betrayed while struggling to conceal it. At other times Indiana had found in Raymon's own confusion those indications which she did not seek, but which forced themselves upon her. One circumstance in particular would have enlightened her further, if she had not closed her mind to all distrust. They had found on Noun's finger a very handsome ring which Madame Delmare had noticed some time before her death and which the girl claimed to have found. Since her death Madame Delmare had always worn that pledge of sorrow, and she had often noticed that Raymon changed color when he took her hand to put it to his lips. Once he had begged her never to mention Noun to him because he looked upon himself as the cause of her death; and when she sought to banish that painful thought by taking all the blame to herself, he had replied:

"No, my poor Indiana, do not accuse yourself; you have no idea how guilty I am."

Those words, uttered in a bitter, gloomy tone, had alarmed Madame Delmare. She had not dared to insist, and, now that she was beginning to understand all these fragments of discoveries, she had not the courage to fix her thoughts upon them and put them together.

She opened her window, and, as she looked out upon the calm night, upon the moon so pale and lovely behind the silvery vapors on the horizon, as she remembered that Raymon was coming, that he was perhaps in the park even now, and thought of all the joy she had anticipated in that hour of love and mystery, she cursed Ralph who with a word had poisoned her hope and destroyed her repose forever. She even felt that she hated him, the unhappy man who had been a father to her and who had sacrificed his future for her; for his future was Indiana's friendship; that was his only treasure, and he resigned himself to the certainty of forfeiting it in order to save her.

Indiana could not read in the depths of his heart, nor had she been able to fathom Raymon's. She was unjust, not from ingratitude, but from ignorance. Being under the influence of a strong passion she could not but feel strongly the blow that had been dealt her. For an instant she laid the whole crime upon Ralph, preferring to accuse him rather than to suspect Raymon.

And then she had so little time to collect her thoughts, and make up her mind: Raymon was coming. Perhaps it was he whom she had seen for some minutes wandering about the little bridge. How much more intense would her aversion for Ralph have been at that moment, if she could have recognized him in that vague figure, which constantly appeared and disappeared in the mist, and which, like a spirit stationed at the gate of the Elysian Fields, sought to keep the guilty man from entering!

Suddenly there came to her mind one of those strange, half-formed ideas, which only restless and unhappy persons are capable of conceiving. She risked her whole destiny upon a strange and delicate test against which Raymon could not be on his guard. She had hardly completed her mysterious preparations when she heard Raymon's footsteps on the secret stairway. She ran and unlocked the door, then returned to her chair, so agitated that she felt that she was on the point of falling; but, as in all the great crises of her life, she retained a remarkable clearness of perception and great strength of mind.

Raymon was still pale and breathless when he opened the door; impatient to see the light, to grasp reality once more. Indiana's back was turned to him, she was wrapped in a fur-lined pelisse. By a strange chance it was the same that Noun wore when she went to meet him in the park at their last rendezvous. I do not know if you remember that at that time Raymon had had for an instant the untenable idea that that woman shrouded in her cloak was Madame Delmare. Now, when he saw once more the same apparition sitting inert in a chair, with her head on her breast, by the light of a pale, flickering lamp, on the same spot where so many memories awaited him, in that room which he had not entered since the darkest night in his life and which was full to overflowing of his remorse, he involuntarily recoiled and remained in the doorway, his terrified gaze fixed upon that motionless figure, and trembling like a coward, lest, when it turned, it should display the livid features of a drowned woman.

Madame Delmare had no suspicion of the effect she produced upon Raymon. She had wound about her head a handkerchief of India silk, tied carelessly in true creole style; it was Noun's usual head-dress. Raymon, fairly overcome by terror, nearly fell backward, thinking that his superstitious fancies were realized. But, recognizing the woman he had come to seduce, he forgot the one whom he had seduced and walked toward her. Her face wore a grave, meditative expression: she gazed earnestly at him, but with close attention rather than affection, and did not make a motion to draw him to her side more quickly.

Raymon, surprised by this reception, attributed it to some scruple of chastity, to some girlish impulse of delicacy or constraint. He knelt at her feet, saying:

"Are you afraid of me, my beloved?" But at that moment he noticed that Madame Delmare held something in her hands to which she seemed to direct his attention with a playful affectation of gravity. He looked more closely and saw a mass of black hair, of varying lengths, which seemed to have been cut in haste, and which Indiana was smoothing with her hand.

"Do you recognize it?" she asked, fastening upon him her limpid eyes, in which there was a peculiar, penetrating gleam.

Raymon hesitated, looked again at the handkerchief about her head, and thought that he understood.

"Naughty girl!" he said, taking the hair in his hand, "why did you cut it off? It was so beautiful, and I loved it so dearly!"

"You asked me yesterday," she said with the shadow of a smile, "if I would sacrifice it to you."

"O Indiana!" cried Raymon, "you know well that you will be lovelier than ever to me henceforth. Give it to me. I do not choose to regret the absence from your head of that glorious hair which I admired every day, and which now I can kiss every day without restraint. Give it to me, so that it may never leave me."

But as he gathered up in his hand that luxuriant mass of which some locks reached to the floor, Raymon fancied that it had a dry, rough feeling which his fingers had never noticed in the silken tresses over Indiana's forehead. He was conscious, also, of an indefinable nervous thrill, it felt so cold and dead, as if it had been cut a long time, and seemed to have lost its perfumed moisture and vital warmth. Then he looked at it again, and sought in vain the blue gleam which made Indiana's hair resemble the blue-black wing of the crow; this was of an Ethiopian black, of an Indian texture, of a lifeless heaviness.

Indiana's bright piercing eyes followed Raymon's. He turned them involuntarily upon an open ebony casket from which several locks of the same hair protruded.

"This is not yours," he said, untying the kerchief which concealed Madame Delmare's hair.

It was untouched, and fell over her shoulders in all its splendor. But she made a gesture as if to push him away and said, still pointing to the hair:

"Don't you recognize this? Did you never admire,

never caress it? Has the damp night air robbed it of all its fragrance? Have you not a thought, a tear for her who wore this ring?"

Raymon sank upon a chair; Noun's locks fell from his trembling hand. So much painful excitement had exhausted him. He was a man of choleric temper, whose blood flowed rapidly, whose nerves were easily and deeply irritated. He shivered from head to foot and fell in a swoon on the floor.

When he came to himself, Madame Delmare was on her knees beside him, weeping copiously and asking his forgiveness; but Raymon no longer loved her.

"You have inflicted a horrible wound on me," he said; "a wound which it is not in your power to cure. You will never restore the confidence I had in your heart; that is evident to me. You have shown me how vindictive and cruel your heart can be. Poor Noun! poor unhappy girl! It was she whom I treated badly, not you; it was she who had the right to avenge herself, and she did not. She took her own life in order to leave me the future. She sacrificed herself to my repose. You are not the woman to have done as much, madame! Give me her hair; it is mine—it belongs to me; it is all that remains to me of the only woman who ever loved me truly. Unhappy Noun! you were worthy of a better love! And you, madame, dare to reproach me with her death; you, whom I loved so well that I forgot her—that I defied the ghastly torture of remorse; you who, on the faith of a kiss, have led me across that river—across that bridge—alone, with terror at my side, pursued by the infernal illusions of my crime! And when you discover with what a frantic passion I love you, you bury your woman's nails in my heart, seeking there another drop of blood which may still be made to flow for you!

Ah! when I spurned so devoted a love to take up with so savage a passion as yours, I was no less mad than guilty."

Madame Delmare did not reply. Pale and motionless, with dishevelled hair and staring eyes, she moved Raymon to pity. He took her hand.

"And yet," he said, "this love I feel for you is so blind that, in spite of myself, I can still forget the past and the present—the sin that blasted my life and the crime you have just committed. So love me, and I will forgive you."

Madame Delmare's despair rekindled desire and pride in her lover's heart. When he saw how dismayed she was at the thought of losing his love—how humble before him, how resigned to accept his decrees for the future by way of atonement for the past—he remembered what his intentions had been when he eluded Ralph's vigilance, and he realized all the advantages of his position. He pretended to be absorbed in a melancholy, sombre reverie for some moments; he hardly responded to Indiana's tears and caresses. He waited until her heart should break and overflow in sobs, until she should realize all the horrors of desertion—until she should have exhausted all her strength in heart-rending emotion; and then, when he saw her at his feet, fainting, utterly worn out, awaiting death at a word from him, he seized her in his arms with convulsive passion and strained her to his heart. She yielded like a weak child; she abandoned her lips to him unresistingly. She was almost dead.

But suddenly, as if waking from a dream, she snatched herself away from his burning caresses, rushed to the end of the room where Sir Ralph's portrait hung on the panel; and, as if she would place herself under the protection of that grave personage with the unruffled brow and tranquil lips, she shrank back against the portrait, wild-eyed, quivering from head to foot, in the clutches of a strange fear. It was this that made Raymon think that she had been deeply moved in his arms—that she was afraid of herself—that she was his. He ran to her; drew her by force from her retreat, and told her that he had come with the purpose of keeping his promises, but that her cruel treatment of him had absolved him from his oath.

"I am no longer either your slave or your ally," he said. "I am simply the man who loves you madly and who has you in his arms, a wicked, capricious, cruel, mad creature, but lovely and adored. With sweet, confiding words you might have cooled my blood. Had you been as calm and generous as yesterday, you would have made me mild and submissive as usual. But you have kindled all my passions, overturned all my ideas. You have made me unhappy, cowardly, ill, frantic, desperate, one after another. You must make me happy now, or I feel that I can no longer believe in you—that I can no longer love you or bless you. Forgive me, Indiana, forgive me! If I frighten you it is your own fault; you have made me suffer so that I have lost my reason!"

Indiana trembled in every limb. She knew so little of life that she believed resistance to be impossible; she was ready to concede from fear what she would refuse from love; but, as she struggled feebly in Raymon's arms, she said, in desperation:

"So you are capable of using force with me?"

Raymon paused, impressed with this moral resistance, which survived physical resistance. He hastily pushed her away.

"Never!" he cried: "I would rather die than possess you except by your own will!"

He threw himself on his knees, and all that the mind can supply in place of the heart, all the poesy that the imagination can impart to the ardor of the blood, he expressed in a fervent and dangerous entreaty. And when he saw that she did not surrender, he yielded to necessity and reproached her with not loving him; a commonplace expedient which he despised and which made him smile, with a feeling of something like shame at having to do with a woman so innocent as not to smile at it herself.

That reproach went to Indiana's heart more swiftly than all the exclamations with which Raymon had embellished his discourse.

But suddenly she remembered.

"Raymon," she said, "the other, who loved you so dearly—of whom we were speaking just now—she refused you nothing, I suppose?"

"Nothing!" exclaimed Raymon, annoyed by this inopportune reminder. "Instead of reminding me of her so continually, you would do well to make me forget how dearly she loved me!"

"Listen!" rejoined Indiana, thoughtfully and gravely; "have a little courage, for I must say something more. Perhaps you have not been as guilty towards me as I thought. It would be sweet to me to be able to forgive you for what I considered a mortal insult. Tell me then—when I surprised you here—for whom did you come? for her or for me?"

Raymon hesitated; then, as he thought that the truth would soon be known to Madame Delmare, that perhaps she knew it already, he answered:

"For her."

"Well, I prefer it so," she said sadly; "I prefer an infidelity to an insult. Be frank to the end, Raymon. How long had you been in my room when I came? Remember that Ralph knows all, and that, if I chose to question him——"

"There is no need of Sir Ralph's testimony, madame. I had been here since the night before."

"And you had passed the night in this room. Your silence is a sufficient answer."

They both remained silent for some moments; then Indiana rose and was about to continue, when a sharp knock at the door checked the flow of the blood in her veins. Neither she nor Raymon dared to breathe.

A paper was slipped under the door. It was a leaf from a note-book on which these words were scrawled in pencil, almost illegibly:

"Your husband is here.

"RALPH."

XVIII

"This is a wretchedly devised falsehood," said Raymon, as soon as the sound of Ralph's footsteps had died away. "Sir Ralph needs a lesson, and I will administer it in such shape——"

"I forbid it," said Indiana, in a cold, determined tone: "my husband is here: Ralph never lied. You and I are lost. There was a time when the thought would have frozen me with horror; to-day it matters little to me!"

"Very well!" said Raymon, seizing her in his arms excitedly, "since death encompasses us, be mine! Forgive everything, and let your last word in this supreme moment be a word of love, my last breath a breath of joy."

"This moment of terror and courage might have been the sweetest moment in my life," she said, "but you have spoiled it for me."

There was a rumbling of wheels in the farmyard, and the bell at the gate of the château was rung by a strong and impatient hand.

"I know that ring," said Indiana, watchful and cool. "Ralph did not lie; but you have time to escape; go!"

"I will not," cried Raymon; "I suspect some despicable treachery and you shall not be the only victim. I will remain and my breast shall protect you——"

"There is no treachery—listen—the servants are stirring and the gate will be opened directly. Go: the trees in the garden will conceal you, and the moon is not fairly out yet. Not a word more, but go!"

Raymon was compelled to obey; but she accompanied him to the foot of the stairs and cast a searching glance about the flower-garden. All was silent and calm. She stood a long while on the last stair, listening with terror to the grinding of his footsteps on the gravel, entirely oblivious of her husband's arrival. What cared she for his suspicions and his anger, provided that Raymon was out of danger?

As for him he crossed the stream and hurried swiftly through the park. He reached the small gate and, in his excitement, had some difficulty in opening it. He was no sooner in the road than Sir Ralph appeared in front of him and said with as much *sang-froid* as if he were accosting him at a party:

"Be good enough to let me have that key. If there should be a search for it, it would be less inconvenient for it to be found in my hands."

Raymon would have preferred the most deadly insult to this satirical generosity.

"I am not the man to forget a well-meant service," said he; "I am the man to avenge an insult and to punish treachery."

Sir Ralph changed neither his tone nor his expression.

"I want none of your gratitude," he rejoined, "and I await your vengeance tranquilly; but this is no time to talk. There is your path—think of Madame Delmare's good name."

And he disappeared.

This night of agitation had overturned Raymon's brain so completely that he would readily have believed in witchcraft at that moment. He reached Cercy at daybreak and went to bed with a raging fever.

As for Madame Delmare, she did the honors of the breakfast table for her husband and cousin with much calmness and dignity. She had not as yet reflected upon her situation; she was absolutely under the influence of instinct, which enjoined *sang-froid* and presence of mind upon her. The colonel was gloomy and thoughtful, but it was his business alone that preoccupied him, and no jealous suspicion found a place in his thoughts.

Toward evening Raymon mustered courage to think about his love; but that love had diminished materially. He loved obstacles; but he hated to be bored and he foresaw that he should be bored times without number now that Indiana had the right to reproach him. However, he remembered at last that his honor demanded that he should inquire for her, and he sent his servant to prowl around Lagny and find out what was going on there. The servant brought him the following letter which Madame Delmare herself had handed him:

"I hoped last night that I should lose either my reason or my life. Unhappily for me I have retained both; but I will not complain, I have deserved the suffering that I am undergoing; I chose to live this tempestuous life; it would be cowardly to recoil to-day. I do not know whether you are guilty, I do not want to know. We will never return to that subject, will we? It causes us both too much suffering: so let this be the last time it is mentioned between us.

"You said one thing at which I felt a cruel joy. Poor Noun! from your place in heaven forgive me! you no longer suffer, you no longer love, perhaps you pity me! You told me, Raymon, that you sacrificed that unhappy girl to me, that you loved me better than her. Oh! do not take it back; you said it, and I feel so strongly the need to believe it that I do believe it. And yet your conduct last night, your entreaties, your wild outbreaks, might well have made me doubt it. I forgave you on account of the mental disturbance under which you were laboring; but now you have had time to reflect, to become yourself once more; tell me, will you renounce loving me in that way? I, who love you with my heart, have believed hitherto that I could arouse in you a love as pure as my own. And then I had not thought very much about the future; I had not looked ahead very far, and I had not taken alarm at the thought that the day might come when, conquered by your devotion, I should sacrifice to you my scruples and my repugnance. But to-day, it can no longer be the same; I can see in the future only a ghastly parallel between myself and Noun! Oh! the thought of being loved no more than she was! If I believed it! And yet she was lovelier than I, far lovelier! Why did you prefer me? You must have loved me differently and better,—That is what I wanted you to say. Will you give up being my lover in the way that you have been? In that case I can still esteem you, believe in your remorse, your sincerity, your love; if not, think of me no more, you will never see me again. I shall die of it perhaps, but I would rather die than descend so low as to be your mistress."

Raymon was sorely embarrassed as to how he should reply. This pride offended him; he had never supposed hitherto that a woman who had thrown herself into his arms could resist him thus outspokenly and give reasons for her resistance.

"She does not love me," he said to himself; "her heart is dry, she is naturally overbearing."

From that moment he loved her no longer. She had ruffled his self-esteem; she had disappointed his hope of triumph, defeated his anticipations of pleasure. In his eyes she was no more than Noun had been. Poor Indiana! who longed to be so much more! Her passionate love was misunderstood, her blind confidence was spurned. Raymon had never understood her; how could he have continued to love her?

Thereupon he swore, in his irritation, that he would triumph over her; he swore it not from a feeling of pride but in a revengeful spirit. It was no longer a matter of snatching a new pleasure, but of punishing an insult; of possessing a woman, but of subduing her. He swore that he would be her master, were it for but a single day, and that then he would abandon her, to have the satisfaction of seeing her at his feet.

On the spur of the moment he wrote this letter:

"You want me to promise. Foolish girl, can you think of such a thing? I will promise whatever you choose, because I can do nothing but obey you; but, if I break my promises I shall be guilty neither to God nor to you. If you loved me, Indiana, you would not inflict these cruel torments on me, you would not expose me to the risk of perjuring myself, you would not blush at the thought of being my mistress. But you think that in my arms you would be degraded——"

He felt that his bitterness was making itself manifest, despite his efforts; he tore up this sheet, and, after taking time to reflect, began anew:

"You admit that you nearly lost your reason last night; for my part, I lost mine altogether. I was culpable—but no, I was mad! Forget those hours of suffering and excitement. I am calm now; I have reflected; I am still worthy of you. Bless you, my angel from heaven, for saving me from myself, for reminding me how I ought to love you. Now, Indiana, command me! I am your slave, as you well know. I would give my life for an hour in your arms; but I can suffer a whole lifetime to obtain a smile from you. I will be your friend, your brother, nothing more. If I suffer, you shall not know it. If my blood boils when I am near you, if my breast takes fire, if a cloud passes before my eyes when I touch your hand, if a sweet kiss from your lips, a sisterly kiss, scorches my forehead, I will order my blood to be calm, my brain to grow cool, my mouth to respect you. I will be gentle, I will be submissive, I will be unhappy,—if you will be the happier therefor and enjoy my agony,—if only I may hear you tell me again that you love me! Oh! tell me so! give me back your confidence and my joy! tell me when we shall meet again. I know not what result the events of last night may have had; how does it happen that you do not refer to the subject, that you leave me in an agony of suspense? Carle saw you all three walking together in the park. The colonel seemed ill or depressed, but not angry. In that case that Ralph did not betray us! What a strange man! But to what extent can we rely on his discretion, and how shall I dare show myself at Lagny now that our fate is in his hands? But I will dare. If it is necessary to stoop so low as to implore him, I will silence my pride, I will overcome my aversion, I will do anything rather than lose you. A word from you and I will burden my life with as much remorse as I am able to carry; for you I would abandon my mother herself; for you I would commit any crime. Ah! if you realized the depth of my love, Indiana!"

The pen fell from Raymon's hands; he was terribly fatigued, he was falling asleep. But he read over his letter to make sure that his ideas had not suffered from the influence of drowsiness; but it was impossible for him to understand his own meaning, his brain was so affected by his physical exhaustion. He rang for his servant, bade him go to Lagny before daybreak; then slept that deep, refreshing sleep whose tranquil delights only those who are thoroughly satisfied with themselves really know. Madame Delmare had not retired; she was unconscious of fatigue and passed the night writing. When she received Raymon's letter she answered it in haste:

"Thanks, Raymon, thanks! you restore my strength and my life. Now I can dare anything, endure anything; for you love me, and the most severe tests do not alarm you. Yes, we will meet again—we will defy everybody. Ralph may do what he will with our secret. I am no longer disturbed about anything since you love me; I am not even afraid of my husband.

"You want to know about our affairs? I forgot to mention them yesterday, and yet they have taken a turn which has an important bearing on my fortunes. We are ruined. There is some talk of selling Lagny, and even of going to live in the colonies. But of what consequence is all that? I cannot make up my mind to think about it. I know that we shall never be parted. You have sworn it, Raymon; I rely on your promise, do you rely on my courage. Nothing will frighten me, nothing will turn me back. My place is established at your side, and death alone can tear me from it."

"Mere woman's effervescence!" said Raymon, crumpling the letter. "Romantic projects, perilous undertakings, appeal to their feeble imaginations as bitter substances arouse a sick man's appetite. I have succeeded; I have recovered my influence; and, as for all this imprudent folly with which she threatens me, we will see! It is all characteristic of the light-headed, false creatures, always ready to undertake the impossible and making of generosity a show virtue which must be attended with scandal! Who would think, to read this letter, that she counts her kisses and doles out her caresses like a miser!"

That same day he went to Lagny. Ralph was not there, and the colonel received him amicably and talked to him confidentially. He took him into the park, where they were less likely to be disturbed, and told him that he was utterly ruined and that the factory would be offered for sale on the following day. Raymon made generous offers of assistance, but Delmare declined them.

"No, my friend," he said, "I have suffered too much from the thought that I owed my fate to Ralph's kindness; I was in too much of a hurry to repay him. The sale of this property will enable me to pay all my debts at once. To be sure, I shall have nothing left, but I have courage, energy and business experience; the future is before us. I have built up my little fortune once, and I can begin it again. I must do it for my wife's sake, for she is young, and I don't wish to leave her in poverty.

She still owns an estate of some little value at Ile Bourbon, and I propose to go into retirement there and start in business afresh. In a few years—in ten years at most—I hope that we shall meet again."

Raymon pressed the colonel's hand, smiling inwardly at his confidence, at his speaking of ten years as of a single day, when his bald head and enfeebled body indicated a feeble hold upon existence, a life near its close. Nevertheless he pretended to share his hopes.

"I am delighted to see," he said, "that you do not allow yourself to be cast down by these reverses. I recognize your manly heart, your undaunted courage. But does Madame Delmare display the same courage? Do you not anticipate some resistance on her part to your project of expatriation?"

"I shall be very sorry," the colonel replied, "but wives are made to obey, not to advise. I have not yet definitely made my purpose known to Indiana. With the exception of yourself, my friend, I do not know what there is here that she should feel any regret at leaving; and yet I anticipate tears and nervous attacks, from a spirit of contradiction, if nothing else. The devil take the women! However, my dear Raymon, I rely upon you all the same to make my wife listen to reason. She has confidence in you; use your influence to prevent her from crying. I detest tears."

Raymon promised to come again the next day and inform Madame Delmare of her husband's decision.

"You will do me a very great favor," said the colonel. "I will take Ralph to the farm, so that you may have a good chance to talk with her."

"Well, luck is on my side!" thought Ralph, as he took his leave.

XIX

Monsieur Delmare's plans fell in perfectly with Raymon's wishes. He foresaw that this love affair which, so far as he was concerned, was drawing near its close, would soon bring him nothing but annoyance and importunity, so that he was very glad to see events arranging themselves in such a way as to save him from the wearisome but inevitable results of a played-out intrigue. It only remained for him to take advantage of Madame Delmare's last moments of excitement, and then to leave to his complaisant destiny the task of ridding him of her tears and reproaches.

So he returned to Lagny the next day, intending to exalt the unhappy woman's enthusiasm to its apogee.

"Do you know, Indiana," he said, when they met, "the part that your husband has requested me to play with respect to you? A strange commission, upon my word! I am to entreat you to go with him to Ile Bourbon; to urge you to leave me; to tear out my heart and my life. Do you think that he made a good choice of an advocate?"

Madame Delmare's sombre gravity imposed a sort of respect on Raymon's cunning.

"Why do you come and tell me all this?" she said. "Are you afraid that I shall allow myself to be moved? Are you afraid that I shall obey? Never fear, Raymon, my mind is made up; I have passed two nights looking at it on every side; I know to what I expose myself; I know what I must defy, what I must sacrifice, what I must disdain to notice; I am ready to pass through this stormy period of my destiny. Will not you be my support and my guide?"

Raymon was tempted to take fright at this cool determination and to take these insane threats seriously; but in a moment he recurred to his former opinion that Indiana did not really love him, and that she was applying now to her situation the exaggerated sentiments she had learned from books. He strove to be eloquent with passion, he devoted his energies to dramatic improvisation, in order to maintain himself on his romantic mistress's level, and he succeeded in prolonging her error. But, to a calm and impartial auditor, this love scene would have seemed a contest between stage illusion and reality. The grandiloquence of Raymon's sentiments, the poesy of his ideas would have seemed a cold and cruel parody of the real sentiments which Indiana expressed so simply: in the one case mind, in the other heart.

Raymon, who however had some little fear that she might carry out her promises if he did not shrewdly undermine the plan of resistance she had formed, persuaded her to counterfeit submission or indifference until such time as she could come forth in open rebellion. It was essential, he said, that they should have left Lagny before she declared herself, in order to avoid a scandal in presence of the servants, and Ralph's dangerous intervention in the affair.

But Ralph did not leave his unfortunate friends. In vain did he offer his whole fortune, his Bellerive estate, his English consols, and whatever his plantations in the colonies would bring; the colonel was inflexible. His affection for Ralph had diminished; he was no longer willing to owe anything to him. Ralph might perhaps have been able to move him had he possessed Raymon's wit and address; but when he had plainly set forth his ideas and declared his sentiments, the poor baronet believed that he had said everything, and he never attempted to secure the retraction of a refusal. So he let Bellerive and followed Monsieur and Madame Delmare to Paris, pending their departure for Ile Bourbon.

Lagny was offered for sale with the factory and the appurtenances. The winter was a melancholy and depressing one to Madame Delmare. To be sure, Raymon was in Paris, he saw her every day, he was attentive and affectionate; but he remained barely an hour with her. He arrived just after dinner, and when the colonel went out on business, he also took his leave to attend some social function or other. Society, you know, was Raymon's element, his life; he must have the noise, the bustle, the crowd, to breathe freely, to display all his intellectual power, all his ease of manner, all his superiority. In the privacy of the boudoir he could make himself attractive, in society he became brilliant; and then he was no longer the man of a small coterie, the friend of this one or that one; he was the man of intellect who belongs to all alike, and to whom society is a sort of fatherland.

And then, as we have said, Raymon had some principle. When the colonel manifested such confidence in him and esteem for him, when he saw that he regarded him as the very type of honor and sincerity and desired him to act as mediator between his wife and himself, he determined to justify that confidence, to deserve that esteem, to reconcile that husband and wife, to repel any attachment on the part of the latter which might endanger the repose of the other. He became once more a moral, virtuous, philosophical person. You will see for how long.

Indiana, who did not understand this conversion, suffered horribly to be so neglected; and yet she still had the satisfaction of feeling that her hopes were not entirely destroyed. She was easily deceived; she asked nothing better than to be deceived, her real life was so bitter and desolate! Her husband had become almost impossible to live with. In public he affected the heroic courage and indifference of a brave man; but when he returned to the privacy of his own home he was simply an irritable, severe, absurd child. Indiana was the victim of his disgust with life, and, we must confess, she was largely to blame. If she had raised her voice, if she had complained, affectionately but forcibly, Delmare, who was only rough, would have blushed at the idea of being considered unkind. Nothing was easier than to touch his heart and govern him absolutely, if one chose to descend to his level and enter into the circle of ideas that were within the scope of his mind. But Indiana was stiff and haughty in her submissiveness; she always obeyed in silence; but it was the silence and submissiveness of the slave who has made of hatred a virtue and of unhappiness a merit. Her resignation was the dignity of a king who accepts fetters and a dungeon rather than voluntarily abdicate his throne and lay aside a vain title. A woman of a commoner mould would have mastered that commonplace man; she would have said what he said and reserved the right to think differently; she would have pretended to respect his prejudices and secretly have trampled them under foot; she would have caressed him and deceived him. Indiana saw many women who acted thus; but she felt so far above them that she would have blushed to imitate them. Being virtuous and chaste, she thought that she was not called upon to flatter her master by her words so long as she respected him in his actions. She did not care for his affection because she could not respond to it. She would have considered it far more blameworthy to make a show of love for the husband whom she did not love, than to give her heart to the lover who inspired love in her. To deceive was the crime in her eyes, and twenty times a day she felt that she must declare her love for Raymon; naught detained her but the fear of ruining him. Her impassive obedience irritated the colonel much more than a cleverly managed rebellion would have done. Although his self-esteem would have suffered if he had ceased to be master in his own house, it suffered much more from the consciousness that he was master in a hateful and absurd fashion. He would have liked to convince and he simply commanded; to reign, and he governed. Sometimes he gave an order that was awkwardly expressed, or, without reflection, issued orders that were injurious to his own interests. Madame Delmare saw that they were carried out without scrutiny, without question, with the indifference of the horse that draws the plough in one direction or another. Delmare, when he saw the result of the failure to understand his ideas, of the misconstruction of his wishes, would fly into a rage; but when she had proved to him with a few tranquil, icy words that she had simply caused his orders to be obeyed, he was reduced to the necessity of turning his wrath against himself. It was a cruel pang, a bitter affront to that man of petty self-esteem and of violent passions.

Several times he would have killed his wife, if he had been at Smyrna or at Cairo. And yet he loved with all his heart that weak woman who lived in subjection to him and kept the secret of his ill-treatment with religious prudence. He loved her or pitied her—I do not know which. He would have liked to win her love, for he was proud of her education and of her superiority. He would have risen in his own eyes if she would have stooped so far as to parley with his ideas and his principles. When he went to her apartments in the morning with the purpose of picking a quarrel with her, he sometimes found her asleep and dared not wake her. He would gaze at her in silence; he would take fright at the delicacy of her constitution, the pallor of her cheeks, at the air of calm melancholy, of resignation to misfortune expressed by that motionless and silent face. He would find in her features innumerable subjects of self-reproach, remorse, anger and dread. He would blush at the thought of the influence which so frail a creature had exerted over his destiny—he, a man of iron, accustomed to command others, to see whole battalions, spirited horses and frightened men march at a word from his lips.

And a wife who was still but a child had made him unhappy! She forced him to look within himself—to scrutinize his own decisions, to modify many of them, to retract some of them—and all this without saying: "You are wrong; I beg that you will do thus or thus." She had never implored, she had never deigned to show herself his equal and to avow herself his companion. That woman, whom he could have crushed in his hand if he had chosen, lay there, an insignificant creature, dreaming of another before his eyes, perhaps, and defying him even in her sleep. He was tempted to strangle her—to drag her out of bed by the hair, to trample on her and force her to shriek for mercy and to implore his forgiveness; but she was so pretty, so dainty and so fair, that he would suddenly take pity on her, as a child is moved to pity as he gazes at the bird he intended to kill. And he would weep like a woman, man of bronze as he was, and would steal away so that she might not enjoy the triumph of seeing him weep. In truth I know not which was the unhappier, he or she. She was cruel from virtue, as he was kind from weakness; she had too much patience, of which he had not enough; she had the failings of her good qualities and he the good qualities of his failings.

Around these two ill-assorted beings swarmed a multitude of friends who strove to bring them nearer together, some in order to have something to occupy their minds, others to give themselves importance, others as the result of ill-advised affection. Some took the wife's part, others the husband's. They quarrelled among themselves on the subject of Monsieur and Madame Delmare, who, on the other hand, did not quarrel at all; for, with Indiana's systematic submission, the colonel could never succeed in picking a quarrel, whatever he might do. And then there were those who knew nothing, but wanted to make themselves necessary. They counselled submission to Madame Delmare and did not see that she was only too submissive; others advised the husband to be inflexible and not to allow his authority to pass into his wife's hands. These last, stupid mortals who have so little feeling that they are always afraid that some one is treading on them and who mistake cause and effect for each other, belong to a species which you will find everywhere, which is constantly getting entangled in other people's legs and makes a deal of noise in order to attract attention.

Monsieur and Madame Delmare had made a particularly large number of acquaintances at Melun and at Fontainebleau. They met these people again at Paris, and they were the keenest in the game of evil-speaking that was being played about them. The wit of small towns is, as you doubtless know, the most ill-natured in the world. Good people are always misunderstood there, superior minds are sworn foes of the public. If a battle is to be fought for a fool or a boor you will see them running from all directions. If you have a dispute with any one, they come to look on as at the theatre; they make bets; they crowd upon your heels, so eager are they to see and hear. The one who falls they will cover with mud and maledictions; the weakest is always in the wrong. If you make war on prejudices, petty foibles, vices, you insult them personally, you attack them in what they hold most dear, you are a treacherous and dangerous man. You will be summoned before the courts to make reparation by people whose names you do not know, but whom you will be convicted of having referred to in your slurring allusions. What advice shall I give you? If you meet one of these people, avoid stepping in his shadow, even at sunset, when a man's shadow is thirty feet long; all that ground belongs to the inhabitant of the small town, and you have no right to set foot upon it. If you breathe the air that he breathes, you injure him, you destroy his health; if you drink at his fountain, you cause it to run dry; if you lend a hand to business in his province, you increase the price of the articles he purchases; if you offer him snuff, you poison it; if you think his daughter pretty, you intend to seduce her; if you extol his wife's domestic virtues, it is insulting irony, and in your heart you despise her for her ignorance; if you are so ill-advised as to pay him a compliment in his own house, he will not understand it, and he will go about everywhere saying that you have insulted him. Take your penates and carry them into the woods or to the desolate moors. There only will the man of the small town leave you in peace.

Even behind the manifold girdle of the walls of Paris

the small town pursued that ill-starred couple. Well-to-do families from Melun and Fontainebleau took up their abode in the capital for the winter and brought thither the blessing of their provincial manners. Cliques were formed around Delmare and his wife, and all that was humanly possible was attempted in order to make their position with respect to each other more uncomfortable. Their unhappiness was increased thereby and their mutual obstinacy did not diminish.

Ralph had the good sense not to meddle in their dissensions. Madame Delmare had suspected him of embittering her husband against her, or at least of seeking to put an end to Raymon's intimacy with her; but she soon realized the injustice of her suspicions. The colonel's perfect tranquillity with respect to Monsieur de Ramière was irrefutable evidence of her cousin's silence. Thereupon she felt that she must thank him; but he sedulously avoided any conversation on that subject; whenever she was alone with him, he eluded her hints and pretended not to understand them. It was such a delicate subject that Madame Delmare had not the courage to force Ralph to discuss it; she simply endeavored, by her loving attentions, by her delicate and affectionate deference to him, to make him understand her gratitude; but Ralph seemed to pay no heed, and Indiana's pride was wounded by this display of supercilious generosity. She was afraid that she should seem to play the rôle of the guilty wife imploring the indulgence of a stern witness; she became cold and constrained once more with poor Ralph. It seemed to her that his conduct in this matter was the natural consequence of his selfishness; that he loved her still, although he no longer esteemed her; that he simply desired her society for his own diversion, that he disliked to abandon habits which she had formed for him in her home and to deprive himself of the attentions that she was never weary of bestowing upon him. She fancied that he was by no means anxious to invent grievances against her husband or herself.

"That is just like his contempt for women," she thought; "in his eyes they are simply domestic animals, useful to keep a house in order, prepare meals and serve tea. He doesn't do them the honor of entering into a discussion with them; their faults have no effect on him provided that they do not interfere with his comfort or with his mode of life. Ralph has no need of my heart; so long as my hands retain the knack of preparing his pudding and of touching the strings of the harp for him, what does he care for my love for another man, my secret suffering, my deathly impatience under the yoke which is crushing me? I am his servant, he asks nothing more of me than that."

XX

Indiana had ceased to reproach Raymon; he defended himself so badly that she was afraid of finding him too worthy of blame. There was one thing which she dreaded much more than being deceived, and that was being abandoned. She could not live without her belief in him, without her hope of the future he had promised her; for her life with Monsieur Delmare and Ralph had become hateful to her, and if she had not expected soon to escape from the power of those two men, she would have drowned herself at once. She often thought of it;

she said to herself that if Raymon treated her as he had treated Noun there would be no other way for her to avoid an unendurable future than to join Noun. That sombre thought followed her everywhere and she took pleasure in it.

Meanwhile the time fixed for their departure from France drew near. The colonel seemed to have no suspicion of the resistance which his wife was meditating; every day he made some progress in the settlement of his affairs, every day he paid off one more creditor; and Madame Delmare looked on with a tranquil eye at all these preparations, sure as she was of her own courage. She was preparing, too, for her struggle with the difficulties she anticipated. She sought to procure an ally in her aunt, Madame de Carvajal, and dilated to her upon her repugnance to the journey; and the old marchioness who—to give her no more than her due—built great hopes of attracting *custom* to her salon upon her niece's beauty, declared that it was the colonel's duty to leave his wife in France; that it would be downright barbarity to expose her to the fatigues and dangers of an ocean voyage when her health had just begun to show some slight improvement; in a word, that it was his place to go to work at rebuilding his fortune, Indiana's to remain with her old aunt and take care of her. At first Monsieur Delmare looked upon these insinuations as the doting talk of an old woman; but he was forced to pay more attention to them when Madame de Carvajal gave him clearly to understand that her inheritance was to be had only at that price. Although Delmare loved money like a man who had worked hard all his life to amass it, he had some pride in his composition; he pronounced his ultimatum with decision, and declared that his wife should go with him at any risk. The marchioness, who could not believe that money was not the absolute sovereign of every man of good sense, did not look upon this as Monsieur Delmare's last word; she continued to encourage her niece in her resistance, proposing to assume the responsibility for her action in the eyes of the world. It needed all the indelicacy of a mind corrupted by intrigue and ambition, all the shuffling of a heart distorted by constant devotion to mere external show, to close her eyes thus to the real causes of Indiana's rebellion. Her passion for Monsieur de Ramière was a secret to no one but her husband; but as Indiana had as yet given scandal nothing to seize upon, the secret was mentioned only in undertones, and Madame de Carvajal had been confidentially informed of it by more than a score of persons. The foolish old woman was flattered by it; all that she desired was to have her niece *à la mode* in society, and an intrigue with Raymon was a fine beginning. And yet Madame de Carvajal's moral character was not of the Regency type; the Restoration had given a virtuous impulse to minds of that stamp; and as *conduct* was demanded at court, the marchioness detested nothing so much as the scandal that ruins and destroys. Under Madame du Barry she would have been less rigid in her principles; under the Dauphiness she became one of the *high-necked*. But all this was for show, for the sake of appearances; she kept her disapprobation and her scorn for notorious misconduct, and she always awaited the result of an intrigue before condemning it. Those infidelities which did not cross the threshold were venial in her eyes. She became a Spaniard once more to pass judgment on passions inside the blinds; in her eyes there was no guilt save that which was placarded in the streets for passers-by to see. So that Indiana, passionate but chaste, enamored but reserved, was a precious subject to exhibit and exploit;

such a woman as she was might fascinate the strongest brains in that hypocritical society and withstand the perils of the most delicate missions. There was an excellent chance to speculate on the responsibility of so pure a mind and so passionate a heart. Poor Indiana! luckily her fatal destiny surpassed all her hopes and led her into an abyss of misery where her aunt's pernicious protection did not seek her out.

Raymon was not disturbed as to what was to become of her. This intrigue had already reached the last stage of distaste, deathly ennui, so far as he was concerned. To cause ennui is to descend as low as possible in the regard of the person whom one loves. Luckily for the last days of her illusion, Indiana had no suspicion of it.

One morning, on returning from a ball, he found Madame Delmare in his room. She had come at midnight; for five mortal hours she had been waiting! It was in the coldest part of the year; she had no fire, but sat with her head resting on her hand, enduring cold and anxiety with the gloomy patience which the whole course of her life had taught her. She raised her head when he entered, and Raymon, speechless with amazement, could detect on her pale face no indication of anger or reproach.

"I was waiting for you," she said gently; "as you had not come to see me for three days, and as things have happened which it is important that you should know without delay, I came here last night in order to tell you of them."

"It is imprudent beyond belief!" said Raymon, cautiously locking the door behind him; "and my people know that you are here! They just told me so."

"I made no attempt at concealment," she replied coldly; "and as for the word you use, I consider it ill-chosen."

"I said imprudent, I should have said insane."

"And I should say *courageous.* But no matter; listen to me. Monsieur Delmare starts for Bordeaux in three days, and sails thence for the colony. You and I agreed that you should protect me from violence if he employed it; there is no question that he will, for I made known my determination last evening and he locked me into my room. I escaped through a window; see, my hands are bleeding. They may be looking for me at this moment, but Ralph is at Bellerive so that he will not be able to tell where I am. I have decided to remain in hiding until Monsieur Delmare has made up his mind to leave me behind. Have you thought about making ready for my flight, of preparing a hiding-place for me? It is so long since I have been able to see you alone, that I do not know what your present inclinations are; but one day, when I expressed some doubt concerning your resolution, you told me that you could not imagine love without confidence; you reminded me that you had never doubted me, you proved to me that I was unjust, and thereupon I was afraid of remaining below your level if I did not cast aside such puerile suspicions and the innumerable little exactions by which women degrade ordinary love-affairs. I have endured with resignation the brevity of your calls, the embarrassment of our interviews, the eagerness with which you seemed to avoid any free exchange of sentiments with me; I have retained my confidence in you. Heaven is my witness that when anxiety and fear were gnawing at my heart I spurned them as criminal thoughts. I have come now to seek the reward of my faith; the time has come; tell me, do you accept my sacrifices?"

The crisis was so urgent that Raymon did not feel bold enough to pretend any longer. Desperate, frantic to find himself caught in his own trap, he lost his head and vented his temper in coarse and brutal maledictions.

"You are a mad woman!" he cried, throwing himself into a chair. "Where have you dreamed of love? in what romance written for the entertainment of lady's-maids, have you studied society, I pray to know?"

He paused, realizing that he had been far too rough, and cudgelling his brains to find a way of saying the same things in other terms and of sending her away without insulting her.

But she was calm, like one prepared to listen to anything.

"Go on," she said, folding her arms over her heart, whose throbbing gradually grew less violent; "I am listening; I presume that you have something more than that to say to me?"

"Still another effort of the imagination, another love scene," thought Raymon.—"Never," he cried, springing excitedly to his feet, "never will I accept such sacrifices! When I told you that I should have the strength to do it, Indiana, I boasted too much, or rather I slandered myself; for the man is no better than a dastard who will consent to dishonor the woman he loves. In your ignorance of life, you failed to realize the importance of such a plan, and I, in my despair at the thought of losing you, did not choose to reflect——"

"Your power of reflection has returned very suddenly!" she said, withdrawing her hand, which he tried to take.

"Indiana," he rejoined, "do you not see that you impose the dishonorable part on me, while you reserve the heroic part for yourself, and that you condemn me because I desire to remain worthy of your love? Could you continue to love me, ignorant and simple-hearted woman that you are, if I sacrificed your life to my pleasure, your reputation to my selfish interests?"

"You say things that are very contradictory," said Indiana; "if I made you happy by remaining with you, what do you care for public opinion? Do you care more for it than for me?"

"Oh! I do not care for it on my account, Indiana!"

"Is it on my account then? I anticipated your scruples and to spare you anything like remorse I have taken the initiative; I did not wait for you to come and carry me away from my home, I did not even consult you with regard to crossing my husband's threshold forever. That decisive step is taken, and your conscience cannot reproach you for it. At this moment, Raymon, I am dishonored. In your absence I counted on yonder clock the hours that consummated my disgrace; and now, although the dawn finds my brow as pure as it was yesterday, I am a lost creature in public opinion. Yesterday there was still some compassion for me in the hearts of other women; to-day there will be no feeling left but contempt. I considered all these things before acting."

"Infernal female foresight!" thought Raymon.

And then, struggling against her as he would have done against a bailiff who had come to levy on his furniture, he said in a caressing fatherly tone:

"You exaggerate the importance of what you have done. No, my love, all is not lost because of one rash step. I will enjoin silence on my servants."

"Will you enjoin silence on mine who, I doubt not, are anxiously looking for me at this moment. And my husband, do you think he will quietly keep the secret? do you think he will consent to receive me to-morrow, when I have passed a whole night under your roof? Will you advise me to go back and throw myself at his feet, and ask him, as a proof of his forgiveness, to be kind enough to replace on my neck the chain which has crushed my life and withered my youth? You would consent, without regret, to see the woman whom you loved so dearly go back and resume another man's yoke, when you have her fate in your hands, when you can keep her in your arms all your life, when she is in your power, offering to remain there forever! You would not feel the least repugnance, the least alarm in surrendering her at once to the implacable master, who perhaps awaits her coming only to kill her!"

A thought flashed through Raymon's brain. The moment had come to subdue that womanly pride, or it would never come. She had offered him all the sacrifices that he did not want, and she stood before him in overweening confidence that she ran no other risks than those she had foreseen. Raymon conceived a scheme for ridding himself of her embarrassing devotion or of deriving some profit from it. He was too good a friend of Delmare, he owed too much consideration to the man's unbounded confidence to steal his wife from him; he must content himself with seducing her.

"You are right, my Indiana," he cried with animation, "you bring me back to myself, you rekindle my transports which the thought of your danger and the dread of injuring you had cooled. Forgive my childish solicitude and let me prove to you how much of tenderness and genuine love it denotes. Your sweet voice makes my blood quiver, your burning words pour fire into my veins; forgive, oh! forgive me for having thought of anything else than this ineffable moment when I at last possess you. Let me forget all the dangers that threaten us and thank you on my knees for the happiness you bring me; let me live entirely in this hour of bliss which I pass at your feet and for which all my blood would not pay. Let him come, that dolt of a husband who locks you up and goes to sleep upon his vulgar brutality, let him come and snatch you from my transports! let him come and snatch you from my arms, my treasure, my life! Henceforth you do not belong to him; you are my sweetheart, my companion, my mistress——"

As he pleaded thus, Raymon gradually worked himself up, as he was accustomed to do when *arguing* his passions. It was a powerful, a romantic situation; it offered some risks. Raymon loved danger, like a genuine descendant of a race of valiant knights. Every sound that he heard in the street seemed to denote the coming of the husband to claim his wife and his rival's blood. To seek the joys of love in the stirring emotions of such a situation was a diversion worthy of Raymon. For a quarter of an hour he loved Madame Delmare passionately, he lavished upon her the seductions of burning eloquence. He was truly powerful in his language and sincere in his behavior—this man whose ardent brain considered love-making a polite accomplishment. He played at passion so well that he deceived himself. Shame upon that foolish woman! She abandoned herself in ecstasy to those treacherous demonstrations; she was happy, she was radiant with hope and joy; she forgave everything, she almost accorded everything.

But Raymon ruined himself by over-precipitation. If he had carried his art so far as to prolong for twenty-four hours the situation in which Indiana had risked herself, she would perhaps have been his. But the day was breaking, bright and rosy; the sun poured floods of light into the room, and the noise in the street increased with every moment. Raymon cast a glance at the clock; it was nearly seven.

"It is time to have done with it," he thought; "Delmare may appear at any moment, and before that happens I must induce her to return home voluntarily."

He became more urgent and less tender; the pallor of his lips betrayed the working of an impatience more imperious than delicate. There was in his kisses a sort of abruptness, almost anger. Indiana was afraid. A good angel spread its wings over that wavering and bewildered soul; she came to herself and repelled the attacks of cold and selfish vice.

"Leave me," she said; "I do not propose to yield through weakness what I am willing to accord for love or gratitude. You cannot need proofs of my affection; my presence here is a sufficiently decisive one, and I bring the future with me. But allow me to keep all the strength of my conscience to contend against the powerful obstacles that still separate us; I need stoicism and tranquillity."

"What are you talking about?" angrily demanded Raymon, who was furious at her resistance and had not listened to her.

And, losing his head altogether in that moment of torture and wrath, he pushed her roughly away and strode up and down the room, with heaving bosom and head on fire; then he took a carafe and drank a large glass of water which suddenly calmed his excitement and cooled his love. Whereupon he looked at her ironically and said:

"Come, madame, it is time for you to retire."

A ray of light at last enlightened Indiana and laid Raymon's heart bare before her.

"You are right," she said.

And she walked toward the door.

"Pray take your cloak and boa," he said, detaining her.

"To be sure," she retorted, "those traces of my presence might compromise you."

"You are a child," he said, in a coaxing tone, as he adjusted her cloak with ostentatious care; "you know very well that I love you; but really you take pleasure in torturing me, and you drive me mad. Wait until I go and call a cab. If I could, I would escort you home; but that would ruin you."

"Pray, do you not think that I am ruined already?" she asked bitterly.

"No, my darling," replied Raymon, who asked nothing better than to persuade her to leave him in peace. "Nobody has noticed your absence, as they have not come here yet in search of you. Although I should be the last one to be suspected, it would be natural to inquire at the houses of all of your acquaintances. And then you can go and place yourself under your aunt's protection; indeed, that is the course I advise you to take; she will arrange everything. You will be supposed to have passed the night at her house."

Madame Delmare was not listening; she was gazing stupidly at the sun, as it rose, huge and red, over an expanse of gleaming roofs. Raymon tried to rouse her from her preoccupation. She turned her eyes on him but seemed not to recognize him. Her cheeks had a greenish tinge and her parched lips seemed paralyzed.

Raymon was terrified. He remembered the other's suicide, and, in his alarm, not knowing which way to turn, dreading lest he should become twice a criminal in his own eyes, but feeling too exhausted mentally to be able to deceive her again, he pushed her gently into an easy-chair, locked the door, and went up to his mother's room.

XXI

He found her awake; she was accustomed to rise early, the result of habits of hard-working activity which she had formed during the emigration, and which she had not abandoned when she recovered her wealth.

Seeing Raymon enter her room so late, pale and excited, and in full dress, she realized that he was struggling in one of the frequent crises of his stormy life. She had always been his refuge and salvation in these periods of agitation, of which no trace remained save a deep and sorrowful one in her mother-heart. Her life had been withered and used up by all that Raymon had acquired and reacquired. Her son's character, impetuous yet cold, reflective yet passionate, was a consequence of her inexhaustible love and generous indulgence. He would have been a better man with a mother less kind; but she had accustomed him to make the most of all the sacrifices that she consented to make for him; she had taught him to seek and to advance his own well-being as zealously and as powerfully as she sought it. Because she deemed herself created to preserve him from all sorrows and to sacrifice all her own interests to him, he had accustomed himself to believe that the whole world was created for him and would place itself in his hand at a word from his mother. By an abundance of generosity she had succeeded only in forming a selfish heart.

She turned pale, did the poor mother, and, sitting up in bed, gazed anxiously at him. Her glance said at once: "What can I do for you? Where must I go?"

"Mother," he said, grasping the dry, transparent hand that she held out to him, "I am horribly unhappy, I need your help. Save me from the troubles by which I am surrounded. I love Madame Delmare, as you know——"

"I did not know it," said Madame de Ramière, in a tone of affectionate reproof.

"Don't try to deny it, dear mother," said Raymon, who had no time to waste; "you did know it, and your admirable delicacy prevented you speaking of it first. Well, that woman is driving me to despair, and my brain is going."

"Tell me what you mean!" said Madame de Ramière, with the youthful vivacity born of ardent maternal love.

"I do not mean to conceal anything from you, especially as I am not guilty this time. For several months I have been trying to calm her romantic brain and bring her back to a sense of her duties; but all my efforts serve only to intensify this thirst for danger, this craving for adventure that ferments in the brains of all the women of her country. At this moment she is here, in my room, against my will, and I cannot induce her to go away."

"Unhappy child!" said Madame de Ramière, dressing herself in haste. "Such a timid, gentle creature! I will go and see her, talk to her! that is what you came to ask me to do, isn't it?"

"Yes, yes," said Raymon, moved involuntarily by his mother's goodness of heart; "go and make her understand the language of reason and kindness. She will love virtue from your lips, I doubt not; perhaps she will give way to your caresses; she will recover her self-control, poor creature! she suffers so keenly!"

Raymon threw himself into a chair and began to weep, the divers emotions of the morning had so shaken his nerves. His mother wept with him and could not make up her mind to go down until she had forced him to take a few drops of ether.

Indiana was not weeping and rose with a calm and dignified air when she recognized her. Madame de Ramière was so little prepared for such a dignified and noble bearing, that she felt embarrassed before the younger woman, as if she had shown lack of consideration for her by taking her by surprise in her son's bedroom. She yielded to the deep and true emotion of her heart and opened her arms impulsively. Madame Delmare threw herself into them ; her despair found vent in bitter sobs and the two women wept a long while on each other's bosom.

But when Madame de Ramière would have spoken, Indiana checked her.

"Do not say anything to me, madame," she said, wiping away her tears ; "you could find no words to say that would not cause me pain. Your interest and your kisses are enough to prove your generous affection ; my heart is as much relieved as it can be. I will go now ; I do not need your urging to realize what I have to do."

"But I did not come to send you away, but to comfort you," said Madame de Ramière.

"I cannot be comforted," she replied, kissing her once more ; "love me, that will help me a little ; but do not speak to me. Adieu, madame ; you believe in God—pray for me."

"You shall not go alone!" cried Madame de Ramière ; "I will myself go with you to your husband, to justify you, defend you and protect you."

"Generous woman!" said Indiana, embracing her warmly, "you cannot do it. You alone are ignorant of Raymon's secret ; all Paris will be talking about it to-night, and you would play an incongruous part in such a story. Let me bear the scandal of it alone; I shall not suffer long."

"What do you mean? would you commit the crime of taking your own life? Dear child! you too believe in God, do you not?"

"And so, madame, I start for Ile Bourbon in three days."

"Come to my arms, my darling child! come and let me bless you! God will reward your courage."

"I trust so," said Indiana, looking up at the sky.

Madame de Ramière insisted on sending for a carriage; but Indiana resisted. She was resolved to return alone and without causing a sensation. In vain did Raymon's mother express her alarm at the idea of her undertaking so long a journey on foot in her exhausted, agitated condition.

"I have strength enough," she said; "a word from Raymon sufficed to give me all I need."

She wrapped herself in her cloak, lowered her black lace veil and left the house by a secret door to which Madame de Ramière showed her the way. As soon as she stepped into the street she felt as if her trembling legs would refuse to carry her; it seemed to her every moment that she could feel her furious husband's brutal hand seize her, throw her down and drag her in the gutter. Soon the noise in the street, the indifference of the faces that passed her on every side and the penetrating chill of the morning air restored her strength and tranquillity, but it was a pitiable sort of strength and a tranquillity as depressing as that which sometimes prevails on the ocean and alarms the far-sighted sailor more than the howling of the tempest. She walked along the quays from the Institute to the Corps Législatif; but she forgot to cross the bridge and continued to wander by the river,

SIR RALPH SAVES INDIANA

In that moment of vertigo she leaned against a wall and bent forward, fascinated, over what seemed to her a solid mass. But the bark of a dog that was capering about her distracted her thoughts and delayed for some seconds the accomplishment of her design. Meanwhile, a man ran to the spot, guided by the dog's voice, seized her around the waist, dragged her back, and laid her on the ruins of an abandoned boat on the shore.

absorbed in a bewildered reverie, in meditation without ideas, and walking aimlessly on and on.

She gradually drew nearer to the river, which washed pieces of ice ashore at her feet and shattered them on the stones along the shore with a dry sound that suggested cold. The greenish water exerted an attractive force on Indiana's senses. One becomes accustomed to horrible ideas; by dint of dwelling on them one takes pleasure in them. The thought of Noun's suicide had soothed her hours of despair for so many months, that suicide had assumed in her mind the form of a tempting pleasure. A single thought, a religious thought, had prevented her from deciding definitely upon it; but at this moment no well-defined thought controlled her exhausted brain. She hardly remembered that God existed, that Raymon ever existed, and she walked on, still drawing nearer the bank, obeying the instinct of unhappiness and the magnetic force of suffering.

When she felt the stinging cold of the water on her feet, she woke as if from a fit of somnambulism, and on looking about to discover where she was, saw Paris behind her and the Seine rushing by at her feet, bearing in its oily depths the white reflection of the houses and the grayish blue of the sky. This constant movement of the water and the immobility of the ground became confused in her bewildered mind, and it seemed to her that the water was sleeping and the ground moving. In that moment of vertigo she leaned against a wall and bent forward, fascinated, over what seemed to her a solid mass. But the bark of a dog that was capering about her distracted her thoughts and delayed for some seconds the accomplishment of her design. Meanwhile a man ran to the spot, guided by the dog's voice, seized her around the waist, dragged her back and laid her on the ruins of an abandoned boat on the shore. She looked in his face and did not recognize him. He knelt at her foot, unfastened his cloak and wrapped it about her, took her hands in his to warm them and called her by name. But her brain was too weak to make an effort; for forty-eight hours she had forgotten to eat.

However, when the blood began to circulate in her benumbed limbs, she saw Ralph kneeling beside her, holding her hands and watching for the return of consciousness.

"Did you meet Noun?" she asked him. "I saw her pass along there," she added, pointing to the river, distracted by her fixed idea. "I tried to follow her, but she walked too fast, and I am not strong enough to walk. It was like a nightmare."

Ralph looked at her in sore distress. He too felt as if his head were bursting and his brain running wild.

"Let us go," she continued; "but first see if you can find my feet; I lost them on the stones."

Ralph saw that her feet were wet and paralyzed by cold. He carried her in his arms to a house near by, where the kindly care of a hospitable woman restored her to consciousness. Meanwhile Ralph sent word to Monsieur Delmare that his wife was found; but the colonel had not returned home when the news arrived. He was continuing his search in a frenzy of anxiety and wrath. Ralph, being more perspicacious, had gone to Monsieur de Ramière's, but he had found Raymon, who had just gone to bed and who was very cool and ironical in his reception of him. Then he had thought of Noun and had followed the river in one direction, while his servant did the same in the other direction. Ophelia had speediiy found her mistress's scent and had led Ralph to the place where he found her.

When Indiana was able to recall what had taken place during that wretched night, she tried in vain to remember the occurrences of her moments of delirium. She was unable therefore to explain to her cousin what thoughts had guided her action during the last hour; but he divined them and understood the state of her heart without questioning her. He simply took her hand and said to her in a gentle but grave tone:

"Cousin, I require one promise from you; it is the last proof of friendship which I shall ever ask at your hands."

"Tell me what it is," she replied; "to oblige you is the only pleasure that is left to me."

"Well then," rejoined Ralph, "swear to me that you will not resort to suicide without notifying me. I swear to you on my honor that I will not oppose your design in any way. I simply insist on being notified: as for life, I care about it as little as you do, and you know that I have often had the same idea."

"Why do you talk of suicide?" said Madame Delmare. "I have never intended to take my own life. I am afraid of God; if it weren't for that!——"

"Just now, Indiana, when I seized you in my arms, when this poor beast"—and he patted Ophelia—"caught your dress, you had forgotten God and the whole universe, poor Ralph with the rest."

A tear stood in Indiana's eye. She pressed Sir Ralph's hand.

"Why did you stop me?" she said sadly; "I should be on God's bosom now, for I was not guilty, I did not know what I was doing."

"I saw that, and I thought that it was better to commit suicide after due reflection. We will talk about it again if you choose."

Indiana shuddered. The cab stopped in front of the house where she was to confront her husband. She had not the strength to mount the steps and Ralph carried her to her room. Their whole retinue was reduced to a single maid servant, who had gone to discuss Madame Delmare's flight with the neighbors, and Lelièvre, who, in despair, had gone to the morgue to inspect the bodies brought in that morning. So Ralph remained with Madame Delmare to nurse her. She was suffering intensely when a loud peal of the bell announced the colonel's return. A shudder of terror and hatred ran through her every vein. She seized her cousin's arm.

"Listen, Ralph," she said; "if you have the slightest affection for me, you will spare me the sight of that man in my present condition. I do not want to arouse his pity, I prefer his anger to that. Do not open the door, or else send him away; tell him that I haven't been found."

Her lips quivered, her arms clung to Ralph with convulsive strength, to detain him. Torn by two conflicting feelings, the poor baronet could not make up his mind what to do. Delmare was jangling the bell as if he would break it, and his wife was almost dying in his chair.

"You think only of his anger," said Ralph at last; "you do not think of his misery, his anxiety; you still believe that he hates you. If you had seen his grief this morning!"

Indiana dropped her arms, thoroughly exhausted, and Ralph went and opened the door.

"Is she here?" cried the colonel, rushing in. "Ten thousand devils! I have run about enough after her; I am deeply obliged to her for putting such a pleasant duty on me! Deuce take her! I don't want to see her, for I should kill her!"

"You forget that she can hear you," replied Ralph in

an undertone. "She is in no condition to bear any painful excitement. Be calm."

"Twenty-five thousand maledictions!" roared the colonel. "I have endured enough myself since this morning. It's a good thing for me that my nerves are like cables. Which of us is the more injured, the more exhausted, which of us has the better right to be sick, I pray to know,—she or I? And where did you find her? what was she doing? She is responsible for my having outrageously insulted that foolish old woman, Carvajal, who gave me ambiguous answers and blamed me for this charming freak! Damnation! I am dead beat!"

As he spoke thus in his harsh, hoarse voice, Delmare had thrown himself on a chair in the ante-room; he wiped his brow from which the perspiration was streaming despite the intense cold; he described with many oaths his fatigues, his anxieties, his sufferings; he asked a thousand questions, and, luckily, did not listen to the answers, for poor Ralph could not lie, and he could think of nothing in what he had to tell that was likely to appease the colonel. So he sat on a table, as silent and unmoved as if he were absolutely without interest in the sufferings of those two, and yet he was really more unhappy in their unhappiness than they themselves were.

Madame Delmare, when she heard her husband's imprecations, felt stronger than she expected. She preferred this fierce wrath, which reconciled her with herself, to a generous forbearance which would have aroused her remorse. She wiped away the last trace of her tears and summoned what remained of her strength, which she was well content to expend in a day, so heavy a burden had life become to her. Her husband accosted her in a harsh and imperious tone, but suddenly changed his expression and his manner and seemed sorely embarrassed, overmatched by the superiority of her character. He tried to be as cool and dignified as she was; but he could not succeed.

"Will you condescend to inform me, madame," he said, "where you passed the morning and perhaps the night?"

That *perhaps* indicated to Madame Delmare that her absence had not been discovered until late. Her courage increased with that knowledge.

"No, monsieur," she replied, "I do not propose to tell you."

Delmare turned green with anger and amazement.

"Do you really hope to conceal the truth from me?" he said, in a trembling voice.

"I care very little about it," she replied in an icy tone. "I refuse to tell you solely for form's sake. I propose to convince you that you have no right to ask me that question?"

"I have no right, ten thousand devils. Who is master here, pray tell, you or I? Which of us wears a petticoat and ought to be running a distaff? Do you propose to take the beard off my chin? It would look well on you, hussy!"

"I know that I am the slave and you the master. The laws of this country make you my master. You can bind my body, tie my hands, govern my acts. You have the right of the stronger, and society confirms you in it; but you cannot command my will, monsieur; God alone can bend it and subdue it. Try to find a law, a dungeon, an instrument of torture that gives you any hold on it! you might as well try to handle the air and grasp space."

"Hold your tongue, you foolish, impertinent creature; your high-flown novelist's phrases weary me."

"You can impose silence on me, but not prevent me from thinking."

"Silly pride! pride of a poor worm! you abuse the compassion I have had for you! But you will soon see that this mighty will can be subdued without too much difficulty."

"I don't advise you to try it; your repose would suffer, and you would gain nothing in dignity."

"Do you think so?" he said, crushing her hand between his thumb and forefinger.

"I do think so," she said, without wincing.

Ralph stepped forward, grasped the colonel's arm in his iron hand and bent it like a reed, saying in a pacific tone:

"I beg that you will not touch a hair of that woman's head."

Delmare longed to fly at him; but he felt that he was in the wrong and he dreaded nothing in the world so much as having to blush for himself. So he simply pushed him away, saying:

"Attend to your own business."

Then he returned to his wife.

"So, madame," he said, holding his arms tightly against his sides to resist the temptation to strike her, "you rebel against me, you refuse to go to Ile Bourbon with me, you desire a separation? Very well! *Mordieu!* I too——"

"I desire it no longer," she replied. "I did desire it yesterday, it was my will; it is not so this morning. You resorted to violence and locked me in my room; I went out through the window to show you that there is a difference between exerting an absurd control over a woman's actions and reigning over her will. I passed several hours away from your domination; I breathed the air of liberty in order to show you that you are not morally my master, and that I look to no one on earth but myself for orders. As I walked along I reflected that I owed it to my duty and my conscience to return and place myself under your control once more. I did it of my own free will. My cousin *accompanied* me here, he did not *bring me back.* If I had not chosen to come with him, he could not have forced me to do it, as you can imagine. So, monsieur, do not waste your time fighting against my determination; you will never control it, you lost all right to change it as soon as you undertook to assert your right by force. Make your preparations for departure; I am ready to assist you and to accompany you, not because it is your will, but because it is my pleasure. You may condemn me, but I will never obey anyone but myself."

"I am sorry for the derangement of your mind," said the colonel, shrugging his shoulders.

And he went to his room to put his papers in order, well satisfied in his heart with Madame Delmare's resolution and anticipating no further obstacles; for he respected her word as much as he despised her ideas.

XXII

Raymon, yielding to fatigue, slept soundly after his curt reception of Sir Ralph, who came to his house to make inquiries. When he awoke, his heart was full of a feeling of intense relief; he believed that the worst crisis of his intrigue had finally come and gone. For a long time he had foreseen that there would come a time when he would be brought face to face with that woman's love and would have to defend his liberty against the exacting demands of a romantic passion; and he encouraged himself in advance by arguing against such pretensions. He had at last reached and crossed that dangerous spot: he had said no, he would have no occasion to go there again, for everything had happened for the best. Indiana had not wept overmuch, had not been too insistent. She had been quite reasonable; she had understood at the first word and had made up her mind quickly and proudly.

Raymon was very well pleased with his providence; for he had one of his own, in whom he believed like a good son, and upon whom he relied to arrange everything to other people's detriment rather than his own. That providence had treated him so well thus far that he did not choose to doubt it. To anticipate the result of his wrong-doing and to be anxious concerning it would have been in his eyes a crime against the good Lord who watched over him.

He rose, still very much fatigued by the efforts of the imagination which the circumstances of that painful scene had compelled him to make. His mother returned; she had been to Madame de Carvajal to inquire as to Madame Delmare's health and frame of mind. The marchioness was not disturbed about her; she was, however, very much disgusted when Madame de Ramière shrewdly questioned her. But the only thing that impressed her in Madame Delmare's disappearance was the scandal that would result from it. She complained very bitterly of her niece, whom, only the day before, she had extolled to the skies; and Madame de Ramière understood that the unfortunate Indiana had, by this performance, alienated her kinswoman and lost the only natural prop that she still possessed.

To one who could read in the depths of the marchioness's soul, this would have seemed no great loss; but Madame de Carvajal was esteemed virtuous beyond reproach, even by Madame de Ramière. Her youth had been enveloped in the mysteries of prudence, or lost in the whirlwind of revolutions.

Raymon's mother wept over Indiana's lot and tried to excuse her; Madame de Carvajal tartly reminded her that she was not sufficiently disinterested in the matter to judge.

"But what will become of the unhappy creature?" said Madame de Ramière. "If her husband maltreats her, who will protect her?"

"That will be as God wills," replied the marchioness; "for my part, I'll have nothing more to do with her and I never wish to see her again."

Madame de Ramière, kind-hearted and anxious, determined to obtain news of Madame Delmare at any price. She bade her coachman drive to the end of the street on which she lived and sent a footman to question the concierge, instructing him to try to see Sir Ralph if he were in the house. She awaited in her carriage the result of this manœuvre, and Ralph himself soon joined her there.

The only person, perhaps, who judged Ralph accurately was Madame de Ramière; a few words sufficed to make each of them understand the other's sincere and unselfish interest in the matter. Ralph narrated what had passed during the morning; and, as he had nothing more than suspicions concerning the events of the night, he did not seek confirmation of them. But Madame de Ramière deemed it her duty to inform him of what she knew, imparting to him her desire to break off this ill-omened and impossible liaison. Ralph, who felt more at ease with her than with anybody else, allowed the profound emotion which her information caused him to appear on his face.

"You say, madame," he murmured, repressing a sort of nervous shudder that ran through his veins, "that she passed the night in your house?"

"A solitary and sorrowful night, no doubt. Raymon, who certainly was not guilty of complicity, did not come home until six o'clock, and at seven he came up to me to ask me to go down and soothe the poor child's mind."

"She meant to leave her husband! she meant to destroy her good name!" rejoined Ralph, his eyes fixed on vacancy and a strange oppression at his heart. "Then she must love this man, who is so unworthy of her, very dearly!"

Ralph forgot that he was talking to Raymon's mother.

"I have suspected this a long while," he continued; "why could I not have foretold the day on which she would consummate her ruin! I would have killed her first!"

Such language in Ralph's mouth surprised Madame de Ramière beyond measure; she supposed that she was speaking to a calm, indulgent man, and she regretted that she had trusted to appearances.

"Mon Dieu!" she said in dismay, "do you judge her without mercy? will you abandon her as her aunt has? Are you incapable of pity or forgiveness? Will she not have a single friend left after a fault which has already caused her such bitter suffering?"

"Have no fear of anything of the sort on my part, madame," Ralph replied; "I have known all for six months and I have said nothing. I surprised their first kiss and I did not hurl Monsieur de Ramière from his horse; I often intercepted their love messages in the woods and did not tear them in pieces with my whip. I met Monsieur de Ramière on the bridge he must cross to go to join her; it was night, we were alone and I am four times as strong as he; and yet I did not throw the man into the river; and when, after allowing him to escape, I discovered that he had eluded my vigilance and had stolen into her house, instead of bursting in the doors and throwing him out of the window, I quietly warned them of the husband's approach and saved the life of one in order to save the other's honor. You see, madame, that I am indulgent and merciful. This morning I had that man under my hand; I was well aware that he was the cause of all our misery, and, if I had not the right to accuse him without proofs, I certainly should have been justified in quarreling with him for his arrogant and mocking manner. But I bore with his insulting contempt because I knew that his death would kill Indiana; I allowed him to turn over and fall asleep again on the other side, while Indiana, insane and almost dead, was on the shore of the Seine, preparing to join his other victim. You see, madame, that I practise patience with those whom I hate and indulgence with those I love."

Madame de Ramière, sitting in her carriage opposite Ralph, gazed at him in surprise mingled with alarm. He was so different from what she had always seen him that she almost believed that he had suddenly become deranged. The allusion he had just made to Noun's death confirmed her in that idea; for she knew absolutely nothing of that story and took the words that Ralph had let fall in his indignation for a fragment of thought unconnected with his subject. He was, in very truth, passing through one of those periods of intense excitement which occur at least once in the lives of the most placid men, and which border so closely on madness that one step farther would carry them across the line. His wrath was restrained and concentrated like that of all cold temperaments; but it was deep, like the wrath of all noble souls; and the novelty of this frame of mind, which was truly portentous in him, made him terrible to look upon.

Madame de Ramière took his hand and said gently:

"You must suffer terribly, my dear Monsieur Ralph, for you wound me without mercy: you forget that the man of whom you speak is my son and that his wrongdoing, if he has been guilty of any, must be infinitely more painful to me than to you."

Ralph at once came to himself, and said, kissing Madame de Ramière's hand with an effusive warmth of regard, which was almost as unusual a manifestation on his part as that of his wrath:

"Forgive me, madame; you are right, I do suffer terribly, and I forget those things which I should respect. Pray, forget yourself the bitterness I have allowed to appear! my heart will not fail to lock itself up again."

Madame de Ramière, although somewhat reassured by this reply, could not rid herself of all anxiety when she saw with what profound hatred Ralph regarded her son. She tried to excuse him in his enemy's eyes, but he checked her.

"I divine your thoughts, madame," he said; "but have no fear, Monsieur de Ramière and I are not likely to meet again at present. As for my cousin, do not regret having enlightened me. If the whole world abandons her, I swear that she will always have at least one friend."

When Madame de Ramière returned home, toward evening, she found Raymon luxuriously ensconced in front of the fire, warming his slippered feet and drinking tea to banish the last vestiges of the nervous excitement of the morning. He was still cast down by that artificial emotion; but pleasant thoughts of the future revivified his faculties; he felt that he had become free once more, and he abandoned himself unreservedly to blissful meditations upon that priceless condition, which he had hitherto been so unsuccessful in maintaining.

"Why am I destined," he said to himself, "to weary so quickly of this priceless freedom of the heart which I always have to buy so dearly? When I feel that I am caught in a woman's net, I cannot break it quickly enough, in order to recover my repose and mental tranquillity. May I be cursed if I sacrifice them in such a hurry again! The trouble these two creoles have caused me will serve as a warning, and hereafter I do not propose to meddle with any but easy-going, laughing Parisian women—genuine women of the world. Perhaps I should do well to marry and have done with it, as they say——"

He was absorbed by such comforting, commonplace thoughts as these, when his mother entered, tired and deeply moved.

"She is better," she said; "everything has gone off as well as possible; I hope that she will grow calmer and——"

"Who?" inquired Raymon, waking with a start among his castles in Spain.

However, he concluded on the following day that he still had a duty to perform, namely, to regain that woman's esteem, if not her love. He did not choose that she should boast of having left him; he proposed that she should be persuaded that she had yielded to the influence of his good sense and his generosity. He desired to govern her even after he had spurned her; and he wrote to her as follows:

"I do not write to ask your pardon, my dear, for a few cruel or audacious words that escaped me in the delirium of my passion. In the derangement of fever no man can form perfectly coherent ideas or express himself in a proper manner. It is not my fault that I am not a god, that I cannot control in your presence the turbulent ardor of my blood, that my brain whirls, that I go mad. Perhaps I may have a right to complain of the merciless *sang-froid* with which you condemned me to frightful torture and never took pity on me; but that was not your fault. You are too perfect to play the same rôle in this world that we common mortals play, subject as we are to human passions, slaves of our less-refined organization. As I have often told you, Indiana, you are not a woman, and, when I think of you tranquilly and without excitement, you are an angel. I adore you in my heart as a divinity. But alas! in your presence the *old Adam* has often reasserted his rights. Often, under the perfumed breath from your lips, a scorching flame has consumed mine; often when, as I leaned toward you, my hair has brushed against yours, a thrill of indescribable bliss has run through my veins, and thereupon I have forgotten that you were an emanation from Heaven, a dream of everlasting felicity, an angel sent from God's bosom to guide my steps in this life and to describe to me the joys of another existence. Why, O chaste spirit, did you assume the alluring form of a woman? Why, O angel of light, did you clothe yourself in the seductions of hell? Often have I thought that I held happiness in my arms, and it was only virtue.

"Forgive me these reprehensible regrets, my love; I was not worthy of you, but perhaps we should both have been happier if you would have consented to stoop to my level. But my inferiority has constantly caused you pain and you have imputed your own virtues to me as crimes.

"Now that you absolve me—as I am sure that you do, for perfection implies mercy—let me still raise my voice to thank you and bless you. Thank you, do I say? Ah! no, my life, that is not the word; for my heart is more torn than yours by the courage that snatches you from my arms. But I admire you; and, through my tears, I congratulate you. Yes, my Indiana, you have mustered strength to accomplish this heroic sacrifice. It tears out my heart and my life; it renders my future desolate, it ruins my existence. But I love you well enough to endure it without a complaint; for my honor is nothing, yours is all in all. I would sacrifice my honor to you a thousand times; but yours is dearer to me than all the joys you have given me. No, no! I could not have enjoyed such a sacrifice. In vain should I have tried to blunt my conscience by delirious transports; in vain would you have opened your arms to intoxicate me with celestial joys—remorse would have found me out; it would have poisoned every hour of my life, and I should have been more humiliated than you by the contempt of men. O God! to see you degraded and brought to shame by me! to see you deprived of the veneration which encompassed you! to see you insulted in my arms and to be unable to wipe out the insult! for, though I should have shed all my blood for you, it would not have availed you. I might have avenged you, perhaps, but could never have justified you. My zeal in your defence would have been an additional accusation against you; my death an unquestionable proof of your crime. Poor Indiana! I should have ruined you! Ah! how miserably unhappy I should be!

"Go, therefore, my beloved; go and reap under another sky the fruits of virtue and religion. God will reward us for such an effort, for God is good. He will reunite us in a happier life, and perhaps—but the mere thought is a crime; and yet I cannot refrain from hoping! Adieu, Indiana, adieu! You see that our love is a sin! Alas! my heart is broken. Where could I find strength to say adieu to you!"

Raymon himself carried this letter to Madame Delmare's; but she shut herself up in her room and refused to see him. So he left the house after handing the letter secretly to the servant and cordially embracing the husband. As he left the last step behind him, he felt much better-hearted than usual; the weather was finer, the women fairer, the shops more brilliant. It was a red-letter day in Raymon's life.

Madame Delmare placed the letter, with the seal unbroken, in a box which she did not propose to open until she reached her destination. She wished to go to take leave of her aunt, but Sir Ralph with downright obstinacy opposed her doing so. He had seen Madame de Carvajal; he knew that she would overwhelm Indiana with reproaches and scorn; he was indignant at this hypocritical severity, and could not endure the thought of Madame Delmare exposing herself to it.

On the following day, as Delmare and his wife were about entering the diligence, Sir Ralph said to them with his accustomed *sang-froid:*

"I have often given you to understand, my friends, that it was my wish to accompany you; but you have refused to understand, or, at all events, to give me an answer. Will you allow me to go with you?"

"To Bordeaux?" queried Monsieur Delmare.

"To Bourbon," replied Sir Ralph.

"You cannot think of it," rejoined Monsieur Delmare;

"you cannot shift your establishment about from place to place at the caprice of a couple whose situation is precarious and whose future is uncertain. It would be abusing your friendship shamefully to accept the sacrifice of your whole life and of your position in society. You are rich and young and free; you ought to marry again, found a family—"

"That is not the question," said Sir Ralph, coldly. "As I have not the art of enveloping my ideas in words which change their meaning, I will tell you frankly what I think. It has seemed to me that in the last six months our friendship has fallen off perceptibly. Perhaps I have made mistakes which my dulness of perception has prevented me from detecting. If I am wrong, a word from you will suffice to set my mind at rest; allow me to go with you. If I have deserved severe treatment at your hands, it is time to tell me so; you ought not, by abandoning me thus, to leave me to suffer remorse for having failed to make reparation for my faults."

The colonel was so touched by this artless and generous appeal that he forgot all the wounds to his self-esteem which had alienated him from his friend. He offered him his hand, swore that his friendship was more sincere than ever, and that he refused his offers only from delicacy.

Madame Delmare held her peace. Ralph made an effort to obtain a word from her.

"And you, Indiana," he said in a stifled voice, "have you still a friendly feeling for me?"

That question reawoke all the filial affection, all the memories of childhood, of years of intimacy, which bound their hearts together. They threw themselves weeping into each other's arms, and Ralph nearly swooned; for strong emotions were constantly fermenting in that robust body, beneath that calm and reserved exterior. He sat down to avoid falling and remained for a few moments without speaking, pale as death; then he seized the colonel's hand in one of his and his wife's in the other.

"At this moment, when we are about to part, perhaps forever, be frank with me. You refuse my proposal to accompany you on my account and not on your own?"

"I give you my word of honor," said Delmare, "that in refusing you I sacrifice my happiness to yours."

"For my part," said Indiana, "you know that I would like never to leave you."

"God forbid that I should doubt your sincerity at such a moment!" rejoined Ralph; "your word is enough for me; I am content with you both."

And he disappeared.

Six weeks later the brig *Coraly* sailed from the port of Bordeaux. Ralph had written to his friends that he would be in that city just prior to their sailing; but, as his custom was, in such a laconic style that it was impossible to determine whether he intended to bid them adieu for the last time or to accompany them. They waited in vain for him until the last moment, and when the captain gave the signal to weigh anchor he had not appeared. Gloomy presentiments added their bitterness to the dull pain that gnawed at Indiana's heart, when the last houses of the town vanished amid the trees on the shore. She shuddered at the thought that she was thenceforth alone in the world with the husband whom she hated! that she must live and die with him, without a friend to comfort her, without a kinsman to protect her against his brutal domination.

But, as she turned, she saw on the deck behind her Ralph's placid and kindly face smiling into hers.

"So you have not abandoned me after all?" she said, as she threw her arms about his neck, her face bathed in tears.

"Never!" replied Ralph, straining her to his heart.

XXIII

LETTER FROM MADAME DELMARE TO MONSIEUR DE RAMIÈRE

"Ile Bourbon, June 3d, 18—

"I had determined to weary you no more with reminders of me; but, after reading on my arrival here the letter you sent me just before I left Paris, I feel that I owe you a reply because, in the agitation caused by horrible suffering, I went too far. I was mistaken with regard to you, and I owe you an apology, not as a *lover* but as a *man*.

"Forgive me, Raymon, for in the most ghastly moment of my life I took you for a monster. A single word, a single glance from you banished all confidence and all hope from my heart forever. I know that I can never be happy again; but I still hope that I may not be driven to despise you; that would be the last blow.

"Yes, I took you for a dastard, for the worst of all human creatures, an *egotist*. I conceived a horror of you. I regretted that Bourbon was not so far away as I longed to fly from you, and indignation gave me strength to drain the cup to the dregs.

"But since I have read your letter I feel better. I do

not regret you, but I no longer hate you, and I do not wish to leave your life a prey to remorse for having ruined mine. Be happy, be free from care; forget me. I am still alive and I may live a long while.

"It is a fact that you are not to blame; I was the one who was mad. Your heart was not dry, but it was closed to me. You did not lie to me, but I deceived myself. You were neither perjured nor cold; you simply did not love me.

"Oh! *mon Dieu!* you did not love me! In heaven's name how must you be loved? But I will not stoop to complaints; I am not writing to you for the purpose of poisoning with hateful memories the repose of your present life; nor do I propose to implore your compassion for sorrows which I am strong enough to bear alone. On the contrary, knowing better the rôle for which you are suited, I absolve you and forgive you.

"I will not amuse myself by refuting the charges in your letter; it would be too easy a matter; I will not reply to your observations with regard to my duties. Never fear, Raymon; I am familiar with them and I did not love you little enough to disregard them without due reflection. It is not necessary to tell me that the scorn of mankind would have been the reward of my downfall; I was well aware of it. I knew too that the stain would be deep, indelible and painful beyond words; that I should be spurned on all sides, cursed, covered with shame, and that I should not find a single friend to pity me and comfort me. The only mistake I had made was the feeling confident that you would open your arms to me, and that you would assist me to forget the scorn, the misery and the desertion of my friends. The only thing I had not anticipated was that you might refuse to accept my sacrifice after I had consummated it. I had imagined that that was impossible. I went to your house with the expectation that you would repel me at first from principle and a sense of duty, but firmly convinced that when you learned the inevitable consequences of what I had done, you would feel bound to assist me to endure them. No, upon my word I would never have believed that you would abandon me undefended to the consequences of such a dangerous resolution, and that you would leave me to gather its bitter fruits instead of taking me to your bosom and making a rampart of your love.

"In that case how gladly I would have defied the distant mutterings of a world that was powerless to injure me! how I would have defied hatred, being strong in your love! how feeble my remorse would have been, and how easily the passion you would have inspired would have stifled its voice! Engrossed by you alone, I would have forgotten myself; proud in the possession of your heart, I should have had no time to blush for my own. A word from you, a glance, a kiss would have sufficed to absolve me, and the memory of men and laws could have found no place in such a life. You see I was mad; according to your cynical expression I had acquired my knowledge of life from novels written for lady's-maids, from those gay, childish works of fiction in which the heart is interested in the success of wild enterprises and in impossible felicities. What you said, Raymon, was horribly true! The thing that terrifies and crushes me is that you are right.

"One thing that I cannot understand so well is that the impossibility was not the same for both of us; that I, a weak woman, derived from the exaltation of my feelings sufficient strength to place myself alone in a romantic, improbable situation, and that you, a brave man, could not find in your will-power, sufficient courage to follow me. And yet you had shared my dreams of the future, you had assented to my illusions, you had nourished in me that hope impossible of realization. For a long while you had listened to my childish plans, my pygmy-like aspirations, with a smile on your lips and joy in your eyes, and your words were all love and gratitude. You too were blind, short-sighted, boastful. How did it happen that your reason did not return until the danger was in sight? Why, I thought that danger charmed the eyes, strengthened the resolution, put fear to flight; and yet you trembled like a leaf when the crisis came! Have you men no courage except the physical courage that defies death? are you not capable of the moral courage that welcomes misfortune? Do you, who explain everything so admirably, explain that to me, I beg.

"It may be that your dream was not like mine; in my case, you see, courage was love. You had fancied that you loved me, and you had awakened, surprised to find that you had made such a mistake, on the day that I went forward trusting in the shelter of my mistake. Great God! what an extraordinary delusion it was of yours, since you did not then foresee all the obstacles that struck you when the time for action came! since you did not mention them to me until it was too late!

"But why should I reproach you now? Are we responsible for the impulses of our hearts? was it in your power to say that you would always love me? No, of course not. My misfortune consists in my inability to make myself agreeable to you longer and more really. I look about for the cause of it and find none in my heart; but it apparently exists, none the less. Perhaps I loved you too well, perhaps my affection was annoying and tiresome. You were a man, you loved liberty and pleasure. I was a burden to you. Sometimes I tried to put fetters on your life. Alas! those were very paltry offences to plead in justification of such a cruel desertion!

"Enjoy, therefore, the liberty you have purchased at the expense of my whole life; I will interfere with it no more. Why did you not give me this lesson sooner? My wound would have been less deep, and yours also, perhaps.

"Be happy! that is the last wish my broken heart will ever form! Do not exhort me to think of God, leave that for the priests, who have to soften the hard hearts of the guilty. For my part, I have more faith than you; I do not serve the same God, but I serve Him more loyally and with a purer heart. Yours is the God of men, the king, the founder and the upholder of your race; mine is the God of the universe, the creator, the preserver and the hope of all creatures. Yours made everything for you alone; mine made all created things for one another. You deem yourselves the masters of the world; I deem you only its tyrants. You think that God protects you and authorizes you to possess the empire of the earth; I think that He permits that for a little time, and that the day will come when His breath will scatter you like grains of sand. No, Raymon, you do not know God; or rather let me repeat what Ralph said to you one day at Lagny: you believe in nothing. Your education and your craving for an irresistible power to oppose to the brute force of the people, have led you to adopt without scrutiny the beliefs of your fathers; but the conviction of God's existence has never reached your heart—I doubt if you have ever prayed to Him. For my part, I have but one belief, the only one probably that you have not: I believe in Him; but the religion you have devised I will have nothing to do with; all your morality, all your principles, are simply the interests of your social order which you have raised to the dignity of laws and which you claim to trace back to God himself, just as your priests instituted the rites and ceremonies of the church to establish their power over the nations and amass wealth. But it is all falsehood and impiety. I, who invoke God and understand Him, know that there is nothing in common between Him and you, and that by clinging to Him with all my strength I separate myself from you, whose constant aim it is to overthrow His works and sully His gifts. I tell you, it ill becomes you to invoke His name to crush the resistance of a poor, weak woman, to stifle the lamentations of a broken heart. God does not choose that the creations of His hands shall be oppressed and trodden under foot. If He vouchsafed to descend so far as to intervene in our paltry quarrels, He would crush the strong and raise the weak; He would pass His mighty hand over our uneven heads and level them like the surface of the sea; He would say to the slave: 'Cast off thy chains and fly to the mountains where I have placed water and flowers and sunshine for thee.' He would say to the kings: 'Throw your purple robes to the beggars to sit upon, and go to sleep in the valleys where I have spread for you carpets of moss and heather.' To the powerful He would say: 'Bend your knees and bear the burdens of your weaker brethren; for henceforth you will need them and I will give them strength and courage.' Yes, those are my dreams; they are all of another life, of another world, where the laws of the brutal will not have passed over the heads of the peaceably inclined; where resistance and flight will not be crimes; where man can escape man as the gazelle escapes the panther; where the chain of the law will not be stretched about him to force him to throw himself under his enemy's feet; and where the voice of prejudice will not be raised in his distress to insult his sufferings and to say to him: 'You shall be deemed cowardly and base because you did not bend the knee and crawl.'

"No, do not talk to me about God, you of all men, Raymon; do not invoke His name to send me into exile and reduce me to silence. In submitting as I do I yield to the power of men. If I listened to the voice which God has placed in the depths of my heart, and to the noble instinct of a bold and strong nature, which perhaps is the genuine conscience, I should fly to the desert, I should learn to do without help, protection and love: I should go and live for myself in the heart of our beautiful mountains: I should forget the tyrants, the unjust and the ungrateful. But alas! man cannot do without his fellow-man, and even Ralph cannot live alone.

"Adieu, Raymon! may you be happy without me! I forgive you for the harm you have done me. Talk of me sometimes to your mother, the best woman I have ever known. Understand that there is neither anger nor vengeance in my heart against you; my grief is worthy of the love I had for you.

"INDIANA."

The unfortunate creature was over-boastful. This profound and calm sorrow was due simply to a sense of what her own dignity demanded when she addressed Raymon; but, when she was alone, she gave way freely to its consuming violence. Sometimes, however, a vague gleam of hope shone in her troubled eyes. Perhaps she never lost the last vestige of confidence in Raymon's love, despite the cruel lessons of experience, despite the distressing thoughts which placed before her mind every day his indifference and indolence when his interests or his pleasures were not concerned. It is my belief that, if Indiana could have persuaded herself to face the bald truth, she would not have dragged out her hopeless, ruined life so long.

Woman is naturally foolish; it is as if Heaven, to counterbalance the eminent superiority over us men which she owes to her delicacy of perception, had implanted a blind vanity, an idiotic credulity in her heart. It may be that one need only be an adept in the art of bestowing praise and flattering the self-esteem, to obtain dominion over that subtle, supple and perspicacious being. Sometimes the men who are most incapable of obtaining any sort of ascendancy over other men, obtain an unbounded ascendancy over the minds of women. Flattery is the yoke that bends those ardent but frivolous heads so low. Woe to him who undertakes to be frank and outspoken in love! he will have Ralph's fate.

This is what I should reply if you should tell me that Indiana is an exceptional character, and that the ordinary woman displays neither her stoical coolness nor her exasperating patience in resistance to conjugal despotism. I should tell you to look at the reverse of the medal, and see the miserable weakness, the stupid blindness she displays in her relations with Raymon. I should ask you where you ever found a woman who was not as ready to deceive as to be deceived; who had not the art to confine for ten years in the depths of her heart the secret of a hope sacrificed so thoughtlessly in a day of frenzied excitement, and who would not become, in one man's arms, as pitiably weak as she could be strong and invincible in another man's.

XXIV

Madame Delmare's home had become more peaceable, however. With their false friends had disappeared many of the difficulties which, under the fostering hand of those officious meddlers, had been envenomed with all the warmth of their zeal. Sir Ralph, with his silence and his apparent non-interference, was more skilful than all of them in letting drop those airy trifles of intimate companionship which float about in the favoring breeze of pleasant gossip. But Indiana lived almost alone. Her house was in the mountains above the town, and Monsieur Delmare, who had a warehouse in the port, went down every morning for the whole day, to superintend his business with the Indies and with France. Sir Ralph, who had no other home than theirs, but who found ways to add to their comfort without their suspecting his gifts, devoted himself to the study of natural history or to superintending the plantation; Indiana, resuming the easy-going habits of creole life, passed the scorching hours of the day in her straw chair, and the long evenings in the solitude of the mountains.

Bourbon is in truth, simply a huge cone, the base of which is about forty leagues in circumference, while its gigantic mountain peaks rise to the height of ten thousand feet. From almost every part of that imposing mass, the eye can see in the distance, beyond the beetling rocks, beyond the narrow valleys and stately forests, the unbroken horizon surrounding the azure-hued sea like a girdle. From her window, Indiana could see between the twin peaks of a wooded mountain opposite that on which their house was built, the white sails on the Indian Ocean. During the silent hours of the day, that spectacle attracted her eyes and gave to her melancholy a fixed and uniform tinge of despair. That splendid sight made her musings bitter and gloomy, instead of casting its poetical influence upon them; and she would lower the curtain that hung at her window and shun the very daylight, in order to shed bitter, scalding tears in the secrecy of her heart.

But when the land breeze began to blow, toward evening, and to bring to her nostrils the fragrance of the flowering rice-fields, she would go forth into the wilderness, leaving Delmare and Ralph on the veranda, to enjoy the aromatic infusion of the *faham* and to loiter over their cigars. She would climb to the top of some accessible peak, the extinct crater of a former volcano, and gaze at the setting sun as it kindled the red vapors of the atmosphere into flame and spread a sort of dust of gold and rubies over the murmuring stalks of the sugar cane and the glistening walls of the cliff. She rarely went down into the gorges of the St. Gilles River, because the sight of the sea, although it distressed her, fascinated her with its magnetic mirage. It seemed to her that beyond those waves and that distant haze the magic apparition of another land would burst upon her gaze. Sometimes the clouds on the shore assumed strange forms in her eyes: at one time she would see a white wave rise upon the ocean and describe a gigantic line which she took for the facade of the Louvre; again two square sails would emerge suddenly from the mist and recall to her mind the towers of Notre-Dame at Paris, when the Seine sends up a dense mist which surrounds their foundations and leaves them as if suspended in the sky; at other times there were patches of pink clouds which, in their changing shapes, imitated all the caprices of architecture in a great city. That woman's mind slumbered in the illusions of the past, and she would quiver with joy at sight of that magnificent Paris, whose realities were connected with the most unhappy period of her life. A curious sort of vertigo would take possession of her brain. Standing at a great height above the shore, and watching the gorges that separated her from the ocean recede before her eyes, it seemed as if she were flying swiftly through space toward the fascinating city of her imagination. Dreaming thus, she would cling to the rock against which she was leaning, and to one who had at such times seen her eager eyes, her bosom heaving with impatient longing and the horrifying expression of joy on her face, she would have seemed to manifest all the symptoms of madness. And yet those were her hours of pleasure, the only moments of well-being to which she looked forward hopefully during the day. If her husband had taken it into his head to forbid these solitary walks, I do not know what thought she would have lived upon; for in her everything centred in a certain faculty of inventing allusions, in an eager striving toward a point which was neither memory, nor anticipation, nor hope, nor regret, but longing in all its devouring intensity. Thus she lived for weeks and months beneath the tropical sky, recognizing, loving, caressing but one shade, cherishing but one chimera.

Ralph, for his part, was attracted to gloomy, secluded spots in his walks, where the wind from the sea could not reach him; for the sight of the ocean had become as antipathetic to him as the thought of crossing it again. France held only an accursed place in his heart's memory. There it was that he had been unhappy to the point of losing courage, accustomed as he was to unhappiness and patient with his misery. He strove with all his might to forget it; for, although he was intensely disgusted with life, he wished to live as long as he should feel that he was necessary. He was very careful therefore never to utter a word relating to the time he had passed in that country. What would he not have given to tear that ghastly memory from Madame Delmare's mind! But he had so little confidence of his ability, he felt that he was so awkward, so lacking in eloquence, that he avoided her instead of trying to divert her thoughts. In the excess of his delicate reserve, he continued to maintain the outward appearance of indifference and selfishness. He went off and suffered alone, and, to see him scouring woods and mountains in pursuit of birds and insects, one would have taken him for a naturalist sportsman engrossed by his innocent passion and utterly indifferent to the passions of the heart that were stirring in his neighborhood. And yet hunting and study were merely the pretext behind which he concealed his long and bitter reveries.

This conical island is split at the base on all sides and conceals in its embrasures deep gorges through which flow pure and turbulent streams. One of these gorges is called Bernica. It is a picturesque spot, a sort of deep and narrow valley, hidden between two perpendicular walls of rock, the surface of which is studded with clumps of saxatile shrubs and tufts of ferns.

A stream flows in the narrow trough formed by the meeting of the two sides. At the point where they meet it plunges down into frightful depths, and, where it falls, forms a basin surrounded by reeds and covered with a damp mist. Around its banks and along the edges of the tiny stream fed by the overflow of the basin grow bananas and oranges, whose dark and healthy green clothe the inner walls of the gorge. Thither Ralph fled to avoid the heat and companionship. All his walks led to that favorite goal; the cool, monotonous plash of the waterfall lulled his melancholy to sleep, When his heart was torn by the secret agony so long concealed, so cruelly misunderstood, it was there that he expended in unknown tears, in silent lamentations, the useless energy of his heart and the concentrated activity of his youth.

In order that you may understand Ralph's character, it will be well to tell you that at least half of his life had been passed in the depths of that ravine. Thither he had gone, in his early childhood, to steel his courage against the injustice with which he had been treated in his family. It was there that he had put forth all the energies of his soul to endure the destiny arbitrarily imposed upon him, and that he had acquired the habit of stoicism which he had carried to such a point that it had become a second nature to him. There too, in his youth, he had carried little Indiana on his shoulders; he had laid her on the grass by the stream while he fished in the clear water or tried to scale the cliff in search of birds' nests.

The only dwellers in that solitude were the gulls, petrels, coots and sea-swallows. Those birds were incessantly flying up and down, hovering overhead or circling about, having chosen the holes and clefts in those inaccessible walls to rear their wild broods. Toward night they would assemble in restless groups and fill the echoing gorge with their hoarse, savage cries. Ralph liked to follow their majestic flight, to listen to their melancholy voices. He taught his little pupil their names and their habits; he showed her the lovely Madagascar teal, with its orange breast and emerald back; he bade her admire the flight of the red-winged tropic-bird, which sometimes strays to those regions and flies in a few hours from Mauritius to Rodrigues, whither, after a journey of two hundred leagues, it returns to sleep under the *veloutier* in which its nest is hidden. The petrel, harbinger of the tempest, also spread its tapering wings over those cliffs; and the queen of the sea, the frigate-bird, with its forked tail, its slate-colored coat and its jagged beak, which lights so rarely that it would seem that the air is its country, and constant movement its nature, raised its cry of distress above all the rest. These wild inhabitants were apparently accustomed to seeing the two children playing about the dwellings, for they hardly condescended to take fright at their approach; and when Ralph reached the shelf on which they had installed their families, they would rise in black clouds and light, as if in derision, a few feet above him. Indiana would laugh at their evolutions, and would carry home, carefully, in her hat of rice-straw, the eggs Ralph had succeeded in stealing for her, and for which he had often to fight stoutly against powerful blows from the wings of the great amphibious creatures.

These memories rushed tumultuously to Ralph's mind, but they were extremely bitter to him; for times had changed greatly, and the little girl who had always been his companion had ceased to be his friend, or at all events was no longer his friend, as formerly, in absolute simpleness of heart. Although she returned his affection, his devotion, his regard, there was one thing which prevented any confidence between them, one memory upon which all the emotions of their lives turned as upon a pivot. Ralph felt that he could not refer to it; he had ventured to do it once, on a day of danger, and his bold act had availed nothing. To recur to it now would be nothing more than cold-blooded barbarity, and Ralph had made up his mind to forgive Raymon, the man for whom he had less esteem than for any man on earth, rather than add to Indiana's sorrow by condemning him according to his own ideas of what justice demanded.

So he held his peace and even avoided her. Although living under the same roof, he had managed so that he hardly saw her except at meals; and yet he watched over her like a mysterious providence. He left the house only when the heat confined her to her hammock; but at night, when she had gone out, he would invent an excuse for leaving Delmare on the veranda and would go and wait for her at the foot of the cliffs where he knew she was in the habit of sitting. He would remain there whole hours, sometimes gazing at her through the branches upon which the moon cast its white light, but respecting the narrow space which separated them, and never venturing to shorten her sad reverie by an instant. When she came down into the valley she always found him on the edge of a little stream along which ran the path to the house. Several broad flat stones, around which the water rippled in silver threads, served him as a seat. When Indiana's white dress appeared on the bank, Ralph would rise silently, offer her his arm and take her back to the house without speaking to her, unless Indiana, being more discouraged and depressed than usual, herself opened the conversation. Then, when he had left her, he would go to his own room and wait until the whole house was asleep before going to bed. If he heard Delmare scolding, Ralph would grasp the first pretext that came to his mind to go to him, and would succeed in pacifying him or diverting his thoughts without ever allowing him to suspect that such was his purpose.

The construction of the house, which was transparent, so to speak, compared with the houses in our climate, and the consequent necessity of being always under the eyes of everybody else, compelled the colonel to put more restraint upon his temper. Ralph's inevitable appearance, at the slightest sound, to stand between him and his wife, forced him to keep a check upon himself; for Delmare had sufficient self-esteem to retain control of himself before that acute but stern censor. And so he waited until the hour for retiring had delivered him from his judge before venting the ill-humor which business vexations had heaped up during the day. But it was of no avail; the secret influence kept vigil with him, and, at the first harsh word, at the first loud tone that was audible through the thin partitions, the sound of moving furniture or of somebody walking about, as if by accident, in Ralph's room, seemed to impose silence on him and to warn him that the silent and patient solicitude of Indiana's protector was not asleep.

PART FOURTH

XXV

Now it happened that the ministry of the 8th of August, which overturned so many things in France, dealt a serious blow at Raymon's security. Monsieur de Ramière was not one of those blindly vain mortals who triumph on a day of victory. He had made politics the mainspring of all his ideas, the basis of all his dreams of the future. He had flattered himself that the king, by adopting a policy of shrewd concessions, would maintain for a long time to come the equilibrium which assured the existence of the noble families. But the rise to power of the Prince de Polignac destroyed that hope. Raymon saw too far ahead, he was too well acquainted with the *new* society not to stand on his guard against momentary triumphs. He understood that his whole future trembled in the balance with that of the monarchy, and that his fortune, perhaps his life, hung by a thread.

Thereupon he found himself in a delicate and embarrassing position. Honor made it his duty to devote himself, despite all the risks of such devotion, to the family whose interests had been thus far closely connected with his own. In that respect he could hardly disregard his conscience and the memory of his forefathers. But this new order of things, this tendency toward an absolute despotism, offended his prudence, his common-sense, and, so he said, his convictions. It compromised his whole existence, it did worse than that, it made him ridiculous, him, a renowned publicist who had ventured so many times to promise, in the name of the crown, justice for all and fidelity to the sworn compact. But now all the acts of the government gave a formal contradiction to the young eclectic politician's imprudent assertions; all the calm and slothful minds who, two days earlier, asked nothing better than to cling to the constitutional throne, began to throw themselves into the opposition and to denounce as rascality the efforts of Raymon and his fellows. The most courteous accused him of lack of foresight and incapacity. Raymon felt that it was humiliating to be considered a dupe after playing such a brilliant rôle in the game. He began secretly to curse and despise this royalty which thus degraded itself and involved him in its downfall; he would have liked to be able to cut loose from it without disgrace before the hour of battle. For some time he made incredible efforts to gain the confidence of both camps. The opposition ranks of that period were not squeamish concerning the admission of new recruits. They needed them, and the credentials they required were so trivial, that they enlisted considerable numbers. Nor did they disdain the support of great names, and day after day adroitly flattering allusions in their newspapers tended to detach the brightest gems from that worn-out crown. Raymon was not deceived by these demonstrations of esteem; but he did not reject them, for he was certain of their utility. On the other hand, the champions of the throne became more intolerant as their situation became more desperate. They drove from their ranks, without prudence and without regard for propriety, their strongest defenders. They soon began to manifest their dissatisfaction and distrust to Raymon. He, in his embarrassment, attached to his reputation as the principal ornament of his existence, was very opportunely taken down with an acute attack of rheumatism, which compelled him to abandon work of every sort for the moment and to go into the country with his mother.

In his isolation Raymon really suffered to feel that he was like a corpse amid the devouring activity of a society on the brink of dissolution, to feel that he was prevented, by his embarrassment as to the color he should assume no less than by illness, from enlisting under the warlike banners that waved on all sides, summoning the most obscure and the least experienced to the great conflict. The intense pains of his malady, solitude, ennui and fever insensibly turned his ideas into another channel. He asked himself, for the first time, perhaps, if society had deserved all the pains he had taken to make himself agreeable to it, and he judged society justly when he saw that it was so indifferent with regard to him, so forgetful of his talents and his glory. Then he took comfort for having been its dupe by assuring himself that he had never sought anything but his personal gratification; and that he had found it there, thanks to himself. Nothing so confirms us in egotism as reflection. Raymon drew this conclusion from it: that man, in the social state, requires two sorts of happiness, happiness in public life and in private life, social triumphs and domestic joys.

His mother, who nursed him assiduously, fell dangerously ill; it was his turn to forget his own sufferings and to take care of her; but his strength was not sufficient. Ardent, passionate souls display miraculous stores of health in times of danger; but lukewarm, indolent souls do not arouse such supernatural outbursts of bodily strength. Although Raymon was a good son, as the phrase is understood in society, he succumbed physically under the weight of fatigue. Lying on his bed of pain, with no one at his pillow save hirelings and now and then a friend who was in haste to return to the excitements of social life, he began to think of Indiana, and he sincerely regretted her, for at that time she would have been most useful to him. He remembered the dutiful attentions she had lavished on her crabbed old husband and he imagined the gentle and beneficent care with which she would have encompassed her lover.

"If I had accepted her sacrifice," he thought, "she would be dishonored; but what would it matter to me now? Abandoned as I am by a frivolous, selfish world, I should not be alone; she whom everybody spurned with contumely would be at my feet, impelled by love; she would weep over my sufferings and would find a way to allay them. Why did I discard that woman? She loved me so dearly that she would have found consolation for the insults of her fellows by bringing a little happiness into my domestic life."

He determined to marry when he recovered, and he mentally reviewed the names and faces that had impressed him in the salons of the two divisions of society. Fascinating apparitions flitted through his dreams; head-dresses laden with flowers, snowy shoulders enveloped in swansdown capes, supple forms imprisoned in muslin or satin: such alluring phantoms fluttered their gauze wings before Raymon's heavy, burning eyes; but he had seen these peris only in the perfumed whirl of the ballroom. On waking, he asked himself whether their rosy lips knew any other smiles than those of coquetry; whether their white hands could dress the wounds of sorrow; whether their refined and brilliant wit could stoop to the painful task of consoling and diverting a horribly bored invalid. Raymon was a man of keen intelligence and he was more distrustful than other men of the coquetry of women; he had a more intense hatred of selfishness because he knew that from a selfish person he could obtain nothing to advance his own happiness. And then Raymon was no less embarrassed concerning the choice of a wife than concerning the choice of his political colors. The same reasons imposed moderation and prudence on him. He belonged to a family of high rank and unbending pride which would brook no mésalliance, and yet wealth could no longer be considered secure except in plebeian hands. According to all appearance that class was destined to rise over the ruins of the other, and in order to maintain oneself on the surface of the movement one must be the son-in-law of a manufacturer or a stock-broker. Raymon concluded therefore that it would be wise to wait and see which way the wind blew before entering upon a course of action which would decide his whole future.

These positive reflections made plain to him the utter lack of affection which characterizes marriages of convenience, so-called, and the hope of having some day a companion worthy of his love entered only incidentally into his prospects of happiness. Meanwhile his illness might be prolonged, and the hope of better days to come does not efface the keen consciousness of present pains. He recurred to the unpleasant thought of his blindness on the day he had declined to kidnap Madame Delmare, and he cursed himself for having comprehended so imperfectly his real interests.

At this juncture he received the letter Indiana wrote him from Ile Bourbon. The sombre and inflexible energy which she retained, amid shocks which might well have crushed her spirit, made a profound impression on Raymon.

"I judged her ill," he thought; "she really loved me, she still loves me; for my sake she would have been capable of those heroic efforts which I considered to be beyond a woman's strength; and now I probably need say but a word to draw her, like an irresistible magnet, from one end of the world to the other. If six months, eight months, perhaps, were not necessary to obtain that result, I would like to make the trial!"

He fell asleep meditating that idea: but he was soon awakened by a great commotion in the next room. He rose with difficulty, put on a dressing-gown, and dragged himself to his mother's apartment. She was very ill.

Toward morning she found strength to talk with him; she was under no illusion as to the brief time she had yet to live and her mind was busy with her son's future.

"You are about to lose your best friend," she said; "may Heaven replace her by a companion worthy of you! But be prudent, Raymon, and do not risk the repose of your whole life for a mere chimera of your ambition. I have known but one woman, alas! whom I should have cared to call my daughter; but Heaven has disposed of her. But listen, my son. Monsieur Delmare is old and broken; who knows if that long voyage did not exhaust the rest of his vitality? Respect his wife as long as he lives; but if, as I believe will be the case, he is summoned soon to follow me to the grave, remember there is still one woman in the world who loves you almost as dearly as your mother loved you."

That evening Madame de Ramière died in her son's arms. Raymon's grief was deep and bitter; in the face of such a loss there could be neither false emotion nor selfish scheming. His mother was really necessary to him; with her he lost all the moral comfort of his life. He shed despairing tears upon her pallid forehead, her lifeless eyes. He maligned Heaven, he cursed his destiny, he wept for Indiana. He called God to account for the happiness He owed him. He reproached Him for treating him like other men and tearing everything from him at once. Then he doubted the existence of this God who chastised him; he chose to deny Him rather than submit to His decrees. He lost all the illusions with all the realities of life; and he returned to his bed of fever and suffering, as crushed and hopeless as a deposed king, as a fallen angel.

When he was nearly restored to health, he cast a glance at the condition of France. Matters were going from bad to worse; on all sides there were threats of refusal to pay taxes. Raymon was amazed at the foolish confidence of his party, and deeming it wise not to plunge into the mêlée as yet, he shut himself up at Cercy with the melancholy memory of his mother and Madame Delmare.

By dint of pondering the idea to which he had attached little importance at its first conception, he accustomed himself to the thought that Indiana was not lost to him, if he chose to take the trouble to beckon her back. He detected many inconveniences in the scheme but many more advantages. It was not in accord with his interest to wait until she was a widow before marrying her, as Madame de Ramière had suggested. Delmare might live twenty years longer, and Raymon did not choose to renounce forever the chance of a brilliant marriage. He conceived a better plan than that in his cheerful and fertile imagination. He could, by taking a little trouble, exert an unbounded influence over his Indiana; he felt that he possessed sufficient mental cunning and knavery to make of that enthusiastic and sublime creature a devoted and submissive mistress. He could shield her from the ferocity of public opinion, conceal her behind the impenetrable wall of his private life, keep her as a precious treasure in the depths of his retreat, and employ her to sweeten his moments of solitude and meditation with the joys of a pure and generous affection. He would not have to exert himself overmuch to escape the husband's wrath; he would not come three thousand leagues in pursuit of his wife when his business interests made his presence absolutely necessary in the other hemisphere. Indiana would demand little in the way of pleasure and liberty after the bitter trials which had bent her neck to the yoke. She was ambitious only for love, and Raymon felt that he would love her from gratitude as soon as she made herself useful to him. He remembered also the constancy and gentleness she had shown during the long days of his coldness and neglect. He promised himself that he would cleverly retain his liberty, so that she would not dare to complain. He flattered himself that he could acquire sufficient control over her convictions to make her consent to anything, even to his marriage; and he based that hope upon numerous examples of secret liaisons which he had known to continue despite the laws of society, by virtue of the prudence and skill with which the parties had succeeded in avoiding the judgment of public opinion.

"Besides," he said to himself, "that woman will have made an irrevocable, boundless sacrifice for me. She will have travelled the world over for me and have left behind her all means of existence—all possibility of pardon. Society is stern and unforgiving only to paltry, commonplace faults. Uncommon audacity takes it by surprise, notorious misfortune disarms it; it will pity, perhaps admire this woman who will have done for me what no other woman would have dared to try. It will blame her, but it will not laugh at her, and I shall not be blamed for taking her in and protecting her after such a signal proof of her love. Perhaps, on the contrary, my courage will be extolled, at all events I shall have defenders, and my reputation will undergo a glorious and indecisive trial. Society likes to be defied sometimes; it does not accord its admiration to those who crawl along the beaten paths. In these days public opinion must be driven with a whip."

Under the influence of these thoughts he wrote to Madame Delmare. His letter was what it was sure to be from the pen of so adroit and experienced a man. It breathed love, grief, and, above all, truth. Alas! what a slender reed the truth is, to bend thus with every breath!

However, Raymon was wise enough not to express the object of his letter in so many words. He pretended to look upon Indiana's return as a joy of which he had no hope; but he had but little to say of her duty. He repeated his mother's last words; he described with much warmth the state of despair to which his loss had reduced him, the ennui of solitude and the danger of his position politically. He drew a dismal and terrifying picture of the revolution that was rising above the horizon, and, while feigning to rejoice that he was to meet its coming alone, he gave Indiana to understand that the moment had come for her to manifest that enthusiastic loyalty, that perilous devotion of which she had boasted so confidently. He cursed his destiny and said that virtue had cost him very dear, that his yoke was very heavy: that he had held happiness in his hand and had

had the strength of will to doom himself to eternal solitude.

"Do not tell me again that you once loved me," he added; "I am so weak and discouraged that I curse my courage and hate my duties. Tell me that you are happy, that you have forgotten me, so that I may have strength not to come and tear you away from the bonds that keep you from me."

In a word, he said that he was unhappy; that was equivalent to telling Indiana that he expected her.

XXVI

During the three months that elapsed between the despatch of this letter and its arrival at Ile Bourbon, Madame Delmare's situation had become almost intolerable, as the result of a domestic incident of the greatest importance to her. She had adopted the depressing habit of writing down every evening a narrative of the sorrowful thoughts of the day. This journal of her sufferings was addressed to Raymon, and, although she had no intention of sending it to him, she talked with him, sometimes passionately, sometimes bitterly, of the misery of her life and of the sentiments which she could not overcome. These papers fell into Delmare's hands, that is to say, he broke open the box which contained them as well as Raymon's letters, and devoured them with a jealous, frenzied eye. In the first outbreak of his wrath he lost the power to restrain himself and went outside, with fast-beating heart and clenched fists, to await her return from her walk. Perhaps, if she had been a few minutes later, the unhappy man would have had time to recover himself; but their evil star decreed that she should appear before him almost immediately. Thereupon, unable to utter a word, he seized her by the hair, threw her down and stamped on her forehead with his heel.

He had no sooner made that bloody mark of his brutal nature upon a poor, weak creature, than he was horrified at what he had done. He fled in dire dismay, and locked himself in his room, where he cocked his pistol preparatory to blowing out his brains; but as he was about to pull the trigger he looked out on the veranda and saw that Indiana had risen and, with a calm, self-possessed air, was wiping away the blood that covered her face. As he thought that he had killed her, his first feeling was of joy when he saw her on her feet; then his wrath blazed up anew.

"It is only a scratch," he cried, "and you deserve a thousand deaths! No, I will not kill myself; for then you would go and rejoice over it in your lover's arms. I do not propose to assure the happiness of both of you; I propose to live to make you suffer, to see you die by inches of deathly ennui, to dishonor the infamous creature who has made a fool of me!"

He was battling with the tortures of jealous rage, when Ralph entered the veranda by another door and found Indiana in the dishevelled condition in which that horrible scene had left her. But she had not manifested the slightest alarm, she had not uttered a cry, she had not raised her hand to ask for mercy. Weary of life as she was, it seemed that she had been desirous to give Delmare time to commit murder by refraining from calling for help. It is certain that when the assault took place

Ralph was within twenty yards, and that he had not heard the slightest sound.

"Indiana!" he cried, recoiling in horror and surprise; "who has wounded you thus?"

"Do you ask?" she replied with a bitter smile; "what other than *your friend* has the *right* and the inclination?"

Ralph dropped the cane he held; he needed no other weapons than his great hands to strangle Delmare. He reached his door in two leaps and burst it open with his fist. But he found Delmare lying on the floor, with purple cheeks and swollen throat, struggling in the noiseless convulsions of apoplexy.

He seized the papers that were scattered over the floor. When he recognized Raymon's handwriting and saw the ruins of the letter-box, he understood what had happened; and, carefully collecting the accusing documents, he hastened to hand them to Madame Delmare and urged her to burn them at once. Delmare had probably not taken time to read them all.

Then he begged her to go to her room while he summoned the slaves to look after the colonel; but she would neither burn the papers nor hide the wound.

"No," she said haughtily, "I will not do it! That man did not scruple to tell Madame de Carvajal of my flight long ago; he made haste to publish what he called my dishonor. I propose to show to everybody this token of his own dishonor which he has taken pains to stamp on my face. It is a strange sort of justice that requires one to keep secret another's crimes, when that other assumes the right to brand one without mercy!"

When Ralph found the colonel was in a condition to listen to him, he heaped reproaches upon him with more energy and severity than one would have thought him capable of exhibiting. Thereupon Delmare, who certainly was not an evil-minded man, wept like a child over what he had done; but he wept without dignity, as a man can do when he abandons himself to the sensation of the moment, without reasoning as to its causes and effects. Prompt to jump to the opposite extreme, he would have called his wife and solicited her pardon; but Ralph objected and tried to make him understand that such a puerile reconciliation would impair the authority of one without wiping out the injury done to the other. He was well aware that there are injuries which are never forgiven and miseries which one can never forget.

From that moment, the husband's personality became hateful in the wife's eyes. All that he did to atone for his treatment of her deprived him of the slight consideration he had retained thus far. He had in very truth made a tremendous mistake; the man who does not feel strong enough to be cold and implacable in his vengeance should abjure all thought of impatience or resentment. There is no possible rôle between that of the Christian who forgives and that of the man of the world who spurns. But Delmare had his share of selfishness too; he felt that he was growing old, that his wife's care was becoming more necessary to him every day. He was terribly afraid of solitude, and if, in the paroxysm of his wounded pride, he recurred to his habits as a soldier and maltreated her, reflection soon led him back to the characteristic weakness of old men, whom the thought of desertion terrifies. Too enfeebled by age and hardships to aspire to become a father, he had remained an old bachelor in his home, and had taken a wife as he would have taken a housekeeper. It was not from affection for her, therefore, that he forgave her for not loving him, but from regard for his own comfort: and if he grieved at his failure to command her affections, it was because he was afraid that he should be less carefully tended in his old age.

When Madame Delmare, for her part, being deeply aggrieved by the operation of the laws of society, summoned all her strength of mind to hate and despise them, there was a wholly personal feeling at the bottom of her thoughts. But it may be that this craving for happiness which consumes us, this hatred of injustice, this thirst for liberty which ends only with life, are the constituent elements of *egotism,* a name by which the English designate love of self, considered as one of the privileges of mankind and not as a vice. It seems to me that the individual who is selected out of all the rest to suffer from the working of institutions that are advantageous to his fellowmen ought, if he has the least energy in his soul, to struggle against this arbitrary yoke. I also think that the greater and more noble his soul is, the more it should rankle and fester under the blows of injustice. If he has ever dreamed that happiness was to be the reward of virtue, into what ghastly doubts, what desperate perplexity must he be cast by the disappointments which experience brings!

Thus all Indiana's reflections, all her acts, all her sorrows were a part of this great and terrible struggle between nature and civilization. If the desert mountains of the island could have concealed her long, she would assuredly have taken refuge among them on the day of the assault upon her; but Bourbon was not of sufficient extent to afford her a secure hiding-place, and she determined to place the sea and uncertainty as to her place of refuge between her tyrant and herself. When she had formed this resolution, she felt more at ease and was almost gay and unconcerned at home. Delmare was so surprised and delighted that he indulged apart in this brutal reasoning: that it was a good thing to make women feel the law of the strongest now and then.

Thereafter she thought of nothing but flight, solitude and independence; she considered in her tortured, grief-stricken brain innumerable plans of a romantic establishment in the deserts of India or Africa. At night she followed the flight of the birds to their resting-place at Ile Rodrigue. That deserted island promised her all the pleasures of solitude, the first craving of a broken heart. But the same reasons that prevented her from flying to the interior of Bourbon caused her to abandon the idea of seeking refuge in the small islands near by. She often met at the house tradesmen from Madagascar, who had business relations with her husband; dull, vulgar, copper-colored fellows who had no tact or shrewdness except in forwarding their business interests. Their stories attracted Madame Delmare's attention, none the less; she enjoyed questioning them concerning the marvelous products of that island, and what they told her of the prodigies performed by nature there intensified more and more the desire that she felt to go and hide herself away there. The size of the island and the fact that Europeans occupied so small a portion of it led her to hope that she would never be discovered. She decided upon that place, therefore, and fed her idle mind upon dreams of a future which she proposed to create for herself, unassisted. She was already building her solitary cabin under the shade of a primeval forest, on the bank of a nameless river; she fancied herself taking refuge under the protection of those savage tribes whom the yoke of our laws and our prejudices has not debased. Ignorant creature that she was, she hoped to find there the virtues that are banished from our hemisphere, and to live in peace, unvexed by any social constitution; she imagined that she could avoid the dangers of isolation, escape the malignant diseases of the climate. A weak woman, who could not endure the anger of one man, but flattered herself that she could defy the hardships of uncivilized life!

Amid these romantic thoughts and extravagant plans she forgot her present ills; she made for herself a world apart, which consoled her for that in which she was compelled to live; she accustomed herself to think less of Raymon, who was soon to cease to be a part of her solitary and philosophical existence. She was so busily occupied in constructing for herself a future according to her fancy that she let the past rest a little; and already, as she felt that her heart was freer and braver, she imagined that she was reaping in advance the fruits of her solitary life. But Raymon's letter arrived, and that edifice of chimeras vanished like a breath. She felt, or fancied that she felt, that she loved him more than before. For my part, I like to think that she never loved him with all the strength of her soul. It seems to me that misplaced affection is as different from requited affection as an error from the truth. It seems to me that, although the excitement and ardor of our sentiments abuse us to the point of believing that that is love in all its power, we learn later, when we taste the delights of a true love, how entirely we deceived ourselves.

But Raymon's situation, as he described it, rekindled in Indiana's heart that generous flame which was a necessity of her nature. Fancying him alone and unhappy, she considered it her duty to forget the past and not to anticipate the future. A few hours earlier, she intended to leave her husband under the spur of hatred and resentment; now, she regretted that she did not esteem him so that she might make a real sacrifice for Raymon's sake. So great was her enthusiasm that she feared that she was doing too little for him in fleeing from an irascible master at the peril of her life, and subjecting herself to the miseries of a four months' voyage. She would have given her life, with the idea that it was too small a price to pay for a smile from Raymon. Women are made that way.

Thus it was simply a question of leaving the island. It was very difficult to elude Delmare's distrust and Ralph's clear-sightedness. But those were not the principal obstacles; it was necessary to avoid giving the notice of her proposed departure, which, according to law, every passenger is compelled to give through the newspapers.

Among the few vessels lying in the dangerous roadstead of Bourbon was the ship *Eugène*, soon to sail for Europe. For a long while Indiana sought an opportunity to speak with the captain without her husband's knowledge, but whenever she expressed a wish to walk down to the port, he ostentatiously placed her in Ralph's charge, and followed them with his own eyes with maddening persistence. However, by dint of picking up with the greatest care every scrap of information favorable to her plan, Indiana learned that the captain of the vessel bound for France had a kinswoman at the village of Saline in the interior of the island, and that he often returned from her house on foot, to sleep on board. From that moment she hardly left the cliff that served as her post of observation. To avert suspicion, she went thither by roundabout paths, and returned in the same way at night when she had failed to discover the person in whom she was interested on the road to the mountains.

She had but two days of hope remaining, for the land-wind had already begun to blow. The anchorage threatened to become untenable, and Captain Random was impatient to be at sea.

However, she prayed earnestly to the God of the weak and oppressed, and went and stationed herself on the very road to Saline, disregarding the danger of being seen, and risking her last hope. She had not been waiting an hour when Captain Random came down the path. He was a genuine sailor, always rough-spoken and cynical, whether he was in good or bad humor; his expression froze Indiana's blood with terror. Nevertheless, she mustered all her courage and walked to meet him with a dignified and resolute air.

"Monsieur," she said, "I place my honor and my life in your hands. I wish to leave the colony and return to France. If, instead of granting me your protection, you betray the secret I confide to you, there is nothing left for me to do but throw myself into the sea."

The captain replied with an oath that the sea would refuse to sink such a pretty lugger, and that, as she had come of her own accord and hove to under his lee, he would promise to tow her to the end of the world.

"You consent then, monsieur?" said Madame Delmare anxiously. "In that case here is the pay for my passage in advance."

And she handed him a casket containing the jewels Madame de Carvajal had given her long before; they were the only fortune that she still possessed. But the sailor had different ideas, and he returned the casket with words that brought the blood to her cheeks.

"I am very unfortunate, monsieur," she replied, restraining the tears of wrath that glistened behind her long lashes; "the proposition I am making to you justifies you in insulting me; and yet, if you knew how odious my life in this country is to me, you would have more pity than contempt for me."

Indiana's noble and touching countenance imposed

respect on Captain Random. Those who do not wear out their natural delicacy by over-use sometimes find it healthy and unimpaired in an emergency. He recalled Colonel Delmare's unattractive features and the sensation that his attack on his wife had caused in the colonies. While ogling with a lustful eye that fragile, pretty creature, he was struck by her air of innocence and sincerity. He was especially moved when he noticed on her forehead a white mark which the deep flush on her face brought out in bold relief. He had had some business relations with Delmare which had left him ill-disposed toward him; he was so close-fisted and unyielding in business matters.

"Damnation!" he cried, "I have nothing but contempt for a man who is capable of kicking such a pretty woman in the face! Delmare's a pirate, and I am not sorry to play this trick on him; but be prudent, madame, and remember that I am compromising my good name. You must make your escape quietly when the moon has set, and fly like a poor petrel from the foot of some sombre reef."

"I know, monsieur," she replied, "that you cannot do me this very great favor without transgressing the law; you may perhaps have to pay a fine; that is why I offer you this casket, the contents of which are worth at least twice the price of a passage."

The captain took the casket with a smile.

"This is not the time to settle our account," he said; "I am willing to take charge of your little fortune. Under the circumstances I suppose you won't have very much luggage; on the night we are to sail, hide among the rocks at the *Anse aux Lataniers;* between one and two o'clock in the morning a boat will come ashore pulled by two stout rowers, and bring you aboard."

XXVII

The day preceding her departure passed away like a dream. Indiana was afraid that it would be long and painful; it seemed to last but a moment. The silence of the neighborhood, the peaceful tranquillity within the house were in striking contrast to the internal agitation by which Madame Delmare was consumed. She locked herself into her room to prepare the few clothes she intended to carry; then she concealed them under her dress and carried them one by one to the rocks at the *Anse aux Lataniers,* where she placed them in a bark basket and buried them in the sand. The sea was rough and the wind increased from hour to hour. As a precautionary measure the *Eugène* had left the roadstead, and Madame Delmare could see in the distance her white sails bellied out by the breeze, as she stood on and off, making short tacks, in order to hold the land. Her heart went out eagerly toward the vessel, which seemed to be pawing the air impatiently, like a race-horse, full of fire and ardor, as the word is about to be given. But when she returned to the interior of the island she found in the mountain gorges a calm, soft atmosphere, bright sunlight, the song of birds and humming of insects, and everything going on as on the day before, heedless of the intense emotions by which she was tortured. Then she could not believe in the reality of her situation, and wondered if her approaching departure were not the illusion of a dream.

Toward night the wind fell. The *Eugène* approached

the shore, and at sunset Madame Delmare on her rocky perch heard the report of a cannon echoing among the cliffs. It was the signal of departure on the following day, on the return of the orb then sinking below the horizon.

After dinner Monsieur Delmare complained of not feeling well. His wife thought that her opportunity had gone, that he would keep the whole house awake all night, and that her plan would be defeated; and then he was suffering, he needed her; that was not the moment to leave him. Thereupon remorse entered her soul and she wondered who would have pity on that old man when she had abandoned him. She shuddered at the thought that she was about to commit what was a crime in her own eyes, and that the voice of conscience would rise even louder than the voice of society, to condemn her. If Delmare, as usual, had harshly demanded her services, if he had displayed an imperious and capricious spirit in his sufferings, resistance would have seemed natural and lawful to the down-trodden slave; but, for the first time in his life, he submitted to the pain with gentleness, and seemed grateful and affectionate to his wife. At ten o'clock he declared that he felt entirely well, insisted that she should go to her own room, and that no one should pay any further attention to him. Ralph, too, assured her that every symptom of illness had disappeared and that a quiet night's sleep was the only remedy that he needed.

When the clock struck eleven all was silent and peaceful in the house. Madame Delmare fell on her knees and prayed, weeping bitterly; for she was about to burden her heart with a grievous sin, and from God alone could come such forgiveness as she could hope to receive. She stole softly into her husband's room. He was sleeping soundly; his features were composed, his breathing regular. As she was about to withdraw, she noticed in the shadows another person asleep in a chair. It was Ralph, who had risen noiselessly and come to watch over her husband in his sleep, to guard against accident.

"Poor Ralph!" thought Indiana; "what an eloquent and cruel reproach to me!"

She longed to wake him, to confess everything to him, to implore him to save her from herself; and then she thought of Raymon.

"One more sacrifice," she said to herself, "and the most cruel of all—the sacrifice of my duty."

Love is woman's virtue; it is for love that she glories in her sins, it is from love that she acquires the heroism to defy her remorse. The more dearly it costs her to commit the crime, the more she will have deserved at the hands of the man she loves. It is like the fanaticism that places the dagger in the hand of the religious enthusiast.

She took from her neck a gold chain which came to her from her mother and which she had always worn; she gently placed it around Ralph's neck, as the last pledge of an everlasting friendship, then lowered the lamp so that she could see her old husband's face once more, and make sure that he was no longer ill. He was dreaming at that moment and said in a faint, sad voice:

"Beware of that man, he will ruin you."

Indiana shuddered from head to foot and fled to her room. She wrung her hands in pitiable uncertainty; then suddenly seized upon the thought that she was no longer acting in her own interest but in Raymon's; that she was going to him, not in search of happiness, but to make him happy, and that, even though she were to be accursed for all eternity, she would be sufficiently recompensed if she embellished her lover's life. She rushed from the house and walked swiftly to the *Anse aux Lataniers,* not daring to turn and look at what she left behind her.

She at once set about disinterring her bark basket and sat upon it, trembling and silent, listening to the whistling of the wind, to the plashing of the waves as they died at her feet, and to the shrill groaning of the *satanite* among the great bunches of seaweed that clung to the steep sides of the cliffs; but all these noises were drowned by the throbbing of her heart, which rang in her ears like a funeral knell.

She waited a long while; she looked at her watch and found that the appointed time had passed. The sea was so high, and navigation about the shores of the island is so difficult in the best of weather, that she was beginning to despair of the courage of the men who were to take her aboard, when she spied on the gleaming waves the black shadow of a *pirogue*, trying to make the land. But the swell was so strong and the sea so rough that the frail craft constantly disappeared, burying itself as it were in the dark folds of a shroud studded with silver stars. She rose and answered their signal several times with cries which the wind whisked away before carrying them to the ears of the oarsmen. At last, when they were near enough to hear her, they pulled toward her with much difficulty; then paused to wait for a wave. As soon as they felt it raise the skiff they redoubled their efforts, and the wave broke and threw them up on the beach.

The ground on which Saint-Paul is built is composed of sea sand and gravel from the mountains, which the Des Galets river brings from a long distance from its mouth by the strength of its current. These heaps of rounded pebbles form submarine mountains near the shore which the waves overthrow and rebuild at their pleasure. Their constant shifting makes it impossible to avoid them, and the skill of the pilot is useless among these constantly appearing and disappearing obstacles. Large vessels lying in the harbor of Saint-Denis often drag their anchors and are cast on shore by the force of the currents; they have no other resource when this off-shore wind begins to blow, and to make the turbulent receding waves perilous, than to put to sea as quickly as possible, and that is what the *Eugène* had done.

The skiff bore Indiana and her fortunes amid the wild waves, the howling of the storm and the oaths of the two rowers, who had no hesitation in cursing loudly the danger to which they exposed themselves for her sake. Two hours ago, they said, the ship should have been under way, and on her account the captain had obstinately refused to give the order. They added divers insulting and cruel reflections, but the unhappy fugitive consumed her shame in silence; and when one of them suggested to the other that they might be punished if they were lacking in the respect they had been ordered to pay the *captain's mistress:*

"Never you fear!" was the reply; "the sharks are the lads we've got to settle accounts with this night. If we ever see the captain again, I don't believe he'll be any uglier than them."

"Talking of sharks," said the first, "I don't know whether one of 'em has got scent of us already, but I can see a face in our wake that don't belong to a Christian."

"You fool! to take a dog's face for a sea-wolf's! Hold! my four-legged passenger, we forgot you and left you on shore; but, blast my eyes, if you shall eat up the ship's biscuit! Our orders only mentioned a young woman, nothing was said about a cur——"

As he spoke he raised his oar to hit the beast on the head; but Madame Delmare, casting her tearful, distraught eyes upon the sea, recognized her beautiful Ophelia, who had found her scent on the rocks and was swimming after her. As the sailor was about to strike her, the waves, against which she was struggling painfully, carried her away from the skiff, and her mistress heard her moaning with impatience and exhaustion. She begged the oarsmen to take her into the boat and they pretended to comply; but, as the faithful beast approached, they dashed out her brains with loud shouts of laughter, and Indiana saw before her the dead body of the creature who had loved her better than Raymon. At the same time a huge wave drew the skiff down as it were into the depths of an abyss, and the laughter of the sailors changed to imprecations and yells of terror. However, thanks to its buoyancy and lightness the *pirogue* righted itself like a duck and climbed to the summit of the wave, to plunge into another ravine and mount again to another foaming crest. As they left the shore behind, the sea became less rough, and soon the skiff flew along swiftly and without danger toward the ship. Thereupon, the oarsmen recovered their good humor and with it the power of reflection. They strove to atone for their brutal treatment of Indiana; but their cajolery was more insulting than their anger.

"Come, come, my young lady," said one of them, "take courage, you're safe now; of course the captain will give us a glass of the best wine in the locker for the pretty parcel we've fished up for him."

The other affected to sympathize with the young lady because her clothes were wet; but, he said, the captain was waiting for her and would take good care of her. Indiana listened to their remarks in deadly terror, without speaking or moving; she realized the horror of her situation, and could see no other way of escaping the outrages which awaited her than to throw herself into the sea. Two or three times she was on the point of jumping out of the boat; but she recovered courage, a sublime courage, with the thought:

"It is for him, Raymon, that I suffer all these indignities. I must live though I were crushed with shame!"

She put her hand to her oppressed heart and touched the hilt of a dagger which she had concealed there in the morning, with a sort of instinctive prevision of danger. The possession of that weapon restored all her confidence; it was a short, pointed stiletto, which her father used to carry; an old Spanish weapon which had belonged to a Medina-Sidonia, whose name was cut on the blade, with the date 1300. Doubtless it had rusted in noble blood, had washed out more than one affront, punished more than one insolent knave. With it in her possession, Indiana felt that she became a Spaniard once more, and she went aboard the ship with a resolute heart, saying to herself that a woman incurred no risk so long as she had a sure means of taking her own life before submitting to dishonor. She avenged herself for the harsh treatment of her guides only by rewarding them handsomely for their fatigue; then she went to her cabin and anxiously awaited the hour of departure.

At last the day broke, and the sea was covered with small boats bringing the passengers aboard. Indiana looked with terror through the port-hole at the faces of those who came aboard the *Eugène;* she dreaded lest she should see her husband, coming to claim her. At last the echoes of the last gun died away on the island which had been her prison. The ship began to cut her way through the waves, and the sun, rising from the ocean, cast its cheerful, rosy light on the white peaks of the Salazes as they sank lower and lower on the horizon.

When they were a few leagues from port, a sort of comedy was played on board to avoid a confession of trickery. Captain Random pretended to discover Madame Delmare on his vessel; he feigned surprise, questioned the sailors, went through the form of losing his temper and of quieting down again, and ended by drawing up a report of the finding of a *stowaway* on board; that is the technical term used on such occasions.

Allow me to go no farther with the story of this voyage. It will be enough for me to tell you, for Captain Random's justification, that, despite his rough training, he had enough natural good sense to understand Madame Delmare's character very quickly; he ventured upon very few attempts to abuse her unprotected condition and eventually was touched by it and acted as her friend and protector. But that worthy man's loyal behavior and Indiana's dignity did not restrain the comments of the crew, the mocking glances, the insulting suspicions and the broad and stinging jests. These were the real torments of the unhappy woman during that journey, for I say nothing of the fatigue, the discomforts, the dangers, the tedium and the sea-sickness; she paid no heed to them.

XXVIII

Three days after the despatch of his letter to Ile Bourbon, Raymon had entirely forgotten both the letter and its purpose. He had felt decidedly better and had ventured to make a visit in the neighborhood. The estate of Lagny, which Monsieur Delmare had left to be sold for the benefit of his creditors, had been purchased by a wealthy manufacturer, Monsieur Hubert, a shrewd and estimable man, not like all wealthy manufacturers, but like a small number of the newly-rich. Raymon found the new owner comfortably settled in that house which recalled so many memories. He took pleasure in giving a free rein to his emotion as he wandered through the garden where Noun's light footprints seemed to be still visible on the gravel, and through those great rooms which seemed still to retain the echoes of Indiana's soft words; but soon the presence of a new hostess changed the current of his thoughts.

In the main salon, on the spot where Madame Delmare was accustomed to sit and work, a tall, slender young woman, with a glance that was at once pleasant and mischievous, caressing and mocking, sat before an easel, amusing herself by copying in water-colors the odd hangings on the walls. The copy was a fascinating thing, a delicate satire instinct with the bantering yet refined nature of the artist. She had amused herself by exaggerating the pretentious finicalness of the old frescoes; she had grasped the false and shifting character of the age of Louis XIV. on those stilted figures. While refreshing the colors that time had faded, she had restored their affected graces, their perfume of courtiership, their costumes of the boudoir and the shepherd's hut, so curiously identical. Beside that work of historical raillery she had written the word *copy*.

She raised her long eyes, instinct with merriment of a caustic, treacherous, yet attractive sort, slowly to Raymon's face. For some reason she reminded him of Shakespeare's Anne Page. There was in her manner neither timidity nor boldness, nor affectation, nor self-distrust. Their conversation turned upon the influence of fashion in the arts.

"Is it not true, monsieur, that the moral coloring of the period was in that brush?" she said, pointing to the wainscoting, covered with rustic cupids after the style of Boucher. "Isn't it true that those sheep do not walk or sleep or browse like sheep of to-day? And that pretty landscape, so false and so orderly, those clumps of many-petalled roses in the middle of the forest where naught but a bit of eglantine grows in our days, those tame birds of a species that has apparently disappeared, and those pink satin gowns which the sun never faded—is there not in all these a deal of poesy, ideas of luxury and pleasure, of a whole useless, harmless, joyous life? Doubtless these absurd fictions were quite as valuable as our gloomy political deliverances! If only I had been born in those days!" she added with a smile; "frivolous and narrow-minded creature that I am, I should have been much better fitted to paint fans and produce masterpieces of thread-work than to read the newspapers and understand the debates in the Chambers!"

Monsieur Hubert left the young people together; and their conversation drifted from one subject to another, until it fell at last upon Madame Delmare.

"You were very intimate with our predecessors in this house," said the young woman, "and it is generous on your part to come and see new faces here. Madame Delmare," she added, with a penetrating glance at him, "was a remarkable woman, so they say; she must have left memories here which place us at a disadvantage, so far as you are concerned."

"She was an excellent woman," Raymon replied, unconcernedly, "and her husband was a worthy man."

"But," rejoined the reckless girl, "she was something more than an excellent woman, I should judge. If I remember rightly there was a charm about her personality which calls for a more enthusiastic and more poetic description. I saw her two years ago, at a ball at the Spanish ambassador's. She was fascinating that night; do you remember?"

Raymon started at this reminder of the evening that he spoke to Indiana for the first time. He remembered at the same moment that he had noticed at that ball the distingué features and clever eyes of the young woman with whom he was now talking; but he did not then ask who she was.

Not until he had taken his leave of her and was congratulating Monsieur Hubert on his daughter's charms, did he learn her name.

"I have not the good fortune to be her father," said the manufacturer; "but I did the best I could by adopting her. Do you not know my story?"

"I have been ill for several months," Raymon replied, "and have heard nothing of you beyond the good you have already done in the province."

"There are people," said Monsieur Hubert with a smile, "who consider that I did a most meritorious thing in adopting Mademoiselle de Nangy; but you, monsieur, who have elevated ideas, will judge whether I did anything more than true delicacy required. Ten years ago, a widower and childless, I found myself possessed of funds to a considerable amount, the results of my labors, which I was anxious to invest. I found that the estate and château of Nangy in Bourgogne, national property, were for sale and suited me perfectly. I had been in possession some time when I learned that the former lord of the manor and his seven-year-old granddaughter were living in a hovel, in extreme destitution. The old man had received some indemnity, but he had religiously devoted it to the payment of debts incurred during the emigration. I tried to better his condition and to give him a home in my house; but he had retained in his poverty all the pride of his rank. He refused to return to the house of his ancestors as an object of charity, and died shortly after my arrival, having steadfastly refused to accept any favors at my hands. Then I took his child there. The little patrician was proud already and accepted my assistance most unwillingly; but at that age prejudices are not deeply rooted and resolutions do not last long. She soon accustomed herself to look upon me as her father and I brought her up as my own daughter. She has rewarded me handsomely by the happiness she has showered on my old age. And so, to make sure of my happiness, I have adopted Mademoiselle de Nangy, and my only hope now is to find her a husband worthy of her and able to manage prudently the property I shall leave her."

Encouraged by the interest with which Raymon listened to his confidences, the excellent man, in true bourgeois fashion, gradually confided all his business affairs to him. His attentive auditor found that he had a fine, large fortune administered with the most minute care, and which simply awaited a younger proprietor, of more fashionable tastes than the worthy Hubert, to shine forth in all its splendor. He felt that he might be the man destined to perform that agreeable task, and he gave thanks to the ingenious fate which reconciled all his interests by offering him, by favor of divers romantic incidents, a woman of his own rank possessed of a fine plebeian fortune. It was a chance not to be let slip, and he put forth all his skill in the effort to grasp it. Moreover, the heiress was charming; Raymon became more kindly disposed toward his providence.

As for Madame Delmare, he would not think of her. He drove away the fears which the thought of his letter aroused from time to time; he tried to persuade himself that poor Indiana would not grasp his meaning or would not have the courage to respond to it; and he finally succeeded in deceiving himself and believing that he was not blameworthy, for Raymon would have been horrified to find that he was selfish. He was not one of those artless villains who come on the stage to make a naïve confession of their vices to their own hearts. Vice is not reflected in its own ugliness, or it would frighten itself; and Shakespeare's Iago, who is so true to life in his acts, is false in his words, being forced by our stage conventions to lay bare himself the secret recesses of his deep and tortuous heart. Man rarely tramples his conscience under foot thus coolly. He turns it over, squeezes it, pinches it, disfigures it; and when he has distorted it and exhausted it and worn it out, he carries it about with him as an indulgent and obliging mentor which accommodates itself to his passions and his interests, but which he pretends always to consult and to fear.

He went often to Lagny, therefore, and his visits were agreeable to Monsieur Hubert; for, as you know, Raymon had the art of winning affection, and soon the rich bourgeois's one desire was to call him his son-in-law. But he wished that his adopted daughter should choose him freely and that they should be allowed every opportunity to know and judge each other.

Laure de Nangy was in no haste to assure Raymon's happiness; she kept him perfectly balanced between fear and hope. Being less generous than Madame Delmare, but more adroit, distant yet flattering, haughty yet cajoling, she was the very woman to subjugate Raymon; for she was as superior to him in cunning as he was to Indiana. She soon realized that her admirer craved her fortune much more than herself. Her placid imagination anticipated nothing better in the way of homage; she had too much sense, too much knowledge of the world to dream of love when two millions were at stake. She had chosen her course calmly and philosophically, and she was not inclined to blame Raymon; she did not hate him because he was of a calculating, unsentimental temper like the age in which he lived; but she knew him too well to love him. She made it a matter of pride not to fall below the standard of that cold and scheming epoch; her self-esteem would have suffered had she been swayed by the foolish illusions of an ignorant boarding-school miss; she would have blushed at being deceived as at being detected in a foolish act; in a word, she made her heroism consist in steering clear of love, as Madame Delmare's consisted in sacrificing everything to it.

Mademoiselle de Nangy was fully resolved, therefore, to submit to marriage as a social necessity; but she took a malicious pleasure in making use of the liberty which still belonged to her, and in imposing her authority for some time on the man who aspired to deprive her of it. No youth, no sweet dreams, no brilliant and deceptive future for that girl, who was doomed to undergo all the miseries of wealth. For her, life was a matter of stoical calculation, happiness a childish delusion against which she must defend herself as a weakness and an absurdity.

While Raymon was at work building up his fortune, Indiana was drawing near the shores of France. But imagine her surprise and alarm, when she landed, to see the tri-colored flag floating on the walls of Bordeaux! The city was in a state of violent agitation; the prefect had been almost murdered the night before; the populace were rising on all sides; the garrison seemed to be preparing for a bloody conflict, and the result of the revolution was still unknown.

"I have come too late!" was the thought that fell upon Madame Delmare like a stroke of lightning.

In her alarm she left on board the little money and the few clothes that she possessed, and ran about through the city in a state of frenzy. She tried to find a diligence for Paris, but the public conveyances were crowded with people who were either escaping or going to claim a share in the spoils of the vanquished. Not until evening did she succeed in finding a place. As she was stepping into the coach an improvised patrol of National Guards objected to the departure of the passengers and demanded to see their papers. Indiana had none. While she argued against the absurd suspicions of the triumphant party, she heard it stated all about her that the monarchy had fallen, that the king was a fugitive, and that the ministers had been massacred with all their adherents. This news, proclaimed with laughter and stamping and shouts of joy, dealt Madame Delmare a deadly blow. In the whole revolution she was personally interested in but one fact; in all France she knew but one man. She fell on the ground in a swoon, and came to herself in a hospital—several days later.

After two months she was discharged, without money or linen or effects, weak and trembling, exhausted by an inflammatory brain fever which had caused her life to be despaired of several times. When she found herself in the street, alone, hardly able to walk, without friends, resources or strength, when she made an effort to recall the particulars of her situation and realized that she was hopelessly lost in that great city, she had an indescribable thrill of terror and despair as she thought that Raymon's fate had long since been decided and that there was not a solitary person about her who could put an end to her horrible uncertainty. The horror of desertion bore down with all its might upon her crushed spirit, and the apathetic despair born of hopeless misery gradually deadened all her faculties. In the mental numbness which she felt stealing over her, she dragged herself to the harbor, and, shivering with fever, sat down on a stone to warm herself in the sunshine, gazing listlessly at the water plashing at her feet. She sat there several hours, devoid of energy, of hope, of purpose; but suddenly she remembered her clothes and her money, which she had left on the *Eugène*, and which she might possibly recover; but it was nightfall, and she dared not go among the sailors who were just leaving their work with much rough merriment and question them concerning the ship. Desiring, on the other hand, to avoid the attention she was beginning to attract, she left the quay and concealed herself in the ruins of a house recently demolished behind the great esplanade of Les Quinconces. There, cowering in a corner, she passed that cold October night, a night laden with bitter thoughts and alarms. At last the day broke; hunger made itself felt insistent and implacable. She decided to ask alms. Her clothes, although in wretched condition, still indicated more comfortable circumstances than a beggar is supposed to enjoy. People looked at her curiously, suspiciously, ironically, and gave her nothing. Again she dragged herself to the quays, inquired about the *Eugène* and learned from the first waterman she addressed that she was still in the roadstead. She hired him to put her aboard and found Random at breakfast.

"Well, well, my fair passenger," he cried, "so you have returned from Paris already! You have come in good time, for I sail to-morrow. Shall I take you back to Bourbon?"

He informed Madame Delmare that he had caused search to be made for her everywhere, that he might return what belonged to her. But Indiana had not a scrap of paper upon her from which her name could be learned when she was taken to the hospital. She had been entered on the books there and also on the police books under the designation *unknown;* so the captain had been unable to learn anything about her.

The next day, despite her weakness and exhaustion, Indiana started for Paris. Her anxiety should have diminished when she saw the turn political affairs had taken; but anxiety does not reason, and love is fertile in childish fears.

On the very evening of her arrival at Paris she hurried to Raymon's house and questioned the concierge in an agony of apprehension.

"Monsieur is quite well," was the reply; "he is at Lagny."

"At Lagny! you mean at Cercy, do you not?"

"No, madame, at Lagny, which he owns now."

"Dear Raymon!" thought Indiana, "he has bought

that estate to afford me a refuge where public malice cannot reach me. He knew that I would come!"

Drunk with joy, she hastened, light of heart and instinct with new life, to take apartments in a furnished house, and devoted the night and part of the next day to rest. It was so long since the unfortunate creature had enjoyed a peaceful sleep! Her dreams were sweet and deceptive, and when she woke she did not regret them, for she found hope at her pillow. She dressed with care; she knew that Raymon was particular about all the minutiæ of the toilet, and she had ordered the night before a pretty new dress which was brought to her just as she rose. But, when she was ready to arrange her hair, she sought in vain the long and magnificent tresses she had once had; during her illness they had fallen under the nurse's shears. She noticed it then for the first time, her all-engrossing thoughts had diverted her mind so completely from small things.

Nevertheless, when she had curled her short black locks about her pale and melancholy brow, when she had placed upon her shapely head a little English hat, called then, by way of allusion to the recent blow to great fortunes, a *three per cent.*; when she had fastened at her girdle a bunch of the flowers whose perfume Raymond loved, she hoped that she would still find favor in his sight; for she was as pale and fragile as in the first days of their acquaintance, and the effect of her illness had effaced the traces of the tropical sunshine.

She hired a cab in the afternoon and arrived about nine at night at a village on the outskirts of Fontainebleau. There she ordered the driver to put up his horse and wait for her until the next day, and started off alone, on foot, by a path which led to Lagny park by a walk of less than quarter of an hour through the woods. She tried to open the small gate but found it locked on the inside. It was her wish to enter by stealth, to avoid the eyes of the servants and take Raymon by surprise. She skirted the park wall. It was quite old; she remembered that there were frequent breaches, and, by good luck, she found one and passed over without much difficulty.

When she stood upon ground which belonged to Raymon and was to be thenceforth her refuge, her sanctuary, her fortress and her home, her heart leaped for joy. With light, triumphant foot she hastened along the winding paths she knew so well. She reached the English garden, which was dark and deserted on that side. Nothing was changed in the flower-beds; but the bridge, the painful sight of which she dreaded, had disappeared, and the course of the stream had been altered; the spots which might have recalled Noun's death had been changed, and no others.

"He wished to banish that cruel memory," thought Indiana. "He was wrong, I could have endured it. Was it not for my sake that he planted the seeds of remorse in his life? Henceforth we are quits, for I too have committed a crime. I may have caused my husband's death. Raymon can open his arms to me, we will take the place of innocence and virtue to each other."

She crossed the stream on boards laid across where a bridge was to be built and passed through the flower-garden. She was forced to stop, for her heart was beating as if it would burst; she looked up at the windows of her old bedroom. O bliss! a light was shining through the blue curtains, Raymon was there. As if he could occupy any other room! The door to the secret stairway was open.

"He expects me at any time," she thought; "he will be happy but not surprised."

At the top of the staircase she paused again to take breath; she felt less strong to endure joy than sorrow. She stooped and looked through the keyhole. Raymon was alone, reading. It was really he, it was Raymon overflowing with life and vigor; his trials had not aged him, the tempests of politics had not taken a single hair from his head; there he sat, placid and handsome, his head resting on his white hand which was buried in his black hair.

Indiana impulsively tried the door, which opened without resistance.

"You expected me!" she cried, falling on her knees and resting her feeble head upon Raymon's bosom; "you counted the months and days, you knew that the time had passed, but you knew too that I could not fail to come at your call. You called me and I am here, I am here! I am dying!"

Her ideas became tangled in her brain; for some time she knelt there, silent, gasping for breath, incapable of speech or thought. Then she opened her eyes, recognized Raymon as if just waking from a dream, uttered a cry of frantic joy, and pressed her lips to his, wild, ardent and happy. He was pale, dumb, motionless, as if struck by lightning.

"Speak to me, in Heaven's name," she cried; "it is I, your Indiana, your slave whom you recalled from exile and who has travelled three thousand leagues to love you and serve you; it is your chosen companion, who has left everything, risked everything, defied everything, to bring you this moment of joy! You are happy, you are content with her, are you not? I am waiting for my reward; with a word, a kiss I shall be paid a hundred fold."

But Raymon did not reply; his admirable presence of

mind had abandoned him. He was crushed with surprise, remorse and terror when he saw that woman at his feet; he hid his face in his hands and longed for death.

"My God! my God! you don't speak to me, you don't kiss me, you have nothing to say to me!" cried Madame Delmare, pressing Raymon's knees to her breast; "is it because you cannot? Joy makes people ill, it kills sometimes, I know! Ah! you are not well, you are suffocating, I surprised you too suddenly! Try to look at me; see how pale I am, how old I have grown, how I have suffered! But it was for you, and you will love me all the better for it! Say one word to me, Raymon, just one."

"I would like to weep," said Raymon in a stifled tone.

"And so would I," said she, covering his hands with kisses. "Ah! yes, that would do you good. Weep, weep on my bosom, and I will wipe your tears away with my kisses. I have come to bring you happiness, to be whatever you choose—your companion, your servant or your mistress. Formerly I was very cruel, very foolish, very selfish. I made you suffer terribly, and I refused to understand that I demanded what was beyond your strength. But since then I have reflected, and as you are not afraid to defy public opinion with me, I have no right to refuse to make any sacrifice. Dispose of me, of my blood, of my life, as you will; I am yours body and soul. I have travelled three thousand leagues to tell you this, to give myself to you. Take me, I am your property, you are my master."

I cannot say what infernal project passed rapidly through Raymon's brain. He removed his clenched hands from his face and looked at Indiana with diabolical *sang-froid;* then a wicked smile played about his lips and made his eyes gleam, for Indiana was still lovely.

"First of all, we must conceal you," he said, rising.

"Why conceal me here?" she said; "aren't you at liberty to take me in and protect me, who have no one but you on earth, and who, without you, shall be compelled to beg on the public highway? Why, even society can no longer call it a crime for you to love me; I have taken everything on my own shoulders! But where are you going?" she cried, as she saw him walking toward the door.

She clung to him with the terror of a child who does not wish to be left alone a single instant, and dragged herself along on her knees behind him.

His purpose was to lock the door; but he was too late. The door opened before he could reach it, and Laure de Nangy entered. She seemed less surprised than exasperated, and did not utter an exclamation, but stooped a little to look with snapping eyes at the half-fainting woman on the floor; then, with a cold, bitter, scornful smile, she said:

"Madame Delmare, you seem to enjoy placing three persons in a very strange situation; but I thank you for assigning me the least ridiculous rôle of the three, and this is how I discharge it. Be good enough to retire."

Indignation renewed Indiana's strength; she rose and drew herself up to her full height.

"Who is this woman, pray?" she said to Raymon, "and by what right does she give me orders in your house?"

"You are in my house, madame," retorted Laure.

"Speak, in heaven's name, monsieur," cried Indiana fiercely, shaking the wretched man's arm; "tell me whether she is your mistress or your wife!"

"She is my wife," Raymon replied with a dazed air.

"I forgive your uncertainty," said Madame de Ramière with a cruel smile. "If you had remained where your duty required you to remain, you would have received cards to monsieur's marriage. Come, Raymon," she added in a tone of sarcastic amiability, "I am moved to pity by your embarrassment. You are rather young; you will realize now, I trust, that more prudence is advisable. I leave it for you to put an end to this absurd scene. I would laugh at it if you didn't look so utterly wretched."

With that she withdrew, well satisfied with the dignity she had displayed, and secretly triumphant because the incident had placed her husband in a position of inferiority and dependence with regard to her.

When Indiana recovered the use of her faculties she was alone in a close carriage, being driven rapidly toward Paris.

XXIX

The carriage stopped at the barrier. A servant whom Madame Delmare recognized as a man who had formerly been in Raymon's service came to the door and asked where he should leave *madame*. Indiana instinctively gave the name and street number of the lodging-house at which she had slept the night before. On arriving there, she fell into a chair and remained there until morning, without a thought of going to bed, without moving, longing for death but too crushed, too inert to summon strength to kill herself. She believed that it was impossible to live after such terrible blows, and that death would of its own motion come in search of her. She remained there all the following day, taking no sustenance, making no reply to the offers of service that were made her.

I do not know that there is anything more horrible on earth than life in a furnished lodging-house in Paris, especially when it is situated, as this one was, in a dark, narrow street, and only a dull, hazy light crawls regretfully, as it were, over the smoky ceilings and soiled windows. And then there is something chilly and repellent in the sight of the furniture to which you are unaccustomed and to which your idle glance turns in vain for a memory, a touch of sympathy. All those objects which belong, so to speak, to no one, because they belong to all comers; that room where no one has left any trace of his passage save now and then a strange name, found on a card in the mirror-frame; that mercenary roof, which has sheltered so many poor travellers, so many lonely strangers, with hospitality for none; which looks with indifference upon so many human agitations and can describe none of them: the discordant, never-ending noise from the street, which does not even allow you to sleep and thus escape grief or ennui: all these are causes of disgust and irritation even to one who does not bring to the horrible place such a frame of mind as Madame Delmare's. You ill-starred provincial, who have left your fields, your blue sky, your verdure, your house and your family, to come and shut yourself up in this dungeon of the mind and the heart—see Paris, lovely Paris, which in your dreams has seemed to you such a marvel of beauty! see it stretch away yonder, black with mud and rainy, as noisy and pestilent and rapid as a torrent of slime! There is the perpetual revel, always brilliant and perfumed, which was promised you; there are the intoxicating pleasures, the wonderful surprises, the treasures of sight and taste and hearing which were to contend for the possession of your passions and faculties, which are of limited capacity and powerless to enjoy them all at once! See, yonder, the affable, winning, hospitable Parisian, as he was described to you, always in a hurry, always careworn! Tired out before you have seen the whole of this ever-moving population, this inextricable labyrinth, you take refuge, overwhelmed with dismay, in the cheerful precincts of a furnished lodging-house, where, after hastily installing you, the only servant of a house that is often of immense size leaves you to die in peace, if fatigue or sorrow deprive you of the strength to attend to the thousand necessities of life.

But to be a woman and to find oneself in such a place, spurned by everybody, three thousand leagues from all human affection; to be without money, which is much worse than being abandoned in a vast desert without water; to have in all one's past not a single happy memory that is not poisoned or withered, in the whole future not a single hope to divert one's thoughts from the emptiness of the present, is the last degree of misery and hopelessness. And so Madame Delmare, making no attempt to contend against a destiny that was fulfilled, against a broken, ruined life, submitted to the gnawings of hunger, fever and sorrow without uttering a complaint, without shedding a tear, without making an effort to die an hour earlier, to suffer an hour less.

They found her on the morning of the second day, lying on the floor, stiff with cold, with clenched teeth, blue lips and lustreless eyes; but she was not dead. The landlady examined her secretary and, seeing how poorly supplied it was, considered whether the hospital was not the proper place for this stranger, who certainly had not the means to pay the expenses of a long and costly illness. However, as she was a woman *overflowing with humanity,* she caused her to be put to bed and sent for a doctor to ascertain if the illness would last more than a day or two.

A doctor appeared who had not been sent for. Indiana, on opening her eyes, found him beside her bed. I need not tell you his name.

"Oh! you here! you here!" she cried, throwing herself, almost fainting, on his breast. "You are my good angel! But you come too late, and I can do nothing for you except to die blessing you."

"You will not die, my dear," replied Ralph with deep emotion; "life may still smile upon you. The laws which interfered with your happiness no longer fetter your affection. I would have preferred to destroy the invincible spell which a man whom I neither like nor esteem has cast upon you; but that is not in my power, and I am tired of seeing you suffer. Hitherto your life has been perfectly frightful; it cannot be more so. Besides, even if my gloomy forebodings are realized and the happiness of which you have dreamed is destined to be of short duration, you will at least have enjoyed it for some little time, you will not die without a taste of it. So I sacrifice all my repugnance and dislike. The destiny which casts you, all alone as you are, into my arms, imposes upon me the duties of a father and a guardian toward you. I come to tell you that you are free and that you may unite your lot to Monsieur de Ramière's. Delmare is no more."

Tears rolled slowly down Ralph's cheeks while he was

speaking. Indiana suddenly sat up in bed and cried, wringing her hands in despair:

"My husband is dead! and it was I who killed him! And you talk to me of the future and happiness, as if such a thing were possible for the heart that detests and despises itself! But be sure that God is just and that I am cursed. Monsieur de Ramière is married."

She fell back, utterly exhausted, into her cousin's arms. They were unable to resume conversation until several hours later.

"Your justly disturbed conscience may be set at rest," said Ralph, in a solemn, but sad and gentle tone. "Delmare was at death's door when you deserted him: he did not wake from the sleep in which you left him, he never knew of your flight, he died without cursing you or weeping for you. Toward morning, when I woke from the heavy sleep into which I had fallen beside his bed, I found his face purple and he was burning hot and breathing stertorously in his sleep; he was already stricken with apoplexy. I ran to your room and was surprised not to find you there; but I had no time to try to discover the explanation of your absence; I was not seriously alarmed about it until after Delmare's death. Everything that skill could do was of no avail, the disease progressed with startling rapidity, and he died an hour later, in my arms, without recovering the use of his senses. At the last moment, however, his benumbed, clouded mind seemed to make an effort to come to life; he felt for my hand which he took for yours—his were already stiff and numb—he tried to press it, and died, stammering your name."

"I heard his last words," said Indiana gloomily; "at the moment that I left him forever, he spoke to me in his sleep. 'That man will ruin you,' he said. Those words are here," she added, putting one hand to her heart and the other to her head.

"When I succeeded in taking my eyes and my thoughts from that dead body," continued Ralph, "I thought of you; of you, Indiana, who were free thenceforth, and who could not weep for your master unless from kindness of heart or religious feeling. I was the only one whom his death deprived of something, for I was his friend, and, even if he was not always very sociable, at all events I had no rival in his heart. I feared the effect of breaking the news to you too suddenly, and I went to the door to wait for you, thinking that you would soon return from your morning walk. I waited a long while. I will not attempt to describe my anxiety, my search, and my alarm when I found Ophelia's body, all bleeding and bruised by the rocks; the waves had washed it upon the beach. I looked a long while, alas! expecting to discover yours; for I thought that you had taken your own life, and for three days I believed that there was nothing left on earth for me to love. It is useless to speak of my grief; you must have foreseen it when you abandoned me.

"Meanwhile, a rumor that you had fled spread swiftly through the colony. A vessel came into port that had passed the *Eugène* in Mozambique Channel; some of the ship's company had been aboard your ship. A passenger had recognized you, and in less than three days the whole island knew of your departure.

"I spare you the absurd and insulting reports that resulted from the coincidence of those two events on the same night, your flight and your husband's death. I was not spared in the charitable conclusions that people amused themselves by drawing; but I paid no attention to them. I had still one duty to perform on earth, to make sure of your welfare and to lend you a helping hand if necessary. I sailed soon after you; but I had a horrible voyage and have been in France only a week. My first thought was to go to Monsieur de Ramière to inquire about you; but by good luck I met his servant Carle, who had just brought you here. I asked him no questions except where you were living, and I came here with the conviction that I should not find you alone."

"Alone, alone! shamefully abandoned!" cried Madame Delmare. "But let us not speak of that man, let us never speak of him. I can never love him again, for I despise him; but you must not tell me that I once loved him, for that reminds me of my shame and my crime; it casts a terrible reproach upon my last moments. Ah! be my angel of consolation; you who never fail to come and offer me a friendly hand in all the crises of my miserable life. Fulfil with pity your last mission; say to me words of affection and forgiveness, so that I may die at peace, and hope for pardon from the Judge who awaits me on high."

She hoped to die; but grief rivets the chain of life instead of breaking it. She was not even dangerously ill; she simply had no strength, and lapsed into a state of languor and apathy which resembled imbecility.

Ralph tried to distract her; he took her away from everything that could remind her of Raymon. He took her to Touraine, he surrounded her with all the comforts of life; he devoted all his time to making a portion of hers endurable; and when he failed, when he had exhausted all the resources of his art and his affection without bringing a feeble gleam of pleasure to that gloomy, careworn face, he deplored the powerlessness of his words and blamed himself bitterly for the ineptitude of his affection.

One day he found her more crushed and hopeless than

ever. He dared not speak to her, but sat down beside her with a melancholy air. Thereupon, Indiana turned to him and said, pressing his hand tenderly:

"I cause you a vast deal of pain, poor Ralph! and you must be patient beyond words to endure the spectacle of such egotistical, cowardly misery as mine! Your unpleasant task was finished long ago. The most insanely exacting woman could not ask of friendship more than you have done for me. Now leave me to the misery that is gnawing at my heart; do not spoil your pure and holy life by contact with an accursed life; try to find elsewhere the happiness which cannot exist near me."

"I do in fact give up all hope of curing you, Indiana," he replied; "but I will never abandon you even if you should tell me that I annoy you; for you still require bodily care, and if you are not willing that I should be your friend, I will at all events be your servant. But listen to me; I have an expedient to propose to you which I have kept in reserve for the last stage of the disease, but which certainly is infallible."

"I know but one remedy for sorrow," she replied, "and that is forgetting; for I have had time to convince myself that argument is unavailing. Let us hope everything from time, therefore. If my will could obey the gratitude which you inspire in me, I should be now as cheerful and calm as in the days of our childhood; believe me, my friend, I take no pleasure in nourishing my trouble and inflaming my wound; do I not know that all my sufferings rebound on your heart? Alas! I would like to forget, to be cured! but I am only a weak woman. Ralph, be patient and do not think me ungrateful."

She burst into tears. Sir Ralph took her hand.

"Listen, dear Indiana," he said; "to forget is not in our power; I do not accuse you! I can suffer patiently;

but to see you suffer is beyond my strength. Indeed, why should we struggle thus, weak creatures that we are, against a destiny of iron? It is quite enough to drag this cannon-ball; the God whom you and I adore did not condemn man to undergo so much misery without giving him the instinct to escape from it; and what constitutes, in my opinion, man's most marked superiority over the brute is his ability to understand what the remedy is for all his ills. The remedy is suicide; that is what I propose, what I advise."

"I have often thought of it," Indiana replied after a short silence. "Long ago I was violently tempted to resort to it, but religious scruples arrested me. Since then my ideas have reached a higher level, in solitude. Misfortune clung to me and gradually taught me a different religion from that taught by men. When you came to my assistance I had determined to allow myself to die of hunger; but you begged me to live, and I had not the right to refuse you that sacrifice. Now, what holds me back is your existence, your future. What will you do all alone, poor Ralph, without family, without passions, without affections? Since I have received these horrible wounds in my heart I am no longer good for anything to you; but perhaps I shall recover. Yes, Ralph, I will do my utmost, I swear. Have patience a little longer; soon, perhaps, I shall be able to smile. I long to become tranquil and light-hearted once more in order to devote to you this life for which you have fought so stoutly with misfortune."

"No, my dear, no; I do not desire such a sacrifice; I will never accept it," said Ralph. "Wherein is my life more precious than yours, pray? Why must you inflict a hateful future upon yourself in order that mine may be pleasant? Do you think that it will be possible for me to enjoy it while feeling that your heart has no share in it? No, I am not so selfish as that. Let us not attempt, I beg you, an impossible heroism; it is overweening pride and presumption to hope to renounce all self-love thus. Let us view our situation calmly and dispose of our remaining days as common property which neither of us has the right to appropriate at the other's expense. For a long time, ever since my birth, I may say, life has been a bore and a burden to me; now I no longer feel the courage to endure it without bitterness of heart and impiety. Let us go together; let us return to God, who exiled us in this world of trials, in this vale of tears, but who will surely not refuse to open His arms to us when, bruised and weary, we go to Him and implore His indulgence and His mercy. I believe in God, Indiana, and it was I who first taught you to believe in Him. So have confidence in me; an upright heart cannot deceive one who questions it with sincerity. I feel that we have both suffered enough here on earth to be cleansed of our sins. The baptism of unhappiness has surely purified our souls sufficiently; let us give them back to Him who gave them."

This idea engrossed Ralph and Indiana for several days, at the end of which it was decided that they should commit suicide together. It only remained to choose what sort of death they would die.

"It is a matter of some importance," said Ralph; "but I have already considered it, and this is what I have to suggest. The act that we are about to undertake not being the result of a momentary mental aberration, but of a deliberate determination formed after calm and pious reflection, it is important that we should bring to it the meditative seriousness of a Catholic receiving the sacraments of his Church. For us the universe is the temple in which we adore God. In the bosom of majestic, virgin nature we are impressed by the consciousness of His power, pure of all human profanation. Let us go back to the desert, therefore, so that we may be able to pray. Here, in this country swarming with men and vices, in the bosom of this civilization which denies God or disfigures Him, I feel that I should be ill at ease, distraught and depressed. I would like to die cheerfully, with a serene brow and with my eyes gazing heavenward. But where can we find heaven here? I will tell you, therefore, the spot where suicide appeared to me in its noblest and most solemn aspect. It is in Ile Bourbon, on the verge of a precipice, on the summit of the cliff from which the transparent cascade, surmounted by a gorgeous rainbow, plunges into the lonely ravine of Bernica. That is where we passed the sweetest hours of our childhood; that is where I bewailed the bitterest sorrows of my life; that is where I learned to pray, to hope; that is where I would like, during one of the lovely nights of that latitude, to bury myself in those pure waters and go down into the cool, flower-decked grave formed by the depths of the verdure-lined abyss. If you have no predilection for any other spot, give me the satisfaction of offering up our twofold sacrifice on the spot which witnessed the games of our childhood and the sorrows of our youth."

"I agree," said Madame Delmare, placing her hand in Ralph's to seal the compact. "I have always been drawn to the banks of the stream by an invincible attraction, by the memory of my poor Noun. To die as she died will be sweet to me; it will be an atonement for her death, which I caused."

"Moreover," said Ralph, "another sea voyage, made under the influence of other feelings than those which have agitated us hitherto, is the best preparation we could imagine for communing with ourselves, for detaching ourselves from earthly affections, for raising ourselves in unalloyed purity to the feet of the Supreme Being. Isolated from the whole world, always ready to leave this life with glad hearts, we shall watch with enchanted eyes the tempest arouse the elements and unfold its magnificent spectacles before us. Come, Indiana, let us go; let us shake the dust of this ungrateful land from our feet. To die here, under Raymon's eyes, would be to all appearance a mere commonplace, cowardly revenge. Let us leave that man's punishment to God; and let us go and beseech Him to open the treasures of His mercy to that barren and ungrateful heart."

They left France. The schooner *Nahandove,* as fleet and nimble as a bird, bore them to their twice-abandoned country. Never was there so pleasant and fast a passage. It seemed as if a favorable wind had undertaken to guide safely into port those two ill-fated beings who had been tossed about so long among the reefs and shoals of life. During those three months Indiana reaped the fruit of her docile compliance with Ralph's advice. The sea air, so bracing and so penetrating, restored her impaired health; a wave of peace overflowed her wearied heart. The certainty that she would soon have done with her sufferings produced upon her the effect of a doctor's assurances upon a credulous patient. Forgetting her past life, she opened her heart to the profound emotions of religious hope. Her thoughts were all impregnated with a mysterious charm, a celestial perfume. Never had the sea and sky seemed to her so beautiful. It seemed to her that she saw them for the first time, she discovered so many new splendors and glories in them. Her brow became serene once more, and one would have said that a ray of the Divine essence had passed into her sweetly melancholy eyes.

A change no less extraordinary took place in Ralph's soul and in his outward aspect; the same causes produced almost the same results. His heart, so long hardened against sorrow, softened in the revivifying warmth of hope. Heaven descended also into that bitter, wounded heart. His words took on the stamp of his feelings and for the first time Indiana became acquainted with his real character. The reverent, filial intimacy that bound them together took from the one his painful shyness, from the other her unjust prejudices. Every day cured Ralph of some *gaucherie* of his nature, Indiana of some error of her judgment. At the same time the painful memory of Raymon faded away and gradually vanished in face of Ralph's unsuspected virtues, his sublime sincerity. As the one grew greater in her estimation, the other fell away. At last, by dint of comparing the two men, every vestige of her blind and fatal love was effaced from her heart.

XXX

It was last year, one evening during the never-ending summer that reigns in those latitudes, that two passengers from the schooner *Nahandove* journeyed into the mountains of Ile Bourbon three days after landing. These two persons had devoted the interval to repose, a precaution quite inconsistent with the plan which had brought them to the colony. But such was evidently not their opinion; for, after taking *faham* together on the veranda, they dressed with especial care as if they intended to pass the evening in society, and, taking the road to the mountain, they reached the ravine of Bernica after about an hour's walk.

Chance willed that it should be one of the loveliest evenings for which the moon ever furnished light in the tropics. That luminary had just risen from the dark waves and was beginning to cast a long band of quick-silver on the sea; but its rays did not shine into the gorge, and the edges of the basin reflected only the trembling gleam of a few stars. Even the lemon-trees on the higher slopes of the mountain were not covered with the pale diamonds with which the moon sprinkles their polished, brittle leaves. The ebony trees and the tamarinds murmured softly in the darkness; only the bushy tufts at the summit of the huge palm-trees, whose slender trunks rose a hundred feet from the ground, shone with a greenish tinge in the silvery beams.

The sea-birds were resting quietly in the crevices of the cliffs, and only a few blue pigeons, concealed behind the projections of the mountain, raised their melancholy, passionate note in the distance. Lovely beetles, living jewels, rustled gently in the branches of the coffee-trees, or skimmed the surface of the lake with a buzzing noise, and the regular plashing of the cascade seemed to exchange mysterious words with the echoes on its shores.

The two solitary promenaders ascended by a steep and winding path to the top of the gorge, to the spot where the torrent plunges down in a white column of vapor to the foot of the precipice. They found themselves on a small platform admirably adapted to their purpose. A number of convolvuli hanging from the trunks of trees formed a natural cradle suspended over the waterfall.

Sir Ralph, with wonderful self-possession, cut away several branches which might impede their spring, then took his companion's hand and drew her to a seat beside him on a moss-covered rock from which in the daytime the beautiful view from that spot could be seen in all its wild and charming grandeur. But at that moment the darkness and the dense vapor from the cascade enveloped everything and made the height of the precipice seem immeasurable and awe-inspiring.

"Let me remind you, my dear Indiana," said Ralph, "that the success of our undertaking requires the greatest self-possession on our part. If you jump hastily in a direction where, because of the darkness, you see no obstacles, you will inevitably bruise yourself on the rocks and your death will be slow and painful; but, if you take care to throw yourself in the direction of the white line which marks the course of the waterfall you will fall into the lake with it, and the water itself will see to it that you do not miss your aim. But, if you prefer to wait an hour, the moon will rise high enough to give us light."

"I am willing," Indiana replied, "especially as we ought to devote these last moments to religious thoughts."

"You are right, my dear," said Ralph. "This last hour should be one of meditation and prayer. I do not say that we ought to make our peace with the Eternal, that would be to forget the distance that separates us from His sublime power; but we ought, I think, to make our peace with the men who have caused our suffering, and to confide to the wind which blows toward the northeast words of pity for those from whom three thousand leagues of ocean separate us."

Indiana received this suggestion without surprise or emotion. For several months past her thoughts had become more and more elevated in direct proportion to the change that had taken place in Ralph. She no longer listened to him simply as a phlegmatic adviser; she followed him in silence as a good spirit whose mission it was to take her from the earth and deliver her from her torments.

"I agree," she said; "I am overjoyed to feel that I can forgive without an effort, that I have neither hatred nor regret nor love nor resentment in my heart; indeed, at this moment, I hardly remember the sorrows of my sad life and the ingratitude of those who surrounded me. Almighty God! Thou seest the deepest recesses of my heart; Thou knowest that it is pure and calm, and that all my thoughts of love and hope have turned to Thee."

Thereupon, Ralph seated himself at Indiana's feet and began to pray in a loud voice that rose above the roar of the cascade. It was the first time perhaps since he was born that his whole thought came to his lips. The hour of his death had struck; his heart was no longer held in check by fetters or mysteries; it belonged to God alone; the chains of society no longer weighed it down. Its ardor was no longer a crime, it was free to soar upward to God who awaited it; the veil that concealed so much virtue, grandeur and power fell away, and the man's mind rose at its first leap to the level of his heart.

As a bright flame burns amid dense clouds of smoke and scatters them, so did the sacred fire that glowed in the depths of his being send forth its brilliant light. The first time that that inflexible conscience found itself delivered from its trammels and its fears, words came of themselves to the assistance of his thoughts, and the man of mediocre talents, who had never said any but commonplace things in his life, became, in his last hour, eloquent and convincing as Raymon had never been. Do not expect me to repeat to you the strange harangue that he confided to the echoes of the vast solitude; not even he himself, if he were here, could repeat it. There are moments of mental exaltation and ecstasy when our thoughts are purified, subtilized, etherealized as it were. These infrequent moments raise us so high, carry us so far out of ourselves, that when we fall back upon the earth we lose all consciousness and memory of that intellectual debauch. Who can understand the anchorite's mysterious visions? Who can tell the dreams of the poet before his exaltation cooled so that he could write them down for us? Who can say what marvellous things are revealed to the soul of the just man when Heaven opens to receive him? Ralph, a man so utterly commonplace to all outward appearance—and yet an exceptional man, for he firmly believed in God and consulted the book of his conscience day by day—Ralph at that moment was adjusting his accounts with eternity. It was the time to be himself, to lay bare his whole moral being, to lay aside, before the Judge, the disguise that men had forced upon him. Casting away the haircloth in which sorrow had enveloped his bones, he stood forth sublime and radiant as if he had already entered into the abode of divine rewards.

As she listened to him, it did not occur to Indiana to be surprised; she did not ask herself if it were really Ralph who talked like that. The Ralph she had known had ceased to exist, and he to whom she was listening now seemed to be a friend whom she had formerly seen in her dreams and who finally became incarnate for her on the brink of the grave. She felt her own pure soul soar upward in the same flight. A profound religious sympathy aroused in her the same emotions, and tears of enthusiasm fell from her eyes upon Ralph's hair.

Thereupon, the moon rose over the tops of the great palms, and its beams, shining between the branches of the convolvuli, enveloped Indiana in a pale, misty light which made her resemble, in her white dress and with her long hair falling over her shoulders, the wraith of some maiden lost in the desert.

Sir Ralph knelt before her and said:

"Now, Indiana, you must forgive me for all the injury I have done you, so that I may forgive myself for it."

"Alas!" she replied, "what can I possibly have to forgive you, my poor Ralph? Ought I not, on the contrary, to bless you to the last moment of my life, as you have forced me to do in all the days of misery that have fallen to my lot?"

"I do not know how far I have been blameworthy," rejoined Ralph; "but it is impossible that, in the course of such a long and terrible battle with my destiny, I should not have been many times without my own volition."

"Of what battle are you speaking?" queried Indiana.

"That is what I must explain to you before we die; that is the secret of my life. You asked me to tell it to you on the ship that brought us here, and I promised to do so on the shore of Bernica Lake, when the moon should rise upon us for the last time."

"That moment has come," she said, "and I am listening."

"Summon all your patience then, for I have a long story to tell you, Indiana, and that story is my own."

"I thought that I knew it, inasmuch as I have hardly ever been separated from you."

"You do not know it; you do not know it for a single day, a single hour," said Ralph sadly. "When could I have told it to you, pray? It is Heaven's will that the only suitable moment for me to do so, should be the last moment of your life and my own. But it is as innocent and proper to-day as it would formerly have been insane and criminal. It is a personal gratification for which no one has the right to blame me at this hour, which you accord to me in order to complete the task of patience and gentleness which you have taken upon yourself with regard to me. Endure to the end, therefore, the burden of my unhappiness; and if my words tire you and annoy you, listen to the waterfall as it sings the hymn of the dead over me.

"I was born to love; none of you chose to believe it, and your error in that regard had a decisive influence on my character. It is true that nature, while giving me an ardent heart, was guilty of a strange inconsistency; she placed on my face a stone mask and on my tongue a weight that it could not raise; she refused me what she grants to the most ordinary mortals, the power to express my feelings by the glance or by speech. That made me selfish. People judged the mental being by the outer envelope and, like an imperfect fruit I was compelled to dry up under the rough husk which I could not cast off. I was hardly born when I was cast out of the heart which I most needed. My mother put me away from her breast with disgust, because my baby face could not return her smile. At an age when one can hardly distinguish a thought from a desire, I was already branded with the hateful designation of egotist.

"Thereupon it was decided that no one would love me, because I was unable to put in words my affection for anyone. They made me unhappy, they declared that I did not feel my unhappiness; I was almost banished from my father's house; they sent me to live among the rocks like a lonely shore-bird. You know what my childhood was, Indiana. I passed the long days in the desert, with no anxious mother to come there in search of me, with no friendly voice amid the silence of the ravines to remind me that the approach of night called me back to the cradle. I grew up alone, I lived alone; but God would not permit me to be unhappy to the end, for I shall not die alone.

"Heaven however sent me a gift, a consolation, a hope. You came into my life as if Heaven had created you for me. Poor child! abandoned like me, like me set adrift in life without love and without protectors, you seemed to be destined for me—at least I flattered myself that it was so. Was I too presumptuous? For ten years you were mine, absolutely mine; I had no rivals, no misgivings. At that time I had had no experience of what jealousy is.

"That time, Indiana, was the least dismal period of my life. I made of you my sister, my daughter, my companion, my pupil, my whole society. Your need of me made my life something more than that of a wild beast; for your sake I threw off the gloom into which the contempt of my own family had cast me. I began to esteem myself by becoming useful to you. I must tell you everything, Indiana; after accepting the burden of life for you, my imagination suggested the hope of a reward. I accustomed myself—forgive the words I am about to use; even to-day I cannot utter them without fear and trembling—I accustomed myself to think that you would be my wife; child that you were, I looked upon you as my betrothed; my imagination arrayed you in the charms of young womanhood; I was impatient to see you in your maturity. My brother, who had usurped my share of the family affection and who took pleasure in peaceful avocations, had a garden on the hillside which we can see from here by daylight, and which subsequent owners have transformed into a rice-field. The care of his flowers occupied his pleasantest moments, and every morning he went out to watch their progress with an impatient eye, and to wonder, child that he was, because they had not grown so much as he expected in a single night. You, Indiana, were my whole vocation, my only joy, my only treasure; you were the young plant that I cultivated, the bud that I was impatient to see bloom. I, too, looked eagerly every morning for the effect of another day that had passed over your head; for I was already a young man and you were but a child. Already passions of which you did not know the name were stirring my bosom; my fifteen years played havoc with my imagination, and you were surprised to see me so often in a melancholy mood, sharing your games, but taking no pleasure in them. You could not imagine that a fruit or a bird was no longer a priceless treasure to me as it was to you, and I already seemed cold and odd to you. And yet you loved me such as I was; for, despite my melancholy, there was not a moment of my life that was not devoted to you; my sufferings made you dearer to my heart; I cherished the insane hope that it would be your mission to change them to joys some day.

"Alas! forgive me for the sacrilegious thought which kept me alive for ten years; if it were a crime in the accursed child to hope for you, lovely, simple-hearted child of the mountains, God alone is guilty of giving him, for his only sustenance, that audacious thought. Upon what could that wounded, misunderstood heart subsist, who encountered new necessities at every turn and found a refuge nowhere? from whom could he expect a glance, a smile of love, if not from you, whose lover and father he was at the same time?

"Do not be shocked to find that you grew up under the wing of a poor bird consumed by love; never did any impure homage, any blameworthy thought endanger the virginity of your soul; never did my mouth brush from your cheeks that bloom of innocence which covered them as the fruit is covered with a moist vapor in the morning. My kisses were the kisses of a father, and when your innocent and playful lips met mine they did not find there the stinging flame of virile desire. No, it was not with you, a tiny blue-eyed child, that I was in love. As I held you in my arms, with your innocent smile and your dainty caresses, you were simply my child, or at most my little sister; but I was in love with your fifteen years, when, yielding to the ardor of my own youth, I devoured the future with a greedy eye.

"When I read you the story of Paul and Virginie, you only half understood it. You wept, however; you saw only the story of a brother and sister where I had quivered with sympathy, realizing the torments of two lovers. That book made me miserable, whereas it was your joy. You enjoyed hearing me read of the attachment of a faithful dog, of the beauty of the cocoa-palms and the songs of Dominique the negro. But I, when I was alone, read over and over the conversations between Paul and his sweetheart, the impulsive suspicions of the one, the secret sufferings of the other. Oh! how well I understood those first anxieties of youth, seeking in his own heart an explanation of the mysteries of life, and seizing enthusiastically on the first object of love that presents itself to him! But do me justice, Indiana—I did not commit the crime of hastening by a single day the placid development of your childhood; I did not let a word escape me which could suggest to you that there were such things as tears and misery in life. I left you, at the age of ten, in all the ignorance, all the security that were yours when your nurse placed you in my arms, one day when I had determined to die.

"Often as I sat alone on this cliff I wrung my hands frantically as I listened to all the sounds of spring time and of love which the mountain gives forth, as I saw the creepers chase each other to and fro, the insects sleeping in a voluptuous embrace in the calyx of a flower, as I inhaled the burning dust which the palm-trees sent to one another—ethereal transports, subtle joys to which the gentle summer breeze serves as a couch. At such times I was frantic, I was mad. I appealed for love to the flowers, to the birds, to the voice of the torrent. I called wildly upon that unknown bliss, the mere thought of which made my brain whirl. But I would see you running toward me, along yonder path, merry and laughing, so tiny in the distance and so awkward about climbing the rocks that one might have taken you for a penguin, with your white dress and your brown hair. Then my blood would grow calm, my lips cease to burn. In presence of the little Indiana of seven I would forget the Indiana of fifteen of whom I had just been dreaming. I would open my arms to you with pure delight; your kisses would cool my forehead. At those times I was happy; I was a father.

"How many free, peaceful days we have passed in this ravine! How many times I have bathed your feet in the pure water of yonder basin! How many times I have watched you sleeping among the reeds, shaded by the leaf of a palm for an umbrella! It was at those times that my tortures would occasionally begin anew. It was a sore affliction to me that you were so small. I would ask myself whether, suffering as I did, I could live until the day when you could understand me and respond to my love. I would gently lift your silken locks and kiss them with passion. I would compare them with curls I had cut from your head in preceding years and which I kept in my wallet. I would joyously make sure of the darker shade that each recurring spring gave to them. Then I would examine the marks on the trunk of a date-tree nearby, that I had made to show the progressive increase in your height for four or five years. The tree still bears those scars, Indiana; I found them on it the last time I came here to suffer. Alas! in vain did you grow taller and taller; in vain did your beauty keep all its promises; in vain did your hair become black as ebony. You did not grow for me; not for me did your charms develop. The first time that your heart beat faster it was for another than me.

"Do you remember how we ran, as light of foot as two turtle-doves, among the thickets of wild rose bushes? Do you remember, too, that we sometimes went astray in the forests over our heads? Once we tried to reach the mist-enveloped peaks of the Salazes; but we had not foreseen that the higher we went the scarcer the fruit became, the less accessible the streams, the more terrible and more penetrating the cold.

"When we saw the vegetation receding behind us you would have returned; but when we had crossed the fern belt we found a quantity of wild strawberries, and you were so busy filling your basket with them that you thought no more about leaving the place. But we had to abandon the idea of going on. We were walking on volcanic rocks covered with little brown spots, and with woolly plants growing among them. Those wretched wind-beaten weeds made us think of the goodness of God, who has given them a warm garment to withstand the violence of the storm. Then the mist became so dense that we could not tell where we were going, and we had to go down again. I carried you in my arms. I crept carefully down the deep slopes of the mountain. Darkness surprised us as we entered the first woods, in the third belt of vegetation. I picked some pomegranates for you and made shift to quench my own thirst with the convolvuli, the stalks of which contain an abundant supply of cool, pure water. Thereupon we recalled the adventure of our favorite heroes, when they lost themselves in the forests of the Rivière-Rouge. But we had no loving mothers, nor zealous servants, nor faithful dog to search for us. But I was content; I was proud. I shared with no one the duty of watching over you, and I considered myself more fortunate than Paul.

"Yes, it was a profound and pure and true passion that you inspired in me even then. Noun, at ten years, was a head taller than you; a creole in the fullest acceptation of the word, she was already developed. Her melting eyes already shone with a curious expression; her bearing and character were those of a young woman. But I did not love Noun, or I loved her only because of you, with whom she always played. It never occurred to me to wonder whether she was beautiful already; whether she would be more beautiful some day. I never looked at her. In my eyes she was more of a child than you; for, you see, I loved you. I staked all my hopes upon you; you were the companion of my life, the dream of my youth.

"Those days of exile in England, that period of pain and grief, I will not describe. If I treated any one badly, it was not you; and if any one treated me badly, I do not propose to complain. There I became more *egotistical,* that is to say more depressed and more distrustful than ever. By being suspicious of me, people had compelled me to become self-sufficient and to rely upon myself. Thus I had only the testimony of my own heart to support me in those trials. It was attributed to me as a crime that I did not love a woman who married me only because she was forced to and who never treated me with anything but contempt. It was afterwards remarked that one of the principal characteristics of my egotism was the aversion I seemed to feel for children. Raymon more than once bantered me cruelly concerning that supposed peculiarity, observing that the care necessary for the education of children was quite inconsistent with the rigidly methodical ways of an old bachelor. I fancy that he did not know that I had been a father, and that it was I who educated you. But none of you would ever understand that the memory of my son was as intensely painful to me after many years as on the first day, and that my sore heart swelled at the sight of flaxen heads that reminded me of him. When a man is unhappy, people are terribly afraid of not finding him blameworthy enough, because they dread being compelled to pity him.

"But what no one will ever be able to understand is the profound indignation, the black despair which took possession of me when I, a poor child of the desert, upon whom no one had ever deigned to cast a pitying glance, was forced to leave this spot and take upon myself the burdens of society; when I was told that I must fill an empty place that had spurned me; when they tried to make me understand that I had duties to fulfil toward those men and women who had disregarded their duties toward me. Think of it! no one of all my kindred had chosen to be my protector and now they all called upon me to undertake the defence of their interests! They would not even leave me to enjoy in peace what pariahs enjoy, the air of solitude! I had but one thing in life that I cherished, one thought, one hope—that you would belong to me forever; they deprived me of that, they told me that you were not rich enough for me. Bitter mockery! for me whom the mountains had nourished and whom my father's roof had cast out! me, who had never been allowed to learn the use of riches, and upon whom was now laid the duty of managing to advantage the riches of other people!

"However I submitted. I had no right to pray that my paltry happiness might be spared; I was despised enough, Heaven knows! to resist would have been to make myself odious. My mother, inconsolable for her other son's death, threatened to die herself if I did not follow out my destiny. My father, who accused me of not knowing how to comfort him, as if I were to blame because he loved me so little, was ready to curse me if I tried to escape from his yoke. I bent my head; but what I suffered even you yourself, although you too have been very unhappy, could never understand. If, after being hunted and maltreated and oppressed as I have been, I have not returned mankind evil for evil, perhaps it is a fair conclusion that my heart is not so cold and sterile as it has been accused of being.

"When I came back here, when I saw the man to whom you had been married—forgive me, Indiana, that was the time when I was genuinely selfish; there must always be selfishness in love, since there was a touch of it even in mine—I felt an indescribably cruel joy in the thought that that legal sham would give you a master and not a husband. You were surprised at the species of affection for him I displayed; it was because I did not look upon him as a rival. I knew well enough that that old man could neither feel nor inspire love, and that your heart would come forth untouched from that marriage.

I was grateful to him for your coldness and your melancholy. If he had remained here, I should perhaps have become a very guilty man; but you left me alone and it was not in my power to live without you. I tried to conquer the indomitable love which had sprung to life again in all its force when I found you as fair and sad as I had dreamed of you in your childhood. But solitude only intensified my suffering and I yielded to the craving I felt to see you, to live under the same roof, to breathe the same air, to drink my fill every hour of the melodious tones of your voice. You know what obstacles I had to meet, what distrust I had to overcome; I realized then what duties I had voluntarily undertaken; I could not connect my life with yours without quieting your husband's suspicions by a sacred promise, and I have never known what it was to trifle with my word. I pledged myself therefore with my mind and my heart never to forget my rôle of brother, and I ask you, Indiana, if I ever was false to my oath.

"I realized also that it would be difficult, perhaps impossible, for me to perform that painful task, if I laid aside the disguise that precluded any intimate relations, any profound sentiment; I realized that I must not play with the danger, for my passion was too intense to come forth victorious from a battle. I felt that I must erect about myself a triple wall of ice, in order to repel your interest in me, in order to deprive myself of your compassion, which would have ruined me. I said to myself that on the day that you pitied me, I should be already guilty, and I made up my mind to live under the weight of that horrible accusation of indifference and selfishness, which, thank Heaven! you did not fail to bring against me. The success of my ruse surpassed my hopes; you lavished upon me a sort of insulting pity like that which is accorded to eunuchs; you denied me the possession of a heart and passions; you trampled me under foot, and I had not the right to display energy enough to be angry and vow vengeance, for that would have betrayed me and shown you that I was a man.

"I complain of mankind at large and not of you, Indiana. You were always kind and merciful; you tolerated me under this despicable disguise I had adopted in order to be near you; you never made me blush for my rôle, you were all in all to me, and sometimes I thought with pride that if you looked kindly upon me in the guise I had assumed in order that you might misunderstand me, you might perhaps love me if you should know me some day as I really was. Alas! what other than you would not have spurned me? what other would have held out her hand to that speechless, witless clown? Everybody but you held aloof with disgust from the *egotist!* Ah! there was one being in the world generous enough not to tire of that profitless exchange; there was one heart large enough to shed something of the blessed flame that animated it upon the narrow, benumbed heart of the poor abandoned wretch. It required a heart that had too much of that of which I had not enough. There was under Heaven but one Indiana capable of caring for a Ralph.

"Next to you the person who showed me the most indulgence was Delmare. You accused me of preferring him to you, of sacrificing your comfort to my own by refusing to interfere in your domestic quarrels. Unjust, blind woman! you did not see that I served you as well as it was possible to do; and, above all, you did not understand that I could not raise my voice in your behalf without betraying myself. What would have become of you if Delmare had turned me out of his house? who would have protected you, patiently, silently, but with the persevering steadfastness of an undying love? Not Raymon surely. And then I was fond of him from a feeling of gratitude, I confess;—yes, fond of that rough, vulgar creature who had it in his power to deprive me of my only remaining joy, and who did not do it; that man whose misfortune it was not to be loved by you, so that there was a secret bond of sympathy between us! I was fond of him too for the very reason that he had never caused me the tortures of jealousy.

"But I have come now to the most ghastly sorrow of my life, to the fatal time when your love, of which I had dreamed so long, belonged to another. Then and not till then did I fully realize the nature of the sentiment that I had held in check so many years. Then did hatred pour poison into my breast and jealousy consume what was left of my strength. Hitherto my imagination had kept you pure; my respect encompassed you with a veil which the innocent audacity of dreams dared not even raise; but when I was assailed by the horrible thought that another had involved you in his destiny, had snatched you from my power and was intoxicating himself with deep draughts of the bliss of which I dared not even dream, I became frantic; I would have rejoiced to see that detested man at the foot of this precipice and to roll stones down upon his head.

"However your sufferings were so great that I forgot my own. I did not choose to kill him, because you would have wept for him. Indeed I was tempted twenty times, Heaven forgive me! to be a vile and despicable wretch, to betray Delmare and serve my enemy. Yes, Indiana, I was so insane, so miserable at the sight of your suffering, that I repented having tried to enlighten you and that I would have given my life to bequeath my heart to that man! Oh! the villain! may God forgive him for the injury he has done me! but may He punish him for the misery he has heaped on your head! It is for that that I hate him; for, so far as I am concerned, I forget what my life has been, when I see what he has made of yours. He is a man whom society should have branded on the forehead on the day of his birth! whom it should have spat upon and cast out as the hardest-hearted and vilest of men! But on the contrary, she bore it aloft in triumph. Ah! I recognize mankind in that, and I ought not to be indignant; for man simply obeys his nature in adoring the deformed creature who destroys the happiness and consideration of another.

"Forgive me, Indiana, forgive me! it is cruel perhaps to complain before you, but this is the first time and the last; let me curse the ungrateful wretch who has driven you to the grave. This terrible lesson was necessary to open your eyes. In vain did a voice from Noun's deathbed and Delmare's cry out to you: 'Beware of him, he will ruin you!'—you were deaf: your evil genius led you on and, dishonored as you are, public opinion condemns you and absolves him. He did all sorts of evil and no heed was paid to it. He killed Noun and you forgot it; he ruined you and you forgave him. You see, he had the art to dazzle the eyes and deceive the mind; his adroit, deceitful words found their way to the heart; his viper's glance fascinated; and if nature had given him my metallic features and my dull intelligence she would have made a perfect man of him.

"Yes, I say, may God punish him, for he was barbarous to you! or, rather, may He forgive him, for perhaps he was more stupid than wicked! He did not understand you; he did not appreciate the happiness he might have enjoyed! Oh! you loved him so dearly!

He might have made your life so beautiful! In his place I would not have been virtuous; I would have fled with you into the heart of the mountains; I would have torn you from society to have you all to myself, and I should have had but one fear, that you would not be accursed and abandoned sufficiently so that I might be all in all to you. I would have been jealous of your consideration, but not in the same way that he was; my aim would have been to destroy it in order to replace it by my love. I should have suffered intensely to see another man give you the slightest morsel of pleasure, a moment's gratification; it would have been a theft from me; for your happiness would have been my care, my property, my life, my honor! Oh! how vain and how wealthy I would have been with this wild ravine for my only home, these mountain trees for my only fortune, if heaven had given them to me with your love! Let us weep, Indiana; it is the first time in my life that I have wept; it is God's will that I should not die without knowing that melancholy pleasure."

Ralph was weeping like a child. It was in very truth the first time that stoical soul had ever given way to self-compassion; and yet there was in those tears more sorrow for Indiana's fate than for his own.

"Do not weep for me," he said, seeing that her face too was bathed in tears. "Do not pity me; your pity wipes out the whole past, and the present is no longer bitter. Why should I suffer now? You no longer love him."

"If I had known you as you are, Ralph, I should never have loved him," cried Madame Delmare; "it was your virtue that was my ruin."

"And then," continued Ralph, looking at her with a sorrowful smile, "I have many other causes of joy.

You unwittingly confided something to me during the hours that we poured out our hearts to each other on board ship. You told me that this Raymon was never so fortunate as he had the presumption to claim to be, and you relieved me of a part of my torments. You took away my remorse for having watched over you so ineffectually; for I had the insolence to try to protect you from his fascinations; and therein I insulted you, Indiana. I did not have faith in your strength; that is another crime for you to forgive."

"Alas!" said Indiana, "you ask me to forgive! me who have made your whole life miserable, who have rewarded so pure and generous a love with incredible blindness, barbarous ingratitude! Why, I am the one who should crawl at your feet and implore forgiveness."

"Then this love of mine arouses neither disgust nor anger in your breast, Indiana? O my God! I thank Thee! I shall die happy! Listen, Indiana; cease to blame yourself for my sufferings. At this moment I regret none of Raymon's joys, and I think that my fate would arouse his envy if he had the heart of a man. Now I am your brother, your husband your lover for all eternity. Since the day that you promised to leave this life with me, I have cherished the sweet thought that you belonged to me, that you had returned to me never to leave me again. I began once more to call you my betrothed under my breath. It would have been too much happiness—or, it may be, not enough—to possess you on earth. In God's bosom the bliss awaits me of which my childhood dreamed. There, Indiana, you will love me; there, your divine intellect, stripped of all the lying fictions of this life, will make up to me for a whole life of sacrifices, suffering and self-denial; there, you will be mine, O my Indiana! for you are heaven! and

RALPH AND INDIANA SEEK DEATH TOGETHER

Their lips met; and doubtless there is in a love that comes from the heart a greater power than in the ardor of a fugitive desire; for that kiss, on the threshold of another life, summed up for them all the joys of this.

Thereupon Ralph took his fiancée in his arms and bore her away to plunge with her in the torrent.

if I deserve to be saved, I deserve to possess you. This is what I had in mind when I asked you to put on this white dress; it is the wedding dress; and yonder rock jutting out into the basin is the altar that awaits us."

He rose and plucked a branch from a flowering orange tree in a neighboring thicket and placed it on Indiana's black hair; then he knelt at her feet.

"Make me happy," he said; "tell me that your heart consents to this marriage in another world. Give me eternity; do not compel me to pray for absolute annihilation."

If the story of Ralph's inward life has produced no effect upon you, if you have not come to love that virtuous man, it is because I have proved to be an unfaithful interpreter of his memories, because I have not been able to exert the power possessed by a man who is profoundly in earnest in his passion. Moreover, the moon does not lend me its melancholy influence, nor do the song of the grosbeak, the perfume of the cinnamon-tree, and all the luxurious and intoxicating seductions of a night in the tropics appeal to your head and heart. It may be, too, that you do not know by experience what powerful and novel sensations awake in the heart at the thought of suicide, and how all the things of this life appear in their true light at the moment of severing our connection with them. This sudden light filled all the inmost recesses of Indiana's heart; the bandage, which had long been loosened, fell from her eyes altogether. Newly awake to the truth and to nature, she saw Ralph's heart as it really was. She also saw his features as she had never seen them; for the mental exaltation of his position had produced the same effect on him that the Voltaic battery produces on paralyzed limbs; it had set him free from the paralysis that had fettered his eyes and his voice. Arrayed in all the glory of his frankness and his virtue he was much handsomer than Raymon, and Indiana felt that he was the man she should have loved.

"Be my husband in heaven and on earth," she said, "and let this kiss bind me to you for all eternity!"

Their lips met; and doubtless there is in a love that comes from the heart a greater power than in the ardor of a fugitive desire; for that kiss, on the threshold of another life, summed up for them all the joys of this.

Thereupon Ralph took his fiancée in his arms and bore her away to plunge with her in the torrent.

CONCLUSION

TO J. NERAUD

On a hot, sunshiny day in January last I started from Saint-Paul and wandered into the wild forests of Ile Bourbon to muse and dream. I dreamed of you, my friend; those virgin forests had retained for me the memory of your wanderings and your studies, the ground had kept the imprint of your feet. I found everywhere the marvellous things with which your magical tales charmed the tedium of my vigils in the old days, and, in order that we might enjoy them together, I called upon old Europe, where obscurity encompasses you with its modest advantages, to send you to me. Happy man, whose intellect and merits no treacherous friend has made known to the world!

I walked in the direction of a lonely spot in the highest part of the island, called *Brulé de Saint-Paul.*

A huge fragment of mountain, which was dislodged and fell during some volcanic disturbance, has formed on the slope of the principal mountain a sort of long arena studded with rocks arranged in the most magical disorder, in the most extraordinary confusion. Here, a huge boulder balances itself on a number of small fragments; there, rises a wall of slender, light, porous rocks with dentilated edges and openwork decoration like a Moorish building; farther on, an obelisk of basalt, whose sides an artist seems to have carved and polished, stands upon a crenelated bastion; in another place, a gothic fortress is crumbling to decay beside a curious, shapeless pagoda. That spot is the rendezvous of all the rough drafts of art, all the sketches of architecture; it would seem that all the geniuses of all nations and of all ages went for their inspiration to that vast work of hazard and demolition. There, doubtless some magically elaborate design of chance gave birth to the Moorish style of sculpture. In the heart of the forests, art found in the palm-tree one of its most beautiful models. The *vacoa* which anchors itself in the ground and clings to it with a hundred arms branched from its main stalk, evidently furnished the first suggestion of the plan of a cathedral supported by its light flying buttresses. In the *Brulé de Saint-Paul* all shapes, all types of beauty, all humorous and bold conceits were assembled, piled upon one another, arranged and constructed in one tempestuous night. The spirits of air and fire undoubtedly presided over this diabolical operation; they alone could give to their productions that awe-inspiring, fanciful, incomplete character which distinguishes their works from those of man; they alone could have piled up those monstrous boulders, moved those gigantic masses, toyed with mountains as with grains of sand, and strewn, amid creations which man has tried to copy, those grand conceptions of art, those sublime contrasts impossible of realization, which seem to defy the audacity of the artist and to say to him derisively: "Try it again."

I halted at the foot of a crystallized basaltic monument, about sixty feet high and cut with facets as if by a lapidary. At the top of this strange object an inscription seemed to have been traced in bold characters by an immortal hand. Those vulcanized rocks often present that phenomenon; long ago, when their substance, softened by the action of fire, was still warm and malleable, they received and retained the imprint of the shells and climbing plants that clung to them. These chance contacts have resulted in some strange freaks, curious hieroglyphics, mysterious characters which seem to have been stamped there like the seal of some supernatural being, written in cabalistic letters.

I stood there a long time, detained by a foolish idea that I might find a meaning for those ciphers. This profitless search caused me to fall into a profound meditation, during which I forgot that time was flying.

Already the mists were gathering about the peaks of the mountains, creeping down the sides and rapidly shutting out their outlines. Before I had descended half way to the plateau, they reached the belt that I was crossing and enveloped it in an impenetrable curtain. A moment later a high wind came up and swept the mist away in a twinkling. Then it fell; the mist settled down once more, to be once more driven away by a terrific squall.

I sought shelter from the storm in a grotto which afforded me some protection; but another scourge came to the assistance of the wind. Torrents of rain swelled the streams, all of which flow from the summit of the mountain. In an hour, everything was inundated and the sides of the mountain, with water pouring down on every side, formed one vast cascade which rushed madly down toward the lowlands.

After two days of most painful and dangerous travelling, I found myself, guided by Providence, I doubt not, at the door of a house built in an exceedingly wild locality. The simple but attractive cottage had withstood the tempest, being sheltered by a rampart of cliffs which leaned over it as if to act as an umbrella. A little lower, a waterfall plunged madly down into a ravine and formed at the bottom a brimming lake, above which, clumps of lovely trees still reared their storm-tossed, tired heads.

I knocked vigorously; but the face that appeared in the doorway made me recoil. Before I had opened my mouth to ask for shelter the master of the house had welcomed me gravely and silently with a wave of his hand. I entered and found myself alone with him, face to face with Sir Ralph Brown.

In the year that had passed since the *Nahandove* brought Sir Ralph and his companion back to the colony, he had not been seen in the town three times; and, as for Madame Delmare, her seclusion had been so absolute that her existence was still a problematical matter to many of the people. It was about the same time that I first landed at Bourbon, and my present interview with Monsieur Brown was the second one I had had in my life.

The first had left an ineradicable impression on me; it was at Saint-Paul, on the seashore. His features and bearing had impressed me only slightly at first; but when, through mere idle curiosity, I questioned the colonists concerning him, their replies were so strange, so contradictory, that I scrutinized the recluse of Bernica more closely.

"He's a clown—a man of no education," said one; "an absolute nullity, who has only one good quality—that of keeping his mouth shut."

"He's an extremely well educated and profound man," said another, "but too strongly persuaded of his own superiority, contemptuous and conceited—so much so that he considers any words wasted that he happens to exchange with the common herd."

"He's a man who cares for nobody but himself," said a third; "a man of inferior capacity, but not stupid; profoundly selfish and, they say, hopelessly unsociable."

"Why, don't you know?" said a young man brought up in the colony and thoroughly imbued with the characteristic narrow-mindedness of provincials, "he's a knave, a villain who poisoned his friend in the most dastardly way in order to marry his wife."

This assertion bewildered me so that I turned to another, older colonist, whom I knew to be possessed of considerable common sense.

As my glance eagerly requested a solution of these enigmas, he answered:

"Sir Ralph was formerly an excellent man, who was not a favorite because he was not communicative, but whom everybody esteemed. That is all I can say about him; for, since his unfortunate experience, I have had no relations with him."

"What experience?" I inquired.

He told me about Colonel Delmare's sudden death, his wife's flight during the same night, and Monsieur Brown's departure and return. The obscurity which surrounded all these circumstances had been in nowise lessened by the investigations of the authorities; there was no evidence that the fugitive had committed the crime. The king's attorney had refused to prosecute; but the partiality of the magistrates for Monsieur Brown was well known, and they had been severely criticised for not having at least enlightened public opinion concerning an affair which left the reputations of two persons marred by a hateful suspicion.

A fact that seemed to justify these suspicions was the furtive return of the two accused persons and their mysterious establishment in the depths of the ravine of Bernica. They had run away at first, so it was said, to give the affair time to die out; but public opinion had been so cold in France that they had been driven to return and take refuge in the desert, to gratify their criminal attachment in peace.

But all these theories were set at naught by another fact which was vouched for by persons who seemed better informed: Madame Delmare, I was told, had always manifested a decided coolness, almost downright aversion for her cousin Monsieur Brown.

I had thereupon scrutinized the hero of so many strange tales carefully—conscientiously, if I may say so. He was sitting on a bale of merchandise, awaiting the return of a sailor whom he had sent to make some purchase or other for him. His eyes, blue as the sea, were gazing pensively at the horizon, with such a placid and honest expression; all the lines of his face were so perfectly in harmony with one another; nerves, muscles, blood, all seemed so tranquil, so perfect, so well-ordered in that robust and healthy individual, that I would have sworn that all the tales were deadly insults, that he had no crime on his conscience, that he had never had one in his mind, that his heart and his hands were as pure as his brow.

But suddenly the baronet's distraught glance had fallen upon me, as I was staring at him with eager and impertinent curiosity. Confused and embarrassed as a thief caught in the act, I lowered my eyes, for Sir Ralph's expression conveyed a stern rebuke. Since then I had often thought of him, involuntarily; he had appeared in my dreams. I was conscious, as I thought of him, of that vague feeling of uneasiness, that indescribable emotion, which are like the magnetic fluid with which an unusual destiny is encompassed.

My desire to know Sir Ralph was very real, therefore, and very keen; but I should have preferred to watch him furtively, without being seen myself. It seemed to me that I had wronged him. The crystalline appearance of his eyes froze me with terror. It was so evident that he was a man of towering superiority, either in virtue or in villainy, that I felt very small and mean in his presence.

His hospitality was neither showy nor vulgar. He took me to his room, lent me some clothes and clean linen; then led me to his companion, who was awaiting us to take supper.

As I saw how young and lovely she still was—she seemed barely eighteen—and admired her bloom, her grace, and her sweet voice, I felt a thrill of painful emotion. I reflected that that woman was either very guilty or very unfortunate: guilty of a detestable crime or dishonored by a detestable accusation.

I was detained at Bernica for a week by the overflowing of the rivers, the inundation of the plains, the rain and the wind; and then came the sun, and it never occurred to me to leave my hosts.

Neither of them could be called brilliant. They had little wit, I should say—perhaps indeed they had none at all; but they had that quality which makes one's words impressive and pleasant to hear; they had intellect of the heart. Indiana is ignorant, but not with that narrow, vulgar ignorance which proceeds from indolence, from carelessness or nullity of character. She is eager to learn what the engrossing preoccupations of her life had prevented her from finding out; and then, too, there may have been a little coquetry in the way she questioned Sir Ralph, in order to bring into the light her friend's vast stores of knowledge.

I found her playful, but without petulance; her manners have retained a trace of the languor and melancholy natural to creoles, but in her they seemed to me to have a more abiding charm; her eyes especially have an incomparably soft expression and seem to tell the story of a life of suffering; and when her mouth smiles, there is still a touch of melancholy in those eyes, but the melancholy that seems to be the contemplation of happiness or the emotion of gratitude.

One morning I said to them that at last I was going away.

"Already!" was their answer.

The accent of regret was so genuine, so touching, that I felt encouraged. I had determined that I would not leave Sir Ralph without asking him to tell me his story; but I felt an insurmountable timidity because of the horrible suspicion that had been planted in my mind.

I tried to overcome it.

"Men are great villains," I said to him; "they have spoken ill of you to me. I am not surprised, now that I know you. Your life must have been a very beautiful one, to be so slandered——"

I stopped abruptly when I detected an expression of innocent surprise on Madame Delmare's features. I understood that she knew nothing of the atrocious calumnies current in the colony, and I encountered upon Sir Ralph's face an unequivocal look of haughty displeasure. I rose at once to take my leave of them, shamefaced and sad, crushed by Monsieur Brown's glance, which reminded me of our first meeting and the silent interview of the same sort we had had on the sea-shore.

Bitterly chagrined to leave that excellent man in such a frame of mind, regretting that I had annoyed and wounded him in return for the happy days I owed to him, I felt my heart swell within me and I burst into tears.

"Young man," he said, taking my hand, "remain with us another day; I have not the courage to let the only friend we have on the island leave us in this way—I understand you," he added, after Madame Delmare had left the room; "I will tell you my story, but not before Indiana. There are wounds which one must not reopen."

That evening we went for a walk in the woods. The trees, which had been so fresh and lovely a fortnight earlier, were entirely stripped of their leaves, but they were already covered with great resinous buds. The birds and insects had resumed possession of their empire. The withered flowers already had young buds to replace them. The streams perseveringly carried seaward the gravel with which their beds were filled. Everything was returning to life and health and happiness.

"Just see," said Ralph to me, "with what astounding rapidity this kindly, fecund nature repairs its losses! Does it not seem as if it were ashamed of the time wasted, and were determined, by dint of a lavish expenditure of sap and vigor, to do over in a few days the work of a year?"

"And it will succeed," rejoined Madame Delmare. "I remember last year's storms; at the end of a month there was no trace of them."

"It is the image of a heart broken by sorrow," I said to her; "when happiness comes back, it renews its youth and blooms again very quickly."

Indiana gave me her hand and looked at Monsieur Brown with an indescribable expression of affection and joy.

When night fell she went to her room, and Sir Ralph, bidding me sit beside him on a bench in the garden, told me his history to the point at which we dropped it in the last chapter.

There he made a long pause and seemed to have forgotten my presence completely.

Impelled by my interest in his narrative, I decided to interrupt his meditation by one last question.

He started like a man suddenly awakened; then, smiling pleasantly, he said:

"My young friend, there are memories which we rob of their bloom by putting them in words. Let it suffice you to know that I was fully determined to kill Indiana with myself. But doubtless the consummation of our sacrifice was still unrecorded in the archives of Heaven. A doctor would tell you perhaps that a very natural attack of vertigo took possession of my wits and led me astray as to the location of the path. For my own part, who am not a doctor at all in such matters, I prefer to believe that the angel of Abraham and Tobias, that beautiful white angel with the blue eyes and the girdle of gold, whom you often saw in your childish dreams, came down from Heaven on a moonbeam, and, as he hovered in the trembling vapor of the cataract, stretched his silvery wings over my gentle companion's head.

The only thing that I am able to tell you is that the moon sank behind the great peaks of the mountain and no ominous sound disturbed the peaceful murmur of the waterfall; the birds on the cliff did not take their flight until a white streak appeared on the horizon; and the first ruddy beam that fell upon the clump of orange-trees found me on my knees blessing God.

"Do not think, however, that I accepted instantly the unhoped-for happiness which gave a new turn to my destiny. I was afraid to sound the radiant future that was dawning for me; and when Indiana raised her eyes and smiled upon me, I pointed to the waterfall and talked of dying.

"'If you do not regret having lived until this morning,' I said to her, 'we can both declare that we have tasted happiness in all its plenitude; and it is an additional reason for ceasing to live, for perhaps my star would pale to-morrow. Who can say that, on leaving this spot, on coming forth from this intoxicating situation to which thoughts of death and love have brought me, I shall not become once more the detestable brute whom you despised yesterday? Will you not blush for yourself when you find me again as you have always known me? Oh! Indiana, spare me that horrible agony; it would be the complement of my destiny.'

"'Do you doubt your heart, Ralph?' said Indiana with an adorable expression of love and confidence, 'or does not mine offer you sufficient guarantee?'

"Shall I tell you? I was not happy at first. I did not doubt Madame Delmare's sincerity, but I was terrified by thought of the future. Having distrusted myself beyond measure for thirty years, I could not feel assured in a single day of my ability to please and to retain her love. I had moments of uncertainty, alarm and bitterness; I sometimes regretted that I had not jumped into the lake when a word from Indiana had made me so happy.

"She too must have had attacks of melancholy. She found it difficult to break herself of the habit of suffering, for the heart becomes used to unhappiness, it takes root in it and cuts loose from it only with an effort. However, I must do her heart the justice to say that she never had a regret for Raymon; she did not even remember him enough to hate him.

"At last, as always happens in deep and true attachments, time, instead of weakening our love, established it firmly and sealed it; each day gave it added intensity, because each day brought fresh obligations on both sides to esteem and to bless. All our fears vanished one by one; and when we saw how easy it was to destroy those causes of distrust, we smilingly confessed to each other that we took our happiness like cowards and that neither of us deserved it. From that moment we have loved each other in perfect security."

Ralph paused; then, after a few moments of profound meditation in which we were equally absorbed, he continued, pressing my hand:

"I say nothing of my happiness; if there are griefs that never betray their existence and envelop the heart like a shroud, so there are joys that remain buried in the heart of man because no earthly voice can describe them. Moreover, if some angel from heaven should light upon one of these flowering branches and describe those joys in the language of his native land, you would not understand them, young man, for the tempest has not bruised and shattered you. Alas! what can the heart that has not suffered understand of happiness? As to our crimes——" he added with a smile.

"Oh!" I cried, my eyes wet with tears.

"Listen, monsieur," he continued, interrupting me; "you have lived but a few hours with the two outlaws of Bernica, but a single hour would suffice for you to learn their whole life. All our days resemble one another; they are all calm and lovely; they pass by as swiftly and as pure as those of our childhood. Every night we bless God; we pray to him every morning, we implore at his hands the sunshine and shade of the day before. The greater part of our income is devoted to the redemption of poor and infirm blacks. That is the principal cause of the evil that the colonists say of us. Would that we were rich enough to set free all those who live in slavery! Our servants are our friends; they share our joys, we nurse them in sickness. This is the way our life is spent, without vexations, without remorse. We rarely speak of the past, rarely of the future; but always of the former without bitterness, of the latter without alarm. If we sometimes surprise ourselves with tears in our eyes, it is because great joys always cause tears to flow; the eyes are dry in great misery."

"My friend," I said after a long silence, "if the accusations of the world should reach your ears, your happiness would answer loudly enough."

"You are young," he replied, "in your eyes, for your conscience is ingenuous and pure and unsoiled by the world, our happiness is the proof of our virtue; in the eyes of the world it is our crime. Solitude is sweet, I tell you, and men are not worth a regret."

"All do not accuse you," I said; "but even those who appreciate your true character blame you for despising public opinion, and those who acknowledge your virtue say that you are arrogant and proud."

"Believe me," replied Ralph, "there is more pride in that reproach than in any alleged scorn. As for public opinion, monsieur, judging from those whom it exalts, ought we not always to hold out our hand to those whom it tramples upon? It is said that its approval is necessary to happiness; they who think so should respect it. For my part, I sincerely pity any happiness that rises or falls with its capricious breath."

"Some moralists criticise your solitary life; they claim that every man belongs to society, which demands his presence. They add that you set an example which it is dangerous to follow."

"Society should demand nothing of the man who expects nothing from it," Sir Ralph replied. "As for the contagion of example, I do not believe in it, monsieur; too much energy is required to break with the world, and too much suffering to acquire that energy. So let this unknown happiness flow on in peace, for it costs nobody anything, and conceals itself for fear of making others envious. Go, young man, follow the course of your destiny; have friends, a profession, a reputation, a fatherland. As for me, I have Indiana. Do not break the chains that bind you to society, respect its laws if they protect you, accept its judgments if they are fair to you: but if some day it calumniates you and spurns you, have pride enough to find a way to do without it."

"Yes," said I, "a pure heart will enable us to endure exile; but, to make us love it, one must have such a companion as yours."

"Ah!" he said, "if you knew how I pity this world of yours, which looks down on me!"

The next day I left Ralph and Indiana; one embraced me, the other shed a few tears.

"Adieu," they said to me; "return to the world; if some day it banishes you, remember our Indian cottage."